TEMPLAR OF ARCHAEA

CALEB FRANKLIN

Danbury, Connecticut

Templar of Archaea
Copyright © 2025 Warrington Publishing

Printed in the United States of America
First Edition
ISBN: 978-1-969359-02-6 (paperback)
978-1-969359-01-9 (ebook)
978-1-969359-03-3 (hardcover)

Book cover designed by JD&J
Edited by Mike Waitz at Stick & Stones

To my best friend and fellow worldbuilder, Jonny. It all started with us, and I will never forget it.

CHAPTER 1

A Storm in Pallerheim

Racing north by northwest through the green and white valleys of Nethel, a forceful gust of wind screamed over hillsides and past mountain ranges, dragging behind it a massive conglomerate of angry clouds from the Black Ocean toward the slightly more mellow Harpol Sea.

With the thunderheads came a dangerous and beautiful fusion of snow, hail, and lightning, unique to the northernmost countries of the planet Archaea.

This weather anomaly would likely blow through the entirety of the country, but one city would receive the lion's share of the storm, the Nethellite megalopolis known as Pallerheim.

Sitting entrenched on the shores of the Harpol Sea where two titanic mountain ranges met, Pallerheim's one and a half million residents knew the signs of such a tempest and had closed the city's doors and gates hours prior. Banners, exterior curtains, and outdoor garnishes of a similar nature had been pulled preemptively into the stone and steel structures they once adorned so that nothing lightweight would be left for the marauding winds to take.

For though the storms of the North were majestic to behold, the winter gale would certainly be violent enough to put a halt to any evening business or travel one had previously hoped to undertake should the climate have remained fair. So, for the night, an ancient and otherwise fair capital would be temporarily stripped of its embellishments for fear of them being swept away.

As the sun receded and plunged Pallerheim into darkness, the storm overtook the city and battered its towering frame with howling winds and interchanging salvos of snow, rain, and hail. Mighty bursts of lightning also lit the swirling sky, attended by bone-rattling claps of thunder.

The winding walkways and far-reaching freeways of the city were all but uninhabited. However, there were some who saw opportunity within the skyward turmoil.

In fact, to a select few individuals standing in a small roadway on one of Pallerheim's thousands of seaside wharves, the chaos was a welcome change, for such an atmosphere would provide excellent cover for the deeds they had planned for the night.

Moving with efficiency and unnerving silence, two cloaked figures approached a man leaning against a motorized transport vehicle. He checked his timepiece and slowly glanced in their direction, causing both newcomers to hesitate.

An armored visor covered his face, but both men could feel his stare melt into their chests and heads. They knew who he was, and he was not to be trifled with.

Lightning flashed, and its luminous ignition announced the presence of two more pairs of men, each approaching from a different direction. In a matter of seconds, the founder of the meeting stood in the crux of a semicircle formed by six shadowy newcomers.

Initially, no one said a word, for the storm would likely drown out any effort to communicate. Instead, the leader reached into the transport behind him and produced facial coverings similar to his own, tossing one to each of the men standing before him.

The armored masks unfolded and wrapped around the heads of their wearers, covering the ears, face, and upper neck with a thin steel plating.

Once the masks were on their heads, each man pressed a small button by his ear, causing the eyes of the visor to light up. With the armored cowls active, the chaos of the storm faded away along with all ambient noise, and the men began to speak to each other.

"Did you take care of the envoy?" the man in the center grunted.

"Bottom of the bay, Lord-Inquisitor."

"The element of surprise is ours, then. This should be quick." The leader reached farther into the carrier and began drawing weapons from its interior. He handed out firearms and blades varying greatly in size to the group. The supplier's motions were efficient and mechanical, but once he reached the last duo of newcomers, he paused.

"Identify yourselves. Starting with your names." The two men stiffened their backs but responded with haste.

"Mahkt Essen Zorn, and my comrade Augen Di Gattchen." Both men pulled their cloaks, waistcoats, and undershirts down from the neck to reveal the upper quarter of a chest tattoo that depicted a red cross boring into a skull.

"Templar, and young ones, too," one of the other newcomers remarked.

"One still has the itch," another added.

Augen quickly halted the instinctive scratching of his forearms that had plagued him for the last couple of weeks, but it was too late to evade notice.

"How long since your augmentation, boy?" the leader inquired.

"Four months and eleven days," the one named Augen sighed, wishing his inexperience as one of their kind had never come to light.

"Bah. Leave it to the Templar to send an initiate to a co-op hit of this criticality," one of the others mumbled. The man in the center did not join in. He grunted to himself but said nothing more on the matter.

Instead, he tossed a number of weapons to the Templar duo, who promptly sheathed and holstered them beneath their long coats.

"We have a short walk ahead of us. You three will breach the *Leoris*. Cripple the ship and make certain that its cargo does not detonate. You will accompany me to the warehouse. The Templar will run intel. Get the balloon."

Obeying the man's orders with mechanical efficiency, the two Templars grabbed a detection console known to them as an Intel-Balloon from the back of the now-empty transport bed.

The seven walked with haste through the tempest, keeping the wide brims of their hats down so that the wind did not carry them away. Rounding the harbor's dull curve, the crew advanced in perfect lockstep despite the powerful wind and the heavy load each man carried.

When their objective came into sight, the leader, who spearheaded the group's triangular formation, ceased his movement, signaling with his right hand for the others to mimic him. The plan he had organized had already gone awry.

Several hundred yards long and designed to hold a crew of one hundred fifty men, the *Leoris* was not a small vessel, yet, by either dumb luck or clever strategy on behalf of the vessel's captain, the two mega carriers she had moored directly between dwarfed her.

Such was the case that these massive ships, held stable by concrete jetties jutting from the mainland, created a wind buffer for the *Leoris* and even calmed the storm-struck waves around her, preventing her crew from feeling the chaos felt by the rest of the harbor.

Utilizing this unique peace, the ship used its onboard crane to unload the bulk of its payload onto several awaiting cargo vehicles. Members of the ship's crew struggled to tie the freight onto the waiting carriers but had already succeeded in preparing one for land travel, and the first of the carriages was warming its engines in preparation for departure.

"It seems the envoy was not the only buyer." The leader paused for a moment and shot a glance at two of the men behind him. His fists tightened around his weapons, projecting a fit of fury as he continued his observation, "It also appears that our cover was blown during a prerequisite hit!" Through the mics and headsets, the whole squad could hear the leader hyperventilate under his visor. His arms began to twitch erratically, contorting slightly with each spasm, and those behind him fought the urge to run, for succumbing to the temptation would certainly guarantee their deaths, through desertion charges in the future or being caught by the enraged inquisitor immediately.

However, just as quickly as the rage poured through the veins of their leader, it, along with all its physiological tells, dissipated into his inner being. His body jerked rigid, and his voice became calm again.

"No! I will punish incompetence later!" he shouted to himself. Turning rapidly, he unleashed a barrage of commands, pointing to each man as he spoke.

"You four secure the cargo on the ground! Those trucks *will not* leave the piers! Templar, run intel and secure the warehouse! I will take the ship and bag its captain myself!" Breaking into inhuman sprints, the team split up as they were ordered. Mahkt and Augen reached the warehouse without any apparent detection. Augen worked to set up their balloon but was not moving at an optimal pace, so Mahkt, the more experienced of them, stepped in.

"You take the warehouse. I will wrangle the balloon." Augen nodded and breached the building. Moments later, his headset crackled to life, and he could hear Mahkt, who had miraculously gotten the balloon into the air despite the violent wind, speak into his ear through his visor.

"Long-range comms established! Eyes in the sky!"

The balloon was a true jack-of-all-trades masterpiece, held sturdy in the wind by magnetic anchors and capable of tying short-range comm-links together over long distances. Sensors on its lower carriage sent bursts of sonic waves into its environment, granting its user a three-dimensional view of whatever battlefield it floated above.

Mahkt could now see everything and made haste to divulge his findings to the others.

"A land-freighter is pulling away! Commander, you are walking into a nest of hostiles!"

"Intel, focus on the warehouse and trucks! I do not need assistance!"

The warehouse Augen combed was nearly empty, but upon reaching the far back of the building, he found some heavy equipment and materials packed and ready to be shipped. Augen could not be certain in the heat of the moment, but it looked like he was staring at pieces of a dismantled hovercraft. Switching his comm to communicate with the whole squad, Augen gave his update.

"Warehouse is clear, no resistance so far, and no sign of ordnance or explosives."

Scattered gunfire rattled the windows facing the harbor, but the thunder covered up the bulk of the sound. Augen turned to leave, but Mahkt stopped him.

"Several hostiles closing in on the warehouse," his headset whispered.

"Finally," Augen whispered back, letting a grin form underneath his visor. Four armed men burst through the far door, jogging toward the hardware Augen had just examined, gun smugglers with no idea how short their remaining life was.

Augen stepped into the darkness and lowered his hat over the glowing eyes of his visor. He had no effective armor on, but he would not need any to take on four men who did not expect him.

Slipping between empty hardware containers with his hood down, Augen waited for the intruders to step far enough away from their exits before he dramatically revealed himself.

"Knight! Kill him! Kill him!" one of the men screamed shakily as he tried to raise his rifle. He got no response from his comrades.

Since the Dread Wars of Cataclysm nearly a century prior, rumors had circulated throughout the civilized world about the physically enhanced mercenaries who could slay ten trained soldiers of any army without taking a blow, but few believed such rumors.

Since those who encountered a knight of any order rarely lived to talk about it, many believed they were but mere legends of times long past. Yet for all those decades, it was not uncommon for criminals and killers who drew too much attention to themselves to learn of the knights' existence the hard way.

Before any of them could believe their eyes or ready their weapons, Augen closed a thirty-three-yard gap between himself and his targets, striking the man readiest with a deadly shoulder check.

The sight of their fellow seaman having his neck broken by an impact to the chest awoke the others from their stunned daze, but they were far, far, too late to do anything. Without the use of his myriad firearms, Augen bludgeoned or gutted the remaining men in seconds with a single dagger he wore on his belt before reverently cleaning the blade and returning it to its sheath.

Another group of sailors and smugglers flew through the front doors, likely fleeing the carnage inflicted by the four other knights outside. They glanced at Augen and scampered up a flight of stairs near the doorways.

Drawing his handguns, Augen cut down two of them as they fled, but was unable to stop the remaining five before they disappeared up the staircase.

Augen heard cursing over the comms as two of the knights outside declared a pursuit. One of the cargo trucks was mobile, but the land freighters were not built for speed, and seconds later, it sounded as though the vehicle was going to be run down by foot.

No injuries had been sustained, and, assuming the commander, who had gone dark on comms, was able to keep the bulk of the smugglers on the ship, the mission was looking clean-cut.

"Engaging in a second-floor pursuit," Augen declared over the comms. "Clean-up duty."

Both the Teutonic Order, whose foot soldiers made up the bulk of the muscle in this raid, and the Templar Order, their rival paramilitary organization, hated loose ends. So, Augen climbed the stairs, running down the slowest of the fleeing men before reaching the second floor.

The warehouse was, like the *Leoris*, a very small addition to the broader harbor of Pallerheim, which boasted some of the largest coastal structures on the planet.

Because the two-thousand-year-old city had grown to such immensity, most of the buildings were intermingled, trussed together with large stone and steel walkways. This architectural marvel made the Pallerheim skyline far more durable in the face of its regular windstorms and even the occasional earthquakes it was expected to endure. Such structural engineering also allowed for easy foot travel through miles of the inner city without the need for a descent to the ground level.

The smugglers fleeing Augen's butchery hoped to escape through such a walkway, passing into one of the larger buildings in the steel mill behind it, but the smugglers were far too slow to get across and pick the lock.

Before the dealers could get through the steel mill's front gate, their pursuer overcame them, shooting three and beating down the last with the grip of a handgun.

"Augen. One of the carriers has pulled out of the harbor. It will pass by you on the other side of the mill in about fifty seconds." Augen knew the balloon would lose sight of the freighter if it pulled onto one of the freeways winding throughout the city, and there would definitely be hell to pay if the truck was lost.

So, acting without forethought, Augen kicked the lock of the gate before him, breaking it open. With unnatural speed, he sprinted down a hallway, around a corner, through a second hallway, then up a small flight of stairs until he reached another bridge.

As he crossed, he was struck once again by the rain, which was now mixed with hail. The headlights of the freighter were just visible from the bridge.

Augen considered jumping onto the machine as it passed, but a glance over the edge made him think twice. Even with his impressive physical modifications, four stories of free fall would likely result in broken limbs.

The next building, a noticeably higher-class structure, had far more than a simple chain lock on its bridge gate.

Improvising, Augen observed a billboard overlooking the streets on the opposite side of the bridge. It was angled to gaze down toward the ground, so jumping directly onto its top frame was impossible, but some of the lights illuminating the sign from below were held up by thin steel arms, which branched outward to form a broken semicircle of steel fingers nine feet below.

A three-story jump was far more feasible.

So, grabbing the long end of the chain he broke to access the bridge, he hurdled the baluster, propelling himself just far enough to clear the ridge of the billboard. Then, reaching backward with an end of the chain in each hand, he snagged the center light fixture with his makeshift grappling hook.

The light shattered and the metal frame bent, but Augen's grip endured, and he found himself hanging about thirty feet above the street. Seeing the headlights below him, he let his hands, now soaking wet, slip from the chain.

Had he desired to minimize the distance of his fall, he would have waited a moment longer so that he could land on the slightly taller cargo trailer his target was pulling. Instead, he let go early and landed directly on the roof of the cab.

Augen's impact with the truck's thin ceiling warped the windshield socket, shattering the windshield and showering the two men in the cab with glass, water, and ice. Augen heard screams briefly, and the truck swerved dangerously to the right and overcorrected.

Just as the rig and its load looked like they were going to roll over, Augen bailed, jumping to the right to avoid being crushed by the now free-drifting trailer to his left.

The truck did not roll. As it pulled onto an entrance ramp, moving far too fast for its size and pulling loose cargo with no grip on the road, the trailer's end plowed through the railing and high-centered between the freeway and a small, two-way road tunneling beneath it.

Augen did roll. Six...nine...twelve times before grinding to a stop on the slick pavement. His coat was matted, and his hat was demolished. His visor kept his face from any major harm, but his arms and legs, save his biceps, had no steel protection and were covered in road rash.

"Truck disabled...targets exiting the vehicle...possible man down," rang through Augen's earpiece, but he was far from down. A man, too small to be a knight, stood above Augen and grabbed him by the back of his coat.

Pure adrenaline kicked in, and for two seconds, he felt nothing. Drawing the embroidered dagger from his belt, as his other weapons had been scattered upon impact with the pavement, Augen slid the blade through the man's chin and into the core of his head. With a quick withdrawal of the sleek weapon and a slight tap to the chest, the newcomer dropped dead without a word.

Augen arose with haste but froze in place after a double-take at his latest victim's face.

"No!" The man he slew was no knight, but he was not a smuggler, either. He was a bystander, wearing the cloak of a clergyman, and despite the gore pouring from his fatal head wound and mingling with the ice falling from the sky, the Templar initiate recognized his victim's face. "No! No! No! No! No!"

The two Teutons who had been pursuing the truck caught up with Augen and paused. One did a quick vital check on Augen and made sure his adrenaline wasn't compelling him to stand on or fight with anything broken. The other sighed, studying the corpse.

"Bloody fool, Templar! You save the integrity of our mission, then slay a priest just in case we start taking you seriously!"

Augen did not respond. His heart sank. Then it leaped back into a frenzy when the Teuton finished his thought.

"Inquisitor Belogo will have your head."

"Wait. Our commander is...him?" Mahkt's voice shook slightly even through the headset. Augen gaped at his victim, then slowly turned to the knight standing next to him.

It all made sense in hindsight. Teutons were arguably the most terrifying, unflinching, unfeeling killers on Archaea, yet Augen witnessed them flinch upon their commander's first movements. Had the Templar soldiers known the identity of their current leader, they would have flinched, too.

Knights were a legend, known by few, and usually not for long. Zhatka Belogo was a legend among the knights of all three orders. Stories of his accomplishments as a commander and an assassin were questioned regularly by those who heard of them. Such unlikely tales were so numerous that the few who did hear them wondered if someone could live long enough to establish such a list. The Supreme Inquisitor was a boogeyman for traitors and a myth to most living, but real nonetheless, all too real.

Staring into the sky, Augen caught sight of the billboard he had hurdled. It was a state-sponsored message quoting the scriptures of the Holy Church. It read:

Deos sees all! Do all things in the knowledge that He is watching!

The Teutons, though likely familiar with failures of their own, had not seen such a response from a knight, and for a moment, were unsure of how to respond. One tugged on his arm.

"We need to secure the cargo," was all he got out before the distracted knight was shot three times in the back.

The two smugglers in the wreck had recovered their wits. Knowing that their cargo would never leave Pallerheim, one had grabbed a low-powered rifle, the only weapon at his disposal, and begun taking potshots at their attackers as the other climbed into the dangling trailer.

The bullets flung from the light weapon were blunt and dreadfully outdated, mere pellets to the body of a knight, but still dreadfully painful.

"This containment unit is packed with explosives! A spark in the wrong place could level three city blocks! Are you so-called holy warriors willing to sacrifice your own people to kill us?" the shooter screamed before shooting again, this time with far less accuracy but making his point regardless.

The newly wounded Teuton hobbled toward cover at the end of the street. His comrade did the same, diving toward the opposite sidewalk and pulling Augen with him. Mahkt, who had been listening in through the visor-mics, hastily responded but sounded unsure of himself.

"Checking for radiation spikes and irregular radio frequencies."

The knights on the ground who had missed their chance to strike the hot iron were now pinned down. Their offensive capacities far outranked those of the man shooting at them, but they had to know what they were up against. Then Zhatka spoke, and the knights froze.

"Is one of them in the cargo hold?"

"Yes, Inquisitor." A slow, exasperated sigh came through the mics before the commanding officer spoke again, this time with a grim sarcasm that oozed through their headsets.

"If the truck is full of explosives, the driver's pinned down, and one of them is now accessing said explosives as their enemy closes in, what do you think he is doing back there?"

The men, all distracted now, had no time to answer, but they knew perfectly well that the man was trying to detonate his cargo.

"Get into gear and secure the payload!" Another second went by as the now-wounded trio tried to come up with a plan that did not involve running headlong into gunfire, but the commander spoke once more, this time perfectly calm. "Never mind. I will do it."

The smuggler continued to yell threats from what he perceived as his safe space, firing periodically into the darkness until a loud crack rang out from a distance and the man dropped where he stood.

Lightning struck and illuminated the smuggler, who had been shot through the knee from an angle, preventing the lead from hitting the trailer. He cursed and groaned in pain as another noisy projectile was sent into the open mouth of the explosive shipment.

No explosion came. Instead, a toxic billow of smoke poured from the trailer's gaping maw. The moment the other smuggler pulled his wheezing purple head above the ridge of the smog-cloaked cargo unit, another shot passed through his right eye from a different angle, dropping him back into the smoke, lifeless as the hold he fell into.

"Templar. Finish the gunman off." Augen stood slowly, his head finally clearing up enough to function independently, and strode toward the last living target. He could still kill easily enough, and the phantom hovering somewhere nearby—none of the knights knew exactly where—demanded it.

The lone, soon-to-be-dead smuggler whimpered and tried to reach for his gun. Augen raised his knife, which he still clutched instinctively by white knuckles despite the shock, and gazed into the eyes of the bleeding man before him. He was no priest.

"The emperor demands your death. The civil world will rejoice in your passing," Augen said before finishing the man off with a jab to the throat.

The Templar turned away from the freighter and was shot before taking a second step. The bullet passed straight through Augen's torso, puncturing his lower abdomen all the way through and narrowly missing his spinal cord. Another heavy round immediately followed, blowing through the opposite side of his torso. Neither shot was fatal, but they would take months to fully heal.

As he fell over backward, Augen got another good look at that billboard before shock kicked in and his vision blurred.

"The penalty for incompetence," he heard Zhatka sneer over his headset.

Deos sees all! He is watching! he read again. Then again. Then once more.

He had heard similar phrases uttered by the higher-ups of Archaea's Gold and Silver Empires, the only powers to remain intact through the Wars of Cataclysm and to whom every other people, in every corner of the planet, answered.

He had never read the holy texts himself, though. No one outside of the top echelon of elites had ever gazed at their pages.

"Now get up and throw the dead priest into the sea. Mahkt, pack up the balloon, and come and pick up your comrade. This mission is over."

At that moment, for the first time in his life, as Augen lay bleeding next to a dead priest who used to be an old friend of his, he doubted that Deos was watching at all.

CHAPTER 2

A CALL FOR THE LOST SOLDIER

Snow fell lightly now over a small house near Pallerheim's border. The storm had passed two days ago, and for the first time since the mission, nearly a week ago, Augen moved about his quarters freely. His breathing was labored, and his body radiated incredible pain, but what hurt far more was his conscience.

Augen sat in his room, praying silently. He had prepared a simple meal for himself, but it sat alone on a small table, getting cold. Food did not seem very important at the moment.

Poor Steven. What was he even doing in that part of Pallerheim? Was there any way of preventing what had happened? Was he destined to such a fate all along? And why did Augen have to be the one to kill him? Such questions made Augen sick, regardless of the answer. It happened, and it was his fault.

Augen joined the Templar Order willingly, endured the hazing, completed the brutal training regimens, and even welcomed the horrific process of physical enhancement required to mold his body into the killing machine it now was. He did it to kill traitors, terrorists, and criminals, not priests.

Killing an innocent bystander was horrible enough; the fact that his victim was a childhood friend made it worse than any of his comrades could have ever understood.

Praying again, he desperately hoped for a voice to respond, but nothing came. The words of Deos were written everywhere, on signs, hoardings, and posters, plastered onto public walls, and stained into elaborate windows. Yet, despite all of it, he could not bring himself to believe the words he saw now.

If truth were universal, then would it not be self-explanatory, and contradictory to the nature of evil man? And if the words strewn across the cultural landscape were true, then why did everyone in power have to try so hard to justify it? It was all too convenient, too filtered, and too...helpful to the empires.

Perhaps the words were truly taken from the holy pages, but so long as the only known copies lay in the Underground Cathedrals and not in the hands of the common man, nobody could be trusted. Perhaps it was all a lie, some scheme to keep the people in check? Augen had never questioned such words throughout his childhood. Even when he joined the Holy Order Templar, he had little cynicism, but now he did not know.

Everything felt wrong, deceitful, as though everyone, even those he had never met, had lied to him.

As he continued reciting vague prayers, a creaking floorboard announced the entrance of another entity. Augen feared that the foreign presence was not Deos.

"How disappointing. Our first mission together, and you kill a civilian. Is your incompetence always visible from the collateral angle, or were you just trying to test my patience?" Augen's spine stiffened, and a knot materialized in his stomach. Most definitely not Deos, more like the devil.

"What do you want, Zhatka?"

Even in the morning light, Augen could not tell where his visitor lurked. His voice seemed to echo through the little house in a way that made him sound everywhere at once. Terrifying and typical of a man with a fatal prestige of his caliber.

"I wanted to check in on my beloved half-brother. How are those bullet wounds?"

Augen snarled at the sarcastic response. "Eating and breathing are painful, but you would know. Now, what do you really want?"

"Find me. And then we'll talk." Augen stood still as a stone. His eyes darted back and forth, but there was no sign of Zhatka's presence anywhere.

There was so little space in the quaint hallways and simple rooms of his house. It should have been impossible for a murderous seven-foot-tall assassin to remain concealed.

"You have to move to see me."

"Clearly not, since you can see me!" Augen shifted his weight to shoot a glance down the hallway. Still no sign of his visitor, just another creaking floorboard in the different room. As Augen slowly worked his way into the hall, Zhatka spoke again.

"Come now! I did not hit your spine! So, show some! I am aware you are just a Templar, and I am still not fully convinced that we are family. Do something to compensate for your pathetic performance on the field!" Augen took another cautious step forward, but it clearly wasn't enough.

"Too late. I'm bored." In an inhuman flash, a shadow appeared in the hallway behind Augen, closed the distance between them, and collided with him before he could flinch.

Augen spun, swinging wildly in hopes of keeping his stalker at bay, but he had no such luck. His fists, toned and hardened by intense hand combat training and weapons in their own right, proved utterly useless against this foe.

Zhatka casually dodged every initial swing, blocked a wide hook at the shoulder, and battered both of Augen's fresh bullet wounds with two precise finger strikes. Before Augen could breathe again, Zhatka had him pinned to the floor.

The inquisitor stared into Augen's eyes with furious hatred. Augen tried to move, but for the first time since his augmentation, he found himself completely overpowered.

"What is wrong with you? If you answered directly to me, I would break you myself! I may even kill you!" A cold blade pressed against Augen's throat. "Maybe I will anyway."

Zhatka wore nothing but loose combat trousers, and his body displayed the full spectrum of war's polychrome rainbow. His exposed chest and back were carpeted with thick speckles of pale scar tissue, and his face and neck fared little better.

No part of his body, as far as Augen could tell, had been spared of cuts, tears, burns, punctures, or some other sinister combination of manmade abuses.

His face was ragged, brutally scarred, adorned with two wicked onyx stones for eyes and crowned with thick but unnaturally white hair. Only the scars of his augmentation and the tattoos of his allegiance, the Teutonic Heralds and the Blood Inquisition remained strangely untouched. It was as if the rest of his body was being sacrificed for the sake of their preservation.

Despite Augen's efforts to break Zhatka's grip, leverage was not on his side, not that he tried his hardest to break free. Even the infamous inquisitor had failed to truly take his mind off the guilt and anger he felt toward himself and Deos. The pain Augen felt from his injuries and at the hands of his superior almost relieved it, and after a moment of direct eye contact, Zhatka could tell.

"It is far less entertaining when you don't fight back," he growled. After a moment of tense silence, Zhatka sighed in disappointment and stood, calmly making his way toward the window to observe the snow.

"When I was notified that I had a half-sibling and that he had just joined the Templar-Eros Order..." The Teuton interrupted himself with a wheezing chuckle that briefly contorted his shirtless body before he went rigid again.

A short turn back to meet Augen's eyes showed a pained attempt at a smile and a small stream of tears dripping down his face from one eye. "I was...so excited! I demanded that I transfer here to lead your first mission." More giggling followed, but this time, it was less enthusiastic, almost mocking. Despite his bodily spasms, Zhatka appeared to have lost his lust for violence. Augen felt safe enough to slowly sit up.

"I was told that I might meet you," he finally responded.

"Hi," Zhatka said, waving dramatically before spinning back toward the window. "And now you have. Do you share my disappointment?" The inquisitor shook his head slowly and allowed his eyes to track the falling snowflakes with mechanical precision.

"What were you hoping to find?" Augen asked, trying and failing to not cough the last word. The question echoed through the house but did not seem to affect its target enough to warrant a response.

Without breaking his gaze on the snow, Zhatka tossed a small sheet of parchment onto the floor and changed the subject, slowly turning his body toward the door and refusing to make further eye contact.

"I wish to invite you to a celebration the rest of the squad is having tonight. The golden emperor has written our formal recognition into law, so we are official soldiers now, recognized by half the world as peacekeepers." He chuckled at the last part before finishing hastily, "The address is written there."

Zhatka got to the door and threw it open. His body was twitching again, but the tics seemed to pause when a frigid gust of wind struck him.

"Get back to your prayers, boy," he said. "Pray that you don't get deployed in the ancient world. Pray that your bleeding heart does not compromise your performance in the future. Pray that I am never your squad leader again. You are unlikely to survive any of these events. Catch you later."

And just as he came, the Reaper was gone without a sound.

The physical modifications every knight went through had a number of negative side effects, including bursts of adrenaline-fueled aggression, but the bipolar mood swings Zhatka displayed were unlike anything Augen had ever seen or felt.

Perhaps his age had something to do with it. Indeed, Zhatka appeared to be much older than him, perhaps even middle-aged, which, for a knight, may as well be one hundred twenty years old. Knights didn't usually live long.

❖

Augen adjusted a chair that had been knocked over during Zhatka's visit and leaned slowly into it, wiping a streak of blood dripping from his mouth. He remained in that chair for a very long time, thinking, hurting, and occasionally praying as Zhatka had suggested.

"Deos. I have buried myself in fatal mistakes. I am undeserving of anything You have to offer. When my time comes, please make my death mean something." As Augen finally worked up the courage to stand once more, he gave one last nod to his Maker before preparing to leave his quarters for the city.

The Holy Orders operated all over the world. Yet, in an ironic and tragic coincidence, Augen's first assignment was in Pallerheim, the city where he grew up. His family was complicated and dead, mostly dead, so he hoped to visit two people before his transfer. He had the unexpected opportunity to see the first a week prior. He was dead now. Perhaps this meeting would go better.

He bandaged up his chest again, covered his marred forearms with powerful coagulants and some soothing gauze, and took a stroll through the urban landscape. Augen could hear the industrial sector winding up miles away, but he was not interested in business.

Augen trudged through the provincial maze of manor houses, crossing the roads periodically and leaving a tiny line of blood drops to accompany his shallow prints in the snow. Eventually, his path led him to The Hideaway, a quaint red inn overlooking a river.

The inn was a small, three-story building built with a classical air and frilled with white trimmings on its outer decks. Augen knew the place well as he had quite nearly grown up in its shadow, playing in the grass of its landscape as a boy, and working on its bottom floor as a youth. His adoptive father, Alexi Glaineacht, owned and ran the small establishment for most of Augen's life.

Working inside the building was one of Augen's only ties to civility, a quaint and lovely young lady who stumbled about the restaurant, preparing it for visitors and ignorant of the shadow of her past lingering outside.

"I did not think I would ever see you here again," a gruff voice echoed toward Augen and ended his gradual approach. Alexi, a stout man with a bushy face and balding head, leaned casually on the outer railing of The Hideaway's deck, smoking a pipe and scowling at the approaching visitor.

"I was not sure I would ever return," Augen responded quietly, taking another step forward. The man opposite him stepped into the entrance, blocking his path.

"Why are you here?" he asked flatly.

"I wanted to see her," the knight responded, sucking the fresh blood from the corners of his mouth and hoping the old man did not notice. "I heard she had recovered."

"Oh, I see. It has been, what, twenty-three months since your last contact? What exactly makes you think she would wish to see you?"

Despite his morning encounter with the world's most dangerous sibling, Augen knew his face was well-preserved and unlikely to show the physical abuse of the rest of his body.

However, deeper scarring of his conscience and mind drove him to keep the brim of his hat low, avoiding eye contact with the man who had almost become his father-in-law and shifting his weight from leg to leg without conscious knowledge of the twitch.

Christine's father was disinterested in a conversation, so he pushed further.

"You think you can leave her on her deathbed and stroll back into her life as though nothing happened? Where have you been all this time?"

Augen took a breath, understanding that he needed to provide an explanation but could not disclose whom he actually worked for, not yet anyway, since the Holy Orders were still considered illegal paramilitary companies.

"I took work for...the government. I wished to avenge what happened to her, or at least prevent it from happening again."

The old man shook his head in frustration, huffing several quick shots from his pipe before stepping closer to Augen. "And growing more than a full foot taller in the process... I suppose the government is feeding you well."

Pulling Augen's collar so that they were eye to eye, Alexi growled into his ear, "Remember how I once served in the Great Foreign Legion? I know about your kind. I even had the displeasure of fighting one. I never thought you would end up joining their ranks."

"I don't know what you are talking about," Augen said, trying not to appear uncomfortable.

Alexi responded with a quick jab to Augen's right biceps, which, by coincidence, was left unarmored that day. The unhealing lesion he struck, a remnant of the augmentation process Augen endured when he became a Templar, flared up with agonizing intensity.

The knight yelped like a dog and pulled away, gripping his arm and fighting the urge to scratch the tender wound.

"I could always tell when you were lying, boy."

Whether by some flaw in his physical enhancements or perhaps the revealing of a deeper, more fundamental blemish, Augen's pain transformed into hot fury in seconds.

The edges of his vision grew red, and for a brief moment, he was no longer talking to the man who raised him most of his life.

"Touch me again, old man!" Augen roared, squaring up to him and grabbing his collar.

Had the grieving soldier's temper pushed him into more misdirected violence, he never would have forgiven himself. Yet, by providence or coincidence, he was interrupted before getting the chance to make such a choice.

"Father? Are you all right?" Augen and Alexi froze as the love of both their lives stepped from the threshold of the building.

"Yes, dearest," Alexi responded calmly.

"I heard yelling," she continued.

Augen gasped but said nothing. Seeing her again was painful, and despite many hours of mental preparations for their meeting, the words he hoped would come refused to show themselves. Her eyes were shrouded with a white mist, and he could see two mechanical hearing aids protruding from her hair like metal antennas. She was beautiful, yet tragically pathetic, leaning on the nearest wall to maintain her balance and avoid tumbling over something.

"Who is with you?" Christine inquired, squinting through her hazy eyes at the two men. Her tone sounded chipper, and a polite smile lined her face, but Augen could tell that she was suspicious of them both.

Her father shared a moment of eye contact with Augen and answered her coldly.

"A stranger. He asked me for directions, and things got political. Where are your contacts?" As Alexi spoke, Augen's mind returned to him and loosened his grip. *Would I have really hurt him?* he pondered to himself, afraid of the answer.

"I could not find them this morning. I think my sight is improving without them anyway," Christine said, turning back inside the building and letting her smile sag for a brief moment before disappearing within. "Please refrain from taking too long; we need to open soon."

"I will be in shortly. Try to find your contacts."

A gentle gust of wind whistled around the two men, nipping at exposed skin with frosty fingers before passing deeper into the city on its pilgrimage to the sea.

Normally, a Nethellite local would be far too desensitized to the humid winter to notice such a mellow gust, but for a brief moment, both Alexi and Augen were made aware of its presence, and their intense temperament was tranquilized by its touch.

Alexi took a huff from his pipe and turned to face the stranger he once knew. Augen stepped back.

"When I heard that she was going to..." Augen started to explain.

"But she didn't," Alexi interrupted. Despite his circumstances, the old veteran's temperament was stifled, and his movements and words were carefully calculated. "Look at yourself. Instead of fulfilling the promise you made her, you fled your powerless position in her time of need." He paused and shook his head again. The old man was truly an adept stoic, but Augen could tell that he was hurting, too. "Now you have immense power, clearly more than you understand, and have paid for it with the things you wished to protect."

Alexi began to turn away, but Augen grabbed his shoulder, not in anger but in desperation.

"Why? Am I not the same man who asked to marry her?"

"You are not the same. Could I believe you if you told me that you would not abuse your new strength? What makes you think she would not eventually become the target of your physical outbursts?"

Shaking his head with a mournful but resolute scowl, he pulled away from his forgotten family member and strode toward the building, adjusting the pipe between his lips and huffing sporadically.

Augen was indignant, but he understood there was nothing honest he could say to put his accuser at ease, so he made no effort to prevent their parting.

Once back on the Hideaway's deck, Alexi paused his withdrawal to speak, his hand resting on the door handle but not opening it.

"You chose to put power into your own hands rather than have faith in providence. You got what you wished for, but to have true power is to be alone. Until you truly understand the weight of your choice, I wish you happiness in the life you have chosen. Do not return here. She is going through enough."

Augen wished to follow the old man. He longed to return to him and his daughter and beg for forgiveness, but what then? He had done such damage to the family even before he killed Steven.

Even if Christine forgave him, was he going to hold that secret over her and Alexi's heads forever? No. It could not be done. There was no redemption awaiting him.

"Could you...play a match of Chatura with her? For my sake?" Augen's odd request bid Alexi pause, and for a brief moment, the old veteran stood on the threshold contemplating whether to respond.

"She does not play anymore." Then the door slammed shut.

It was over; his former fiancée was lost to him, and it was all his fault.

When Christine was on the verge of death, vengeance was motivation enough for him to continue. During his intense two years of training, he had fostered a fantasy in which he returned to her brother Steven and their stoic father. He would let them know that he had brought justice to the beasts who slew her. He believed that such knowledge would mend all their pain and bring about a touch of clarity to his own life.

But now, such a story could never happen. His ties to the whole family had been severed worse than Steven's throat, and he would find no family in his dreadful half-brother. If they truly were related.

After a final forlorn look at the Hideaway, Augen walked, leaving only his footprints and an occasional crimson droplet garnishing the snow for him to be remembered by.

❖

The inner city was incredibly busy, but the streets he wandered through were well outside the chaotic hub, lined only with the occasional passerby in either a motorized vehicle or on foot.

He passed another billboard, this one stating that Deos honored honest behavior, then another advertising something about skincare.

Lies! he thought, reading one superficial quote after another. It is all lies! The empire does not care for me. Neither does Deos!

The storm, which could still be seen looming over the sea, rumbled in the distance, reminding Augen of its existence, despite the peaceful sky and purifying snow.

I thought I knew what I wanted. Now I have nothing. Nothing to fight for. Nothing to live for. Nothing at all!

Augen's pace quickened, as did the daemonic voice echoing through his head, both jointly gathering momentum as he continued through the cold. *Why continue? No one will miss you now.*

Augen sped to a jog, fleeing the pain in his conscience and the voice in his head, and failing to elude either one. Eventually, his damaged lungs hurt, and his conscience altered course, bidding him to stop.

Across the road from Augen was a chapel, smaller than most of the religious buildings in Pallerheim, taking up only a half-block and bordered by two smaller state-funded structures, a library, and a constabulary pen.

The chapel was certainly the figurehead of the block. Beautiful, yet ancient, its sleek, angular, towering design gave off a timeless but intimidating air.

The library to its left was modern and appeared to have been renovated recently. It was by far the newest of the buildings and seemed likely to be the most popular.

The constabulary, on the other hand, stuck out amongst its neighbors. Short, square, undecorated, ugly. Yet, at least to Augen, it felt like it belonged where it stood, as though the unsightly structure's company was fitting, despite their obvious contrast.

Augen gave pause to the block-wide trio and considered entering the center building. *The top spire is tall enough...if you **really** wish to be rid of your pain...*

"Interesting, isn't it?" Augen jumped at the sound of the voice that had rudely interrupted his suicidal musings.

An elderly man had slipped beside the ruminating knight and stood directly beside him, gazing at the same buildings. He was dressed in a ragged undershirt, a blandly colored wool vest, and padded work trousers and boots. His head was adorned with a crude sailor's cap slightly too small for his head and reeking of fish oil. He was a simple and unintimidating man with seemingly little to offer, yet he stood beside Augen's towering frame with confidence.

At first glance, his average figure could disappear into a crowd completely unnoticed, but something about the man demanded respect, though Augen could not pinpoint what it was.

"Are you thinking about entering the chapel?" the stranger asked.

"No. Not genuinely. Under the circumstances, I am not sure I will be welcome."

The man nodded knowingly at Augen's response.

"There are times when I am not welcome either. Tell me, young man, of the trinity you see on this block, which do you think the world needs most?"

Augen raised his eyebrow, as his query felt like a trick question, but something compelled him to answer regardless. Augen paused for a moment and stared at the towering structures.

Since Deos was not listening, the fact that this stranger would do so felt strangely comforting.

"I believe the constabulary is needed most."

"Really? Explain."

"We live in a time when knowledge and faith are revealed only for the convenience of those promoting them. The true words of Deos sit dormant beneath two of Archaea's most impregnable fortresses and not in the hands or hearts of the people.

"As for knowledge and practical wisdom, I have observed firsthand just how much of that is hidden, distorted, and withheld from the eyes of the crowds. It is arguably just as biased as a religion, but without any guiding moral code.

"The only thing I have witnessed in my life is this: that some people cannot be guided gently—they need to be forced, and some behavior cannot be forgiven, just punished. The constabulary stands for both virtues."

"Interesting. You did not learn a thought process bussing tables at the Hideaway...or from training with the Templar."

Augen shot a panicked glance at the man. *How does he know? Does the old man work for them? Does he work for the Blood Inquisition like Zhatka?* The Templar hastily examined his surroundings, looking for assassins, some kind of ambush, or worse yet, Zhatka himself.

Not comforted by the fact he saw nothing out of the ordinary, Augen shuffled a foot to slip away, but the old visitor grabbed his coat sleeve confidently. He said nothing, and despite their obvious difference in size, such a bold move on a physically enhanced foot soldier intimidated Augen all the more.

"How did you..." Augen began to ask fearfully. The old man continued looking at the chapel and did not bother answering.

"You joined an illegal military organization to exact revenge on the men who once wronged you and your loved ones. Tell me, would the deaths of these men really cure you of your pain?"

A tear welled up in Augen's eye but did not fall. He nodded; it was what he had believed for several years now, but a tiny pinch in his heart made him feel guilty for admitting it.

The man with him made no eye contact but grunted in response to Augen's confession.

"What would it take for your faith to be restored? What would Deos have to do for you to put the same faith in Him that you do in your arms?" A final glance at the stranger, and Augen noticed something genuinely unique.

Despite his bland build, the man's eyes were anomalous, deeply nebulous, and striking, simultaneously dawning three different colors in each pupil. Augen had never seen anything like it before and was shocked that he had not caught it earlier.

Is he a prophet of some kind? Or some spiritual entity? Augen was unsure of what to do. He was suddenly far more uncomfortable than before.

If the man was just some stranger or even a spy, he understood what would come next. This was different.

"My days are limited, and my goals are shattered. I just want my..."

"Your death to mean something?" the stranger interrupted. "Yet here you are, contemplating suicide in front of a church."

The old man released Augen's arm and shook his head in frustration. "If you honor Deos in your actions, He will do so much more than what you want. He can make your life mean something. He could make you a hero, an enlightener, a legend. You can be a savior of the powerful and protector of the innocent! You can ascend to great heights! You can fall from the sky and live! You will set the throne room in the Ivory Citadel ablaze!"

Then, seemingly mid-sentence, the man stopped and smiled at Augen. "He does care. Do you?" And with that, the old fisherman began to depart.

Augen was dumbfounded but gathered his wits enough to retort.

"You cannot be serious?" he said. "I am a lonely, contract-bound gun for hire. What makes you think I can do any of those things? All I am trained to do is kill people. That doesn't seem very honorable to The Almighty."

"There is a time for everything under the sun, including killing. You have been chosen by Deos."

"And...to set the Ivory Citadel ablaze! That would be treason! Why would I even consider such a thing?"

"There is a time for everything under the sun, including treason. Should you accept this, you have been chosen." Augen was following the man as he walked away, around a corner toward an alleyway.

"I am not the kind of man you seem to think I am. What does Deos really want from me?" To this, the stranger paused, sighed, and eyed the man standing behind him.

"You want the words of Deos? Here are a couple more. To follow Him means to sacrifice your relationships, your lust for power, and even your will to survive. Give these things up, and when the time comes, you will know what He wants.

"You believe the Empire needs an enforcer? A punisher? Promise to protect the innocent to the best of your ability; He just might make you one. Perhaps you should care less about who you are and trust who He is." The old man rounded the corner of a building with Augen less than a second behind him. Augen was not done talking, but the stranger was, and when the knight cleared the edge of the building, with fresh protests on his mind, the fisherman was gone.

Augen stood alone in an empty alleyway for a moment, contemplating the words spoken to him before slowly and thoughtfully departing. He had never heard of anything like what he had just experienced, but he knew it was special.

Gazing through the window of the nearest building, he spotted a large timepiece hanging from the back wall. *Still several hours before I meet with Zhatka and the team.*

For a moment, Augen considered returning to The Hideaway. Maybe he could tell Alexi about his strange run-in with whoever that man was, but he decided against it. There was still so much he could not say, and he feared that opening up, even a little bit, would cause the dam to collapse.

Christine and her father could never know about Steven. Not if Augen had a say in the matter.

So, he wandered some more, this time keeping an eye out for the mysterious seafarer who confronted him in the shadow of the chapel. He approached a busier district of Pallerheim and took note of the faces he passed.

For the most part, the city folk seemed too engrossed in their own tasks to catch or contemplate the giant man in their midst.

Some did notice, most of them children, but they did not seem to care. In fact, some of them followed him a short distance, whispering to their friends about the "big scary man." Augen paid them little mind and continued scoping the crowd for a face he recognized. Any face would do.

Then, seemingly coming from everywhere at once, sirens located all over the city blew deeply with the force of a small earthquake.

Their deep brass resonance caused all to give pause for but a brief moment. When the trumpeting concluded, the common folk of Pallerheim dropped their work, and a chaotic, city-wide search ensued. Motor vehicles screeched to a halt and were turned off where they sat, and everyone surged into the nearest pub, electronics store, or high-end resort. Within a matter of moments, every establishment with a Hologram-Radio was packed to the point of bursting with eager observers. Even Pallerheim's massive industry buildings briefly powered down.

Understanding what the horns meant in this context, Augen hastened to find a suitable medium for such an occasion, but did not bother going indoors. Sprinting made his arms, legs, and chest hurt, but he knew the city well, and if the golden emperor was going to speak over the wavelengths, he knew where to get the best seat. So, sprint he did.

CHAPTER 3
THE LEGEND, THE MYTH, THE MAN

Near Pallerheim's core, a monstrous hologram projector sat nestled amid three of the city's tallest spires. Usually, it was dormant, reserved for breaking news, city-wide announcements, and occasionally, the new-world sporting tournaments. It would certainly be active for this.

Augen was able to close the distance swiftly, but underestimating both the distance and the severity of his injuries, he was late and in incredible pain by the time he finally did.

The city lights dimmed as the crackling machinery came to life, and suddenly, standing at least sixty feet tall, one of the world's two most powerful sovereign couples addressed the masses of Pallerheim and the western half of the planet Archaea.

Their greyscale images were glitchy and shaky, shifting in and out of focus regularly, but there was little left to the imagination. The emperor and empress of half the world sat on massive thrones high above people, both figuratively and literally.

No skin was visible on either of them as every inch of their bodies was covered in black ornamental armor, thick maroon linen cloth bearing various markings and words in eldritch languages, and several different kinds of gold and silver mail.

Their tall, sharp crowns were built into faceless visors broadcasting a perpetual but invisible gaze of intensity. They did not look human, but rather like ancient pagan deities, and Augen believed this aesthetic was intentional.

When they flickered into focus, most of the masses bowed. Augen did the same but with little enthusiasm. His body throbbed when he bent over, and despite the excitement, the cynicism toward life and the people he served continued gnawing at him.

"People of civil Archaea, the Ivory Citadel greets you. As you are aware, our glorious empire has seen the rise and fall of many enemies since the Wars of Cataclysm, and though many of them have returned to legitimacy under our guidance, some still seek our collapse and will go to any length to witness our demise."

The images overhead shifted and warped into a grotesque display of butchery with which all people of the West, especially Augen, were far too familiar.

The emperor continued to speak, narrating and describing the horrors of what the world knew as Impact Day.

He described in vivid detail how an anarchist terror cell acquired a division of outdated long-range artillery. He recalled the way they positioned the massive guns in hidden locations throughout the continent of Eros through months of meticulous planning. Then, feeding into the fury of the crowds below, he described the hundreds of explosive shells they flung into civilian epicenters all over the Western world in the continent's bloodiest event since the Cataclysm Wars themselves.

Augen felt another emotion ignite in his chest as the tale unwound, and for a moment, his guilt was buried in the same impassioned fury that had driven him into service for the Templar. An orphan from infancy, Augen had no biological family to lose on that day. However, he and Christine were some of the few to survive witnessing the atrocity firsthand.

The day Augen announced his intent for her would forever be marred by the occasion, and like their relationship, seemingly buried by its consequences, for mere days later, a newly vengeful and mourning young man also made contact with a Templar agent to announce his new, more destructive intentions.

The throngs cheered as images of the Great Foreign Legion, as well as numerous national forces, flew across the screen. The holographic armies raised the Imperial Flag over the scorched husk of Rhyad City, whose government had helped fund and organize Impact Day.

Seeing such a spectacle exalted the already cheering crowds into a state of patriotic ecstasy, and initially, Augen felt like joining them, but his brief flare of patriotism faded just as quickly as it came.

Though such a show of dominance was undeniably incredible, in Augen's mind, it was proven to be just that, merely a show; for he and many others were still fighting the same war without a resolution in sight, and the emperor's next words proved it.

"Though the governmental powers that threw their support to such destructive ends are now pounded into ash by my armies and by the armies of the civil world, we must take further measures to ensure that such a catastrophe never reoccurs. I now hold in my hand a law that will ensure that the Golden Empire will never fall under the threat of such a shadow again. Upon my signature, the armies of Alanapas and Eros will be transformed into something new, something unlike anything our enemies have ever encountered."

Augen rolled his eyes. *That is not true.* Nearly two hundred dead international smugglers would say otherwise.

The crowds were enthralled as images of knights in decorative full-plate flex armor were displayed heading up divisions of the international guard.

The scene was undeniably inspiring, as though the emperor himself were with his troops. Augen focused on the image as it reformed into the likeness of the emperor. He noted the similarities between them.

"Feeling better, Augen?" The voice pulled him out of his trance, and Augen recognized the source in an instant.

"Bleeding internally, marred skin and cement-rash on the forearms, shins, and lower back, three broken ribs, four cracked finger bones, a sprained wrist, and a mild concussion. I think I am faring well."

Mahkt had stepped beside him during the momentous episode and chuckled to himself, and smiled at the images on the screen. "Beautiful, isn't she?"

"The empress?"

"A feminine reflection of the emperor is a strange thing to behold. The image of power in a smaller, more unimposing form...but she always gets the last word. Have you noticed that?" As the speech continued, Augen paid closer attention to the empress standing, still as a statue, at the right hand of her husband.

She was significantly smaller than her menacing spouse, and her armor was smoother and less martial than his. Yet, in her own right, she possessed every ounce of ominous regality he did. A presence seen and felt even when not heard.

"I had not given it much thought," Augen said.

"They are two sides of a single coin, the iron fist of the state and the guiding hand of culture. One only goes so far, yet together, they are all but unstoppable! Deos knew what he was doing when he created the female species. It almost makes me wish I knew one."

"Yeah. Me too." A twitch of sharp pain pricked Augen as he spoke.

He did know one, but he gave her up. She did not know him anymore. Even if he could still speak with her, even if her brother's blood were not on his hands, even if her father allowed it, the Order, his new spouse, would not. The Templars' strict celibacy mandates meant that their relationship was doomed to a crippled stasis, with or without Augen's assistance ensuring it.

The more he contemplated it, the more his heart sank, and the louder the wicked voices in his mind grew, demanding an easy escape. But such thoughts were blown away when the crowd let a monstrous cheer erupt from their ranks.

The emperor raised a clenched fist to his forehead in a salute to his people, and everyone in the crowd, including the knights, returned the salute in tandem. Such vast grandeur was hard to shake, and the sight of the imperial couple was enough to blow away even Augen's cynicism for a short time.

Then the empress took the foreground, and Pallerheim went utterly silent while she began her half of the address. The emperor moved directly behind her and loomed in the background, perfectly still, but impossible to miss.

"Words cannot express the pain in my heart that we, as a species, cannot bear the tranquil lull of international accord. The halcyon dreams of our ancestors, who fought and spilled their blood in the Wars of Cataclysm, are yet to be consummated on the fields and seas of Archaea." Even under her helmet, she spoke with a calming, hypnotic tone that could put a child to sleep in a war zone. Her majesty was nothing like her husband's, but no less astonishing.

The city was so quiet, one could hear a copper coin drop in the street. Augen wondered if her voice was modified in some way to sound the way it did. One thing was certain: No woman, save perhaps the Silver Countess from the East, drew the ear and awe of the world as she did.

Despite having never shown her face or spoken in person to the public, her image defined beauty standards, and her words were encoded in the psyche of Western culture. Augen pondered this as she continued. It did not seem believable, yet it was. Far less believable was her next announcement.

"Though we still fall short of such monumental aspirations, Deos, the Maker of all, has His ever-watching eyes on us. For through focused toil, we, our race, will certainly endeavor to actualize a new plane of achievement in the times to come. Our neighbors, the industrious, charismatic, and dangerous Silverens, have already begun to compose a means of perpetuating long-distance aetheric travel. Know now, people of Alanapas and Western Eros, that our glorious empire is, this very day, in pursuit of the same end."

"Well now," Mahkt chuckled. "I did not see that one coming. I guess the conquest of Archaea is not enough anymore."

Augen shook his head. "What do they think they are going to find out there other than swirling masses of noxious gases?"

"Or already found?" Mahkt shot a sideways glance at Augen.

"You think they aren't telling us something?" Augen queried.

"Don't you?"

A group of civilians standing next to the knights motioned for them to be silent. Mahkt found their moxie amusing and humored them. Augen's mind was elsewhere. The knights said nothing more for the duration of the speech.

When the emperor and empress disappeared and were replaced with miscellaneous representatives of the Western Council, the crowd began to act lively again. However, work did not resume in earnest until the international transmission ceased altogether.

The everyday lives of the people would likely be affected by such international changes, and though the district representatives provided a lackluster spectacle compared to that of their masters, their words would provide details of such change. They would also take the blame should the application of the new law be found frustrating in the eyes of the common folk.

Augen figured a call would go out for certain workforce specialists and engineers to be registered in a national census bank so that their skills could be requisitioned by the government. The pay would be more than worthwhile, assuming the performance was satisfactory.

While he thought through the implications of a Void Race between the Great Empires, his mind drifted once more to his own "specialist" work.

The crowds began to fade away in his mind, and once again, Augen would be left to face his guilt and loneliness. As the world began to disappear altogether, Mahkt's hand tapped Augen on the shoulder and jerked him back out of the void.

"Are you sure you are all right? You are bleeding out of your mouth again," Mahkt muttered. Augen wiped his mouth and shrugged.

"A bit worse for wear, I am afraid. My wounds are already healing, but my conscience does not seem to want to."

Mahkt sighed. "I cannot say I understand. You have to know that you are not the first knight to kill a civilian during an op, right? It is never ideal, but it does happen."

In the distance, Pallerheim's towering industrial district reawakened like a massive bronze clock, and the ground shook with the slow mechanical grind of the production facilities' resurrecting apparatuses. Soon, ships would be loaded, unloaded, repaired, and even built within the great docks of Pallerheim and its foundries. For most within its borders, mundane life would return to its normal pace now that the emperor had said his piece.

Augen walked once more with no direction in mind, but Mahkt kept an identical pace.

"You think I make too much of this?"

"No, I think it is good to have a conscience. Just don't let conviction become guilt. One is a motivator for improvement, and the other is a paralytic."

"Where did you hear that?"

"A priest I knew as a youth."

The two continued walking for quite some time until the sun began to duck behind the Nethellite Mountains. The men said little until Augen posed another question.

"Do you think Deos is real?"

Mahkt started at the question and chuckled. "Of course."

"Do you think He cares about what happens to us?" This time, Mahkt did not respond immediately. Instead, he looked into the distance and clicked his tongue.

"I think He does as He pleases, like the emperor." Then Mahkt gestured for them to take a turn on the next roadway.

They had a meeting to get to, and though neither of them particularly desired to see or interact with Zhatka again, there was an opportunity to learn and grow, and at the moment, such an opportunity was enough to push them onward.

....

Alexander took a deep breath and gazed into the eye of the projector lens until the light above it died out, then he strode out of the room as quickly as he could. The guards lining the doorway and walls all bowed in synchronicity as he made his exit.

The hallways ahead were empty save for a handful of heavily ornamental soldiers standing erect at the farthest doorway. The orange hue of setting sunlight flooded the room from the thirty-foot-tall slit windows, illuminating the great structure's interior with a glorious tint.

One would feel as though they were walking through a canyon in such a room, but Alexander took no pause. He had to get into the open. He had to breathe.

On the other side of the hall was a crowded cross-chamber packed with the conglomeration of an empire-state at work. People in different uniforms, some accompanied by guards, strode from one doorway to another. Priests and deacons bearing religious documents, secretaries bearing charts and graphs, and media-guild representatives bearing notepads and projector-cams scurried to and fro, each with his own distinct destination in mind.

The guards clicked their heels upon Alexander's entrance, and the room froze. The crowd parted to make room for their emperor, and as he passed them, they saluted in silence, shifting their feet to face him for the duration of his stay. No one dared to come within ten feet of their leader, who strode through the room as though it were empty.

Passing through a tall slit threshold into an empty elevator hatch, he turned and nodded to the crowds, permitting them to continue their work. Two engraved doors silently slid together, sealing the hoisted room and its inhabitants inside.

Once out of sight, his rigid form melted down as he let himself relax just enough to regain some energy. Leaning against the nearest wall, he bent over in a fashion that allowed him some space to breathe inside his beautiful and constricting regalia.

But he could not remain there for long, for he had one more stretch to clear before respite. The doors opened once more, and the emperor strode with supreme poise through the twelfth and second-to-highest floor of the Ivory Citadel.

This floor was occupied by the more antisocial arm of the Golden Empire. Military staff, many of whom wore masks and garb similar to the emperor's, paused and saluted as their commander-in-chief passed through before they hustled once more to complete their objectives.

Once through the bustling martial cluster, the emperor strode up a staircase and into a massive marble and steel semicircle that sat completely unoccupied at the end of the building. It sat at the base of a towering spire crowned with an ornate dome looming fifty yards overhead.

He turned and gazed into a thick, tinted window adorning a guardhouse suspended above the oblique room. He could not see the armed gatekeepers inside, but they saw him.

A deep rumble grew beneath the emperor's feet, and the floor he stood on ascended the spire's neck toward its gold and ivory peak.

Despite the scientific wonders accomplished to create the floor's indoor propulsion system, the process seemed quite slow for Alexander, who had made this trek thousands of times.

The dome glowed with twilight radiating from its small but numerous slitted skylights, and the floor sealed the emperor into the top floor with an echoing metallic clang. Upon the reverberating signal, Alexander ripped off his heavy helmet and crown, gasping for air before stumbling toward his quarters.

Waiting for him in the next room were two members of the Whitetower Sentinels, an elite and secretive branch of palace guard who occupied only the top floors of the Ivory Citadel, and a clergyman.

"Good day, today?" The clergyman took the emperor's crown and strode alongside him, accommodating his lord's staggered pace.

"Long...very long."

"Will the empress be up soon?"

"Yes. The empress agreed to address the complaints of the reps today and update me when she comes up." Alexander's gait recovered quickly. Though his fatigue was still noticeable, his stride quickened, and the chaplain soon found himself struggling to keep pace.

The emperor was unstrapping, untying, unbuttoning, and loosening his clothes with every step at this point.

"Have you figured out what is going on with…the incidents in the cathedral?" To this, the cleric paused, and his stride hiccupped. He had hoped to bring the topic up on his own time, but the emperor pushed it. "What did you find? Come on, Nathan. I know that you did as I asked. Did you get to the bottom of this?"

"It is happening more often now than ever. Apparently, there are even priests outside the cathedral being driven to this prophecy. Evidence suggests that these are not independent incidents." A visible tension arose in Alexander's countenance.

"So…you think this could be it. You think Deos is poised to strike us?" Nathan avoided eye contact, unsure of what to say. By now, Alexander carried his capes, armor, and outer tunics by hand, handing them off to select household servants, who bore the items to a closet on the other end of his living quarters.

"You know that Impact Day was…"

"Come now, Nathan, do not trouble the emperor further. Impact Day was unique, but that does not make it the first strike of Deos." Another member of the clergy strutted into the room, staring Nathan down before more was said. Alexander redirected his attention to the newcomer, noting an obvious tension between the two. "Little is known about the prophecies you mention so casually. We should all be careful before applying such texts to our time."

Nathan shot a troubled look at the newcomer. "That does not mean we should disregard it altogether."

The two clergymen stared each other down with confidence until Alexander, who was now shirtless, pulled their focus back to him. "I asked for Nathan's opinion, Zavaden. I am interested in his perspective, regardless of his rank compared to yours. Let him finish." The latecomer bowed his head politely and took a step back, but he eyed Nathan pointedly as he continued.

"It is true. Nothing is certain, as my...colleague...has pointed out, but these are uncertain times. It would be wise to tread carefully. Pride, arrogance, impatience, these are all characteristics despised by Deos in the world's leadership. It is imperative that we not test His patience, lest we drive Him to wrath."

Alexander nodded solemnly, but doubt was still written on his countenance. "Of course, but if the first strike has happened, are the wheels not already turning? If Deos has set in motion the end times for our empire, then there is no tangible way of stopping it. What am I supposed to do if the empire is already doomed?"

Nathan sighed, staring at the polished bronze floor before returning eye contact, for he too was unsure. "If you look for guidance, why don't you try praying to Deos yourself, sir? Try talking to Him. He could bring some clarity to..."

"That's *our* job, Nathan! Why don't you return to your studies?" Zavaden's abrupt breach of temper and etiquette soured the conversation and brought it to an untimely end. Alexander shot a displeased look at Zavaden but nodded for Nathan to do as he was told.

When the door latch announced Nathan's departure, Alexander asked once more, "What am I to do if the Rain of Iron has come to pass? Since you were so unwilling to let Nathan answer, you can do it instead."

"Apologies, my emperor. There are times when my patience wears thin around people who say more than they should. Despite my position in the Church, I am still only a man." Zavaden slowly paced the width of the room as he spoke. Alexander leaned against the frame of the washing room door.

By now, the servants had taken all his clothing out of the quarters save the pair of thin trousers he still wore. The two men were now completely alone. "However, very little is certain regarding these prophecies, or your role in them, for that matter. It is prudent to acknowledge the role the clergy takes in addressing such issues with the wherewithal to understand one's own humanity and subsequent fallibility. Are you not reminded of this flaw daily? Your...flaw?"

Alexander's eyes narrowed. He got the message.

"You should be very careful what you say next," he growled.

"My liege, I will say no more. I apologize for any disturbance Nathan or I may have caused you. We will continue looking into these strange occurrences, and if anything is revealed for certain, we will let you know. No, *I* will let you know."

"I do not want anyone to disturb me. Let the guards know on your way out."

Zavaden bowed once more and slipped out of the room. Fatigue returned to Alexander's psyche and body with a whirlwind of force the moment he was truly on his own. He was exhausted, and only now was he finally able to admit it to himself.

After limping into the washroom, he pulled an ointment that had been set out for him on the vanity, lathered his hands with it, and very gently rubbed his grotesque augmentation scars with it. They throbbed miserably upon contact, and Alexander winced with each touch.

He hated doing this, but seventeen hours in the suffocating attire he wore for work had left his body greasy and smelly. He had to bathe. So, despite the searing pain in his arms and back, bathe he did.

Once out of the washroom, he bandaged his arms and chest and dressed in plain clothing. Then, he took a walk in the orchard.

By now, the sun was completely down, but a nearly full moon illuminated the roof of the citadel plenty. Taking a deep breath of fresh air, Alexander slouched onto one of the numerous wooden and steel benches bolted to the citadel roof and gazed into the horizon.

A mountain range stretched across the horizon, walling in three riverfront municipalities and providing a border between the starlit sky and the equally illuminated cityscapes. It was beautiful to behold, at least from where Alexander sat. He had not personally seen the interior of any of those cities in years.

Staring into the land outside his world, Alexander rested his eyes and began to drift into an unconscious dream state until he heard footsteps approaching him. They did not initially register in his exhausted mind until they were close enough to startle him awake.

"There you are, Alexander." A lady, accompanied by several young maidens, slipped through the orchard and took a seat next to the man on the bench.

The young girls with her worked silently, combing and pulling her long hair straight behind her. When she sat, they held it above the bench's back brace and continued working in silence. "You picked a different spot tonight. It took me a while to find you."

Alexander strained his countenance back into the perfect posture usually expected of him, but began to relax again once he realized who he was speaking with.

"Hello, Catherine. How did the meeting go?" The lady shrugged casually and stared into the distance with her husband. "As you would expect, questions about the Void Race, a couple of funding and construction requests. Busy work, mostly. I took care of the bulk of it."

Alexander smiled weakly at Catherine and closed his eyes again. "Thank you."

"How... How much sleep have you been getting lately?" she inquired, shifting her frame uncomfortably.

He knew that she hated to ask, but understood that it was likely the dark purple and grey patches beneath his eyes were going to undermine any excuse he could make up in the moment. So, he chose to be honest. "About four hours a night. The generals convene in the early morning Eastern Time, and I don't stop until our sundown."

"That's...not very healthy."

Alexander opened his eyes enough to shoot her a scowl. It seemed everyone was content with telling him his weaknesses today.

Catherine kept her eyes forward but bit her lip as though she knew that she had hit a sore spot. "I can take another shift tomorrow with the reps if you like."

Alexander scowled again, but this time, he was the target of his own angst. *She shouldn't need to be covering for you at all.*

"I will do it," he grunted.

"It is no issue for me. I don't have the kind of schedule you do."

"I said I would do it!"

Catherine recoiled slightly upon her husband's outburst but kept her cool. The servants did their best to work with her movements, keeping her hair straight without pulling or tangling it. Catherine took a moment to look into the horizon as well.

"I know you can do it... I simply wish to help, that is all." Catherine touched his hand to no response and leaned over to kiss his cheek, but her hair was tugged by one of the servants, and she yelped in his ear instead. She turned to correct her hairdressers, but Alexander, who had been snapped out of sleep yet again, cut in.

"Do that again, girl, and you will be cleaning lavatories for the rest of your life!" The perpetrator, barely a day over seven years old, stood stiff in shock. Catherine tried to step in.

"It is all right, Alexander. I can take care of..."

"It is NOT all right! If you think you can get away with roughshod, lazy, mediocre work, then the citadel is not for you. You had better get your act together, girl, or you will find yourself back in the orphanage!"

The emperor stumbled off the bench and leaned over Catherine and the girls.

"And don't patronize me, Catherine! I can handle things myself! I am going to sleep! I need sleep! I need...some peace and quiet!"

Standing nearly six and a half feet tall, he knew that he did not need his armor to appear intimidating, but his wife's eyes radiated a pity that he despised but could do nothing about. So, after a lengthy moment of intense silence, Alexander stormed away. His first steps were uneven and awkward as though he were drunk, until his run-down mind caught up with his body and evened out his pace.

Catherine leaned back slowly and sighed to herself. A tear rolled down her cheek as she gazed into the moonlit sky. The girl behind her sobbed quietly, and Catherine swallowed her own emotions again to address her.

"Is he really going to get rid of me?" she asked, hands shaking, but still gripping the patch of hair she had accidentally tugged earlier.

"No. He was just angry." A spark of calloused anger materialized in her chest, but she stuffed it.

Taking in some orphans to raise was her idea since she was unable to have children of her own, but Alexander was too engrossed in his work to recognize the good it could do for them both. Though if she were honest, she knew that she, too, had often forgotten the reason they were brought to the citadel.

The power she and Alexander wielded was extraordinary and impossible to ignore—it permeated every part of their life. It was them, and they were made to embody it.

"Your...father...would not disown you. He just bears a tremendous burden, and sometimes, he doesn't have the chance to be just a man."

Another tear came, and she turned away from the girls before finishing. "You may go. Get some rest before your studies tomorrow."

The girls walked solemnly out of the garden, whispering amongst themselves as they went.

Once they were out of sight, Catherine stared into the starry sky and cried quietly. Things were never meant to be this way. She wanted something more for her and Alexander, but she hadn't the faintest idea what that was.

CHAPTER 4

AN EDUCATIONAL MEETING

"I wonder where the Teutons are." Mahkt and Augen sat at an upscale public house packed to the brim with its slightly inebriated clientele. The boisterous crowds swelled with talk about the upcoming Void Race and what it meant for the people in Pallerheim.

There was also talk about the new "super soldiers" enlisted in the military. Mahkt smirked as the group occupying the booth behind them spoke about the end of the wars.

"You think I should tell them that we aren't going to win the war for them? After all, the Orders have been involved for years and.... Would you calm down, Augen? Zhatka and the others will be around soon enough."

Augen visually cleared the room as well as he could once more before acknowledging his comrade. "Sorry. I am certain that they would have been here by now." Augen began to clear the corners again. Mahkt may not be nervous about Zhatka's absence, but Mahkt did not get a surprise visit from Zhatka earlier in the day. If he had, he would be.

The building was quite large and consisted of several rooms, most of which Augen could not see into. He considered going into those rooms and checking to make sure they were not holding up his half-brother, who lurked in some undiscovered corner of the structure, but as luck would have it, Mahkt was right. The Teutons were indeed running late and made their entrance unmistakable.

The double doors at the inn's mouth slapped open dramatically, and the rambunctious crowds near the establishment's throat clammed up. A series of perfectly synchronized footsteps imitating a march echoed across the wood floors of the brewery, heralding the entrance of a truly unique brand of pub hopper.

"Well, I think you can finally calm down now, Augen. It seems our friends are here." The five Teutons rounded the corner, and the rest of the pub went silent.

Unlike Augen and Mahkt, the Teutons did not arrive in civilian garb. Instead, they wore dress uniforms from the armies they had fought in before joining the Teutonic Order.

Their tall hats, elaborately decorated coats that barely fit their enhanced bodies, dress pants, plated boots, and even some medals of honor, were all part of the display.

Most of the patrons stared in awe as the massive men passed them by. Others looked on with more than a hint of fear on their faces.

"Aw. You waited for us, how kind of you." Zhatka, standing at the front of the group, winked at the Templar as he grabbed a drink off a random table and downed most of it in a swallow.

"I see you are making fine use of the new edict," Mahkt said in jest, though Augen noted a slight touch of sarcasm in his voice as well.

"And I see that you aren't."

"Had you told us we were dressing up for the occasion, I may have," Mahkt continued his banter, but Augen kept quiet.

Zhatka knew well that the Teutons were the only order to require military service in a Northern country as a prerequisite to joining their ranks. Even if Mahkt had a uniform to wear, Augen didn't, and Zhatka likely knew this. Regardless of whether it was intentional, the two Templar stuck out next to their new company.

Once the newcomers had seated themselves, the room gradually became lively once more. However, there was a palpable disturbance in the establishment's aura. Augen could not tell if it was awe or fear, but the talk that resumed in the bar had little to do with the Void Race.

Most of the knights spoke of their work in vague terms, without revealing their more recent operations directly. Zhatka was less careful, boasting of his previous mission's kill count through a rather pathetic veil of subtlety, referring to the deceased sailors of the *Leoris* as "chores" and "obstacles" he had to discard in the ocean.

"How about you, Templar?" he finally concluded. "How many, ahem, *chores* did you eliminate last night? Oh, and it doesn't count if you picked them out yourself."

What was meant to be a jab at Augen fell almost entirely on deaf ears. The Teutons snickered briefly to themselves, but what little merriment they gained from an obvious low blow burned out in seconds.

Zhatka visibly wanted to tell his underlings to laugh, but understood that it would not be the same even if they listened to him. Instead, he grunted to himself and leaned back in his chair, muttering about how slow the service was.

Small talk transitioned from there to other topics, but it was awkward and clunky. The more experienced knights clearly did not get out much. Formal events were unheard of before the legalization of their orders. In fact, many knights talked to inanimate objects more commonly than something that could respond, and as a result, the average knight's social skills were gravely handicapped. However, after a short break, Zhatka found plenty more to say.

"This world is so disappointing. Mountains, deserts, tundra, all just terrain to overcome. One is happier to have passed through such a location than to ever have been there.

"The jungles are just as miserable. Grotesque, teeming with filth, and an irritant at best. One would be better off avoiding such places.

"You hear about the cities abroad, spend valuable time traveling there, just to find out that they are made up of steel, wood, and stone, just like everywhere else. It looks different, but it is nothing special, masquerading as order with a chaotic soul. But worse than all these things...are people." Zhatka stared into Augen's eyes as he continued.

Augen cautiously glanced back into the dark orbs of his half-brother, and there was little left to the imagination. He was angry, seemingly about everything, but most of all about Augen himself.

Despite their supposed familial connection, Augen wondered what brought about such vitriol toward him. Could it have been his killing of Steven? It likely was. They were, after all, supposed to be "holy orders," and Deos forbid a relative of his to kill a non-combatant.

"You cannot change a human being—that is what is most dreadful about them. You can push them, punish them, put them through a gantlet of misery, but you can never truly draw them from their failure. Once a washout, always a waste."

"How about the void, then?" Mahkt interrupted. He leaned back in his chair unimposingly, but there was also a touch of arrogance in his posture. He did not seem intimidated, and Augen could not decide whether this trait was impressive or stupid.

The Teutons eyed Mahkt but remained silent. Two of them held or rubbed numerous fresh wounds on their arms and torsos; Augen figured the wounds were the "punishment for incompetence" Zhatka had foreshadowed during their op.

"The void?" Zhatka paused, glancing at the ceiling as though he could see the starry night through the many layers of manmade structure above them. "The void is going to be no more interesting than Archaea. Swirling masses of toxic gas intermingling with superheated rock and steel particles. A hazardous mineral mine without gravity. Boring, just another distraction."

"From what?" Mahkt interrupted again. Zhatka leaned backward, seemingly enjoying the presence of an audience.

"The meaningless and mundane nature of life. The emperor is in charge because he gives people something to do. Without it, we are left to think, and that..." Leaning forward, this time with an emphatic gesture, he concluded, "...would be the greatest curse of all."

Augen paused, pondering the commander's words. His vision of the world was grim, but something about it rang true. At least to him, it did.

A moment went by, and Augen considered chiming in. Zhatka, who peered threateningly at him once more, seemed to want something out of him. Perhaps he could lighten up his currently tense relations with the man if he just knew what he wanted?

"What kind of freaks are you, huuuh?" All eyes went toward an obviously intoxicated man who approached the knights with some less-than-subtle questions. "You guys are big! What are you doing around here, huuuh?" The man looked like a factory worker of some kind, a nobody in the eyes of Zhatka, and someone who could easily be swept aside. Zhatka turned his body to face the man, but one of the Teutons spoke up.

"Showing you what kind of soldiers your taxes are now funding. Now beat it."

Despite the Teuton's uncharacteristic effort to avoid a scene, it became obvious that the civilians in the room were far more thoroughly invested in their booth than they initially let on. Augen saw all eyes fall on them, and some of the patrons even let out supportive whoops. Others murmured amongst themselves, responding to the confirmation of the men's identities as knights.

"You don't seem too tough to me," the man said, belching his last word. Zhatka turned and made eye contact with the man, who, even in his groggy state, shrank slightly under his gaze.

Augen observed and pondered his options. Clearly, this man was asking for mortal trouble, but what was he going to do? At first, the answer seemed obvious: Do nothing. Zhatka could not be crossed, and drunk or not, this man would get what he had coming to him for doing so.

Tensions rose momentarily but were dispersed slightly as one of the barkeeps brought them drinks.

"One of you men paying? Or all of you?"

"I will pay." Zhatka nodded toward the barkeep but kept his eyes on the peon confronting him. "Unless, of course, *you* want to?"

He shot another warning stare at the man to accompany his veiled threat, and the man tentatively began to leave, eyeing them in a way he surely thought intimidating. The knights smiled belittlingly in response.

Augen sighed in relief. Two chances to walk away? Zhatka must have been feeling very generous. Or maybe he didn't want blood on his dress jacket.

"So...you don't think there is anything interesting to be discovered in the void, then?" Mahkt jumped back into conversation, and this time, the Teutons joined in.

"Doubt it. We may never even make it to the void. My guess: If the void is toxic to us, it is toxic to everything. I think they will make a big deal about this, then dismiss it quietly when some other distraction comes along."

"I agree with Zhatka. I think if anything of interest is out there, we would have already discovered it."

"You know…if you guys are so tough…" The drunk was back. This time, some bystanders got involved in a futile attempt to turn the man away. "You could have stopped Impact Day, or these endless wars in the ancient world. You are all frauds to me." Then he vomited, spewing a high-alcohol liquid all over the back of Commander Zhatka's dress jacket.

The Teutons leaped to their feet in synch, and the whole building held its breath.

The two older men, trying to disarm the situation, one of them covered in the man's spew, tried to step between Zhatka and the drunk. He started to say something but was violently thrown aside by the Reaper and lay there silently until he felt safe enough to move again.

"You want to see how tough we are? Why don't I show you firsthand?" A bouncer tried to step in, but three of the Teutons stood in his way. Too late, and far too little compared to the three standing before him, the bouncer froze and backed off, utterly useless.

Panic was now written all over the drunkard's face. In Zhatka's shadow, it seemed the weight of his predicament had finally struck him.

"How about an appetizer?" The massive Teuton grabbed the man by the collar, lifted him off the floor, and backhanded him with the force required to rip the collar off.

Mahkt swore to himself but leaned back into his chair. His calm demeanor remained visible in his posture, but his face showed that such form was forced. He was brazen and cold enough to verbally spar with Zhatka, but even he knew better than to cross the Reaper enraged. He squinted as though he were preparing to take a blow but did not make another move.

Augen sighed to himself. It all seemed inevitable. A man with Zhatka's demeanor should not be allowed in a public area, yet there he was, there they all were.

"Zhatka, enough!" Augen yelled with illogical confidence.

The scarred Teuton paused, his fist closed to strike a second, far more dangerous blow, and looked at Augen, who did not stop. "Look at yourself! Beating on a drunk? Doesn't that seem a bit...below you?"

The Teutons running interference for their commander eyed him menacingly but waited for a response. Zhatka stared at his accuser, and a smile slid onto his face.

"Protecting the weak? You wouldn't be compensating for anything, would you?" The Teutons chuckled to themselves as Zhatka dragged the drunk to the door and tossed him out.

The jab at Augen hurt, but he didn't fight it. He deserved it.

The bouncer looked at the floor in embarrassment as Zhatka passed him again to return to his seat.

"Do your job next time, boy! Or people will certainly get hurt." Zhatka sat, as did everyone else, but his eyes burned with a malevolent glow, and Augen was the new target.

The inn's atmosphere was soured. Patrons who once gazed in awe at the knights as they entered now expressed obvious discomfort at their prolonged presence. They clearly had not considered the idea that such power could be so easily turned on them. Augen felt everyone's eyes, but Zhatka took his attention.

"I would be extremely careful, Augen Di Gattchen. You don't know what depths I have stooped to in order to become the best. Very little is below me. VERY little!"

No one in the group felt like small talk anymore.

Drinks were tentatively brought to them by a waiter who was extra careful not to spill anything. No one drank. Instead, Zhatka pulled a series of manuscripts from the pocket of his begrimed jacket before removing and hanging it up.

"I have political pull in both of our orders and have written up recommendations for your next assignments. It turns out one of you will be staying in Pallerheim, working with the local district militia...great use of our talent," he said, rolling his eyes.

Augen gasped silently, remembering the words of the old man on the street. Perhaps Deos was going to prove His existence after all. A station in Pallerheim was not only logical; it would make an optimistic prediction possible.

"Garroth, Hellik, you two will be working in the Byzican city-states, assisting the local militias in fortifying their citadels in case of a potential invasion." Two of the Teutons nodded as he continued, though disappointment was clearly written on their faces. Apparently, they hoped for something more dangerous.

Augen fought the urge to roll his eyes at their response and focused on Zhatka as he continued.

"Ranyen, you will be transferred to the Araby Plateau. The Forty-fifth Islican Grenadiers are spearheading a push into the war zone in Babyl. You will be co-leading them." As Zhatka spoke, he handed the papers containing transfer information and travel times to the men, each according to what was allotted to them.

"Co-leading?" Ranyen accepted his papers but surveyed them in confusion.

"Yes. You will be providing tactical analysis from the front lines to the divisional commander. Read it yourself.

"Lyzev, you will be heading up the Thirty-second Cassadirs. Same base of operations, but you are going to be an enforcer for the locals."

"Urban combat, close quarters, irregular formations. Sounds like my kind of party if I wasn't working with unkempt Southerners," Lyzev grunted, spitting on the floor and taking his papers.

Zhatka glanced at his manuscripts, then at Augen and Mahkt, and pocketed the last papers.

"Mahkt Essen Zorn. I have...recommended you for the Pallerheim shift."

Mahkt said nothing but shot a glance at Augen before posing a question. "I have a great deal of experience in intelligence. Why this post?" Zhatka gave no response, but instead, he focused his gaze on Augen.

"Augen Di Gattchen will be transferred to the Eleventh Alampian Sharpshooters and...the Seventh Reds. I think you could use some time on the front lines. Don't you?" The Teutons sneered, Mahkt was taken aback, and Augen slumped into his chair.

Spearheading the 7th Islican Musketers or "The Reds," a battalion known for their unwillingness to give ground under any circumstances, meant guaranteed deployment in the far corners of the world. This was the position of envy for the kill-crazy Teutons and, at least at the moment, was the very last thing Augen was interested in partaking in.

"It seems that I have neither the skills nor the will to deal with people formally. I may see you again. Maybe not." Zhatka stared into Augen's eyes, soaking in his disappointment before grabbing his messy coat and striding out.

The Teutons snarled at Augen and followed suit. Mahkt reached for one of the untouched drinks they had requested.

"You should have let him do his thing—better some nobody than you."

"He could have killed him. I thought I was doing the right thing."

"Yes, he likely would have killed him," Mahkt said, gulping down the last of a drink and starting another.

Augen was bothered by his nonchalant attitude about this. "We don't need another needless casualty of our visit. Some poor sap who was just in the wrong place at the wrong time. Like Steven."

"Who?" Mahkt downed another drink and squinted at his comrade.

"The, uh, priest I killed. I read about his identity in the local news-pamphlets."

"I get it. You were trying to atone for your mistake by saving some drunk. Do you feel better now that you have?"

Augen frowned. He didn't. The words of the old man still lingered in his head, but he threw them out. Some promise. There was no chance those predictions, or prophecies, or whatever Augen wanted to call them, would come true now.

Mahkt put his hand on Augen's shoulder. "Let the priest go. The ancient world is no place to try to play the part of a god."

Augen considered leaving, but something, a minuscule voice in his head, a hook in his conscience, compelled him to stick around just a bit longer.

Mahkt slid the last drink toward his sulking compatriot. "Come on. Have a drink. I am buying since our…ehem…friends have flown the coop. Besides, I owe you for my new low-risk station."

The two drank for a short while. The alcohol had little effect on the massive men except for a slight numbing of their shallow injuries. Eventually, the conversation died out, and for a short time, neither of them said anything. Nothing interesting or useful seemed to come to mind until Augen broke the silence.

"Well, I did learn something from this meeting."

"What did you learn?"

"That I was not cut out for this kind of work. I have too big a mouth and too bloody a heart to last long as a Templar."

Mahkt sighed and rubbed his chin.

"Yet here you stand. The only one with the brass to stand up to Commander Belogo when he was clearly out of line. Even the Reaper was thrown off by your behavior. I could tell." Another pause as Mahkt drank again before continuing. "You know..." He finished the last drink and slammed the goblet onto the table before standing. "I think you are wrong. I do not think you are incompetent. I think there is something special in you. I am a good soldier; I don't question orders or the behavior of commanding officers. I don't take it personally when I kill. You do both and have already paid the price for it."

"Thanks," Augen said sarcastically, but Mahkt was not finished.

"And yet. I have a strange feeling that the Reaper will be caught off-guard by you yet again. A knight like you would have had little chance of survival in the past, but there is a time for everything. And I have a feeling that times are changing indeed. Perhaps Deos has chosen you for something a normal knight would never be able to do?"

As Mahkt walked away to pay for the booth and drinks, Augen pondered his words. *A time for everything*. The man on the street had said something similar. *Chosen.*

As his fellow Templar nodded once more to him and departed, Augen whispered a silent prayer once more, with all the sincerity he could muster.

"Deos. I am completely reliant on You now. Get me through these times, let me fulfill my purpose, and I will never doubt You again. I will honor You the best I can for the rest of my life. If You did speak to me through that man, please keep Your promise."

Augen scoped out the crowd as he stood. The people had largely returned to their personal chatter, talking about politics, sports, and the trivial things normal people spoke of. But many did eye him, murmuring cautiously amongst themselves as he passed them.

Drinks and conversation with strangers seemed unlikely and unattractive to the Templar, so he returned to his quarters alone, pondering his future as he shuffled through the wet snow.

Since Zhatka had kept his instructions and written assignment, doubtless so that he could alter the papers as a cruel final punishment, Augen would likely receive the papers sometime tomorrow night via an encrypted message.

Then he would be gone. The renowned 7th Islican Musketers had not left a combat zone since the Wars of Cataclysm. They boasted some of the most veteran, battle-hardened men the Western Armies possessed.

Their leader, a man by the name of Pazkt Lomat, possessed an intimidating reputation as the face and mind of his war-hardened men. Menacing, yet cold, the commander had endured and survived numerous courts-martial and investigations for his disregard of casualties, eventually clawing his way into the uniform of an all but untouchable senior field commander.

Another Zhatka, just unaugmented. Perfect. At least I will be able to hold my own when things inevitably come to blows.

Despite the weight of his circumstances, a glance at the moonlit sky helped alleviate the burden. It certainly was beautiful.

As Augen walked, his mind shifted to the Void Race. Was it just another distraction? Perhaps it was, but for the moment, a distraction did not seem too bad.

CHAPTER 5

A DIFFERENT PERSPECTIVE

The next days went just as Augen suspected they would. The Order contacted him via a handheld letter delivered to the door of the house he lodged in.

Inside the letter were instructions guiding him to a specific runway stretching along the eastern border of Pallerheim's single airfield. He was told what to wear, what baggage to bring, and the precise time he was expected to arrive.

Once there, he was hastily directed into the baggage hold of a massive airship that Augen recognized as a Deathwatch Moth. Most people knew it by the civilian name given to it after reconfiguration, the Eroan Moth, but it had a much deeper history than that of a simple cargo freighter.

Whether for the sake of convenience or the maintenance of a stubborn tradition, Augen would not travel like a normal soldier. He would be alone for the duration of his journey through the air. He had joined the Templar Order expecting nothing less.

The contact stuffed another letter into his jacket pocket just before the two of them were separated by the closing bay door. Once inside, Augen removed his jacket and found a comfortable place to lie down.

His mind wandered into sleep temporarily, but true rest eluded him. Nightmarish visions of his distant past and recollections of his more recent traumas crept about the storage facility, pouncing on his conscience whenever he lowered his guard.

Eventually, Augen gave up on the prospect of a silent and relaxing reprieve between locations. Drawing a large combat dagger from its sheath, he pulled one of the pads from the handle and drew a small piece of paper from the patch it left behind.

Each knight was permitted to carry a single weapon of choice on his person when outside of combat zones. It was never any kind of powder weapon but something medieval, usually as a calling card or lucky charm for the successful and lonely crusader to busy himself with while traveling between bloodbaths. For Augen, it was a reminder of what he fought for and left behind in order to avenge the North after Impact Day.

The parchment contained a detailed sketch of Christine, his beautiful former betrothed, on the day he spoke for her. Augen did not know the man who drew it, but he was clearly an expert in his craft, for the artist had captured her essence in excellent detail on that paper.

Augen stared at it, utilizing a beam of moonlight to take in the presence. He wished she were with him and that things were different.

As he contemplated her beauty, he remembered Impact Day and the death that enshrouded the couple so quickly, sparing them but smothering nearly nine hundred other innocents on their block alone.

A spark of intense hatred ignited in his chest. *If not for dumb luck, those beasts would have smothered her, too.* The spark grew, warming his body and giving him an unnatural energy.

He no longer desired sleep. So, after carefully rolling up the image of his love and returning it to the hilt of his dagger, he toured the lower deck of the airship, dreaming of what it must have looked like in its day.

It did not take long for him to find the steel patches in the floor where the Gullet-Cannons, the main guns of the

Deathwatch Moth, were once used to liquidize enemy armor divisions from orbit with frightening accuracy. The braces used to absorb shock and hold the cannon frames were still present, built into the very core of the airship.

"These were used on the wrong people. The Cataclysm Wars were fought as nothing more than the culmination of the Northern World's petty rivalries. These great weapons should have been turned south, to tame the wildlands before they ever had the strength to rise and stab us in the back. They were nothing then, and had our ancestors been wiser, they could be nothing but ash now."

A light flashed by from outside, possibly from another airship on an intersecting route, illuminating the room.

At that moment, Augen could practically see the Deathwatch Warmoth in its prime, run by a large and highly trained crew of men rushing from the internal loading crane controls and Gullet-Cannons to the numerous Organ-Pipers lining the exterior walls to ward off gunships. The Pipe-Cannons were also long gone, and their sockets welded shut. It did not matter, though, for their history left an essence of its own.

The sight, though never truly seen, emboldened the knight strolling through the airborne beast's belly and beckoned him to see the rest. Such a move was likely a breach of protocol, but he was on a roll.

Nearly two stories above the storage unit, a single captain manned the helm of the airship with two underlings—a copilot and a navigator. They shuffled about in a cockpit too large for a group of three.

"Whoever designed these quarters was an idiot," the navigator, a rookie in his early twenties, grumbled to himself as he walked across the room for a tool he needed.

"Yes, we know. You have grumbled about it since our ascent. Keep it to yourself," the copilot sighed.

Their captain, an older man with a grey, well-trimmed beard, kept silent. His eyes jumped between dials measuring wind speeds and trajectory. He had no interest in succumbing to the young man's complaints.

"I learned aircraft design when I studied..." the navigator broke the silence again, but this time, the copilot cut him off.

"Yes, yes. You could do better, I am sure. Now shut up and get back to work."

The navigator rolled his eyes and grumbled before leaving the room to grab a tool. "Blasted crank-box. I keep having to re-oil it," he said, returning to the room a couple of minutes later. "This ship is a piece of..."

"Art, I would call it," a new voice interrupted.

The navigator dropped his oil tin and gasped. The copilot turned to yell at him, but did the same. Both men stared at a giant standing in the middle of the room like he had been there forever. The copilot's body was barely able to muster the strength to poke the pilot.

"Sir..." was all he got out before Augen, who had slipped in under the cover of the noisy navigator, stretched his hand toward the rear of the ship and interrupted again.

"No need to panic. I am just looking around." Turning to the stunned navigator and picking up his oil can, Augen addressed him first. "This ship is an artifact of war. It was never made to travel as far as it regularly does under your captain."

"Are you..."

"Yes. I am the cargo you were paid to carry, no questions asked. Tell me, is the upper gun-deck still intact? I would love to see it."

The pilot stared at his towering visitor and nodded. "The upper storage cell is in the rear of the ship. I assume that is what you mean. There is nothing up there except more cargo."

"Cargo like me?" Augen asked, knowing perfectly well that there were no other knights onboard.

"No, there is not enough oxygen in the atmosphere to keep someone alive outside the sealed quarters for long."

As the pilot spoke, Augen wandered about the room, staring at consoles like a tourist before taking his leave. Passing by the navigator, he grabbed the young man's arm and tugged him along.

"Then I will not be long. Mind if I take him with me?" Then, with his other hand, he pulled a sealed oxygen tank from the wall and handed it to his hostage.

"But…" was all the pilot got out before Augen and the navigator were outside the cockpit and in the vacuum chamber. Once the inner door was sealed shut, the navigator, who put up very little struggle, posed a question.

"You are one of the new soldiers, aren't you? The ones the Golden Empire is now funding."

"What makes you think that?"

"We are going into Iba, right outside the hot zone from the coup in Babyl. Besides, you are…rather menacing for a passenger, even for one who has to be smuggled across borders."

"Good to know your taxes are paying for something effective."

"Is your body that way naturally?"

"No." Augen glanced at the young man, whose curiosity was visible even under the oxygen mask.

After a short moment of silence, the room depressurized with a hiss, and the air got noticeably thinner.

"So, you can breathe out here?"

"My muscles and blood have better oxygen efficiency than the unaugmented, but no. The toxins in the Aether will get to me if I remain out here too long." Augen wasted no time getting across the suspended walkways and onto the upper deck. The navigator followed him, clearly wanting to know more.

"This spot once served as the tail-gundeck. Ammunition for the Gullet-Cannons was stored up there, where the armor was heaviest. There should also be..." Augen wandered about in the unsealed room as he spoke. The space was cluttered with heavy crates chained to the floor, but Augen shuffled around them until he found what he was looking for. "There they are. The bay doors. In the event of a fire or a bad puncture, the crew could manually dump their ammunition to keep the airship from exploding.

"Interestingly, there are recorded incidents wherein the crew detonated their ammunition on purpose to keep it from falling into enemy hands. It killed them, of course, but the enemy had to be destroyed, not helped." Augen shut his eyes and leaned against the guardrails. His captive audience was clearly captivated.

"I had no idea there was such history behind this old thing."

"I could tell. Our people have tried to forget the Cataclysm Wars, but it was a time of bravery and dedication. The Empires would be utterly untouchable if this generation possessed a mere spark of its ancestral drive. Instead, we load these war memorials with food to supply the nations we are currently warring with."

Augen glanced into the distant horizon and could see both greater layers of the atmosphere. The purple and black swirls of the Aether hovered just above him with tendrils puncturing the first atmosphere and caressing the ship. Another storm was visible on the horizon, but for a moment, he felt beyond it.

Augen sighed, his lungs burning just slightly with the inhale. His head also began to swim. *That was fast,* he thought before turning back toward the sealed cockpit.

"I am ready to go back. You?"

"Uh...sure."

Augen walked the young man back to the helm and banged on the door until the seal-chamber repressurized and its door reopened.

As Augen entered, the pilot and copilot stared at him, hoping that the knight had not done away with their talkative navigator and sighing in relief when he stumbled in.

"Well, you have made my flight quite interesting for me. In return, I will tell you the reasons I travel." The men at the helm did not leave their positions, save the navigator, who removed his oxygen mask and shuffled back to his station.

"As your navigator successfully deduced, and I am sure you both were guessing, I am being transferred to the Imperial Forces outside Babyl with the target of restoring order and exterminating insurgents. I am part of the Golden Empire's latest effort to solidify military dominance across the planet."

"I did not think that the Empire was still using Apex. Those drugs were banned after the Cataclysm Wars," the pilot tentatively interjected.

Augen raised an amused eyebrow. "You know your history."

"I was a captain in the Seventy-second Regulars and am well studied in our military history."

"Hmmm. You should educate your navigator, then. I am not on Apex. That viral substance was destroyed. Its long-term side effects were too...extreme to remain on the field. I am on something better. I am here because I am a survivor of the Nethel Impact, where I...lost my fiancée." The crew said nothing, but all eyes were on him.

"I lost a brother in the Islica Impact," the copilot said solemnly.

"Well, I am here to get my own back. And I will do so with..." The pilot had taken his eyes off the monitors during Augen's return and was snapped back into focus when the

Moth shook and tilted to one side. All those inside slid to the far wall, save the pilot, whose feet were strapped to the floor.

"Eastern turbulence. Making adjustments." The copilot recovered quickly and worked his way back to his station. Augen leaned against the wall, physically unfazed, but irritated with the interruption. While the crew worked to recover equilibrium, a porthole next to his head grabbed his attention.

Outside, the storm had closed a considerable distance and lurked just miles away now, but the storm was not what took Augen's attention. The clouds below them had parted, allowing a field of vision all the way to the planet's surface.

The airship flew thousands of feet above the ocean, and the one thing knights feared more than anything else was water.

It took a powerful numbing ointment rubbed on the arms to merely bathe. The ointment barely worked, but it was the best way to make contact with water tolerable. Augen spoke of side effects making Apex obsolete, but the potent drugs granting his strength still had this considerable flaw.

Seeing the ocean sent flashbacks of Augen's final day of training flying through his head. The day his trainers "proved" the potency and effect of his augmentation and pain tolerance by tying him to a table and pouring half a quart of water onto his unhealing wounds was impossible to forget and just as scarring as the enhancement process itself.

The pain put him into shock and caused seizures before finally knocking him completely out. When he woke, he possessed "the itch," the hellish sensation that coated his arms after contact with water and, nearly nine months later, was still present from a single moment of contact.

Augen gasped aloud and fell over backward. His hands shook violently, and the itch instantly grew worse.

Once the airship was rebalanced, the crewmen were surprised to see that the imperial super soldier was the only one to have lost his footing during the commotion. Augen stumbled clumsily back to his feet, scratching both his arms angrily.

"Don't do that again!" he yelled.

"Are you scared of heights?" the copilot chuckled.

"You do seem a bit heavy on your feet," the navigator chimed in. Augen was furious but said nothing in response. He had said far too much already, and letting slip his only major weakness would be unforgivable.

Instead, he regained his composure and silently walked back toward the sealed containment area, scratching his arms all the way.

How embarrassing, Augen thought.

The trapdoor into sealed storage lay open, just as he had left it. After a second's hesitation, he jumped into the porthole and dropped all the way to the bottom of the unit, nearly eighteen feet below, landing with ease.

Heavy on my feet indeed.

Augen fought the urge to scratch his marks and returned to the space between containers he tried sleeping in.

There was once a time when he loved the ocean, the seas, and every major body of water he encountered in the wilderness. A younger Augen would have loved such a view, but not anymore. Water in the wrong place would literally kill him, so his days of walking the beaches or wading in the riversides with Christine were long over.

Such memories were sore spots to the jaded soldier, but Augen meditated on them and realized he was indeed very tired.

He hoped that, after a deep rest, he would wake up and the seas would be long gone.

On the other side of Archaea, Alexander sat staring into the interior of his visor. His body was far from stable, and he fought the urge to scratch his arms as the men before him spoke.

Before him sat the Stratagem Table, a complex holograph system controlled by the men standing around it. Those who occupied such positions, each a general or admiral of some capacity, controlled models on the three-dimensional map, moving them at will to illustrate the collective strategies of the Imperial War Court.

"The Shoga fleet will support troop deployments into Iba through the Hot Sea. Islica has already deployed troops into Iba, and they are currently awaiting our reinforcements. Tolea and Scil have landed in Byzica and are beginning preparations to move through Araby."

"What of the situation in Babyl? Have we airlifted the chief of state out yet?"

"Not yet, my lord."

Alexander sighed dramatically to show his displeasure. "Why not?" he responded.

"We sent a drone team into Barbasul, but they are MIA, and the local militia are not responding to our contact efforts."

"How can an entire drone team go MIA?" Alexander tried to rub his forehead, forgetting that he had a strangulating helmet on. *It is too early in the morning for this,* he thought, but he was needed, so he would be present, with or without rest.

"It is safe to say that the militia is incapacitated," the emperor concluded aloud.

"Or deserted," a general added, nodding.

"Cease contact efforts with them—we do not want to show the enemy our hand."

Upon hearing their emperor's words, the War Council voiced their agreement. Then, from the margins of the council room, dozens of tech-scribes typed hasty orders to various underlings on the ground floor. From there, an encrypted reiteration would be sent moments later to its intended recipients all over the world.

"I have still not received an answer," Alexander pressed.

"Based on how fast we lost contact with them, we fear that the insurgents shot them down. They likely built an Air-Ribault system of some kind."

"Built?"

"Or rebuilt, sir. Barbasul was one of the iron dome cities in the last Cataclysm War."

"Excellent! So, the militias now have an iron dome over their battlefield! For it is indeed *their* battlefield if our troops remain on the coast and outside of Babyl! And if the insurgents get hold of the king..." Alexander stuttered as he spoke and paused at "king," partially out of anger, but also because he had forgotten the name of the statesman he had assigned to run the Babyl and Iba Districts.

The chief commanders were all visibly uncomfortable, even beneath their masks. All eyes were on the emperor, and he was irate.

"A hostage crisis is something we cannot allow. The media guilds are already capitalizing on this revolt, calling it 'The Great Military Failure of the Golden Empire.' And for once, I am beginning to think they may be right."

One of the partially masked, a representative and head of the Teutonic Order by the name of Manfred von Snaer, spoke up.

"With all due respect, your eminence, the guilds are coin-grubbing play-actors. They will say anything they can to get an audience. If imagery is the issue that concerns you, why not restrict their content coverage? Call it a national secrets breach."

The Teuton, an official newcomer for the War Cabinet and an unofficial long-term specialist for the same cabinet, was the youngest and most impulsive of its members.

The head Templar standing beside Snaer, an old man named Blodian Altegard, played the part of a natural balance for his young colleague and spoke up before Alexander did.

"Everyone knows that nothing the guild has made public is any real threat to the Empire or our troops. Though I share my colleague's opinions about their general intent and character, such an overreach would certainly be a breach of the Free Press Act. The citadel had worked for decades to increase the freedom of the independent guilds, even when it came at the short-term expense of the state."

"What is your point?" Snaer shot back. "It is far from unprecedented to censor information that could lead to unrest or mistrust within the Empire. What is a small cutback in the liberties of the press? We give them the power they have; his majesty is well within his rights to temporarily remove them."

"You would see all civilian and guild liberties erased if you could! Am I the only one to notice that choking restrictions such as this are always suggested from the same side of the table?"

As the heads of the holy orders partook in their intellectual dueling, those lining the remainder of the Stratagem Table elected to chime in, picking sides and arguing morality from myriad angles. Mild insults and insinuations were also thrown about, as was the nature of such a gathering of elites, each believing himself to be the most knowledgeable.

Alexander checked his posture and tried again to rub his forehead. His head throbbed, though not much worse than the day before, and his back had begun to slouch under the weight of his ornamental uniform.

There was much talk, but no audible progress was being made, and though the emperor would have intervened on a regular day, he found himself falling behind.

A slow blink was followed by a slower one, and the next thing Alexander knew, the debate transpiring before him was skipping about like a broken recording. He was falling asleep, but a rush of angry adrenaline yanked him out of his throne before he lost all consciousness.

"Enough! This bickering is getting us nowhere!" Alexander loosened his shoulders and circled the table, gesturing wildly as he walked. It felt and looked strange, but it halted the pointless infighting and woke him back up.

"Damage control is not yet on the table because our troops are not even in the field! Until it is absolutely necessary, we will relegate the consequences of this campaign to the field of battle alone. Not everything requires the altering of laws, Snaer." Alexander chose to catch his breath there, letting his words echo around the War Council and stretching his shoulders again before continuing. "Since our intel is limited, we will assume that Babyl is an insurgent state, the militias are either inoperative or treacherous, and we WILL have all our troops deployed within the week!"

"Seven days, sir?"

"That is what 'within the week' means, General Blass. Now, how many divisions have we already deployed in Iba?" The men he circled typed furiously into their consoles, and their answers flickered into existence on the table as they spoke.

"We have two divisions of urban skirmishers, the Eleventh and the Twelfth Sharps. A marine division, the Thirty-second Bays, and the Seventh Islican Muskets."

Only one regular division, and it isn't even from Alampia, Alexander thought, disgusted. "Does the Seventh have their support artillery prepped?" More typing led to more disappointment.

"No, sir, the Longbow Rockets and Leather Cannons are sitting in the harbor outside Eris Port. The crews are with them, but we are struggling to find space to unload it all. Eris is incredibly crowded, and its docks are located at the base of a sheer cliff."

"Once on land, do we have transports?"

"Yes, my lord. Enough for all the divisions scheduled, but they have no access to the docks. They are sitting at the top of the cliff outside the city's manufacturing district." Alexander stopped pacing and rubbed the chin of his helmet, trying to formulate some kind of solution.

Based on the information at his disposal, there was very little opportunity for him to seize, but progress had to be made. For every second the council sat arguing, the enemy was given time to prepare for their army's arrival.

There was always a chance that they were not preparing, but were merely a disorganized rabble wishing to create chaos and grab attention.

However, it was the emperor's job to assume the worst, and if the enemy could create a no-fly zone over a city with a fifty-mile minimum radius, the worst scenario was likely the realistic one.

"What are the Thirty-second Bays doing?" Alexander queried, pausing his orbit of the table to stand behind one of the empire's three supreme admirals.

"Their current orders are to secure the dockland and run intel on the city, as per protocol. Their naval support is..."

"Redirect them. I want every mariner moving that artillery up the cliffside. If they have to strap chains to the ordnance and pull it up by hand, I do not care. I want the support artillery dry and mobile as soon as physically possible."

"Sir, Eris Port is considered neutral territory, but it is certainly a high-risk area. Removing the security detail is...hazardous to say the least."

"How about our new recruits? Do we have any deployed yet?"

Altegard raised his chin slightly with a smirk. "We have one dropping into Iba today. Keep him away from the water, and he will work miracles for you."

"Good. I am expecting as much."

"So, will he and the Reds run security in Eris Port then?"

"No. They and the Sharps are moving out of Eris and clearing the path for support."

"With all due respect, my lord, a single division of men trying to hold a line for such a distance will leave them stretched thin. Even with artillery support, such a move will be extremely dangerous for the soldiers on the ground. Should the enemy launch any kind of major offensive..."

"I AM AWARE!" Alexander exclaimed with gusto.

His composure slipped away for a moment, but it was quickly regained with the slow folding of steel-clad arms and a crisp verbal conclusion. "The Shoga Navy will support them from the coast for as far inland as possible, and others will reinforce them as they disembark. Am I clear?"

"Abundantly, my liege. We are playing this one close to the chest. The Reds will have to do the same."

CHAPTER 6

FEVERED ASCENSION AND HOT DESCENT

In the age of its prime, the Deathwatch Warmoth was launched, fueled, loaded, and even assembled on the hilts of skyscraping military spires located throughout Eros. Deathwatch Co. built the airships with the presumption that they would never fly very close to the ground. But by the end of the last Cataclysm War, only a handful of their towering "Skydaggers" remained intact. To compensate for the lack of ideal landing sites, cheap landing gear was fashioned for the surviving airships, so that ground landing became possible even with limited room for movement.

Augen braced himself for an awkward arrival, leaning against the wall until the Moth came to a stop. Though the initial impact was barely noticeable, the pained screeching of the Moth's rusted landing gear as it slid across the cobblestone platform put Augen's teeth on edge.

When the bay doors slid open, Augen wasted no time grabbing his coat, his dagger, and his papers before heading on his way.

Eris Port, the city Augen landed outside of, was unimpressive compared to the immensity of Pallerheim, but the heat of the day was unlike anything Augen had ever experienced in the North. Such intense land-fever made his movement through the city a deeply unpleasant experience.

It did not take long for Augen to reach the city's namesake, known by Northerners as the Cliffs of Eris, and the sight he beheld led him to take pause.

Nearly two hundred feet below, steel ships bunched tightly into knots, creating what looked like a cobblestone road across a winding pathway of salt water. The sun reflected off the horizon, but Augen could see patches of steel bulk creating a semicircle around the Eris seaside, likely a blockade created by an allied naval force.

The dockland itself looked like a chaotic mess, but Augen was not interested in anything over the sea. He was looking for the 7th Islican Muskets, who were supposed to be on dry land already.

An Intel-Balloon swaying over a structure on the bottom level looked promising. So, he started there, traversing the narrow roadway down a near-vertical cliff and passing a crowded industrial commune largely chiseled out of the cliffside. At sea level, an imperial outpost sat guarded by two mariners.

"Where is the rest of the guard? I did not see a single perimeter line. How long has your division been landlocked?"

The two guards initially scoffed at the approaching stranger until he reached the gate, and they recognized the Templar Knight whose arrival they were told to expect.

"Well, sir...the rest of our guard has been recalled. Only we were left on guard duty."

"They recalled all the inland guards? Where are you redeploying?"

"Don't know...from what I heard, we are not."

Had circumstances changed since Augen received his papers? To recall stationed guards in a hostile zone seemed highly irregular.

The visibly anxious guards were not being very helpful, and Augen wanted answers, so he passed through the chain gate leading into the camp. As he strode toward the command tent, which housed the anchor of the Intel-Balloon, he was cut off by columns of soldiers in tight formation marching the length of the camp. These moving walls contained nearly three hundred men in total, all of whom looked absolutely miserable.

The soldiers bore heavy plate armor garnished with flamboyant crimson coats, combat helmets topped with decorative caps, and heavy combat packs containing a plethora of specialist munitions, as well as several ammunition-bars. Many of them also carried grenades, spades, handpicks, and other various tools for flexible and prolonged mid- to close-quarters combat.

Augen stopped impatiently and waited for the nearest column to pass. Though his presence was certainly noted, not a single soldier flinched, twitched, or even shot a glance at the towering knight they marched past. Instead, they continued stiffly onward until the front column reached the far wall and the division received an order to adjust their formation. Then, without bending their perfect lines, they rotated one hundred eighty degrees before starting back again.

When Augen finally found an opening between the columns, he strode into the command tent, staring down the tent guards as he passed them.

He had never met General Lomat before, but of the command staff leaning over the table before him, Augen knew exactly whom he answered to after a single glance.

"You are late, Templar," Pazkt Lomat growled. Saliva dropped onto the table as he spoke, but no one said a word about it.

"It could not be helped," Augen responded. General Lomat grunted and wiped the table with his handkerchief. He eyed Augen for a moment before tossing him a headset.

"Keep in touch with me. Your armor and uniform are in the armory. Dress up, then go onto the docks and move the cannons to the exit."

The knight understood his orders but paused for a moment, unsure if he should say anything about his aversion to water. The commander glanced up from his table and, noting that his new subordinate was hesitating, added, "I have ordered the leather cannons to be deployed onto the central stone jetty. Nothing short of a seismic anomaly will put water onto that dock. If you can manage to keep your footing on an unmoving stone walkway, you will not come into any contact with the seawater."

Augen saluted respectfully and strode toward the armory to accomplish his first order.

The armor waiting for him there was visually beautiful yet brutally effective, containing state-of-the-art killing devices built into the officer's garb from both the Golden and Silver Empires.

Even inside the sweltering armory, the soldier wanted to admire the craftsmanship of his new uniform rather than put it on, but he had his orders. He connected his headset to his combat visor and donned the new official outfit of the Imperial knight.

Despite the brilliant design of his uniform, the impact-resistant joints, the gothic blast visor, and the reflexive plate, there was one thing that the armor offered no protection from—the heat, and the moment Augen left the armory, he felt the acute effects of that flaw.

Unfortunately for him, there was no time to bemoan the temperature and nobody to complain to. He had to move. The central jetty was impossible to miss, as were the leather cannons lining its edge. So, Augen got to work moving the light artillery off the jetty.

The leather cannon was an outdated remnant of the first Cataclysm War, but its simple design, low maintenance requirements, and relative mobility kept the small field gun from total obsolescence. A hand-crank engine on its rear wheels allowed a single foot soldier to maneuver the weapon with impressive speed. A skilled skirmisher could fire the cannon, remove its kick-braces, relocate a considerable distance, rebrace, and fire again in less than a minute.

"This will be a cinch," Augen said to himself as he pulled the crank on the engine. Nothing happened. He did it again to no avail.

"The engine fuel is in the Squire Transports atop the cliff. Those cannons are not going to move themselves," some marines yelled as they lowered another big gun onto the jetty.

"What is the point of having transports full of fuel if they cannot reach their targets?" Augen yelled angrily while checking the fuel tank to make sure it was really empty.

The heat already bore down on him, and the thought of having to push nearly two dozen 600 lb. cannons all the way to the Squire Transport Vehicles at the cliff's peak was excruciating.

"We take it you are Lieutenant Di Gattchen? This is the last of the big guns. We, and the men disembarking, are now under your command." Augen nodded to the men approaching him and ordered them to begin pushing the cannons toward the outpost gate.

As his men split into groups, about eight soldiers for each cannon, Augen began to push his own with the remaining three men until a voice rang into his ear.

"Meet me in formation, Templar. On the double."

Augen returned to where the Reds marched to and fro and found them standing in tight formation. They were at ease, but their shoulders sagged, and the men swayed slightly with the wind.

Their commander, who was also in his dress garb, strode before the scorched men, shouting raspy commands.

"Get water. Then march to the top of the cliff. Once there, top off your canteens and clear out an opening for the Squires to pull up to the cliff's edge. Mariners are moving our support artillery up the cliffside. I do not want them pushing those pieces an inch farther than they need to."

Augen stopped at the end of the farthest line and stood at ease, but General Lomat had other ideas.

"Templar, beside me." Pazkt Lomat did not look at Augen but pointed to the place where he was supposed to stand. Augen took the position as quickly as he could, and the commander continued, "You men wanted to see the emperor's new attack dogs. Well, here you go. I have promoted him to the rank of second lieutenant. He answers to me, you answer to him. Nothing outside of this will be tolerated."

Augen stood as still as the soldiers before him, sweat beading into his eyes, and he honestly wondered how the unaugmented men before him were tolerating the heat as well as they seemed to be.

The General issued a final burst of commands, giving precise details to his men regarding their behavior and roles once they reached the caravan, then he dismissed them. After a brisk salute, his men split off to do as they were told, marching to the outpost interior so that they could take their much-needed, albeit short, reprieve.

Augen eyed the men he had left to push the leather cannons up the hill and stepped away so that he could join them. Without breaking his gaze on the departing 7th, General Lomat noticed this and interrupted the knight's withdrawal.

"Are they all moving artillery?" he asked without glancing at his new lieutenant.

"Yes, sir," Augen responded, casually sliding back to his side.

The stoic field general did not move, but his eyes slowly redirected their focus on the mariners that Augen had left to move the cannons.

"Do you think that is efficient?" More saliva dripped from his chin as he spoke. It fell to the ground and evaporated immediately. Augen was unsure of what to say.

"Every man is working," he responded, feigning confidence.

"That does not make it efficient..." The commander's eyes were drawn to the remaining three men straggling behind the rest. Then he drew his own conclusions.

"Have the stragglers leave their cargo where it is and walk to the top of the cliff. The unused Squires have spare fuel containers they can fill and haul back down. Have them do this for the group farthest from the top. As each group is freed up, have them perform the same task, carrying more fuel to the group performing the slowest. You will halve the time it takes and not give anyone sunstroke." As he spoke, the commander's movements were precise and minimalistic, reinforcing his words but conveying nothing else. "Make these adjustments," he concluded. "Then follow me to the base of the cliff."

With haste, Augen did as he was told.

There was an unnerving air to Pazkt Lomat, for in his early days of service, he suffered a unique and messy form of facial trauma. His injury resulted in the tip of his jaw being replaced with an iron prosthetic. His skinless, glistening jawbone and matching bottom teeth looked intimidating and must have felt obscenely uncomfortable.

Augen was curious about the unusual circumstances of such a deformity, but he didn't dare bring it up.

The exhausted mariners sighed with relief, or annoyance, at the new orders, but Augen did not stick around to discern which.

General Lomat was speaking with a senior officer from another division when Augen returned to him. The general was clearly unhappy about what he had been told.

When Augen stepped into the triangle, Pazkt waved off the other commander and strode slowly toward the cliffside, where the mariners worked diligently in the heat. The 7th had already almost cleared the cliff, marching with perfect form and impressive tempo all the way up.

The leather cannons could feasibly be pushed around by a small group of men; however, the massive and unwieldy Longbow Rocket Launchers were an entirely different conundrum. The thin, zipper-shaped path up Eris Cliff could never provide passage for such instruments.

Because of this, an uneasy alternative was found, for the walls of the ancient carved buildings lining the edges of the path were linear and smooth as any highway. One section, in particular, created a wide vertical path to the plateau, provided its walls were thick enough to carry such weight.

Monstrous chains had been slung from the peak of the cliff down to the sea level, where the first of four Longbows waited to be pulled up by a small train of Squires at the top.

"This seems dangerous," Augen said aloud.

Pazkt shot him a glance but said nothing in response. As the Longbow was hoisted into the air and tilted so that its tires were against the wall, Augen heard a deep cracking from the structure it leaned upon. He eyed General Lomat, who initially stood motionless and quiet, staring at the now vertical super-heavy artillery piece ascending into the heavens.

"Move the next one into position!" the commander shouted to the mariners who had been tasked with maneuvering the Longbows. Witnessing his orders carried out post-haste, he wiped his chin and started up the cliff himself. Augen followed, eyeing the machinery already making its vertical journey.

"This does not seem safe. Why risk the soldiers' lives by putting them directly below the hanging artillery?"

"Orders from the citadel say we should have been out of Eris four hours ago. We have to clear the port so that the other divisions can disembark." Augen listened intently, the crackling and groaning stone structure voicing its complaints even as the artillery gained a significant distance on the duo taking the walkway.

"The situation in Babyl is dire. Insurgents have taken the capital city of Barbasul, and as far as we know, the king of the district is holed up in the imperial embassy surrounded by them.

"Intel is limited, but there is evidence to suggest that they have created an iron dome over the city using old flak cannons and Ribaults. A drone team was sent in, two Drakes and a Hydra Attack Chopper. All three are now MIA, presumed to be destroyed.

"Our orders are simple. We will provide a defensive line for the Eleventh and Twelfth Sharps and secure the city from the ground when enough reinforcements arrive."

"One division providing a buffer for two? Would it not be wiser to..." Augen began to interject, but he was abruptly cut off.

"Let us get something straight right now! We are not equals. I do not know how your squads worked when you were terrorists, but here, we have a chain of command. That chain is never to be broken. The men know this, and it is high time you learn it, too. When I give orders, you don't talk back, you don't complain or interrupt." The commander's tone was severe, but without emotion, and his injury made facial expressions impossible to read. "I never wanted a knight in my division," he continued, wiping his jaw to keep his uniform dry. "However, despite my wishes, I was assigned one. Perhaps you can prove to me that you are worth all the talk I hear on the grounds, but so far, you have not come close."

Augen did not flinch but was taken aback by this change in tone. He did not like being talked down to, especially by someone who was not his physical equal.

Yet, something about the man kept Augen from scoffing. Though it did take a moment for him to gather his wits and respond appropriately.

"My apologies, General. I am not accustomed to this kind of leadership. I will follow your lead to the best of my abilities. But with all due respect, if my skills are unwanted, why promote me?" As the two continued, the first of the Longbows crested the cliff, creating a terrible screech, but slowly disappearing over the pinnacle without a visible problem. Moments later, the chains were thrown back down the cliffs so that the troops below could repeat the process.

"Ah, a question worth an answer. You have correctly pointed out that we will be stretched thin holding a line of such length. So, while the men accustomed themselves to the heat this morning, I adjusted their formations, having them march and maneuver in much smaller squads so that we could create a general line without leaving anyone isolated.

"Unfortunately, this makes micromanagement very difficult since I cannot be in several places at once. I need a lieutenant who can understand my tactics but is capable of operating an Intel-Balloon so that specific orders can be given and adjustments made where needed.

"Apparently, your kind had used this old tech in urban areas long before it was deemed legal by the Imperial Law Council. So, for the short term, you were the logical choice for such a position. We will see about the long term."

"Very well, sir. What are our short-term objectives then?"

"We will have naval support for the first fifteen miles inland. A new outpost needs to be set up as soon as we leave their range.

"Ideally, we will receive reinforcements for the rest of the trek. But with or without additional troops, our outpost will be established and held. It will provide a pivotal foothold in this hotbed that the empire needs if we are to restore order in Barbasul."

Augen nodded in support as they passed one of the leather cannons being lugged up the path. There were already three up the hill, and another one's engine was firing up below them.

The Longbows were also making considerable progress as the second was nearing the peak of the cliff.

However, the elderly edifice being used as a road decided that it had suffered enough abuse. The crackling sound echoing about the area crowned with a loud snap, and the wall beneath the Longbow's treads collapsed into itself.

The artillery piece fell sideways into the building, tearing down several internal walls and collapsing the floor beneath it.

General Lomat sprinted the rest of the path toward the Squires, shouting unanswered commands as he went.

Augen saw something else. Below him, a small crowd of locals, many of whom were being ushered away from the tower by mariners, gasped in horror as a woman stuck her head out of the tower's window only a floor beneath the collapse. Augen sped two passes downward, toward the crowd, but paused before passing the tower.

The only real entrance to the tower was a door at its base, but a large wooden-framed window across from the path looked promising. The heavy weapon hanging just above the civilian teetered uneasily, and the cracking sounds quieted down but did not cease altogether.

Augen thought he might have time to get to the tower's base before ascending again from the inside, but such ideas were blown away when the Squires gave another, less-than-gentle tug on the partially suspended Longbow. The sudden shift collapsed yet another interior wall and put enough pressure on the floor above the woman to split its ceiling.

Augen braced himself to jump the gap and narrowly succeeded with a short running start. The wooden frame around the window was thin and weak, crackling under the weight of the giant soldier holding himself up by it. Augen's fingers, several of them damaged during his previous mission, also crackled painfully under the pressure of his body weight.

The window was too narrow to slide through. Augen considered climbing the tower by utilizing thin indents in the back wall, but he knew there was not enough time for such a maneuver. So, he slid to the next wall directly below her, hoping beyond hope that this window would be bigger or perhaps she could climb out of hers.

Unfortunately, another echoing crack heralded the imminent collapse of the next floor, and for lack of a feasible escape route or perhaps pure terror, the woman inside the kill zone did not try to climb out. Instead, she reached into the imploding room and stuck an infant wrapped in a blanket out the window, holding it away from the rubble as the building collapsed onto her.

Augen watched as the arms holding the infant contorted and broke, dropping their cargo as they lost connection with the rest of the woman's body.

Glancing below, Augen saw that the mariners had set a clear perimeter a great distance from the building, and no one would catch the falling child if he failed to.

So, by sticking his foot into the slit window and twisting it awkwardly, he anchored himself to the wall, pushing off with his other foot so that he crouched horizontally with two free hands.

The joint support in his armor helped compensate for carrying more than three hundred pounds in the core, but Augen's rib, lung, and abdominal injuries flared up from the sudden over-exertion. He was quickly reminded that he was hurt, but the little live package plummeted toward him, followed closely by a storm of stone rubble, and he had to do something.

Waiting until the last second, Augen stretched himself out and caught the blanket by two ends, pulling the child into his chest before falling backward into the wall. Bits of the tower's top floors flew past them both and shattered into pieces below. Then, all went still.

It took a great deal of time for Augen to free himself of the window and descend the cliff with the child slung around his shoulder in the blanket.

"Templar. Report to me on the double." Augen caught the shadow of General Lomat's silhouette gazing down at the crowd from where he stood.

With places to be, he desperately tried to pass the child off to someone in the crowd. The locals gave the Templar no leeway or help, shooting him hateful glances and refusing the child as if the knight's very touch tainted it. Eventually, one of the mariners took the child and left Augen to ascend the cliff once more.

By now, it was midday, and the heat was all but unbearable. Augen fought the urge to rip off his helmet and take in some of the relatively cool sea air, but he knew better than to succumb to such a desire.

For such relief would bring his mind off the environmental discomfort and onto his injuries, which now stabbed at his torso. He coughed and tasted blood, but worked his way back up the cliffside once more.

The chains dropped again, and by the time Augen had pulled his weight to the crest of the cliff, the Squire train had done the same to the third Longbow.

The crushed top floors formed a diagonal ramp to the flats, making the final moments of ascension far easier and lessening the chances of further collapse. However, the limp arms still hanging from the broken windowsill gave little comfort to Augen, who shot one more passing glance at the wreckage before quickening his pace to find the commander.

When he finally reached the top floor, Pazkt Lomat stood observing the mariners as they threw the chains over the edge for the last time.

"Where did you go?"

Augen did his best not to show his physical exhaustion, standing at attention directly behind Lomat's right shoulder.

"I was...on the tower, sir. Civilians were in the collapse. I...did not want unnecessary casualties from our op."

Though his superior officer showed no negative response to the answer, staring intensely into the horizon while Augen spoke, the Templar was unnerved by his demeanor and line of questioning. *Did he not see what happened?*

"The tower we are using is ancient, nearly seventeen centuries old. Because of the building's age, there was no steel frame to negate the weight of the artillery pressing against its walls. However, this played to our advantage when the top floors did collapse, for a steel frame would likely have broken the chains. In a sense, we are quite lucky." General Lomat's voice was cold enough to condition Augen's new suit. More slobber, this time mixed with sweat, dripped into the sand as he spoke.

Augen fought the urge to tell his commander about the unnecessary death already brought upon the innocent, not to mention the destruction of an ancient landmark. When he saw the woman's mangled arms hanging outside the window, he saw Steven, too.

When the General observed his underling's shifting weight and clenched fists, he seemed to be visibly confused by his behavior. But his thoughtful explanation continued to its conclusion nonetheless.

"I expect you to stay close enough to me to receive direct orders from now on. No more running off unless I say so. With authority comes the necessity for structure. I need to be capable of relying on you."

To this, Augen said nothing. A long moment of silence ensued as the two men observed the Squires doing their jobs.

The 7th had secured a stable, albeit undermanned, perimeter and was taking shifts maintaining it and fetching water for themselves. Those on break were clustered into patches of shade with their helmets off and much of their gear piled to the side. Such behavior seemed unprofessional for a division of their prestige, but General Lomat did not seem to care, so Augen made no mention of it.

The mariners tasked with pushing the leather cannons up the cliff had finished their assignment and were now partaking in the same shifts as the Reds, likely as a result of General Lomat's silent acceptance of it.

The man was clearly an expert tactician, but his casual disregard for dead civilians was gnawing at Augen. They were not the enemy, and in fact, the 7th was there to maintain order and protect their lands. The Imperial Codex made it clear.

"Commander, do you..." Augen's emotional, and likely illogical, thought was blown to oblivion when a grenade landed between the knight and his commander. The fuse was lit, sputtering high-temperature materials from its neck.

Had the thrower been more experienced, the explosive would have gone off less than a second after landing, but such was not the case, and Augen could tell by the length of the fuse that the handheld bomb still had several seconds before detonation.

So, thinking quickly, Augen pushed his commander aside and snatched the grenade from its landing zone. He meant to fling the explosive a safe distance from harm, but froze, realizing he was surrounded by people. Mariners managing equipment, the 7th maintaining a perimeter, and civilians, many civilians, watching from banisters, windows, the ground level, and even the rooftops.

"Off the cliff!" General Lomat yelled from behind. Upon hearing his words, Augen spun to throw the grenade but was knocked off balance by a burst of energy behind him. Two other handheld explosives, unnoticed by the commander and his knight, had been thrown into the ranks of soldiers. One of them had detonated early.

What would have been an impressive heave past the tower was whiffed, and the sparking grenade floated just past the cliff's edge before exploding magnificently, spewing rock chunks, sand, and gravel into the sky.

When the third bomb went off, the detonation seemed lighter than the previous two, but the moment of silence a soldier expected after overstimulation was buried by a final and completely unexpected blast, the scale of which made the previous three seem adolescent.

In the seconds of chaos, someone had slipped a final crude hand-bomb under the fuel cell of one of the Squire train's two leads. When it went off, it ignited the vehicle's fuel tank and sent the transport nearly thirty feet into the air.

The airborne fireball stopped abruptly midair before careening into the transport tethered to it.

What was once a six-truck train had been reduced in seconds to three Squire Transports pulling on one side, and only one damaged STV pulling the other, and the vehicle working alone had nowhere to go but backward.

This sudden mismatch in distribution jerked the whole Squire train toward the cliff, the weight of its tractors unable to compensate for the cargo dangling below.

Some brave mariners ran behind it and tried to unwind the chains, but a safety mechanism on the STVs locked the winches into place. The trucks would have to be parked for the chains to unwind, but attempting to lock their tires now would mean going over the edge.

A man in the crowd whooped, and several others cheered as the Squires lurched toward the cliff, crushing one of the mariners in the process.

"Templar! Cut it loose!" General Lomat ordered, but Augen needed no encouragement. Unhinging a combat mace from his belt, he flung himself toward the wreckage.

The numerous utility chains, which had been neatly balanced to distribute the weight evenly, shook violently and hummed as the load grew more asymmetric by the second.

Three mariners still tried to unhinge the chains, backing up as the trucks did, to avoid sharing their comrade's fate. Augen dove between the two converging lines and threw the valiant sailors aside.

Then, with an elegant series of coordinated blows, the Templar struck the lone Squire's chains, letting the last one snap before he moved to the other three.

He correctly assumed that leaving the complete group for last would buy him the most time, but he still underestimated how quickly they would give way to the cliff.

Three strides and four more broken chains left Augen dangling over the edge of the wreckage, suspended only by the rear bumper of the last Squire, which he clasped for dear life with his free hand.

The crowds roared their approval to the sound of the Longbow striking the ground and shattering under its own weight, but such cheers and whoops died down when Augen stepped out from behind the recovering Squires unhurt.

The first grenade, unrecovered by Augen, had slain three of the mariners, one of whom had greeted him on the wharf.

The third grenade slew a member of the 7th, who dove onto the explosive and soaked up the detonation so that the surrounding mariners and his unhelmed comrades were untouched by shrapnel. One of them, a younger soldier, stood over his friend's messy corpse in shock.

A fast-acting mariner had tackled one of the fleeing saboteurs before he could disappear into the crowd. Together, with assistance from two of the Reds, the mariner dragged their assailant to Pazkt Lomat's feet.

He was unarmed, without a uniform, and seemed unfazed by his capture. In fact, he smirked defiantly at the men as if he had been caught performing a childish prank on a friend.

"Where is your uniform?" General Lomat inquired stoically.

The young man scoffed, uttered something in his native tongue, and spat onto the commander's shoe.

If Zhatka had been wearing those shoes, he would have wrung the boy's neck until his head came off, then thrown it into the crowd to make a statement, but this commander was more patient than that.

"I asked you for your uniform," he stated unflinchingly as Augen stepped behind him, mace still clenched in his hand. "If you have no uniform, then Imperial Law dictates that you be condemned as a saboteur. The penalty for such a crime is immediate execution."

The young man was covered in dust and deeply tanned by the sunlight; these environmental factors aged him. Yet, as Augen studied his features, he realized the captured bomber was far younger than he looked. He was, in fact, just a boy.

But he acted like no child. He snarled at the commander and screamed profanity at everything under the sun before calming and chuckling to himself.

"It does not matter. If you kill me, my friends will avenge my death with yours! If you let me go, I will do everything in my power to kill you! Either way, you die, and I get what I want. Maveth Shedim will rise from the ashes and burn your pitiful empire to the ground. Long live Maveth!"

General Lomat sighed to himself and wiped his chin and shirt. "Very well. Lieutenant...don't waste ammunition."

Augen nodded solemnly and drew his knife.

The blind hatred, the illogical drive toward mayhem, even to the point of self-destruction, the boy embodied everything that had driven Augen from a quiet life with Christine, and yet he had trouble killing someone so young with his hands, so the knife was fitting.

He stepped behind the prisoner, placed the tip of the blade onto the cuff of his neck, and lodged it into the spinal column with a tap. It was messy, but not nearly as gruesome as a cut throat or anything involving the mace.

"The emperor demands your death; the civil world will rejoice in your passing." Even Augen, in his cynical nature, had trouble doubting those words. The boy would likely not be missed by anyone, yet killing him brought far less satisfaction than he hoped.

"True," the commander muttered as the condemned saboteur dropped to the ground, lifeless.

The crowd went from mocking to silent once more, and the familiar spirit of hatred that Augen had tasted earlier on behalf of the citizenry was back in his mouth.

It made no sense to him—they all saw what the boy did, they knew the law, so why did they see him as the villain? He hated their difference of mind almost as much as the crowds seemed to hate him.

"Get used to this, Templar. You are the emperor's attack dog, and it seems that nobody is off your potential hit list. The infants you save today just might be the assailants blowing us up tomorrow. Now walk with me." General Lomat strode toward his soldiery, shouting commands to the 7th, who wasted no time readying the remaining Squires.

The surviving Longbows and leather cannons were hastily strapped to their transports, ready for their death march through the wastes of Iba.

CHAPTER 7

A STORM IN IBA

As the Reds made their way to Barbasul, their leader quickly learned that the roadways in Iba were untrustworthy. Major freeways lay covered in sand, seemingly unused, and so poorly kept that the convoy oftentimes lost track of them beneath the environment's shifting elements.

Each time this happened, General Lomat, whose attention never left a set of old maps he had acquired in Eris, was forced to correct the errors from the Squire in the front of the caravan.

The 7th Reds, their engineers, and the two Sharps divisions accompanying them were subsequently forced to alternate between riding on the Squires and artillery and marching between the iron columns in the heat.

The two Squires destroyed in Eris were meant to lighten the load of the marching vanguard. General Lomat's adjusted marching system, which he designed on the fly to compensate for the loss and give the men as much rest as possible, could not truly make up for the missing transports. It took only a handful of hours into the trek to make such a reality abundantly clear.

"We are off course again! Adjust your trajectory six degrees northwest," Pazkt Lomat shouted before quietly sighing to himself. "We are never going to make the deadline at this rate."

Initially, the other commanding officers marched with the men, taking shifts with the rest of the division, but after their first course aberration, which went unnoticed for nearly fifteen minutes, General Lomat took his place atop the lead Squire, with maps in hand, so that such errors would not be repeated.

He commanded Augen to join him atop the first Squire, and the two Sharps commanders found excuses to suspend their marching time as well. The men themselves were clearly struggling; some leaned on the shoulders of their more durable comrades, while some clutched wires and chains dangling from the artillery pieces and let the machines pull them forward.

Over time, marching form grew ugly. Though no weapon was ever allowed to touch the ground, the men looked as though their bodies were ready to succumb to the heat any second. Yet, the pace never slowed, for the men seemed to share the adaptability and stone-faced focus of their commanding officer, and Augen respected them for that.

However, such admiration did nothing to sway his worry for the parading soldiers behind. Even when sitting still, he was sweating profusely in his armor, and though a pair of numbing gauze bandages on his arms prevented a bad reaction with his augmentation flaws, the hellish afternoon heat was making him nauseated. He could only imagine what the men marching behind him felt.

"Commander, are the men going to be combat-ready in this heat?" Augen's question snapped the commander out of his focus.

Pazkt Lomat turned toward his lieutenant, clearly ready to chew him out, but hesitated. Instead, he examined the men behind them and sighed to himself.

Eventually, the Squire hit a familiar bump that Augen recognized as their return to the buried freeway, and the commander ordered an all-stop.

"Men of the Seventh, helmets off! Into the shade! Lieutenant, grab a water bin and take it to the back." Augen did as he was told, heaving a keg of liquid over his shoulder and striding toward the tail of the iron caravan.

The 7th was utterly exhausted, leaning into the shade with their helmets off. Many had swollen tongues, and a couple of them vomited what little liquid they had drunk earlier before taking more in.

The midday was well underway, and it would likely get cooler from there, but would the men last another couple of hours marching at this pace? It did not seem likely.

After dropping his supply near the back end of the column, he stared into the wastelands before him, taking it in.

Iba, or at least this part of it, was the polar opposite of Nethel, or anywhere in Eros for that matter. The land was flat, barren, and dead, as though the soil itself grew so dehydrated that its very lifeforce evaporated, leaving nothing but a mummified skeleton behind. Mountains were essentially a memory, for above the cliffs overhanging the sea lay a plateau that seemingly went on for hundreds of miles. When Augen squinted, he could see a mountain range in the far distance, but it was merely a shadowed silhouette outlining the horizon, so tiny that it could barely be seen at all.

He could see some kind of prickly shrub in clusters near the occasional indent in the ground. *Perhaps there is water underneath it?* He shook his head and fought the urge to remove his helmet again, even though the warm, dirty, well water from the vats looked incredibly refreshing. What took his mind off the heat was a word from one of the 7th.

"What a storm..." he said dreamily, gazing into the distance. Augen turned once more and tried to match his vision. There was not a cloud in the sky.

"Yep. You are not going to see anything like that in Islica," another soldier commented, handing his comrade a portable goblet to drink from.

Augen tilted his head in confusion as he slowly returned to the front line.

Up front, the commander stood completely alone, gazing at his map and wiping his chin with a handkerchief.

"Grab some water, Templar. We are moving out again."

Augen hesitated but felt he needed to say something about the soldiers in the back. "Commander, I think there may be something wrong with the men. I heard them talking about a storm..."

"And?" General Lomat interrupted.

Augen sighed to himself as subtly as he could. Did he really have to spell it out? "Sir, they claimed to see a storm, and there is nothing nearby."

"Look again, Templar. A storm is coming, which is why we need to move." Augen turned once more to the horizon. Was he joking?

There were no clouds in the sky, just sand, dirt, brush, and the mountains.

But with a second glance, he noticed that the mountain range had grown larger. In fact, it appeared to be moving before his eyes, like a sea of brown and grey, shifting and waving with a mind of its own.

As time progressed, the decision to move proved to be a wise one.

For what was once a formless mass in the distance quickly became an unignorable wall of encroaching death, rolling toward them at breakneck speeds and illuminating itself with orange and yellow blasts of static lightning.

When the sandstorm hit them, it proved the most terrifying thing Augen had ever seen. Wind that was once unnoticeable caused the Squires to slide sideways as they trekked forward.

General Lomat tapped Augen on the shoulder and motioned for him to turn on his headpiece.

"Get to the back of the convoy and tell me if the cargo is leaving the ground. Always touch the Squire closest to you and tell everyone you pass to do the same."

"Yes, sir. Are we going to keep moving?"

"That depends on what you tell me about the cargo."

Augen jumped off the top of the Squire and worked his way back down the train, keeping his hand on the Squires, Longbows, and leather cannons as they passed him.

The men marching beside the convoy did not need to be told twice about keeping physical contact with the machines, for, between flashes of electricity, the airborne sand grew so thick that the lights mounted on the STVs did effectively nothing. The flashing web of lightning was all that could illuminate the otherwise pitch-black, tangible, stinging darkness.

Two of the Squires and their cargo passed by, the second one and its artillery pieces roughly tied to the third with small utility chains. The brilliant men responsible for such quick thinking clasped the chains and marched in tight formation between the giant guns before them and the larger vehicle behind.

As the third Longbow passed, Augen's earpiece buzzed to life, but he could hear nothing understandable. The transmitters in their headsets were designed to be exclusively short-range unless supported by an Intel-Balloon, but it should have been fine at this distance.

Did the commander need something from him? Were his orders being changed? Augen considered returning to the front, but he did not have far to go, and what he heard may have been only interference.

Each Longbow was followed by a small group of leather cannons that were strung together and held down by several soldiers apiece.

As Augen worked his way past the last Squire, taking mental notes and pulling stray soldiers toward the column, he encountered no single gust of wind that would give him cause to worry seriously about the cargo. The Squires and cannons groaned and drifted slightly toward one side, but Augen saw nothing that would give the caravan cause to stop, save the increased possibility of getting lost.

It was not until he reached the very end of the caravan that things became grim. The remaining two leather cannons were held by only three men, with another straggling behind, just barely visible in the bursts of electric light.

Augen gestured dramatically for the lone soldier to catch up and grab hold of the machine, but dared not let go of it himself. When the man disappeared altogether, Augen fought the urge to go fetch him, for he understood that he too would likely meet the same fate if he did.

A uniquely violent burst of wind nearly threw Augen sideways and picked one of the leather cannons up off the ground. It seemed to hover in the air for a moment, held down by a single set of chains and an engineer clinging to one of the wheels, before jerking horizontally and dropping onto the man trying to hold it.

The sand likely gave way enough to distribute what would otherwise have been a fatal impact to the chest. However, the man unfortunate enough to have an artillery piece thrown onto his ribs was put completely out of commission, suffering from a collapsed lung at the very best.

Augen saw the injured man moving and jumped the chains he held to grab him, but another blistering gust of stinging wind flipped the unmanned gun and snapped the chain Augen clung to.

He picked up the wounded soldier as hastily as he could and spun toward the caravan, but it was already gone. The other two soldiers were tossed into the sand by the windstorm, their grips no match for the coarse airborne tide.

"How?" Augen stood dumbfounded by how fast he lost sight of the Squires. After a moment of contemplation, he grabbed the hands of the other men and pulled them northwest, or at least the direction he presumed to be northwest.

His headset was useless, screeching obnoxiously into his ears until he powered it down.

Even his visor, which helped dull the biting wind and nullify the contrasts between blasts of light and smothering blackness, gave no real assistance as he shuffled forward. He was not technically blind, but he might as well have been.

With no chance of communication and little chance of rescue, Augen trudged onward for hours with one man on his shoulders and two more clinging to his trailing hand like children.

Initially, he tried to keep on the highway, doing his best to feel for the slight contrast between the level roads and the uneven fields of sand surrounding them, but the winds blew with such ferocity that the land itself felt periodically crooked and diagonal. So, despite his best efforts, Augen soon knew without doubt that he had left the beaten path.

He swore to himself before sliding to a stop, desperately trying to formulate another plan. It was likely that General Lomat ordered the train to stop shortly after losing contact with his lieutenant, but if he did, it was very likely that Augen passed them long ago.

But what if the commander didn't stop? The Squires were equipped with basic tracking equipment that let the drivers know their trajectory as well as the distance they had traveled. Such gear would enable them to keep moving even with limited vision. They would certainly lose the freeway again as Augen had, but the commander could feasibly continue until he reached the general location requested for the outpost construction and then make an estimated guess.

Either way, there was little chance Augen could find the rest of the division until the storm broke, but how long would it take for such an occasion—days, weeks, even? Augen hadn't the faintest clue, so he stopped, took a knee, and tried pointlessly to regain his bearings. He whispered a short prayer, but put little effort into it.

Nothing could be seen in any direction save the two men less than a foot behind him. The lightning splashed a sharp orange hue onto everything, but Augen caught a glimpse of another color amidst the chaos. For a microscopic instant, a beam of light penetrated the storm from the Aether, splashed over the frenzied dust particles, and created an oasis of blue, red, and yellow shades over the horizon before dissipating just as quickly.

Augen glanced backward to keep track of the men with him and deduced from their body language that they had not seen the anomaly. When he looked again, he saw something stranger: A man's silhouette on the horizon, distant yet somehow visible through the storm, stood pointing calmly to the right of their position.

The knight stared intently at the man, but couldn't believe his eyes, and the image flickered in the dust and vanished after a moment, confirming his disbelief. The image was likely an instinctual hallucination or natural mirage, but something inside told him to alter his course to the right regardless.

Onward they trudged for what seemed like hours until Augen could not continue any longer. The heat was miserable, his armor was growing cumbersome, and its weight was made worse by the man he carried through the beastly wind that fought him with every step he took. His course alteration pitted him directly against the storm's current, and the difference was beyond tangible; it quickly became unbearable.

Taking a knee once more, he sarcastically thanked Deos for his help and fell sideways into the sand, losing consciousness seconds after his head hit the ground.

❖

Gulls called to each other, the Harpol Sea shimmered in the sunlight, and Christine sat on a blanket watching the birds fly overhead. Augen sat awkwardly beside her, observing some youths tossing a ball nearby. He wanted to say something, but did not know what would be appropriate.

"Nice weather we are having..." was all he got out. *Real smooth.*

"I love the rural districts. It is so much more peaceful around here," Christine responded with a smile. "The weather certainly does add to it." Augen smiled too, but snapped out of his ecstasy immediately afterward. He had been here before; he knew what came next.

Of the few dreams Augen had, most of them consisted of memories with Christine, or at least that was how they always started.

As was typical with dreams, the moment he became conscious of his state, his memories became a sandbox of surreal interactions and unrealistic transformations reflecting his current state in a grotesque contrast with the memory he began with.

Augen possessed complete control of the environment, yet, no matter what he did or altered, the dream always ended with Impact Day, the day he lost her. Some things could not be changed, even within his own dreams.

"Deos has certainly blessed us, that we enjoy such tranquility."

"Deos hates me," he said flatly, breaking the memory's script. Christine glanced at him, surprised.

"I don't think so..." she said. "What has He ever done to hurt you?"

"You do not know the half of it. He dragged you away from me, took your hearing and vision..." Augen teared up as he spoke. Christine touched her ear, and the hearing aids appeared under her hands. "He let Steven die, then He picked me up off the face of the planet and dropped me into hell's sandbox."

Upon his words, the sand on the beach swirled into a wild whirlwind and engulfed the couple, but neither of them flinched. Christine's face was deadpan as the sandstorm dropped out of sight suddenly and left them back in Nethel, but this time in the midst of a crowded city packed with pedestrians and motor vehicles.

"I think you are confused about what really happened. You left me, you killed my brother, then you went to fight a war in hell's sandbox. Deos did none of those things, but He saw them."

The crowds occupying Augen's dream stared at him in perfect unison as Christine's voice warped from her own gentle tones to a metallic scream.

"He always sees!"

Augen recognized the tone that her throat used to form words; it was a noise he knew well, for it was his first taste of war, given to him on Impact Day and sticking with him in his nightmares for all the years since. As the shrill howl of a howitzer shell falling from the sky echoed through the dreamscape, he knew it was coming to an end.

Christine broke character again and became as she was in his memories, looking up at the sound in worried curiosity as unseen and imminent catastrophe loomed over them. Despite her appearance, which matched his memory again perfectly, her words were new and hurt more than anything Augen could have expected in a dream.

"Deos may not hate you, but who are you to judge Him for it if He does? After all, I don't even know about you killing my brother, and I hate you with everything in me..." Then the shells struck the building next to the couple, shattering it like a porcelain dish and turning all its occupants into tragic memories.

Pieces of glass, stone, steel, and even some flesh flew past them in exactly the manner Augen remembered it. He sighed to himself and watched the events unfold in slow motion.

He and Christine were standing directly next to each other, but a large motor vehicle that happened to be passing was in the perfect place to partially shield Augen from the concussive blast without granting the same vital protection to the lady standing by his side.

While he was tossed to the ground, she was violently flung into the wall closest to them. When Augen looked up, he saw her sitting limply against the wall she had hit, eyes open but unfocused, blood pouring from her ears. She looked dead.

As always, this moment struck Augen harder than any other because, for just a split second, he truly believed she was dead. He believed it when it happened, and every time he dreamed of it since then, he was convinced that it was real and that this time, she would never wake up.

"I hate you, Augen. You are not worth my love, or His, so why don't you just die already? 'Hell's Sandbox' sounds like a good place for someone like you to do it." Her body, eyes, and general countenance were as still as a painting, yet her mouth opened to form the words as though her body were being used as a hand puppet.

Augen sat up and cried into his hands while more buildings fell and more people died in slow motion around him.

The two engineers who had followed their lieutenant through the storm ripped off the unconscious knight's facemask and poured some water into his open mouth.

He didn't seem to take it, so the second did his best to check for a pulse.

"I cannot feel anything!" the man screamed to his comrade, who leaned in to read his lips. The man with the near-empty flask took a swig and tapped his fellow engineer on the shoulder with it until he did the same.

"He could be dead!" the man leaning over Augen continued, but the other man shook his head.

"He could be alive, and a commander so willing to save his men deserves the very best from us." The man standing beside him heard only bits of his response, but got the idea and nodded in agreement.

So, they worked to remove the unconscious Templar's armor, propping the cuirass and pauldrons above Augen's head and tucking the decorative short cape he wore over them to create a makeshift tent above his upper body.

It was not much, but it would help with the heat and keep the stinging sand from being inhaled and doing further damage.

Then, after using other pieces of his armor to make a sloppier replica for the injured man whose lieutenant had faithfully carried, they checked his vitals as well. They got little visual response but were convinced that he, too, was still alive.

Then they rested, sitting back-to-back with their coats over their heads and their weapons clasped in their arms. They would not move until they knew their commander was recovering or dead, so they waited for the storm to clear.

Periodically, a booming sound in the distance woke them, but their exhaustion was finally allowed to show itself, and they slept deeply until the winds died down and the sky was dark.

❖

Augen awoke before they did, his head ironically swimming from a lack of water, but he sat up and surveyed his surroundings as thoroughly as he could.

The sky was dark, and the environment was blurred with a filthy earthen fog preventing any long-distance vision, but he could vaguely see the moon glistening overhead. Had it been a day? Several days? Augen had no idea.

His exhausted body did not wish to don the armor lying around him, but his brain told him to do so. For a deep booming sound periodically shook the very atmosphere, and an orange glow manifested in what Augen assumed must have been the horizon.

Though he could not discern the distance he would have to travel to reach it, he girded himself as hastily as he could and awoke the two men sitting back-to-back next to him, for he knew exactly what he was hearing and seeing—explosions, likely from heavy artillery fire.

The slumbering men jumped in surprise as the Templar, fully ironclad and bearing the wounded engineer on his shoulders like a backpack, tapped their shoulders and bid them awake. What little water remained in the soldiers' canteens was distributed amongst the group, and the men began marching as another explosion lit the way.

The blistering wind and hellish temperature had given way to a cold, dead, atmospheric coma that somehow left their path uncomfortable even at night.

Pushing onward, they found another soldier sleeping atop a lone leather cannon that had been flipped in the wind.

He explained that he was the first man Augen saw disappear behind the convoy. He, too, had gotten terribly lost once he lost sight of the column but traveled onward until he came across the cannon and stopped, knowing that he was still on the road and unwilling to risk losing his way again.

Another explosion led them to pause. The burst was noticeably closer, so they continued forward with the extra man.

Augen's knees felt like buckling. His body was bolstered by Hybrid, and he was trained to carry unusual amounts of weight, but not over such ludicrous distances. He heard one final boom in the distance, but when the noises stopped altogether, a new fear that the 7th was in some kind of distress gripped the lieutenant.

It did not seem likely that the commander would waste munitions, yet the explosions seemed consistent, intentional, even uniform.

A couple of hours later, the band finally reached the caravan. The 7th and its support teams had circled the Squires to form a makeshift steel wall around their position atop a hill with a considerable cliff to the east. The commander had decided that the Imperial Outpost would be set up there. Lights dotted the campsite, and the artillery pieces they had not lost faced outward in every direction.

The weakened lieutenant received a hero's welcome from the lookouts sitting atop the Squires, and the men accompanying him encouraged such a reception. The commotion dissolved considerably when the commanders strode through the camp headed up by Pazkt Lomat.

"Get the lieutenant water and take the man he is carrying to the medical tent."

"Accounted for and present..." Augen mumbled, doing his best to stand at attention.

"Take the lieutenant to medical, too." Soon, the whole camp was awakened with the news that the Templar had marched through a sandstorm for nearly a day with a man on his shoulders, though the knight himself was barely functional and had no chance to enjoy his short-lived fame.

He lay in the tent with water feeds injected into his neck for nearly three days, and the caravan experienced nothing of note for the duration of that time. The men kept themselves busy dismantling the Squires' exterior armor and building barricades around the outpost with them.

The commander spent most of his time communicating with his higher-ups through the outpost's Intel-Balloon. Several times, it got noisy, and Augen wished he could hear what was being said. But he stayed bedridden until the third day, when another nightmare memory of Christine startled him awake.

He lay there gasping for air, with a liquid in his eyes that he wished was just sweat, before yanking the vial from his neck and storming from the medical tent.

"When do we head for Barbasul?" he said, striding toward General Lomat, who paused what he was doing and grinned slightly at the half-dressed Templar addressing him.

"I do believe that we are pulling out this morning."

Chapter 8

Sand, Steel, and Blood

By the time Augen had dressed and rejoined the 7th, they had already formed into groups of twenty with the two supporting sharpshooter divisions following their heavy counterparts in a scattered tail formation.

Three of the Squires, each carrying spare ammunition and living supplies for the marching troops, were farther behind with their own small skirmisher guard.

The Squire farthest back had deployed an Intel-balloon, and Augen, who had been put in charge of intel, was confined to the tail vehicle for the duration of the transition.

It was very early in the morning, but the sun was already starting to superheat the soil around the marching men. Though it had been several days since the terrible sandstorm that had nearly killed him, the stale dust fog that had followed it up remained ever present, so Augen switched his visor to detect abnormal thermal energy so he could vaguely see the whole division. The visions he received from the machine were imperfect, as even the balloon's advanced sensors seemed to be put off by the heat, but the images were enough to keep his job from being utterly useless.

From his mobile quarters, Augen had little to personally fear from the heat, but he was curious about the state of the Iba invasion on a larger scale, so after switching his comm system to isolate the general, he asked about it.

"How is the situation looking? Have we received word from Barbasul?" A moment of silence passed, and Augen assumed he would not get an answer from his superior officer, but the headset buzzed to life, and his assumption was disproved.

"We have received no reinforcements over the past three days and have been unable to contact the base at Eris. We are also leaving the range of Shoga's battlefleet, so any future support will have to come from our own artillery."

Augen raised his eyebrow questioningly but kept quiet as the commander continued. "Our Longbows can shatter any organized division we encounter. However...I have a feeling that we will encounter more than infantry when we reach Barbasul.

"For if the enemy has been able to shut out our aircraft, it is likely that they have access to some super-heavy artillery themselves. Monster-Ribaults are the most likely." Another long moment of silence ensued, and the commander sighed.

"I know that you have questions, Templar. Get them out. You wonder why we are moving on without reinforcements? The short answer is this: The comms issues are likely a result of the storm, but if reinforcements have stopped, then it is possible the enemy has taken the fight to them.

"No intel suggests that they are organized enough to launch a multifront offensive, so it could be that the bulk of the enemy's force bypassed us during the storm and is now behind, trying to keep the empire out of Barbasul by filling the chokepoint in Eris until the mob inside the capital reaches and kills the king.

"Assuming that this is true, then it is highly possible that we can take the city without facing an organized force," the commander posits.

"This seems like a gamble," Augen sighed.

"War is a gamble, Templar, and unfortunately, the pressure to take action is on us, not them."

Augen contemplated this as the columns progressed, but nothing more was said until gunfire could be heard in the distance. "Comms for Squads 16 through 18, report. Who is shooting?" Augen opened the comm system to include all the men with headsets and awaited a response.

"Captain Salac, Twelfth Sharps. Mounted men spotted northeast of our position. They are armed." General Lomat, who was the only other officer connected to all comms, spoke to Augen in response.

"Any visual, Lieutenant?"

"No heat signatures outside of our formation... They must be out of range."

"They could be civilians. Tell the men to stop wasting ammunition. If they are not certain, they should continue their advance. Taking potshots at men on camels, armed or not, is far more likely to cause problems than it is to solve any."

"Captain Salac, order your men to hold fire. They could be civilians." As Augen forwarded General Lomat's orders, he continued to check his visor, searching for irregularities and periodically switching between various ocular scanners.

Hours went by, and as the day progressed, the heat got worse. Periodic breaks were permitted, and the Water-Squire made regular trips across the width of the formation, and like a mindless machine, the men continued forward into the wastes. The grind was tedious and little changed until the early evening. Augen detected heat signatures in the distance, and his comms buzzed back to life.

"Captain Harr, Eleventh Sharps. Structures spotted dead ahead. Approximately 400 yards to contact."

"Copy that, Captain," Augen exclaimed with apparent relief.

"We should be reaching one of Barbasul's satellite towns. Which means we are only hours away from the embassy," General Lomat stated. "Contact the outpost. Tell them to pack up the Longbows and bring them to our location."

Augen began recalibrating the balloon to send a long-distance message, but when gunfire broke out to the east again, he stopped short and rapidly reconnected the short-range comms.

"Captain Salac, your men have been ordered to hold fire. State your condition."

"Heavy casualties! Deos help us! It is massive..." The gunfire continued, and Augen heard a large explosion in the distance, but the audio cut out before the captain finished. A leather cannon fired off its rounds amongst the cacophony, and Augen's commander came back onto comms.

"What is going on, Lieutenant?" Augen gave no immediate answer because at the moment he did not have one, but he had a bad feeling that civilians were not the cause of this disturbance, for another noise pierced the chaos—a noise Augen recognized from his training years with the Templar.

"I believe the two easternmost squads have engaged with the enemy. I cannot get a response from 18, but I suggest we brace for a C2-Class Warmachine."

Augen seriously doubted that the commander would believe him, but his gut said that such chaos could not be caused by any infantry squad. Even the Monster Ribauldequins the enemy was rumored to possess could not make the sound Augen heard in the distance.

So, while waiting for further orders, he contacted their own artillery as the commander had asked, but he had no intention of getting them mobile. Instead, he frantically told the Longbow engineers to set back up and prepare anti-armor missiles to strike near his position.

Another shot from a leather cannon rang out as General Lomat answered his lieutenant.

"Tell squads 18 through 16 to fall back to your position. We will do the same and form a line on the right flank. Whatever they are hitting us with will face the full force of our troops."

"Commander! Captain Salac is non-responsive. I have a comms unit in my helmet and request permission to move until I have a visual and can take his place if necessary."

"Request denied, Lieutenant. You have to use thermal vision to locate the far squads and direct them into the correct formation."

"Commander, any tight formation will be blown to bits. I am trained in irregular warfare. Have your men continue toward the city at double time. Direct the western squads to fill your gap. I will reroute the eastern flank to me, and we will surround the armor as it passes us. When it becomes visible, shoot in the treads."

No immediate response came from his commander. *He is considering it.* To Augen, that was permission enough.

So, grabbing an engineer in the Squire charged with maintaining cargo, he shoved the headset onto the man's head and gestured hastily as he spoke.

"Keep the commander updated! To talk, press this. Do not touch anything else." Then Augen was gone.

The untrained engineer would not be nearly as versatile on the balloon as Augen was, but he had left the comms aligned to all commanders, including himself, so he could hear everything and, if need be, respond as necessary.

The obnoxious dust fog that had followed the soldiers since the storm still lingered, and Augen's vision was frustratingly limited. But every couple of seconds, Augen passed men of the 12th fleeing from their positions, so it was not difficult to deduce where they came from.

His armor seemed slightly heavier than it would have been nearly a week ago, and his joints still hurt, but despite the abuse his body had taken since the Pallerheim op, Augen felt more himself as he sped toward the chaos. The adrenaline pumping through his veins awoke something in him, and he felt like a killer again.

When Augen reached the battlefield, the Empire's forces were in disarray. The farthest squad looked to be completely gone, and the next two had been blown into chunks. In all three cases, the men of the 12th were all but scattered to the winds.

The 7th, who had clearly taken far worse casualties, had gathered themselves into small groups of survivors and desperately fired their hotshot rounds toward a single target that sat concealed in the dust and smoke clouds.

Augen could not identify exactly where their target was, but when it unloaded shot into a cluster of men, shredding their corpses, armor, and all, and blowing up the leather cannon with them, he knew that his suspicions were correct. He also understood that the desperate attempts of the 7th to puncture the armor of any Cataclysm-War Sandcrawler from the front were utterly pointless.

Rushing headlong down a small hill toward the pinned-down men of the 7th, Augen pulled routing soldiers toward him before redirecting them to the top of the hill he had just descended.

When men of the 7th saw him, they formed up around him to create a small defensive barrier for their lieutenant, but that was the last thing Augen wanted, for clusters of men were precisely what a Sandcrawler's gunners would be searching for. Why waste ammunition when one can kill many at once with a single well-placed burst of howitzer fire?

Clearly emboldened by the fleeing sharpshooters and limited remaining resistance, the twin engines of the warmachine roared, and like a boar provoked from its den, the massive tank came barreling out of the fog to meet its targets.

Camel-mounted men armed with large guns guarded the flanks of the steel beast, picking off wounded soldiers and killing those who would try to get around it.

"To the hill!" Augen screamed, gesturing wildly to the men around him. As the Sandcrawler approached them, its primary gun, a fully automatic cannon that had been banned after the Cataclysm Wars, rattled off another lethal barrage of grapeshot into a small group of footmen trying to regroup with Augen. Then it slowly turned its gaze onto him.

"Fly, men! Fly! Or you will certainly die here! To the hill, I say!" The men ran with him the best they could, and despite being far slower than their augmented commander, they left the range of the mini cannon before it had a chance to reload and fire again.

Some of the mounted men broke ranks with their comrades to run down the fleeing Reds, but a group of sharps who had assembled on the hill as Augen commanded put them down as they approached before they could do any harm.

Glancing back at the Sandcrawler, Augen sighed in relief even as he ran, for the machine, as well as the bulk of its support cavalry, did not alter course to finish them off. Instead, he watched them press forward, likely in hopes that, despite the chaos that had certainly given away their position, the rebels could use the smog to descend on the rest of the invasion force before General Lomat could fully reform their lines to respond.

They were playing into Augen's hands, and he knew it. As long as General Lomat and the rest of their division had maneuvered as he suggested, the flanks of the machine would be exposed, and even without artillery support, they could cripple the warmachine and destroy the mounted troops encircling its shoulders.

When Augen and his small, newly assembled shock team crested the hill, the regrouped sharpshooters lobbed several more well-placed volleys into the camel riders, dropping several of them. Augen commanded them to cease fire once he was sure that their aggressive cover was no longer saving lives.

"Hold fire! Everyone, on your stomachs! The enemy must not spot us!" The rallied troops did as they were told, lying prone on the peak of the hill until the last of the enemy force had passed them. A handful of the more aggressive skirmishers saw themselves in a solid position to retaliate and were visibly confused by the order, but they too obeyed without question.

Augen stared into the clouds of smoke, waiting for the right time to strike back.

"Lieutenant Di Gattchen, what is your current position?" the man on the comms spoke up, likely on behalf of General Lomat, who could no longer micromanage him personally.

"I have gathered survivors about four hundred yards north by northeast of your position. Squads sixteen through eighteen have been routed or destroyed, but I am poised to strike the enemy from the rear with a couple of dozen survivors. Where are General Lomat and Captain Harr? Have they repositioned their men? A C2 Sandcrawler is right on top of their last position."

Augen tried to stay still as he had ordered his men to do, but it was growing difficult to wait. He could hear cheers and mocking whoops from behind the warmachine as rebel infantrymen shot the wounded soldiers who were left alive by their cavalry.

Trying to keep his temper from flaring up, Augen distracted himself by counting the hostiles guarding the Sandcrawler's tail. It was everything he could hope for—the rear of the crawler was lightly armed, lightly armored, and guarded by a small, unprofessional rabble of footmen. The cavalry was distracted with guarding the crawler's flanks and would likely be slow to respond when they struck.

Patience, Augen, he thought. If you time this correctly, the foe will certainly not escape. You will avenge those soldiers. You just have to wait a little longer...

Not satisfied with the intel man's response time, Augen gave him another question.

"Can you figure out how to contact the Longbows on the broad scanner? If you can, tell them to fire upon the thermal flare between our divisions. We should be able to mark it almost immediately after engagement."

Without waiting for a response from the radio, Augen spoke to the men around him. "You six with the long rifles, stay on the high ground and out of sight. Each of you pick a target from the rear guard and kill them the moment we are spotted. The rest of you, follow me."

The new squad, made up of only fourteen survivors from the Seventh, sped as hastily as they could down the hill until they were paralleling the enemy. Then, while the men caught their breath, Augen waited, just behind a small dune, for some kind of signal.

The rebels and their secret weapon continued to trudge forward, but even as they passed General Lomat's previous position, no guns were fired. The rebels, who had initially struck so surely and passed up the opportunity to kill a knight in hopes of inflicting another devastating flank on the imperial army, found no one to flank.

His division, marked for devastation by the enemy, had disappeared altogether, light artillery and all. Even Augen was impressed by the unexpected speed of their maneuver, and it was obvious that the enemy was not ready for such a move.

The arrogant chuckling and cheering turned into uncomfortable mumbling, and as they continued farther into the yellow smog searching for the other two-thirds of a disappearing army, the enemy grew visibly and audibly worried. A dark side of Augen loved it: He was now the hunter, and his quarry was already in the snare. Any newfound awareness of the rebels' predicament changed nothing, for it was already too late.

No audible signal came, but when three orange hotshot rounds flew into the sky from the north, followed by three more to the south, each spread out with surprising consistency and creating a broken semicircle around the rebel force, Augen knew the wait was over.

Before the blazing bolts of phosphorus came to a stop in the sky, Augen grabbed one of his comrades' rifles and fired its already-loaded hotshot vertically, finishing the airborne crescent.

"Kill the infantry first! Those with hotshot hit the crawler in the exhaust ports!" Augen stood up from his crouch, and the men with him followed suit.

The rest of the ambush remained hidden, spraying lead and phosphorus into the rebels from every conceivable angle at once from behind the drifting desert curtain.

Augen shared no interest in their choice to stay hidden. The sadistic guerrillas had their fun at the expense of his comrades, and now Augen would happily show them what it was like to be suddenly crushed by an unexpected superweapon.

The men of the 7th tried to follow their leader into the fray but were left behind by the lieutenant as he careened forward and hurtled into the traitors' ranks.

Numerous rebels were taken apart before they knew what hit them, but as their assailant passed by the ammunition carts, several remaining camel riders converged on his position, hoping to score a lucky hit with their jezail-howitzers.

This did not matter, for once a knight had negated the advantage of range, he had little to fear from the unaugmented, mounted or not.

The most intelligent among the rebel rearguard tried to create distance between themselves and the juggernaut wreaking havoc behind the crawler. However, those who separated themselves from their column were singled out by the sharpshooters and lasted no longer than the ones being bludgeoned to death in the melee from which they fled.

The sand smog that had once played to the rebels' advantage was now their biggest weakness. For with a little luck and some impressive maneuvering from the 7th, the rebel forces found themselves surrounded by an enemy they could no longer see.

The element of surprise was gone, and in mere moments, the entire defense division surrounding the Sandcrawler, mounted and unmounted, was destroyed. All that remained was the tank itself and its armored ammunition carriages, and without flexible support, it was only a matter of time before they too were felled.

Waves of hotshot flooded over the shell of the crawler, bouncing off it in every comprehensible direction but doing nothing of note except to make a terrible cacophony and light up the clouded horizon with the warmachine's menacing silhouette.

The men following Augen stood between the ammunition carriages and unloaded their rifles into the exhaust ports on the crawler's newly unguarded backside.

The armor of the beast was unfazed, and the secondary guns, which still had ammunition, kept anyone —including the knight—from getting too close. Despite the immense amounts of light ordnance initially flung at the crawler, no noticeable damage was being done to the ancient warmachine.

Despite this temporary standstill, Augen smiled under his helm when one of the engines coughed up a steady plume of smoke. He knew that if they could heat it enough, the Longbow Rockets could spot the machine with their thermal visors, then the killing blow would be struck.

"Focus fire on that exhaust port!" he yelled, aware that the machine would not be felled by such a move. Staring into the sky, Augen hoped that those who could finish the battle were watching and prepared, and as it turned out, they were.

A whistling howl tore through the chaotic ambiance, heralding impending doom before a well-placed rocket struck the Sandcrawler on its hot side, splitting the machine in two and vaporizing the side that took the impact.

The soldiers surrounding Augen cheered triumphantly as a handful of the shattered rebel force emerged from the smoke with their hands in the air. The Templar shared none of the 7th's revelry, for the screech of the friendly artillery dragged traumatic memories of his past back to the surface, and while he ultimately refrained, it took a feat of will for Augen not to slay the surviving rebels himself as they surrendered.

The battle was over, for the secret weapon of the rebellion was ruined, and the threshold of Barbasul was now ripe for the picking.

CHAPTER 9

BURDENS AND PAINS COME TO LIGHT

The 7th wasted no time preparing the final phase of the invasion. First, the men commandeered a local constabulary structure to set up their final outpost, knowing that its walls and stockades would ensure a naturally defensible position. The balloon used during the battle was set up over the facility, acting as its own small scout team for the officers to use as a means of detecting potential counterattacks. It also served as a flag to christen the structures below for the arrival of those scattered by the Sandcrawler battle.

Of the 248 men in the 7th Reds who left Eris Port, sixty-four were slain in the first couple of seconds of the ambush. Another seven were lost during the battle from stray gunfire and unlucky shrapnel. Nineteen of them were wounded badly enough to warrant exclusion from the frontlines, and of the wounded, most were participants in Augen's rear charge.

The 11th and 12th Sharpshooters had suffered far fewer casualties than their armored counterparts, but General Lomat was far from impressed with their performance. As stragglers and cowards who had fled the battle trickled into the imperial base, the commander had them arrested and court-martialed on the spot, executing a handful for desertion and ordering the rest publicly beaten according to the laws of the Empire.

The surviving commander of the 11th Sharps protested many of the sentences but was hastily overruled by the hardened Islican War-Master.

Augen was no exception—his rank and association with the Templar Order held no sway, so for disobeying orders and leaving his post, he too found himself court-martialed by the general. The Templar made the point that he filled a necessary space in the chain of command and that the casualty count would have certainly been far higher had he not acted.

"I had already fulfilled the bulk of my duty on intel and left someone behind to tend to details. So, with or without orders, it seemed less than efficient to continue working where I was not truly needed. In my opinion..."

"We do not want your opinion, Templar," General Lomat interrupted, wiping his mouth as he spoke. "Your impulsive behavior presents an apparent threat to the unit. According to the law of the empire, you could be publicly flogged for disregarding orders."

Augen did not flinch. He had faced worse. The commander sighed as his associate mumbled into his ear, but Lomat waved him off and drew his conclusion.

"However, in recognition of the lives you doubtlessly saved among those hit the hardest by the attack, your punishment will be as follows: You will be stripped of your rank and sentenced to three days in the stockades. Once your time has been served, your position will be reconsidered. Guards..."

"I will see myself to my new quarters," Augen interrupted, shrugging off the man who approached him.

❖

The stockades were old-fashioned cells dedicated to prisoners of special interest to the military. Small, dark, and uncomfortable stone rooms with no power, such alcoves were little more than holes in the ground with a door. Augen had thoughts about his new accommodations, but did not bother to share them with the man stationed outside his cell.

The guard, on the other hand, a local who worked for the constabulary, had much to say to the giant man in the cell.

"Are you one of the new soldiers? The ones the Empire claims will help end the wars?"

The guard brought a large metal flask to his lips between words and tilted it enough to barely draw liquid. Augen shifted his weight around in his cell, attempting to find a comfortable position but eventually recognizing that there was little chance he would be successful in a room designed to serve punishment.

"What wars? The siege of Barbasul is just over a week old, and our counterstrike has just begun. If we have our way, this conflict is weeks from its end at the longest."

"Are you from Eros or Alampia?" the guard inquired further. Augen humored him in hopes that conversation would take his mind off his physical discomfort.

"Eros. My homeland is in Nethel."

"Ah. Very far away. The cores of the Golden Empire and its eastern brother see very little conflict, but here is...different. War is never far away, as the miscellaneous kings put in place by the Empire are always trying to solidify their power, and such politicking brings bloodshed, with or without interference from the North.

"This king, the one you come to save, is the sixth I have seen in my lifetime, and he is no different. I cannot even remember his name," he chuckled to himself as he finished.

Augen sighed to himself, trying to keep the muscles in his back from cramping. Rather than grunting or crying out when he failed, he posited his response. "It seems irresponsible to know so little about your country's leadership," he said, trying not to let the pain alter his voice.

"You think so?" the guard muttered, seemingly agitated by Augen's response. "You Northerners do not understand. You receive your laws straight from the top. The leadership in your countries is stable, with ample protection and an established government system that the people are used to.

"Each time we are given a king, he reveals himself to be nothing more than a petty tyrant, a random member of a noble house thrown into power by a foreign empire without training, preparation, or any apparent forethought. And as the new leadership purges his competition out of fear of assassination, those who put them in charge look on, unwilling to even dignify the bloodshed with their attention."

Augen leaned back as he listened and noticed the words *Maveth Shedim* scratched into the stone wall beside his free shoulder. The youth he had executed in Eris died saluting that name, and Augen wondered how this political environment played into his existence, if at all.

He considered asking about it, but when a door down the hall slammed open, and the guard saluted and walked out, he knew that his questions would have to wait.

"Do you need my help again already, General?" Augen quipped.

General Lomat, still in his dress garb, stepped before the cell door and opened it.

"Funny," he responded with a tone as deadpan as his facial expression. He wiped his chin and shook his head. "I made a mistake."

Augen did not expect such a statement from the cold commander. "Mistake?"

"Yes. Your performance today was irrational and reckless, but it proved beyond a doubt that I misplaced you during deployment."

"Well, I..."

"I am not finished, Templar. Your unwillingness to acknowledge established strategy and obvious freelancing tendencies could have easily jeopardized the mission.

"What would have happened if our Longbows had not received your message? Our forces were spread out and vulnerable from nearly every flank, and that battle could have gone on for hours until an experienced man was able to contact the artillery again.

"How about the enemy? Your strategy trapped the Sandcrawler we saw, but what if there had been another? Had enemy reinforcements come in from farther behind, your men would have been crushed between a hammer of hot lead and a hundred-ton anvil."

"I gambled," Augen responded. He did his best not to sound facetious, for he had no desire to be.

Pazkt Lomat wiped his jaw in frustration and leaned against the threshold of the cell door.

"Indeed," he mumbled. His eyes glared into the back of his own arm, darting back and forth as though he were hastily reading something on his sleeve.

After a moment of intense mental debate that Augen wished he could have overheard, the War-Master grunted to himself and let out a long, wheezing sigh, seemingly settled on something yet simultaneously unhappy about it. He continued slowly, calculating each word.

"However, Deos has clearly blessed you with a favorable wind of fate, for your little stunt experienced no major hookups and doubtlessly halved our casualty count. That much is undeniable, regardless of how I choose to observe it."

The commander sighed to himself, and his countenance sagged slightly as he finished.

"You received a light sentence today because you acted consistently and tried to save lives. I had enough precedent at my disposal to predict that you would get antsy in the rear guard, yet I chose not to adapt."

Augen said nothing in response, largely because he did not know what would be appropriate.

"You should know that war is no place to play a hero," he continued to his underling.

"What makes you think I am a hero?" Augen responded, visibly surprised by his leader's change of heart. "I thought I was a terrorist."

"A terrorist who climbs a tower to save a child and his mother? A terrorist who jumps off a cliff to save the life of a trapped Squire driver, and carries a dead man through a sandstorm in hopes of saving him?"

The commander made eye contact with Augen and let those words sink in. "Yes, Templar, by the time you reached us, the man you carried had been dead for nearly a day..."

Augen's heart sank at the news of another person he was unable to save. Images of the people he lost flashed through his head, and though no one could see it, it wore on his body and spirit.

"You are no terrorist. Deos knows how you were able to join the Templar at all. But next time you try to save the day, remind yourself that you may be carrying a corpse through the storm. Understand that one of these days, if you do not adopt a more...honest perspective on the nature of war, your bloody heart is going to get you killed, one way or another. You can choose to let it, but I pray it doesn't drag others to their deaths, too."

The commander sighed once more and wiped his mouth again, and seemingly satisfied with what was said, he turned to leave.

Augen's posture sagged as the words of the commander weighed on him and made his heart hurt almost as much as his seating arrangements affected his back. He knew he did not fit in amongst his peers, but for all his efforts, his visions of conformity with his order had never emerged as he hoped. I did not come naturally to him.

General Lomat stepped away from the cell and let its steel frame slam back into place, but upon reaching the end of the hallway, something else came to him, and he spoke, focusing his voice concisely into the wall on his right, knowing that the stone structure would relay his voice to his intended audience.

"I have made arrangements to have you promoted to the late Captain Salac's position once your sentence is served; it will suit your skill sets far better. Perhaps you will even beat some much-needed discipline into your new division.

"Despite your origins, I think I can grow to like you, Templar. Do not make me regret my choices here." A dab to his chin with the handkerchief, and he was gone. The guard, who had apparently been eavesdropping through the door, shuffled back in and chuckled to himself.

"You seem to have it good with the man in charge." Augen did not bother to respond. He was completely disinterested in the man on the other side of the door.

The words of the General's warning ate at him, and as he sat with nothing to do but stew on his failures, the self-criticisms grew more personal and aggressive with every passing repetition. Eventually, the knight cracked and broke the pattern of silence he had started.

"Do you have a rock?"

"A rock?"

"Or a piece of steel... Something I can chisel the wall with?"

The guard shifted his weight around uncomfortably at Augen's request.

"Are you trying to break out?"

"I want to write on the wall." Slowly, the guard handed Augen a thin steel chisel with a sharp edge on one side; it was relatively easy to handle and created lines on the wall identical to the ones forming Maveth Shedim's moniker.

The guard watched as Augen chiseled at the back wall to form the names of Christine and Steven above where he rested his head.

Augen made a point to angle his body so that the man could not see the words, but the guard did not seem to take the hint.

"You, too, huh? What do you write? A poem? The name of a loved one?"

"What does it matter?"

"It is said that what one writes in the darkest places shines the brightest light in their life. I would like to know what shines light in yours."

Augen paused his work momentarily and glanced back at him before continuing. "Well, whoever said that must never have known me. I write the name of my greatest burdens. The failures that will likely get me killed someday when my unnatural luck finally runs out, and the guilt that will drag me to Hell when death does show itself."

"And what is that?" the guard continued. To this, Augen spun to face him angrily.

"Don't you have anything better to do?" The man backed off and stood over his post in silence. In truth, Augen knew he did not have anything better to do, but the man clearly understood that he was pushing his luck with a very dangerous inmate.

Once Augen finished writing, he slid the crude instrument back under the door for the guard to pick up and put in his bag.

Then he sat, doing nothing until an uncomfortable sleep took him for a while. He did not have one of his usual nightmares. Instead, he dreamed about the emperor, his bride, and what he believed it was like to be in his shoes.

When he awoke, it was still dark out, but the images of a life of immense power and unwavering prestige loomed over him even as the dream itself drifted away with the vestiges of lasting rest.

What would it be like to sit on that throne? To never feel tired? To always be rested, knowledgeable about the future, and ready to face it?

...

Nathan hurried through the garden to where Catherine sat crying near its core. The night was well underway, and he had much to do in the morning, but this was an emergency. One of the royal couple's adopted girls had awoken him in a panic.

"He hit Mommy!" was all she said, and he flew. His older body could not move like it did when he was in his prime, but he dashed with all the speed he could conjure. As Catherine sat on a bench holding the side of her face and stifling sobs, the old man crouched to meet her eyes.

"Why did he do this?" he asked, holding her in his arms.

"He is losing his mind. I barely recognize him anymore!" She sobbed. "I found him pacing back and forth up here, yelling gibberish and punching everything within his reach as he walked. I tried to stop..." She choked on her words and could not continue, but Nathan got the idea.

A couple of maid-servants who had hastily followed Nathan into the garden tended to their mistress, and she recovered quickly.

Nathan surveyed his surroundings, making sure that Alexander was not lurking somewhere, though if his state matched Catherine's description of it, then the emperor would be heard coming from the other side of the building.

"I will be back. Catherine, alert the sentinels. I will sort him out."

"Nathan! He is irrational, animalistic, and even dangerous. He could hurt you!" Her calls fell on deaf ears as Nathan strode away.

Alexander was easy to find, not because he was noisy, but because he was far closer than expected, collapsed on another bench down the walkway, tears in his eyes and cold sweat all over his body. His arms were shaking spasmodically, and his skin was cold and pale.

He almost appeared to be asleep, but his eyes were wide open, and he jumped back and forth nearly as quickly as his arms shook.

"Deos, have mercy!" Nathan exclaimed to himself quietly as he approached the fallen king.

❖

A day later, Alexander awoke in the medical ward, tied to his bed, and hooked to five different hoses. His body throbbed, and his head spun wildly.

"Where am I?" he queried aloud. His words summoned nearly a dozen nurses and a handful of doctors, who were upon him in seconds. A glance at their uniforms and he knew where he was, the underbelly of the Ivory Citadel, where the sick, dying, or dead of the government's elite were treated and processed.

Built well after the citadel's official founding, but before his lifetime, the grungy grey and white catacombs housed many of the world's best physicians, largely from the Order of Hospitaliers, so that those of the utmost importance to the Empire may be treated for any affliction under the sun without identity exposure or security risk.

He had toured this part of the citadel before and hated everything about it. For while the bulk of the citadel ran like a beautiful, well-oiled machine far above them, it was here, in the core of the mountain the citadel rested, that the true weakness and frailty, the humanity, of the world government was on full display.

The moment his shock dissipated, a deeply embedded panic he had grown so accustomed to returned to him like a wicked spirit, haunting him even as he lay tied to the table.

Why are you lying down? Time waits for no one, not even you! If you cannot fix the Empire, then it will fall, and everything will end. How long have you wasted time sleeping today?

Such voices screamed into his ears simultaneously, and he knew of no way to pull them out, so instead, he began to pull the tubes from his arms until one of the nurses stopped him.

"You need these."

"No, I don't! I need to return to work! How long have I been down here?"

"You are not going anywhere," Nathan interrupted, stepping through the entryway and sliding past the medical staff swarming the hyperintense, aggressive, and emaciated lord.

Alexander's arms bore the black scars of augmentation, and his large frame and dense muscles were proof of his ascension. However, such physical improvement was largely hollow, for the emperor's bodily enhancements bore a painful and life-threatening fault.

The hideous scars that marked the arms of every augmented man stretched around Alexander's chest and down his back, leaving blistering pitch-black cysts on the spinal column and near the heart. Had it not been for his status within the government and his subsequent access to unique medical help, the chemical compound known by the initiates of the orders as "Hybrid" would have certainly killed him on the day he was introduced to it.

The emperor's faulty augmentation was gruesome, but it was something the high clergyman was used to seeing. What surprised him was the apparent deterioration of his health beyond such norms.

Alexander appeared as though he had not eaten in days, his skin was sallow and thin, and his already-marred body bore a new mark the old man recognized immediately, a deep injection mark in the neck.

Nathan was a patient, relatively quiet man with a meek disposition and a peaceful old soul, but when he saw the mark on the emperor's neck, his eyes grew wide, and his tone was infused with white-hot fury.

"I am a member of the citadel's Crown! Everybody out!" The noisy medical staff halted what they were doing and stared at the man through their half-visors.

It was a well-established axiom of the medical facility that any who entered had his or her identity and status within the fortress above kept secret. Anyone who entered, save the medical staff themselves, came anonymously so that the odds of political favoritism or assassination attempts were minimized.

This rule was not established by the Golden Empire itself, but rather by the Holy-Order Hospitaliers, who had built this section of the fortress and overseen its machinations ever since.

Unlike their war-bent brethren, the black-clad specialists were dedicated to international damage control, building great fortresses all over Archaea where the sick and injured could take refuge from torrents, both natural and manmade.

Though she held the technical power in the circumstance, the lead practitioner nodded solemnly to her compatriots, and the crew exited the room.

"I should have known! The sudden bursts of energy, the changes in temperament, the refusal to sleep in your quarters with your wife, you have been drugging yourself again!"

Alexander glared at the old man confronting him and contemplated whether he would tell the truth.

Had Nathan merely been another cog in the government apparatus, he would have told the old man to go jump off a spire, but the cleric was nothing of the sort—he knew Alexander well. In fact, Nathan knew Alexander before he was elected to the emperor's throne, a claim only he and Catherine could boast, not that either of them ever did.

Despite the embarrassment and anger boiling inside the bedridden emperor, Alexander could not escape the fact that he had a genuine regard for the old priest, so he told the truth.

"Yes, for three days now. I could not stay awake." Though Nathan's guess was correct, the emperor's confirmation of it provoked visible disappointment.

"I...I thought you were past that," Nathan said, slowly rubbing his temples.

"I was."

"What have you been on?"

Now Alexander sighed. At this point, it would all certainly be found out when Nathan returned to the citadel's crown quarters, so begrudgingly, he continued.

"An adrenal cocktail I mixed in the medical room." Nathan was now pacing the breadth of the room, rubbing his head, and muttering to himself. Alexander snickered, seemingly amused by Nathan's fit. "You had better knock that off. You are starting to look like me."

"Do you think this is a joke? Had your wife not called the medical staff when she did, you would be dead! Dead! Overdosed on your homemade drugs!" Nathan fumed. His eyes were bloodshot, and his elderly frame was energized by an adrenal cocktail of his own, though it was never mixed in a test tube.

Alexander, on the other hand, deflated slightly as Nathan spoke. He was not afraid, but he was saddened by what he heard.

"So...Catherine knows then?"

Nathan shook his head.

"She confronted you in the garden, and you nearly knocked her unconscious after she accidentally touched your augmentation flaw. By the time I reached her, she had already called someone to help you. She is not as stupid and uncaring as you treat her."

"I hit her?" Alexander gasped and sprang up as much as he could.

Nathan sighed again and shook his head solemnly before responding. "It did not look terrible. My guess is that you threw an elbow when she took hold of your shoulder, but flawed or not, Alexander, you are still augmented, and her face took a very hard blow... You will have some sincere apologies to make upon your return, to your wife first, and then to the girls who witnessed it."

Alexander said nothing in response, but tears welled up in his eyes, and he stared at the ceiling.

Nathan said nothing more. Instead, he took a seat, hit a button to summon the medical staff again, and watched as they tended to the broken man tied to the bed before him. As time progressed, he drifted in and out of sleep but chose not to leave the room for more than a full day.

Periodically, he shot worried prayers into the catacomb ceiling as the emperor slept before him.

Since he came to power, Alexander spent nearly a full year adjusting the traditional workload of the Royal Couple until, between Catherine and him, they directly overlooked all but the most menial of tasks within the Ivory Citadel. This was largely done through implemented limitations of the supporting staff. Efficiency was greatly improved through these methods when the emperor was active, but now, with its head bedridden for the foreseeable future, the government would have to run at half capacity.

Nathan knew that Catherine would do her best to fill in where she could, but it would not be nearly enough. She was diligent and capable, but, like her husband, she was already working harder than was healthy.

When it became apparent that she had hit her limit, Alexander stopped appointing her new tasks but continued picking them up himself until his first incident two years ago, when Nathan caught him taking pain medications in unhealthy doses so that he could remain active.

The old man sighed to himself once more and slouched into his chair.

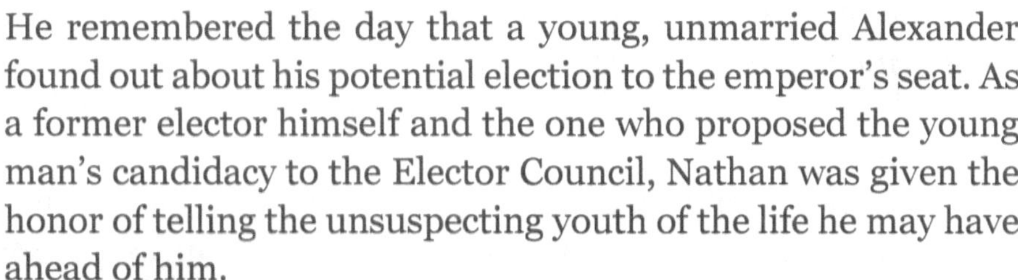

He remembered the day that a young, unmarried Alexander found out about his potential election to the emperor's seat. As a former elector himself and the one who proposed the young man's candidacy to the Elector Council, Nathan was given the honor of telling the unsuspecting youth of the life he may have ahead of him.

He spared no detail, proud of the young noble and pitying him as he took the news stoically, as Nathan knew he would.

"If I am elected to this position, would I be merely a figurehead, or can I make a real difference? For, while I am honored that you would consider me for such an important role, you know that I do not take my jobs lightly."

A much younger Nathan, who was a candidate for a place in the Holy Church and mentor to the newly graduated youth, smiled brightly and placed his hand on his shoulder.

"I haven't the faintest doubt about that. That is precisely why I recommended you. Our current emperor sits on his hands and lets the bureaucracy lead in his stead. As a result, the Empire has fallen into slow decay. The Golden Empire needs a man like you."

Alexander looked toward a distant sunset and grinned to himself.

"Of him who is given much…" he started. Nathan knew the adage well and smiled to himself before finishing it. "Much will be required. I believe that you can do it! I truly believe you can help preserve the civilized world."

Neither man said anything for a while. Eventually, Alexander broke the silence.

"Perhaps Deos has chosen me for something important? Rest assured that if I am elected, I will do my very best to bring the world back to where it needs to be. One way or another."

Nathan opened his eyes and started a bit. The bright streets of his memories were replaced by the bleak catacombs of today. He was no longer in his prime, and Alexander appeared to be past his, too.

Worst of all, Nathan feared the emperor would never fulfill the promise of his youth. He feared that his promise would kill him instead.

Chapter 10

Stepping Into Iron Skin

The next few days dragged on for Augen, who sat confined in a stone cell that was far too small for him.

Nights were miserable, long, and restless. Dreams about other lives alternated with nightmares about his own and prevented any meaningful respite or resolution. Inside the evening, shadows lurked. The wicked voice in Augen's head had seemingly followed him from Pallerheim.

In between bouts with the demonic whispers encouraging him to slit his wrists, the miserable knight spent his remaining nocturnal hours engaging in physical battles with the wall opposite him. His bloodied knuckles eventually put a crack into the stones bearing Christine's name, but any victory over the masonry appeared to be pyrrhic.

Ironically, the days were far more tolerable. Periodically, men of the 7th came to visit him, bringing updates from the outside about the status of the invasion, maps of the city to study, and occasional advice from General Lomat about how to manage troops in a chaotic environment.

Some of the consultations seemed redundant to Augen, as though the general had forgotten about his training for the Templar, but he took mental notes regardless, understanding that his superior officer was giving him an honest shot at leadership before his skills were to be tested. He even managed to fall asleep studying a map during the heat of the day, the uniquely uneventful slumber strengthening his mind between midnight cell battles.

The guard outside his door also spoke regularly with him, asking about the mission in between sips of his hefty iron flask. Augen humored him for his honest and seemingly gentle soul, though he never got any extra water for doing so.

As they exchanged small talk, he found himself relating to the man posted on the other side of the door; they were both out of place, not really cut out for the jobs they were assigned.

Augen never got around to asking him how he ended up working for the constabulary, but he could take some guesses with confidence.

By the end of his third day in confinement, Augen's back and shoulders hurt miserably, and he had developed a slight twitch in his left leg. He was more than ready to leave when the door finally came open.

The knight limped to the armory to dress down, rubbing his badly bruised knuckles and stretching his cramped and sleepy limbs along the way.

Based on what he had been told by the men of the 7th, nothing of note had happened for the duration of his time in confinement. Occasionally, some kind of light mortar fire could be heard from inside the city, but the men were ordered to hold their position.

Evidently, there was some kind of hang-up in the upper echelons of the military complex, resulting in no further orders, and despite promises from the higher-ups, no reinforcements from Eris either, but only a camera crew sent by an Alampian Media Guild to keep track of the siege's progress.

Once the newly dressed Captain Augen finally found General Lomat, he was addressing the guildsmen himself.

"If I had my way, I would send you back across the desert!"

"By law, we are allowed to be here and are entitled to your protection for the duration of our stay. You will hear from your superior officers should you refuse us," the headman of the expedition calmly countered as Augen stepped into the huddle to receive his orders.

When the new captain entered his peripheral vision, the cameraman jumped and turned his attention to him. The man standing toe to toe with General Lomat did the same.

"Ah. One of the new imperial super soldiers! We have much to discuss."

"You will not discuss anything with the captain right now. We have a meeting to attend regarding our march into the city, and you cannot follow us there...legally." The guildsman sighed and waved his hand.

"Very well. I am sure the opportunity will arise eventually. I am inquisitive about your rapid rise through the ranks. But do what you must. We will have a look around in the meantime."

As the parties split ways, the general seethed. "Rabble-rousers. Entitled eavesdroppers. This changes everything."

Augen kept pace as they approached their intel station, but he wished silently for more information. As they crossed into the building, the commander pulled his two captains' attention toward the images that their newly erected balloon projected onto their monitors.

"Here is an image of the embassy where Priority Target One is holed up. It sits about twenty-six miles from here, inside the heart of the city. As you can see, there is no evidence of a breach in the walls or on the roof. However..." As the general gestured, the simple hologram they viewed adjusted slightly to put emphasis on a large boxy object next to the building.

"Is that what I think it is?" Captain Harr gasped, and Augen shook his head in disbelief and finished Harr's sentence.

"A C3-Breach Cannon? It looks like it."

"How is that possible? First, the Ribaults, which we still have not pinpointed, then the Sandcrawler, and now this! How are they getting hold of this kind of technology?"

"They must have been finding ways to restore these machines, or someone is circumventing the law to supply them..." Augen chimed in. "How old is this image?"

"Less than a day. I ordered the previous outpost dismantled and unmanned, save a skeleton crew, and brought their tech to an undisclosed space in the city. These images come from the balloon they have set up."

Augen started at this news. He had heard nothing of this from the men he spoke with in the stockade. Perhaps they didn't even know? "I thought we had orders to hold our ground?"

"We do, and the bulk of our forces have," the general stated flatly. Augen pursed his lips and stuffed a smirk, stunned by such an uncharacteristic breach of protocol, especially from a man of his reputation, but he did not push it any further. If the commander chose to disobey orders, even indirectly, there had to be a very good reason for him to do so.

"Our responsibility is to protect the king of Iba, and once that Breacher is assembled, we will have mere minutes before the enemy is inside. So, orders or not, we will have to move out as soon as possible."

Augen grinned to himself as the commander finished. He had no idea where this side of Pazkt Lomat came from, but he liked it!

Captain Harr, on the other hand, made his complaints apparent. "We have no idea what we could be walking into! You executed three of Captain Salac's men for disobeying orders, and now you are going to do it yourself!"

The commander wiped his mouth and shirt, then his forehead, and for the first time, Augen noticed that he looked visibly nervous. "I executed those men for cowardice. I also understand all too well that not all orders are...for the best. The purpose of each mission must be fulfilled. The rest is detail work.

"Templar, you will rendezvous with the Twelfth at the forward base and await word from us. They moved under the cover of night to their current position, and I ensured that even here, only a select few men noticed their absence. You should have a stealth advantage, but I recommend silence on the matter. And keep away from the guildsmen—they will blow your men's cover without hesitation, should they be given a chance.

"I am planning on all three platoons converging on the target as soon as possible, but I will have to figure something out regarding our...visitors before we can do the same. Be prepared to move in with us on my orders.

"Until then, the Twelfth is in place as a last resort should we suddenly need action on the front without preparation time."

Augen noted that for the duration of the briefing, General Lomat did not hesitate or slow his words to think. It appeared that all second-guessing and doubt were either suppressed or already resolved in his mind, so Augen chose to emulate the same confidence.

The briefing was, like its speaker, largely concise and impersonal, but as the general concluded, he grabbed a cloth patch on Augen's sleeve and pulled the knight's eyes to meet his through the visor. "You are not there to act as a shock team or freelance vanguard. I do not want any surprises from you."

Upon being released, Augen stiffened his spine into an enthusiastic salute. "We will be ready to receive your orders. Whatever they may be," he responded, smiling under his visor.

General Lomat gave him a sheet of paper inscribed with a set of coordinates. "The men are waiting for you here. Prepare them for stiff resistance and gather as much intel as you can without giving up your position. Dismissed."

Augen strode to the entrance of the building but halted his enthusiastic strut upon reaching the door. Very carefully, he cracked the hatch and peered outside, scanning his surroundings for the unwelcome visitors until he spotted his old cell guard and some of the local constables.

"Where are the media guildsmen?" he asked, slipping cautiously from the command center. The guards stopped their conversations and eyed the approaching knight.

"Uh, I think they are standing by the gate. That's where I saw them last," the guard who watched his cell responded. Augen figured as much.

"I have to leave camp without them knowing. Keep them busy."

The men looked at each other and nodded in sync. They strode toward the gate to confront the guildsmen with whatever time-consuming conversation they could conjure. When he saw that the men were distracted, he took his leave, scaling the outer wall in seconds with nothing but a small running start.

His time in solitary left his muscles feeling weak and his joints stiff. He hoped that in the future, he could start a mission in good health, or perhaps the sore body was simply a burden all knights had to carry in one way or another.

Once beyond the risk of detection from those inside, Augen made his way toward the meeting location with considerably more speed.

Despite avoiding the busiest streets, he made excellent time for a man on foot, throwing a large cloak over his war gear to avoid catching unnecessary attention from potential hostiles. He still looked rather ridiculous, as though a giant leather umbrella had collapsed and was fleeing its handlers on unseen metal feet, but none of his neo-steel gear was reflecting sunlight, and that would suffice for the moment.

When Augen finally spotted the balloon, he was impressed with the clever location his commander had chosen for it.

It was packed between an old tower and bulky clusters of seemingly abandoned dormitories, where even an experienced scout would have trouble picking it out from the towering city skyline unless he knew precisely what to look for.

Unsure of how his comrades of the 7th had reached their new base and fearing a potential ambush in one of the conventional entrances, he climbed the outer wall of the dormitory, working his way toward the lookout point without the use of the doors or windows.

As he reached the anchor of the balloon and prepared to reveal himself to the men guarding it, the dusty sky grew dark, and he heard a deep bellowing coming from above.

"Whoa, where did that come from?" he heard one of the scouts petitioning his confederates. The guards gazed up at the vast object floating above them. Augen almost did the same, but finished his climb instead, for with the men's eyes drawn skyward, the knight's cover was blown just as he reached his dropping point.

"What the..." The two riflemen spotted the glowing eyes of Augen's visor and reached for their weapons, but the Templar dropped into their stone pocket and grabbed the barrels of the firearms before either man could make use of them.

"Don't pull the trigger," Augen warned. "You would throw the others into a panic. We don't need that." Pulling off his hood, Augen revealed his identity, and the two men, who expected his arrival but were unprepared for his method of approach, relaxed their grips on their guns.

"How many of those Warmoths have you seen?" Augen inquired as the shadow passed them over.

"The airship? This is the first one."

"They would never fly so low unless they are landing nearby," Augen observed, staring into the sky as the flying behemoth floated over their jagged city skyline, slowly making its way into the core of the metropolis.

"Track it," he commanded.

"We can, but at the rate it's dropping, it will be well out of range before it touches down."

Augen adjusted the dials on his earpiece and connected his visor radio to the Intel-Balloon's mainframe. With the headset synced up, he threw his cloak back over his helmet.

"Tell General Lomat that I have arrived and that we may be running out of time. With the current no-fly zone in place, nothing should be overhead unless it is summoned by our enemies. Keep your comrades ready but hidden for now. Keep close tabs on that Breach Cannon as well, and report to the commander the moment you see enemy movement in its vicinity."

"That thing outside the embassy is a Breach Cannon? Like the ones from the..."

"...Third Cataclysm War. Yes, and I fear that it will not remain in pieces for long. When you report, tell the General that I am doing an intel sweep. If you are not speaking with him, keep me on comms until I am out of range." Augen found some useful cracks in the stone wall and used them to disappear from his men's field of vision once more.

If he was in no real hurry before, Augen sped farther into the city with genuine haste now. The Warmoth passing overhead had horrid implications for the state of the mission, for if it was indeed dropping off cargo for the rebels, then the illegal superweapons being used against his men were not reassembled from scavenged scrap; they were being supplied by exterior forces well beyond the means of any rebel cell, even one with years of preparation.

Such thoughts were daunting, but Augen pushed them aside. He had to catch where that airship was landing, and if he could, identify its cargo as well. The invasion force may not survive another surprise clash with ancient war-crime machinery.

The farther he waded into the once-great capital of Iba, the more difficult it became for him to remain inconspicuous, for the swarms of locals grew dense and chaotic even as he approached the siege line in Barbasul's core.

At the time, Augen had no interest in the siege itself. He needed to confirm his suspicion about the Warmoth, which meant getting above ground level and locating its landing site.

Initially, the knight stuck to dirty back alleys and small, unkempt walkways reserved for the city's impoverished and deplorable. Keeping his eyes on the giant grey entity casting a shadow across the populace below, Augen was aware that he could be identified by the pathetic beings crouching about in the shade, but he knew it was unlikely their observations would travel far.

As the day heated up, the street life grew slightly less intense, as citizens who could afford to wait out the afternoon calefaction did so without hesitation. This played to Augen's advantage since he had no such privilege and could no longer afford to remain fully incognito.

His methods of avoiding the roads highly traveled were beginning to cost him, and despite his best efforts, it became clear that his target was gaining distance even as it descended.

Doing his best to keep his pace, he pondered his options. He did not like the idea of returning to the skyline, for though he could avoid the bulk of Barbasul's civilian foot traffic, he ran a considerable risk of falling through a roof if he had the misfortune of stepping onto the wrong dilapidated building. There was also a fair chance he would be spotted on the rooftops by a diligent rebel lookout, so initially, Augen transitioned his avenue of pursuit to the roadway.

The major paths quickly proved untraversable, for the civilians still on the roads screamed at the sight of the giant metal soldier, and several civilians even attempted to block his path.

Augen's temper began to flare up, and he considered making an example of a particularly belligerent merchant who made it his business to announce the knight's presence, following him around shouting about how much he hated Westerners. But another glance at the evasive grey object in the sky, and Augen chose to bypass the civilian-riddled highways altogether. He would risk the rooftops.

Just as the floating carrier disappeared behind the crumbling city skyline, he slid into the tallest building in his immediate vicinity and began ascending its staircase. A man behind a counter objected in his native language, but Augen paid no mind.

His large, cloaked figure glided down a hallway past some living quarters and what appeared to be some kind of brothel before climbing several more flights. His limbs were loosening up, and he was getting excited again. Killing terrorists was what he had joined up to do, and with the proper motivations, he was quite skilled in the craft.

It took more time than he had hoped, but he eventually found a trapdoor onto the roof and back into the embrace of the elements. Once struck by the daunting heat and dirty air of Barbasul's atmosphere, he had to take a moment for his eyes and body to adjust to its discomforting touch, but such respite was short-lived, for Augen knew he had to continue.

From where he stood, his field of vision was greatly increased, but the dust fog from the storm handicapped the improvement. It settled into the vast spaces between towering structures, growing more obvious and heavier as it approached the bottom floors. In the distance, the crest of the Warmoth disappeared behind the manmade horizon like the dorsal crest of a diving whale. The distance he would have to cover was considerable but manageable.

"Captain Di Gattchen to Falcon Nest, I will be out of your range momentarily. Let the commander know that weather conditions will restrict conventional sniping without ocular-tech."

Crouching on the roof and trying to calculate the most efficient rooftop path to the landing site, Augen kept himself from moving until his men gave their response. When he made up his mind on an acceptable route, he was still waiting.

"Falcon Nest to Captain Di Gattchen. We have relayed your message."

"Good. What is the status of the target?" Another long pause, and Augen sighed impatiently to himself. He wondered if he should have given the two men a run-through for effective use of the balloon before he left them, for they were not performing at the speed he expected.

"No movement, sir."

Satisfied with their answer, the knight leaped from his perch across a nine-foot gap, landing with surprising agility and silence for someone of his weight.

Augen estimated that his second-story jaunt would take nearly an hour one way if he were expedient. The early afternoon heat would have been unbearable had the rooftops in Barbasul proved more difficult to traverse. But the knight quickly found the structures to be far more forgiving than the cityscapes in the North would have been, for the bulk of its walkways were built exclusively for foot traffic and quite narrow.

Barbasul's structures were made mostly of cut stone and subsequently flat-topped and broad. Even the city's great architectural works, most of which predated the Golden Empire's absorption of Iba, were stocky, thick, and more horizontal than vertical. These foreign constructs contrasted sharply with the newer, more imposing structures built by the Great Western Power after Iba's conquest. Such imperial buildings stuck out in Barbasul's skyline like shards of stained glass shoved vertically between the cobblestones in one of

Pallerheim's sidewalks. Augen made a point to avoid their sleek and intrusive silhouettes and keep to the crowns of the native structures.

Despite his visual limitations, Augen could tell that the roadway traffic was not thinning. The streets sounded replete with civilian life despite the bloodshed that had commenced mere miles from their location and the looming siege of the embassy. The local citizenry seemed more than capable of keeping such details from interfering with their daily lives, and when Augen stopped to catch his breath on the ridge of a large living complex, he took in the manmade ambiance and considered how war-hardened the people below him must be. Perhaps they were simply ignorant of the invasion? That seemed unlikely. The man who guarded his cell spoke of warfare being common in this part of the world, and Augen took the lively behavior as confirmation.

When the Warmoth began its ascension, its overworked escalation engines screamed as they tried to push the aerial grampus back to its natural altitude. They only narrowly succeeded, and the metal leviathan struck the decorative crest of an inn before clearing its landing zone, ripping the molding apart and taking a portion of the structure's top floor with it into the sky.

By this time, Augen had lost track of its precise location and only followed in its vague direction, knowing that he would have to be blind to miss a landing zone large enough to contain it. But when the airship announced its leave, the noise and spectacle it created were enough to startle him. A faster aircraft would have made him visibly jump.

Excellent timing! he thought, continuing to the landing site with renewed vigor.

He was uncertain that the Moth would leave the city without taking or leaving anything else, and was disappointed in himself for not being able to reach it while it was grounded.

As the Moth briefly blotted out the scorching sun before passing him, he concluded that whatever the airship left behind would certainly affect the outcome of the upcoming battle for Barbasul.

Knowledge of what the enemy had planned could make a lifesaving difference for the men planning to take Barbasul. Up until now, the rebels had every element of surprise, and for the first time, the Empire may now have the upper hand in intel.

Sliding down a semicircular rooftop and climbing onto a balcony overlooking the city square being used as an insurgent aerial loading bay, Augen crouched low to stay inconspicuous and took in the blurry tumult occurring below. The engines of the departed Moth had sucked the fog into swirling pillars that roamed the busy plaza and briefly provided a clean view of the workings of the ground, but even as Augen chose his reconnaissance space, they were already beginning to release their dusty contents back into the environment.

Wooden crates were haphazardly scattered all over the cobblestone roads, where crews of armed men scurried about trying to organize them. Camels and a few cheap automobiles were being loaded with cargo and carried in the direction of the embassy.

"We are on a deadline! Get that cargo out of here!" someone bellowed as one of the motor carriers sped off with a single, quite heavy container weighing its back end down. Augen tried to pinpoint the source of the commanding voice amidst the chaos but could not quite track it.

By luck, or perhaps an act of mercy from Deos, the Warmoth's brief thinning of the fog allowed Augen a chance to eye the words painted over the base of the impromptu landing site. Parts of the message were covered by the moving cargo, but it was easy to decipher the parts he needed.

"'S.O.S. Imperial Safe Zone?'" Augen read aloud. The voice below called out once more, ordering the men under him with confidence.

After a moment of careful observation, he was able to spot the leader inside the crowd when a rebel rode into the chaos on a camel and handed him a small metal object. The man pulled some kind of pamphlet from its interior and made an announcement to the men working around him.

"We have what we need! The Imps sit on the outskirts of our city and are preparing to push in! Those not chosen to follow me, finish up here and prepare for the third phase."

"Yes, Prince Shedim!"

Augen snapped to attention upon hearing the unnamed rebel's response. *Shedim? That man is Maveth Shedim?* Augen unslung a carbine from his arm and loaded it with an armor-piercing round, but hesitated before trying to pin his target.

"The general said not to blow my cover," he mumbled to himself, lowering his rifle but keeping his finger inside the trigger guard.

The short rifle acted as the average knight's sidearm of choice, replacing most conventional handguns, which usually provided no extra mobility to accommodate for their inability to use specialized rounds. Like most knights, Augen preferred hand combat over gunslinging, but he had grown to recognize the firearm's flexible potential. However, he also knew the rifle was not made for sniping and was unlikely to land a fatal blow at long range, so after a moment of weighing risks, he resuspended the gun and turned to leave.

As he stole a final look at the scene unfolding below, another detail caught his eye. On the opposite side of the plaza, it appeared as though the rebels were constructing some kind of stone structure. Its exterior design was appealing enough, but the nearly finished walls were too thin to keep out heat, and only a single window adorned the structure's face. Its presence also threw an obvious dent into what was once a perfectly symmetrical courtyard.

"Strange," he mumbled before climbing back onto the roof and disappearing into the dirty firmament.

It was a long run back to his checkpoint, but when Augen had finally returned to where he lost contact with the hidden outpost, his headset buzzed to life, and the man heading Falcon's Nest spoke into his ear.

"Moving out. Captain Di Gattchen, do you read me?" Aware of why his men were contacting him, Augen halted his bounding and stooped into a crouch to rest his legs, then he hastily responded.

"Falcon's Nest, I read. How long since General Lomat left base?" Augen could hear the man sigh in relief through his headset before answering.

"About ninety minutes, sir."

I really should have made a contingency plan in case I was held up during reconnaissance, he thought.

He still had considerable ground to cover before reuniting with his men, but thankfully, he was not delayed long enough to make a difference. If General Lomat and the 7th made good time, and they certainly would, they would still be about fifteen minutes from their location and about forty-five from the embassy doors.

"Are there any direct orders from the commander?"

"Negative. Our orders remain the same."

"...And I take it that the Breach Cannon is..." A sharp pop shook the buildings around him and nearly knocked the resting Templar off his feet. In the distance, he heard crumbling stones falling to the ground.

"They just blew a hole in the wall! It's going down!"

Augen paused, knowing that his time was short. One shot should not have taken down the wall, but if it did, only the

Consulate Guard stood between Maveth Shedim and their priority objective. He now heard scattered bursts of gunfire in the distance, and the rebels fired their massive siege gun once more.

"The Guard has engaged, sir! What are your orders?" Augen hastily contemplated his options. He now feared that unless he was able to kick the 7th into gear, the general would not make it to the rescue in time at all.

He knew his own men carried no armor and their rifles were designed for medium- to long-range combat. So, charging into the enemy's rear guard seemed like a stupid choice.

"How many spare headsets does the balloon carry? With haste! We need to launch a counteroffensive, and I need to know what I am working with." Augen kicked himself for not thinking this through earlier. He should have known they would likely be separated when the enemy engaged.

But there was no time to sit on regret. Lives had to be saved, the mission had to succeed, or their trek through the sands would have been for nothing, and there would be hell to pay.

CHAPTER 11

A STORM OF SCREAMING LEAD

Before the first Cataclysm War, armies fought largely in open fields, valley chokepoints, or rural forts guarding the nearest population hub.

But when the Great Wars came, many desperate countries trying to defend or retake their lands formed militia groups designed for long-range hit-and-run tactics within the cities themselves.

Such groups were trained exclusively for roles in claustrophobic inner-city battlefields, supporting the traditional armored infantry divisions as they occupied the grounds.

Throughout the Three Wars of Cataclysm, such tactics had been built upon considerably, but the empire's subsequent de-escalation movements left the well-trained forces of urban fighters in a specialist role with little to no training in general and close-range combat.

Hailing from Alampia, the seat of the Golden Empire, the sharpshooter divisions were perfect embodiments of this hybridized infantry role. While their training and cumbersome long rifles were deadly in specific circumstances, Augen understood all too well that without the stalwart 7th to draw enemy fire and clear grounds at close range, the 12th would be unable to interfere with the embassy siege directly.

If the force led by Maveth Shedim was as well-equipped and organized as the rebels guarding the Sandcrawler had been, then Augen feared his options were suffocatingly limited.

Knights were trained in the same long-range "irregular" combat as the 12th, which was likely one of the reasons Pazkt Lomat gave Augen command over them.

But unlike the knight, whose physical augmentation, hand combat training, and thick plate armor permitted closing distance on the belligerent target who refused to drop at long range, Augen's men were completely untrained and unequipped to accomplish the same. They needed a vantage point and heavy infantry, ideally en masse, to maintain their ranged advantage. While Augen was beyond confident in his own abilities, especially against normal men, he knew that even he could not provide an entire battalion's worth of cover for anyone, regardless of location.

Options were few, and though Augen's presence provided a unique advantage for his own side, he also understood all too well just how much he needed the general to arrive before any real progress could be made. Success almost certainly hinged on his arrival, but Pazkt Lomat was at least an hour from the embassy, so Augen got to work preparing what little he could.

"Have the Twelfth pack up and move out! Tell them to split into three groups and give someone in each band a headset so that I can communicate with them directly. Is that understood?"

Augen endured a short pause while the inteleer relayed the command to the guard accompanying him and handed out the headsets. Augen opted to use the moment of silence to return to ground level.

"Yes, sir. It is being done as you speak."

Augen descended the structure's stairwell and returned to the streets through the same doors from which he left them that morning. He tried to remain inconspicuous, but with the rebels occupied, his focus was now primarily on expedience. There was little use in maintaining the element of surprise if the objective was lost before a trap could be sprung, so Augen braved the civilians and made his way up the road toward the target as quickly as he could.

"Good. Have a look at the opening in front of the embassy. Are there any structures bordering it that we can use for cover?"

The man was getting accustomed to the balloon's mechanics, and Augen barely had to await an answer before it was provided. "Yes, sir. There is a cluster of business structures as well as a group of dilapidated buildings…"

"I am on my way there. Send one group to me, and send the other two to buildings east and west of that space. At your discretion, have them form an indoor perimeter around the breach.

"Tell the men to keep under cover the best they can and prepare for combat upon arrival. We cannot keep the enemy from entering the embassy, but assuming their exit plan involves the same breach, we can certainly make their escape less pleasant."

"Understood, Captain. The men will meet you there."

Augen flew with all his might toward the sounds of conflict ahead. The rebel forces might have already occupied the semicircle of buildings he ordered his men to take.

The 12th would be at a fatal disadvantage in enclosed hallways and narrow rooms, so Augen needed to ensure his men encountered no resistance when they got there.

His plan required a stealthy and unimpeded entrance to the border. If the 12th could accomplish this, they would keep Maveth and his men from going anywhere until the 7th and 11th arrived and the advantage made thoroughly their own.

This was not ideal, for if the rebels killed the king before reinforcements arrived, then their only consolation would be to put the assassins down while they made their exit.

As he careened toward his objective, scrambling through the murmuring crowds to maximize efficiency, the words of the old man he met in Pallerheim came flashing back to him.

"Tell me, Augen, would the deaths of these men really cure you of your pain?"

He could hear the words ringing through his head as though they were being spoken to him at the moment, but as he contemplated the question, his foot caught a misshapen deformity in the road, and he narrowly avoided tumbling over.

"Stay focused, Di Gattchen!" he barked to himself, shoving the thought aside. He had no time for philosophy; he had a job to do.

The heat of the day had not yet left its zenith, but as the knight's mind homed in on the battle ahead, it seemed to disappear. Augen saw an opportunity to finish his job, to end the conflict in Iba, and to get out of the ancient world, and his focus on that grew to such intensity that he not only forgot the heat, but he also forgot every other detail in his dash to the embassy.

When the knight regained self-awareness, he stood at a window, gazing at the crumbled embassy gate across from him. The building he occupied was quite empty, and the two neighboring structures he had searched were no different. Whatever guild usually occupied the structure apparently had little interest in losing workers to stray gunfire. There was a difference between violence-desensitized and stupid.

Civilians who once occupied the neighboring buildings had left in haste quite some time ago, all to Augen and the 12th's advantage, as noncombatants complicated missions and Augen had no interest in trying to deal with them.

Unless there were rebel lookouts in the distant crowds, Augen had arrived in good time without being spotted by the enemy. His silent arrival, paired with the chaotic gunfire inside the embassy, told Augen that even now, his men may still possess the advantage of surprise. It seemed that Maveth Shedim had dedicated the remainder of his force to this final push, leaving only a handful of men running the Breach Cannon outside the fortress they beset.

Those men had stopped working the massive gun and stood atop the cooling barrel to get a better view of the carnage occurring inside the walls. They were completely distracted, and Augen considered sneaking up behind and quietly killing the lot. Instead, he moved back onto the central building overlooking the gate and contacted his men.

"Where are the troops?"

"They should be reaching you any moment!" the comms-handler responded.

"Good. Tell them to move straight to the second and third floors, find a window, and await my orders. Every man should have his weapon fixed on the men working the cannon. But no one is to fire until I give the order." The battle inside could not be seen from where Augen stood, but he could hear that it would not last much longer. The alternations of platoon fire from the Embassy Guards' rifles grew slightly fainter with every salvo.

The rebels' disorganized volleys were also weakening, but the obvious numerical advantage held by the attackers meant that such equal losses short term spelled defeat for the beleaguered guards in the long run.

"Any word from the commander?" No response came right away, and Augen was feeling hot again, though the temperature came from inside him rather than out. He made his way to the fourth floor and found an entrance to the rooftop.

"Nothing."

"Tell him that he has minutes left before we lose our priority target."

The battle in the embassy was well into its final phase, and Augen could tell, for the remaining sounds of combat came from deep inside the building, and rebel soldiers began to emerge from the breach carrying their wounded with them.

They don't need their full force anymore! Maveth knows it! Augen paced anxiously atop the roof. He had to stall, to draw the enemy forces back out and buy some time for whatever guards were left.

A direct assault on foot would be idiotic, but the idea manifested itself inside his consciousness, and the Templar had no time to question it.

"Falcon's Nest, I am on the roof of the central structure. Are the men in position?"

"They are unpacking their equipment."

"Tell them to open fire on the men around the Breacher. If you can, spare the wounded and those carrying them. But I want every gun to fire at least once."

"Uh. With all due respect, sir. I spot only five targets. Wouldn't using 240 rounds be a waste of ammunition?"

"Do not question my orders! Have them all ready to fire on my mark! And have squads fire separately, too. Second-floor fires first, starting with the men under me. Are they in position?"

"Yes, sir."

When Augen received the confirmation, he gave no response. Instead, he flung himself back downstairs until he ran into his men.

"Thirty seconds! Then fire at the cannon! When the floor below you has fired their heavy rounds, alternate shooting with your light rounds into the gap. One shot every four seconds for eight rounds. Do not fire the light rounds together. Alternate your volleys as much as possible."

Many of the men tilted their heads in confusion, but Augen was already moving to the next floor down.

Augen repeated himself to the men waiting for him on the second floor and watched the fireworks unfold through one of the windows. When more than two hundred heavy slugs struck the cannon and slew the engineers standing atop it, the sound of ricocheting lead echoed dreadfully through the city and into the embassy.

Then came the eight volleys of light shots. For having no preparation or practice time, the men were able to alternate their shots with impressive consistency, and the resulting sound was precisely what Augen wished to create: the sound of a massive army dropping onto the heads of the rebel forces like an anvil.

The men carrying the wounded were untouched, but the sound of hundreds of guns firing at them drove the group back into the embassy with a comically visible panic. The wounded were left where their carriers dropped them.

"Why spare the men on the ground?" a soldier queried as Augen turned to ascend the stairs once more. He probably should have scolded the man for speaking out of place, but the job had already been done, and Augen felt proud of his plan.

"I needed them to return to the bulk of their force, convinced that General Lomat and two supporting divisions awaited them outside. Worst-case scenario, they conclude the siege with unnecessary haste and get clumsy. Best case..." As Augen spoke, his headset came to life, and the battle inside the embassy paused for a second before dying down altogether.

"Sir. Thermal readings indicate a large group of hostiles approaching the gate." Hearing this, the Templar smiled to himself again and continued back up the stairs.

"They take the bait and split their forces. Prepare to fire on the men who walk through the gate. Use your remaining ammunition wisely."

Striding quite proudly back to the rooftop, where he could oversee the battle, he contacted his intel man again, trying to get an estimated time of arrival from the commander and desiring a better view of the now mostly empty battlefield.

In Augen's mind, the engagement would involve a single initiating volley from the 12th to drive the rebel rear guard back into the embassy, where they would either have to wait the siege out, or ideally, drag more of their comrades out of combat to help them engage a larger force than what was really present. What he saw was something else entirely.

"Hold your fire!"

Maveth's men did come out to meet the Templar and his division of entrenched skirmishers, but they did not come to fight. They came to bargain.

Each rebel soldier held a hostage, miscellaneous workers within the embassy, and a couple of wounded guardsmen from the firefight, helplessly in front of him. The siege was over. The empire was too late.

"Are you looking for this?" a confident voice echoed across the empty plaza as Maveth Shedim, clad in a purple cape and expensive lamellar armor, strutted between the forces pushing a fat, dirty, whimpering king before him.

The supposed leader of the district tried to say something, but was too frightened to speak with any fluency. All he could squeeze out was a high-pitched, effeminate mew.

His clothing, which was once expensive and luxurious, was soiled with blood, dirt, and excrement produced in the final moments of the siege and during his capture. He did not appear royal anymore. He looked pathetic.

"You are surrounded, Maveth! Three divisions of men await your pathetic force within the buildings below me. You cannot escape, and you certainly cannot fight your way out. If you think some hostages will save your men's lives, understand that you are sorely mistaken."

The crumbling hole in the embassy partially concealed movement behind Maveth and his forces, but Augen caught it.

The rebel warlord standing before him, captive in hand, had not yet revealed the bulk of his own forces.

Had the Templar not been bluffing about his own manpower, the movement would not have worried him. He was certain the rebel numbers came nowhere near three platoons, but until the arrival of General Lomat and his reinforcements, the balance of power could be anything from evenly matched to wildly mismatched in the rebels' favor.

The scenario was a waiting game as much as it was a guessing game, and Maveth Shedim made the first move.

The men with hostages, nearly a dozen soldiers, some dressed in makeshift uniforms imitating those of imperial officers, moved forward with their recent catches.

Several wounded and dying embassy guardsmen, as well as a handful of pencil pushers and passersby who happened to be working in or visiting the embassy when the siege commenced, were held at the end of a blade and pushed before their captors under threat of immediate execution.

The king of Babyl, or the former king at least, grunted as Maveth tapped him forward with a handgun held to his center mass.

"Three divisions in those buildings? You should be able to take us easily then, Templar!" he roared from behind his captive.

Augen cursed under his breath. The renegade called his bluff. Now he had to do something or risk a messy escape and probable failure.

His headset clicked to life, bearing with its awakening more bad news.

"Captain Di Gattchen. This just in from the general: The guildsmen from the camp snuck out shortly after you did and may be at your location now. The commander asks you to confirm." Augen's heart quickened, and his eyes scanned the buildings around him. He did not see the guildsmen, but they were the least of his problems now.

"I am occupied at the moment and cannot confirm their location. What is the general's ETA? I am running out of time!"

As casually as he could, he muted his visor so that only those on comms could hear him respond. He blinked to himself as Maveth reached for his visor and did the same. *Is he speaking to someone on shortwave as well? What if he has reinforcements incoming, too?*

An eerie silence hung over the two forces until a mechanical stuttering broke it up from the sky.

"Another airship?" one of the 12th inquired over shortwave. Augen did not answer. He knew what that sound was, and it was no airship—it was worse.

The curious banner he had observed over the Warmoth's landing site served a purpose, and now he understood what that was.

The three drones sent by the empire for reconnaissance had not been shot down. They had been lured onto the ground and hijacked by men wearing imperial uniforms and working for Maveth. They were the rebels' ticket out, and their presence would spell less than a minute for Augen to do anything about it.

"By all that is holy—! Where is the commander?" he yelled to his intel man, expecting another uncertain answer, but a grizzled and perfectly calm voice responded from the other side.

"My men are delayed and will not make it in time, Captain. Do not risk the success of the mission or the lives of your men with a short-range assault. Shoot the hostage and his takers before they have a chance to escape and turn this war into an international incident. Once the leader and their prize are dead, escape through the back of the structures you occupy and return to Falcon's Nest post-haste. That is an order."

The words physically hurt Augen as he calculated them. He shook his head, knowing that what the commander proposed was the most pragmatic solution, but he had made a promise to an old man in Pallerheim, and to himself, and a voice deep inside him told him to wait.

"I...will not kill the innocent. How long would you need me to stall before your men arrive?" Augen said, sighing to himself. He knew that this move defied logic, the commander who put his faith in him, and likely his own life. But his days were numbered anyway.

"Templar! Don't you dare!" the commander's voice growled through the headset, but Augen flew down the stairs to address the men below him, disconnecting his headset as he ran.

Pazkt Lomat knew all he needed to know, and at this point, further conversation would be redundant. He may send his reinforcements, he may not, but either way, the general understood what would happen next.

"Men of the Twelfth. We make our stand now! Their escape is imminent, but I am going to personally interfere.

"Once I make first contact, I will maneuver into the center of their formation, forcing them to turn their backs to you. If I succeed here, you will have clean shots! Do not kill the hostages."

As Augen finished his orders, one of the soldiers with a headset began to protest, but their captain was long gone, and the men of the 12th were left with a choice to make.

The sun was descending toward the horizon, but the heat of the hellish desert was somehow worse on the ground. It struck Augen with a visible impact once he strode from his cover, but the heat was not what bothered him most. The captain was sweating out of fear long before the environment got to him. He still did not know what hid behind the walls of the embassy, but understood that by folding, he would in a moment.

If the men of the 12th, who at this point were likely receiving different orders from the commander, withdrew or broke the stalemate by shooting the king, the full force of a desperate rebel army would fall on Augen at once, and he knew there was little chance he would survive it.

But footsteps behind the lone Templar alleviated his fear, for he knew the men of the 12th had chosen to help him.

"We will follow you, sir. Once you break up their formation, we will follow up and try to rescue the hostages by hand. Those in the building will provide cover fire."

"You have no armor, and your weapons of melee are short daggers," Augen protested mildly. In truth, he was relieved to see them, but he knew they were risking even more than he was by stepping away from their cover.

"The men in the other two buildings are returning to Falcon's Nest, but we know the risks, sir. The men with you now have volunteered to do this."

Maveth and his men tensed up as the Templar emerged from the shadows with mace and shield in hand and a force of men at his tail. The seemingly foolhardy decision to face them in the open did not look like the desperation that it was. To the enemy, it looked like a taunt.

The rebel leader shouted a command to his reserve forces, and Augen decided it would be best to take his response time away. So, raising his shield to deflect any small arms fire, the knight broke into a full sprint and left his support squad in a cloud of dust.

As the hulking mass of steel super soldier barreled toward the small formation of rebels and their hostages, the insurgents flinched and shuffled backward. Some fired their handguns toward their assailant to no effect, and a few fled back into the embassy with their hostages, but Maveth Shedim was unfazed. While his comrades slunk back into the hole in the wall, he pulled his hostage closer and squared up to his foe.

"We are seconds from escape! Goliath, do not let the Templar get behind us!" The prince's words echoed across the courtyard, and something emerged from the shadows behind him like a demon. An equally swift mass of metal and leather barreled past Maveth toward the incoming Templar with three hostages in his arms and two colossal swords strapped to his back.

In order for a knight to be physically enhanced, he had to already be considerably larger and more muscular than the average man, for the negative effects of Apex, Hybrid, and their chemical brethren were drastically lessened if their host was already large enough to keep an effective dose from becoming too concentrated within his body. Periodically, negative reactions and fatalities would still occur to a newly initiated knight for any number of reasons.

Despite the risks, men still volunteered to subject themselves to the enhancement processes offered for the foot soldiers of the orders, for if successful, the positive results of the process were obvious and strikingly consistent. The augmented soldier would grow nearly a foot in height and put on dozens of pounds of lean muscle, their bones would increase in density, their red blood cell count would exponentially increase, and their shallow nervous system would fray, greatly improving a carrier's pain tolerance.

As a result, the shortest and least athletic knight, discounting those crippled by negative side effects, would be no shorter than seven feet and no lighter than around three hundred pounds. Augen was just above the weight and height threshold, but the man emerging from behind Maveth, if he was to be called a man, was far beyond it. Maveth Shedim's bodyguard was larger than anyone he had trained with or fought alongside; larger than any knight he had ever heard of.

Plummeting toward him with breakneck speed, a ten-foot-tall colossus holding three wounded men over his torso like a living shield caused every imperial soldier, including Augen, to freeze their advance.

The ones to panic most obviously were, ironically, the men who remained behind cover, and their nerves resulted in a hysterical flurry of gunshots toward the encroaching giant. Their rounds slew two of his hostages and left tiny scratches on his helmet and shoulder braces.

Augen was cut off from his target and had to hastily slide into a somersault to avoid being hit by two flying corpses hurled by his foe.

The third hostage, who barely covered his captor's torso alone, outlived his use as a shield and was thrown into the recovering Templar with fatal force.

Augen stumbled with the impact and quite nearly fell over backward, but the joint support in his armor kept him vertical.

With the rebel's arms now free, the mammoth five-and-a-half-foot swords, which were usually held by royal guardsmen with two hands, were out of their sheaths and in each one of Goliath's hands.

Devastating slashes and stabs capable of cleaving through a man crashed into Augen's shield and forced him to maintain a defensive posture. The neo-steel shield and reinforced armor Augen brought to battle were enough to keep him from being wounded as long as he focused on deflecting the blows correctly. Unfortunately, Goliath's unpredictable attacks came in such quick succession, it was all Augen could do to keep up defensively.

The Templar could hear the choppy growls of the enemy drones and felt a powerful wind pushing down onto him from directly above. The rebel aircraft was now on location, and Augen had not yet reached the hostages or their captors' formation.

The men who left cover to assist their captain circled past the dueling knights in an effort to assail the untouched enemy formation without shooting the captives. However, with Augen occupied by Goliath and Maveth's chisel formation unchanged, the insurgents were able to shoot their attackers from safely behind their living shields.

The men fell in droves, nearly thirty casualties in seconds, and no one was saved. Augen tried desperately to reach the volunteers of the 12th as they were gunned down, but his foe possessed nearly ten feet of reach and was almost as quick with the massive blades as Augen was without them. Every time the Templar attempted to maneuver around his adversary, he was pinned down again by an equally well-placed countermaneuver.

A shadow fell over Augen's head, and he glanced up to see the drones just above him. Maveth Shedim motioned for the large hovercraft to land between his forces and the dueling knights.

Two of the transports obeyed, swerving toward the stranded rebels and touching down between them and the dueling knights in the courtyard. The last of the airships, an assault-class Hydra, moved over Augen and dropped abruptly.

The Templar saw this coming and narrowly dove to safety before the craft struck the ground with crushing force and bounced back into the air.

His foe, who merely had to step back to avoid the incoming aircraft, bolted through the sandstorm left by its impact and shoulder-checked the recovering imperial.

The duel would likely have ended there, but for a group of impatient marksmen crouched inside a border structure waiting for a clean shot. Augen's fall provided them with a good, and very large, target.

Bursts of sporadic gunfire struck the towering man standing over Augen from several angles as men of the 12th hastily corrected their sights and fired potshots at their only exposed target.

The chaotic barrages struck in great numbers, but couldn't seem to strike truly, for Goliath's helmet, gauntlets, shinpads, and parts of his breastplate were lined with the same angled neo-steel plates Augen wore.

These personal protections, paired with the haste of the sharpshooters in their efforts to reposition and fire anew, meant that the barrages bounced about on impact or barely grazed his lighter brigandine armor, doing no real damage but sending a clear message.

Unwilling to risk sticking around, Goliath sheathed his weapons and fled into the belly of a drone where his fellow outlaws awaited.

The remaining rebel forces followed suit, shooting their unwanted hostages before boarding their escape vessels. Only the king remained, packed inside a military-class hovercraft with his captors and destined for points unknown.

Augen stumbled to his feet and careened toward the airships, desperate to strike some kind of blow against Maveth and his forces, but with a whirlwind of pressure, the rebel craft shot into the air before he could get close enough to do anything.

The pilot of the Hydra decided to add injury to insult, unloading thousands of phosphorus rounds into the buildings that once served to protect Augen's remaining men.

The mostly empty buildings were turned into white-hot fireballs in seconds, and the soldiers inside who were not slain instantly took their leave, tumbling out of any available exit in droves. Many of them were burned, and several others were already dead but unaware of it, covered in a sticky white chemical that would eat its way through armor, clothes, limbs, and organs alike. It was a hideous sight to behold, and there was nothing that could be done.

This was Augen's first mission as head of the 12th Sharps, and in less than ten minutes of combat, his objective was lost, and his casualties amounted to nearly a third of his total force.

Augen hastily worked to pull the flaming cloak off one of his men, but as he observed the carnage around him, he quickly realized there was no victory to be pulled from this gamble. Augen tried to push his luck and failed, and soon Pazkt Lomat would be present to witness the wages of his choice.

CHAPTER 12

PUNISHMENTS FOR PLAYING HERO

Alexander strode through the pearly halls of the citadel with renewed strength in his body but a dark, burning sensation in his heart. His conscience ached incessantly—he needed to see Catherine, to beg her forgiveness, and to try to rebuild a modicum of their once-happy relationship, but as usual, he could not see her. He had things to do.

The royal couple worked in the same colossal building day after day, but never saw each other unless they were addressing the masses in the transmission studios, and during such times, neither of them was ever really available anyway.

Their bodies were certainly present on such occasions, covered and unrecognizable as they may have been, but their personalities were subdued, buried beneath the colossal and immortal personalities of four-hundred-year-old demigods, chosen by Deos to guide the Golden Empire by carrot or by stick.

His first and most pressing chore for the day was addressing the War Council in the Stratagem Chamber, where he would face the usual amalgam of sideways blame and bureaucratic scheming from some of the most powerful men in the world. Over the years, Alexander had thinned their ranks to what he believed was the council's most efficient and least bloated form. Now, only the best of the imperial warmachine sat at its helm, and though the remaining council members had earned their right to be spared the culling, they were still politicians at heart, and force of will was still their primary language.

Five days prior, the emperor had declared personal oversight of the insurrection in Babyl and the Empire's subsequent response, relegating the War Council to weightless advisors and making the forces of the Imperial Military his personal weapon of punishment.

Then, as fate would have it, he overdosed that same night and spent the remainder of the week, a time he had demanded be used to reinforce the wayward vassal state, chained to a bed.

The declaration stood, with or without his physical presence in the military chambers, and so the military begrudgingly screeched to a halt upon its first tactical hangup.

Altegard, the head of the Templar Order and a primary advisor on the War Council, fought to maintain the traditions of old as he always did, and succeeded in winning a slim majority of the council into following the emperor's declaration for the duration of his absence, despite the urgency of the situation.

Those who were against such a move were visibly infuriated by the costly setback, and let their qualms be known indirectly during their update of the disastrous military failure. No accusation was ever leveled at the emperor, but Alexander could sense the anger steaming from their helmets and feel the eyes of those who disapproved of his methods boring into him.

"During Your Majesty's...moratorium...three divisions of our men entered Babyl independently. They were never reinforced and failed to rescue the king. Intel is choppy, but it appears the Templar sent into the area went rogue and dragged the Twelfth into a deathtrap, resulting in terrible losses," Snaer monologued, alternating obvious glares between the emperor and Altegard while doing so.

"We do not know precisely what has happened or who is to blame for the losses in Barbasul. The high commander of the Reds is still sorting that out," the old man snapped back, inspiring several discontented grumbles from Snaer's allies.

"Well, Altegard, if we look at this...traditionally, then the commanding officer of the division would be held responsible for a suicide mission in which he was one of the few survivors."

"Leadership issues aside, our men were woefully unprepared for what they faced in Babyl," Oxeihov, the Nethellite minister of arms, chimed in. "We received reports of numerous contraband weapons being used on the field by the enemy, including a Manticore II Sandcrawler. We need to equip our troops with less-dated equipment if we are to see more success on the field."

Alexander sat quietly on his throne and listened, but under his helmet, he stifled a frustrated sigh. He knew where this conversation was going, and the council was not going to appreciate his answer.

"We still have working crawlers of our own. Including Manticore III and IV variants. Since our enemy is unwilling to follow the rules of warfare, why not pull our own back into commission? We could grind that city..."

"No," Alexander abruptly interrupted. Several of the councilmen leaned back, and one tapped his fist on the table. Their gestures of disapproval empowered Oxeihov to press further.

"My lord. Restricting ourselves during times of war is...well, inefficient at the very least. What is the purpose of keeping such weapons under lock and key if we cannot use them? When our enemy refuses to follow the rules of combat, they should not be allowed the benefits of just warfare."

The assembly's murmuring grew in volume and gesture as several small debates flared up around the Stratagem Table. Initially, Alexander silently allowed the discussions to commence, believing that the more conservative members of the council would shut out their pragmatic counterparts, but as the fighting commenced, it did not take long for him to recognize the error of his trust. The emperor stood, and the others went silent.

"So, to be clear, you believe that because a band of terrorists is willing to use contraband, we should abandon the pursuit of just warfare, too? If we give up our standard of war, do you believe the Silverens would not do the same? What then, Maz Oxeihov?

"Does anyone remember the Cataclysm Wars? The toxic clouds, the atmospheric bombings, the civilian losses—does anyone here remember that?" Alexander slammed his fist onto the table so hard that the images emerging from its core flickered, and the vaulted room was silent. Now that he had the room's attention, he sighed dramatically and leaned back into his throne. "The Empire...no...my empire was founded on creating a safer world than that of our ancestors. I have spent nearly two hundred years pulling half of Archaea away from world-ending warfare. But apparently, I cannot expect petty politicians to understand such matters. So, you will be silent regarding this until I believe you to be educated enough to speak!" Alexander forced his posture to relax to the point of arrogant disregard before the council.

He was truly present now, embodying the image of the emperor the common man believed in: the demigod. Logically, everyone knew that Alexander had to be in his early thirties. But his visage was ancient, and his purpose divinely inspired, and for that moment, his detractors had nothing more to say. So, the emperor concluded the matter for his mortal supporters with a calm but threatening finale of his own.

"Maz, you and the whole council know why we keep old tech, and it is not to grind down insurgents, regardless of the annoyance they present. So, drop it.

"You suggested that we needed stronger shock troops for inner city warfare. We now have the Knight-Corps Programs. That is enough escalation for two lifetimes, and you will utilize what you have been given instead of mewling for more. Which brings me to this!"

Taking advantage of a seamless, though unplanned, transition to his next point of discussion, Alexander adjusted the projector to display a news article written the previous day by a small media guild of less-than-favorable repute.

Upon seeing the image, the young Teutonic overlord scoffed aloud at the sight of two knights, both in modern armor, fighting each other, hovering in the center of the room.

"Divided Loyalties: What the Empire Doesn't Want You to Know About the Super Soldier Program," Snaer read aloud for dramatic effect.

"Whose knights are they?" Altegard queried as the men studied the mid-motion picture of Augen's duel with Goliath.

"I was hoping you would tell me," Alexander answered.

Snaer, who had already read the article, gave a more precise answer. "One of them is yours, Altegard. This was supposedly taken during the assault on Barbasul, and according to the pigs who dragged this into the light, the other is mine."

"Ah. This explains your accusations of desertion by my men. *Is* the other man yours?"

"How dare you even pose such a question! Of course not! I assumed you had sent more than one of your ill-disciplined initiates and they couldn't decide who would lead the Twelfth. After all, neither one of them was confirmed among the casualties..."

So, the infighting continued, the two outsiders from the Templar and Teutonic Orders pulling the remainder of the council into bickering camps. As they squabbled, Alexander rolled his eyes, knowing that what he was witnessing could summarize the week of his absence.

Eventually, he decided to step in and end the dispute, but the question of who the interfering knight worked for remained a problem.

Despite the fact that both the Templar and Teutonic Orders hunted their own deserters to the death, it was reasonable to presume that they had both lost initiates who were never tracked down, filling the mercenary pool with augmented men willing to sell their skills to any local warlord or crime boss who could afford them. After pressing the issue, he got both parties to admit the possibility.

"At the moment, we will assume that this rogue knight is a mercenary. You had both better pray this is the case, and do some serious house-cleaning in the meantime."

"We should have silenced the media as I suggested," Snaer murmured under his breath. Altegard straightened his back again, preparing for another debate between his tradition and his rival's practicality, but Alexander did not let the conversation proceed.

"But I did not, and you will not make this suggestion again. Our people must be given a choice in whom to listen to, or they will have no choice at all."

By midmorning, the War Council decided to leave the situation as it stood, allowing the Templar to be judged by his superior officer and a casual occupation of Barbasul to commence.

Understanding that other media guilds would likely pounce on the controversy, and recognizing that when the insurgents revealed their captive to the world, another storm of bad press would follow, a counter-message would be set up to help balance the scales.

This plan involved acknowledging the loss of the king at the hands of terrorists and projecting the military peacefully marching into Barbasul to restore peace to the district.

The insurgency could officially be declared over, for a single political hostage was less damaging to the leadership than the continued loss of a whole country, and the inevitable tumult caused by the loss of Babyl's king could be preemptively minimized until a replacement was chosen to fill his place.

As Alexander moved to his less urgent tasks, he began to rub his temples again. His time chained to a hospital bed served only as a temporary break from the crushing pressure of everyday life, and though such respite, coupled with the supplements given to him by the nursing staff, had temporarily stabilized his mental and physical health, he was still nowhere near healthy. Withdrawals from the adrenal supplements wreaked havoc on his head, and the suffocating helmet and armor constricting his augmentation flaws were beginning to take their toll on him once more, and it had been only a day.

As Alexander went about his business, speaking with the miscellaneous representatives, guild leaders, politicians, and talking heads, his mind wandered elsewhere.

He wondered what Catherine was doing, knowing full well she was doing the same high-pressure busywork and micromanagement as him. He wondered if she was still in pain from the wound he had inflicted on her.

When the haze of chemical toxins was still in his system, memories of the incident were clouded, and the precise details of his overdose were unretained, but he remembered enough now.

Catherine accidentally touched a bad part of his back, and he struck her with his elbow, as Nathan had deduced. The blow was partially born of reflex, as when one is jabbed in the ribs or touched on the inner thigh, but there was more to it than that.

In that moment of weakness, when his guard was down and any facade that may have remained in his psyche was scrubbed away by drugs, he treated Catherine with the contempt of an emperor scorned rather than a husband hurt.

She was not his wife, trying to help him in a moment of weakness. At that moment, for a mere second, she was a peon, an underling to be punished for daring to touch the emperor.

His career was getting to his head, as Nathan feared, and though he once vowed never to allow it to happen, a few seconds of synthetic honesty proved him a liar.

As Alexander pondered this, he recognized similar symptoms growing in his wife, largely through her treatment of their adopted children, but at this point, who was he to say so? She never physically assaulted any of her family members.

He needed to speak with her, even if his precious work took the back seat for once because of it. But when would such a time be possible? He could not communicate with her directly, and her schedule was as clustered and chaotic as his. Any reconciliation would have to wait, and he hated everything under the sun for it.

When night finally came, Alexander slogged back to the top floor, achingly removed his garb, carefully cleaned himself, and trudged toward the palace garden.

Catherine awaited him there, sitting on the bench he occupied before his meltdown. She stared into the horizon with stoic features, save a touch of pain and fear in her eyes.

He slowly took a seat beside her and waited to see if she wanted the first words. Neither said a word for several minutes, so Alexander cautiously initiated.

"Are you hurt?"

Catherine shot an indecisive glance in his direction and shrugged, returning her eyes to the dimming horizon before speaking.

"No more than you are, I am sure," she stated flatly. "I should have known better than to grab your shoulder as I did."

A tear began to slide down her cheek, but she swept it aside with haste, turning it away from her husband as casually as she could.

Alexander endured another long pause and felt himself struggling to wait before responding, but waited until it was apparent that she wanted a response.

"I...want to apologize. What I did was inexcusable. The circumstances, my pain, my...flaw, none of them justify what I did to you, and you should never feel the need to excuse me for it. Hitting you was..."

"It was not the blow!" Catherine barked, cracking her polished facade in the process. She turned to face him directly, showing both her eyes and revealing that the one he struck was still bloodshot, swollen, and lined with a bitter shadow. "It is your constant disregard for me and the girls. A year ago, you never would have dreamed of laying hands on me. A year ago, I knew you. You knew me. When we were brought here, we thought nothing could separate us. Yet here we are!"

The broken-hearted queen choked on a sob and turned away again. It took a moment, but she concealed her anger and pain before turning to face him, stuffing them back into her inner being so she could continue.

The smooth and elegant voice with which she addressed the throngs was barely maintained through sheer force of will.

"Your job, this place, this obsession of yours, it is destroying you and dragging me through hell. We have not spoken honestly in nearly a year. You will not sleep with me. You barely even know I exist. For months, I have prayed earnestly for your heart to be as it once was, and night after night, I come to meet you in the garden so you can ignore me and wander away without a good word."

Alexander wanted to get angry, but something deep down stopped him. He owed her this. When Catherine paused to regain her composure once more, he put his arm over her shoulder and answered for himself the best he could.

"I made a promise to the people of the Western world, to Nathan, and to myself. You know I cannot go back on my word. The man I represent is bigger than either one of us. Deos chose me to do this, and until He makes it clear, I need to follow through."

At this, Catherine's honest sorrow turned into a jealous rage, and she sneered, pushing off and standing to leave. Alexander stood, too, taking her hand and keeping her from doing so. "I...I assumed my respect for your work was a given."

"It is not about my work, Alexander. You made a promise to me, too. Apparently, not all promises are created equal." Then she pulled her hand from his and stormed away.

...

The garden atop the Ivory Citadel was, like everything else, massive and extravagant, sporting open walkways, winding dirt trails, and four open brick plazas, each the size of a small-town square.

One could walk the length of a trail as Alexander often did, without encountering another soul, but privacy was an illusion inside the garden.

The decorated and colorful greenhouse walls and their domed ceilings created an unusual acoustic effect, allowing for a speaker on one side of the building to be heard by another on the opposite side without effort.

As Alexander sat in silence, contemplating his life and every decision he had ever made in it, a number of eavesdroppers, three young girls, also began silently shuffling about. Now that their parents' quarrel had reached a conclusion, they slipped away to their quarters.

The fourth, who for different reasons had been growing as jaded and disconnected as her adoptive father, did not bother to attend.

In yet another part of the garden, an old priest knelt on the brick pathway, praying for wisdom and some kind of closure for the heavy-laden couple and their wilting marriage.

It hurt him to see them embroiled in such pain and uncertainty. As Alexander's mentor, he blamed himself.

"Oh, Deos! What am I to do?" The priest heard a weak groan from across the atrium. "My heart is ripped apart, and I am becoming a monster. What can I do for my precious wife without failing in my calling?"

A tiny flash of yellow, red, and blue passed by the priest through the stained-glass windows, and Nathan's elderly frame found the boldness and drive of a prophet. The old man strode toward the emperor with little subtlety and inquired aloud,

"Was the Golden Empire to be run by the laws of Deos or by you?"

The emperor, though surprised by the sudden appearance of his old mentor, turned to face him with an unnatural calm, as though deep down, he understood that Nathan may just provide the answer he wished for.

"I swore that it was to be run by Him," Alexander answered with confidence.

"And have you allowed Him to do it?" Nathan shot back with fire in his eyes and soul. Alexander paused, for he knew he had tried to do it, but the very fact that he was in the garden pleading for help suggested that he had gone astray somewhere along the way.

"I do not understand," he finally let out, for it was the only statement he could come to that was fully honest.

He did not understand why his life was in the state it was, he did not understand what was wrong with his marriage, and he did not understand what Deos was doing through it all.

"Indeed, you don't. You made a promise to see the laws of Deos spread through the entirety of Archaea, you swore to hold the civil worlds and the ancient worlds together, yet you cannot even keep your own household in one piece. The scriptures you claim to uphold sit behind lock and key both in the physical realm and within your heart."

Alexander recoiled at the accusation. "The weight of a planet sits atop my shoulders, and I am somehow expected to live a normal life as well? How is it possible to do both?"

Nathan smiled, trying to alleviate some of the pressure from his pupil, but the words continued coming. "You forget, young Alexander, that Deos sees the heart before contemplating the accomplishments of men. Leading a nation begins behind the doors of your house, not in the towers of your castle. You would remember this if you spent more effort actually reading His words rather than keeping them buried in the Underground Cathedral."

Alexander took a seat, partially out of physical exhaustion, but primarily out of shock. He was educated amongst the best in the world and tutored by some of Archaea's most prominent priests. These words were fundamental, yet he found them refreshing, as though they had never crossed his mind at all. His shortness of memory shocked him.

He knew this, he always did, but it took a late-night lecture from an old mentor to bring it back. A fire emerged in Alexander's eyes, and despite his exhaustion, his posture was made straight, and a tiny bit of his burden was alleviated.

"What should I do?"

"Get your priorities in order. Even the best intentions can become idols that weigh down your soul. Put the effort forward where you have the most control and leave up to Deos that which you cannot control." At this, Nathan calmed down and began to look elderly again. Putting a hand on the emperor's shoulder and smiling warmly, he finished. "You are wrong about one thing, Alexander. Nobody appointed by Deos is called to live a normal life. Least of all, you."

"Do you think there are others like me out there?" he sighed, walking toward the living chambers and staring into the distant cityscape.

"Those who have spoken with the Almighty? Of course!"

"Well...I certainly hope that they fare better than I..."

————————— ❖ —————————

Despite the shades of Augen's past haunting his previous visit to the stockades, his first time there was laced with pride and silver linings. He knew he was in trouble, but only before the boring and impersonal law. Everyone with any kind of morality knew better than to hold it over his head, even General Lomat.

Being temporarily jailed for saving dozens of lives the wrong way was both forgivable and forgettable, not something to bear down on one's conscience.

This time, it was different, as he saved no one. In fact, his actions not only caused the deaths of nearly three dozen men, all his own, but they also prolonged a war that would claim untold more. He had failed, completely and utterly, and he knew it.

So, Augen sat in the cell once more, accompanied by the same lone guard, for doing the very thing that Pazkt Lomat warned against, playing hero.

There was no sympathetic visit from the commander this time, and during the court-martial, there was no mercy given for circumstances or outcomes.

Augen was given his orders, the right ones, and chose to not follow them, and the consequences were disastrous, all because of some promise he made to an old man in Pallerheim. It was that simple, and he was disgusted by it.

His first day back in his cell was physically painful enough, but his heart was the primary target of agony. He could not sleep, for he feared the images his subconscious would conjure in the night. Eventually, exhaustion would pull him into stints of restless purgatory, but to Augen, it appeared as a distressing blur. He did not remember sleep for the duration of his stay, a fact that, while grossly unhealthy, he found preferable to dreams of his past.

He was going to be transferred back to the Templar Headquarters in Diona, where the very men who trained him would decide his fate, and they were not known for their mercy toward defective knights.

At best, he would likely be posted as some inconsequential guard or lookout in a space where he could cause no trouble, similar to the Pallerheim assignment given to Mahkt after his first mission. There would likely be severe physical punishments dealt out first to communicate the Order's disappointment. Such thought made his hands shake, for the newly legalized cabal knew how to break people, to force information from them, or to keep them silent, and it was unlikely that their tactics had changed in the last couple of months.

A more likely scenario involved a similar initiation followed by a bullet in the back of his head, a much more concise punishment to be sure, and one that Augen considered to be not totally inferior to the first.

Out of nerves, or perhaps an effort to be polite given the circumstances, the guard kept to himself for the first twenty hours or so. However, time seemed to loosen his tongue, and on the second day, he was back to his usual self. "I heard that an Imperial field marshal drove in with reinforcements today."

He made no response. The prisoner behind him sat in silence, lightly striking the stone wall he faced with a closed fist. Augen didn't feel like talking, so the lonely guard continued on his own.

"He may be the most important man I have ever seen in person. Not much to talk about with him, though. I think that his rank has gotten to him, if you know what I mean."

Augen grunted and continued deep massaging the wall. He did not want to talk about reinforcements, soldiers who should have arrived days ago and could have kept the mission from going amok.

The guard, who was apparently convinced that Augen was enjoying the one-way conversation, continued to flippantly banter with or without acknowledgment. For nearly fifty hours, no replies came until the guard got a bit more personal.

"I heard from some of the soldiers about what happened on your mission... I think that what you did was brave," he stated cautiously.

"Stupid," Augen replied, trying to stretch his cramping torso and flex his bruised hands.

The man across the bars flinched at the response, completely unprepared for his captive audience to talk back.

"Stupid?"

"I went into combat to avenge the life I lost in Eros, forgetting that I was not cut out for this at all. The desire to kill casually is there, as is the physical and mental prowess. But...I care too much. The cynical, utilitarian mind of war and its successful participants is something I thought I could connect with. But there is no place for right or wrong here, and I discovered that truth too late."

A deep creak and a metallic slam announced the presence of a newcomer in the stockades, cutting off Augen's confession midway and pulling all attention down the stone hall.

The newcomer strutted into the room with pomp, the breast of his long coat covered in different medals announcing rank and honor for its bearer, and his chin held so high that it was a surprise he did not bump into things when he walked.

The relatively old man marched straight toward the only occupied cell and stood over its occupant.

"You are to salute a superior officer when he enters a room," he commanded with indignance toward the guard, who hastily corrected his posture and shot a crisp salute to the marshal. The man grunted unhappily at the response.

"Better. Now kindly leave this hallway until I do. I have matters to discuss with the Templar." The guard glanced about the room uncomfortably for a moment but knew better than to talk back. After the unwanted man slipped from the room, the marshal lowered his chin just enough to make eye contact with the imprisoned Templar and scoffed.

"I would expect unprofessional behavior from the riffraff who live here, but am disappointed to have to remind a citizen of Eros that protocol still exists here."

Augen sighed to himself, did his best to stand in the tiny cell, and performed the best salute he could for the man standing before him. A slight grin slid onto the marshal's face, and he continued.

"It seems you have gotten yourself into a bind, Templar. Don't bother explaining; your commander has told me enough. Disobeying orders, disregard for the lives of your men, etcetera, etcetera," he said, flippantly waving his hand as though the weight of such charges were petty. Perhaps they were to someone like him.

"I want to tell you something," he continued, leaning toward the bars and grinning deviously. "You may feel like this is the end of the road for you, but it doesn't have to be. I do not know much about you, but I can see that you have what it takes to climb the ladder to success."

Augen blinked at the man standing over him, and without realizing it, leaned toward the officer as the field marshal spoke. This was the opposite of what he expected, a twist he could not decide he liked, but certainly something worth his attention.

"There are qualities General Lomat and his ilk will never understand. Such traits grant immeasurable success yet go unnoticed by the masses. Indifference. Indifference to everything is the key." Augen shifted his weight, trying to free his foot, which was asleep, but the monologuing superior took no notice. "Now make no mistake, you must keep sharp, well aware of your surroundings and circumstances, but a man who sits indifferent to the world and its...pathetic occupants is the man who ascends above them. That is where you slipped up."

"Oh?" the Templar queried.

"Yes. You fought that other knight for power over your men, which is very admirable, but you chose the wrong time to do it. Such a choice has cost you in the short term, as it should, but I...I admire your ambition and willingness to grasp for power even at the expense of your lessers. An unusual quality indeed. Therefore, I wish to give you a second chance and do my best to guarantee that you can continue in your quest."

The old man pulled a piece of paper from his coat and waved it in front of Augen's cell. "You see, your Order is very tight-knit and difficult to penetrate in any way. In fact, it is one of the only branches of the military I have no sway over. And like you, this old man still has some ambition."

Augen glanced at the parchment, some kind of inscribed formal document he could not read.

"This is a pardon on your behalf. I don't know where the other knight ran off to, but it seems as though time and chance are on your side for a change."

Augen straightened up, and his eyes locked onto the pamphlet. *A pardon? What are the chances?* Instinctively, Augen reached through the bars for the paper like a starving man grasping for crumbs. He wanted to read the paper's contents, but the official playfully withdrew, holding the pages just out of Augen's reach.

"All I will need from you is a benign favor once you return to your headquarters."

There was an obvious pull toward the field marshal and his message, but something inside warned the Templar against accepting.

He knew that such a favor, initially benign or not, would only begin a chain of other, more compromising favors to follow.

Deep inside, he understood that any other knight would have taken such an offer, even if just to kill the old man later when his requests grew impractical. Augen considered his chances of escape, but a memory of a fellow Templar walking through Pallerheim with him came to his mind and disarmed such thoughts.

"A knight like you would have had little chance of survival in the past, but there is a time for everything. And times are changing... Perhaps Deos has chosen you for something a normal knight could never do?"

"Times are changing indeed," Augen responded, mumbling at first but growing in confidence as he gathered himself and sat back into his cell. "I have no interest in your offer. I have made my choice and will face the consequences honestly! If I am innocent, Deos will be the judge of that. He always watches."

The marshal started at the response and scoffed. "How dare you! I am your superior officer. You owe me."

"I made a vow to the Templar Order to slay the enemies of Deos and remain unbought until the day I die. I owe them more. My loyalty is not for sale."

"This offer will be given only once. Think about what you can do with your freedom."

"So long as I toil under the burden of life, true freedom is illusory. You are offering freedom from one burden by giving me another. Deos is the only master who is truly just."

"Your Deos is not real!" the man screamed, pausing for a moment to regain some composure. "He is just an ancient method of maintaining the uneducated masses. The only true morality is power. A man of your strength and experience should understand that."

Augen stared defiantly at the man standing outside his cell. The marshal had turned bright red in rage, but after a moment of eye contact, briefly broke his gaze and straightened his coat.

"I seem to have underestimated your backward fealty toward the state Church. Pardon my...discomposure... I did not have such problems with the Teutons. It seems they are ahead of your kind in that regard as well."

"I think we are done here," Augen mumbled, leaning back into the pit and redirecting his gaze to the names on the wall.

"Yes, I think we are." The man shook his head and strode down the hallway.

When he reached the door and yanked it open, the guard, who had been leaning on it from the other side, lost his balance and stumbled into the room.

"Pathetic!" the marshal mumbled to himself before disappearing around the corner. The eavesdropper shuffled back to his spot beside Augen's cell as if nothing had happened. Though the man was gone only for a moment, and likely standing outside the door the entire time, Augen could tell that something was different about his composure upon returning.

"You turned down a free pass out of trouble? I agree with you. I do not think you are right for this job." Augen shuffled farther away from the door in an attempt to show his disinterest in conversation.

Though doubt lingered inside his head, there also came a finality to his decision, similar to when he made his initiation vow to the Order and the succeeding promise to the old fisherman to protect the innocent in Pallerheim. He would never go back on his word now, for in a way, his loyalty was all he had left.

"I think you are a good man. Perhaps you shouldn't be marching in the parade with the others today." Though Augen initially gave no response, the words ate at his vocal hesitancy. He had killed his best friend and abandoned his love—he did not like being called good. He did not think he deserved it.

"I am just trying to do my best. I do not deserve the pedestal you are putting me atop. Had I known years ago what I know now, I would have gone about my life, happy with what I had, but now I am beholden to ruthless ends and cannot do anything about it."

"Except have faith? In your Deos? That is what I mean by a good Templar. Your faith is what sets you apart, not your past..." The guard bowed his head slightly, his back to the cell, but Augen could tell he was near tears.

"You see... I, too, am beholden to ruthless powers, regretting past decisions...loyalties I have become entangled with. In a way, we are the same, I think."

Augen's eyes drifted to the words chiseled into the wall beside him. "We are not the same. I am sitting in a cell for doing what I thought was right, and now my men were slaughtered, and the war I could have ended will likely continue for months now. You are just a guard in an unused prison."

"Perhaps you not being with your old commander is for the best?"

"I would much rather be there than here."

"I do not think you will."

The guard's dissent was said with unnerving confidence that Augen picked up on, and suddenly, it seemed strange to him that the guard would have the chisel likely used to scratch

Maveth Shedim's name into the rock. Augen looked the man up and down again, noting that the guard's flask looked oddly familiar. If his memory served him well, he saw a rebel give something much like it to their leader, and Maveth did not use it to drink.

"How many prisoners have used this cell since you started working here?"

"I don't think any have, other than you…"

"Then who wrote this?" Augen wanted to raise his voice, but kept his composure.

The guard shifted his weight uncomfortably and did not answer, which was enough of an answer for the prisoner. Despite his old injuries and stiff joints, Augen's body moved with stunning speed, reaching through the bars and yanking the unsuspecting guard into them without resistance.

"You wrote it, didn't you! Is that why the media guildsmen knew of my early leave? Is that why your leader knew my squad was alone? How he knew that he had time to call my bluff and conclude the siege without interference?"

The guard tried to struggle, but Augen's fingers had nearly recovered from the crash in Pallerheim, and his grip was inhuman.

"You do not understand. I had no choice."

"Is that a fact? You have a couple of seconds to prove it!" The sidearm that sat crookedly on the guard's belt had been smoothly unholstered by his prisoner and aimed directly into the man's right eye.

"You use those flasks to carry notes around to your boss because nobody would question seeing a large flask in a desert." Augen glared as he ripped the flask from the guard with his free hand, snapping its old leather strap and opening its cap with his teeth.

Initially, Augen could see only water and feared that he had made a miscalculation, but a quick shake of the dusty tumbler revealed that it did indeed carry more than what it was made to.

He promptly dumped the water onto the cell floor, and a small, rusted tube with a sealed lid pinged onto the ground and bounced about at Augen's feet. Both the prisoner and the guard followed the object with their eyes as the pressure of impact ruptured the container's seal and ejected its contents onto the floor.

Two pieces of paper floated onto the ground, and Augen quickly holstered the pistol in the back of his pants, reached down, and scooped them up before they were soiled by the water.

The first piece was a crudely drawn map showing what appeared to be a segment of Barbasul's roadways.

Words in one of Iba's native languages were strewn lightly over one particular spot where several larger roads connected. Augen could not read it, but the man he held against the iron bars told him enough to get the idea.

"The parade. Your commander and the Reds. Maveth is going to ambush them." Staring intently at the map, Augen began to recognize some of the spaces depicted on the paper.

"A large-scale ambush in the middle of the city? But there are going to be hundreds of civilians."

The guard teared up, and Augen stole a glance at the second parchment, a sketch of a young woman who appeared to be with child and holding another to her chest.

"I believed in him...in his cause. I believed that he could end the cycle of interference and upheaval that plagues my people. But he does not care... Just like all who came before, Maveth is a tyrant, and he will kill any bystander who gets in his way. Including my family, who will be watching the parade today."

"You knew this and did nothing?" Augen lifted the man off the ground in a hot fury and shoved the barrel of the firearm into his forehead until it left a mark. "We are clearly not as alike as you would think!"

"I did not know! I swear by your god and mine! I read the plans while you spoke with the marshal! I had no idea! But it is too late for me to do anything. When they unleash the firepower of those artillery pieces into the plazas, there will be nothing left for either of us. I am sorry."

The guard's eyes gushed as he reached up and pulled back the hammer on the handgun. "Kill me and escape. I am a wretched being who tried to avenge his brother and failed everybody he loved. You are a godly man. Perhaps you can put in a good word in to your Deos? As an act of mercy?"

Augen stared into the man's eyes. *Mercy?* he thought, remembering the old man who accompanied him in the name of Deos and prevented his suicide.

At that moment, it was obvious that the talkative guard and rebel spy he had in his clutches was his own mirror image— poor, less capable, and perhaps on the wrong side of the war, but Augen saw no personal guilt in the man that he himself did not also possess.

His bloodlust withered, and Augen lowered both the firearm and the man he was prepared to shoot. However, after a long second of silence, the intensity of the situation returned to the knight, who reached out once more to the guard, this time with the papers in hand.

"Take these and alert the marshal! Tell them what was going to happen! The Empire may still be able to save the parade and its onlookers!"

The man looked up, stunned, and shook his head. "I cannot tell the marshal. He would never believe me until it was too late, then he would hang me for treason. I...will turn myself in, but don't expect anyone to be saved by it. I have neither the influence nor the physical strength to make any real difference."

"You have to try!"

"You misunderstand me, knight. We are similar, but not the same. I am not a hero. You cannot expect me to be."

Augen growled aloud through the bars like a caged animal, wishing he could have grabbed the guard's keys rather than his sidearm. The guard just sat across the small hallway and cried into his hands.

Augen glanced across his cell at the name he had inscribed onto the wall with a chisel, and he whispered the name to himself. Like a mad bullet unleashed into a lead dome that it could not puncture, Christine's moniker ricocheted through Augen's mind, activating all the angst, guilt, wrath, and regret he had associated with her memory.

But as the name struck his core, he realized the tragedy that threatened to strike his commander and hundreds of innocent civilians was not a crippling burden, but an opportunity.

A surge of inhuman motivation stirred within him and as if by divine providence, his mind suddenly understood the strategy of his enemy perfectly and formulated a way to help as many people as possible and fulfill his old wish: to die meaningfully.

"Give me the keys," Augen commanded with emotionless conviction.

The guard made eye contact with his prisoner and reached toward his key ring. But at the last moment, the native man hesitated.

Augen reached through the bars and continued reassuringly. "Give me your keys, and go find your family. While I do my work, you will not be harassed by the soldiers of the empire or your master."

"How do you know?" he said, tentatively handing over his keys and livelihood to the Templar in the cell.

"They will not chase you because they will be chasing me. Now escape, and live the life I will never get to."

CHAPTER 13

RESPONSIBILITY AND CHOICE

Orders from the citadel, and presumably the emperor himself, dictated that the people of Barbasul be made acutely aware of the renewed imperial presence in the area.

Thanks to the relatively young rules of warfare established by the Golden Empire and the religious enforcement of said traditions from the top, this was not to be accomplished through the means of elder empires. Mass executions and the ransacking of formerly hostile cities were shadows of the past.

Instead, Pazkt Lomat was to march his bloodied but proud regiment through the main roadways of the city with all but one of the reinforcing platoons in tow.

Such a move was intended to boost the morale of pro-empire citizens and frighten potential rebels back into the shadows. It was also meant to provide some much-needed positive press for the ravenous critics of the empire to choke on.

Because of the devastating casualties inflicted on the 12th, General Lomat gave them charge of the stockades where their discharged former commander was held. Simple guard duty would be their share in the remainder of the campaign if the iron-jawed veteran had any say.

The newcomer, a field marshal by the name of Koder, was supposed to march through Barbasul with the men but had pulled rank and faked a sickness to get out of it.

After finishing his alone time with the Templar prisoner, he strutted about the stone motte-and-bailey, dragging an unnecessarily large troop of the 12th around the base with him to listen to his critiques of the absent General Lomat's work fortifying it.

The few men left to do real guard work were suddenly in far over their heads without knowing it.

"Though I do respect the work of General Lomat, I must say that these temporary walls are not up to my expectations. We cannot afford to..." A muffled gunshot interrupted the man's monologue and caused the soldiers around him to turn toward the sound.

"That sounded like it came from the holding cells," a rifleman suggested aloud. The remainder of the men rotated back to face the marshal, waiting for a command.

Field Marshal Koder hesitated, suddenly unsure of what to say. Though the vast majority of the Imperial High Command was made up of hardened veterans with years of firsthand combat experience under their belts from a plethora of ranks, Koder was of a rare and uniquely devious breed who had been able to avoid it for the entirety of his career.

"Well, I suppose it may be a mechanical malfunction in the motor pool." The men glanced about uncomfortably. They knew what a rifle discharge sounded like, and it did not come from the mechanical zone, but no one questioned the marshal aloud.

Two more bursts of gunfire, this time unmistakable, echoed about between the walls of the stockades, and Field Marshal Koder flinched at their blaring tones.

"Could we be under attack?" the leader queried the nearest soldier.

None of his underlings gave a response. He was supposed to be drawing the conclusions, and he should have been leading them. Several of the guards glanced nervously at each other, suddenly skeptical of their new leader's competence.

Unhappy with his men's apparent inability to keep him safe, Koder grew impatient and took matters a step further into his own hands, even though he knew it would not look especially good for him.

"Where is the safest space in this ramshackle facility?" The men were slow to answer again, entranced by his strange line of questioning.

Another series of shots, this time followed by yelling and a cry of pain, snapped the guards back out of their daze.

"Probably the arsenal, where we keep the armor, spare weapons, and non-explosives. It has only one entrance," one of the soldiers finally answered, shaking his head in disbelief.

Koder was fully cognizant of the thoughts running through the minds of his men and hated to show any sign of his true motivations to lessers, but he was well aware of how much worse he would look if he were forced to participate in a gunfight for the first time in front of them.

"I think the armory will likely be a high-value target to attackers. You four, come with me, and we will guard that section of the base.

"The rest of you, form into ranks and find the source of the turmoil. Come find me when it is neutralized."

By now, the surviving members of the 12th Sharpshooters were visibly confused. They were not heavy infantry with solid body armor or practice running ground formations; their last mission made that abundantly clear.

Some of the men worked up the nerve to protest the strategy, but a particularly bold and level-headed soldier among them interrupted the dissent and drew attention to himself, organizing the troops into a somewhat orderly formation and trying to remember the commands Pazkt Lomat used to maneuver the Reds in Eris Port.

Koder took advantage of the man's initiative and slinked away with his guards while the rest of the troop marched awkwardly toward the last sound of combat.

Ironically, Koder and his unprepared guardsmen were the only ones walking toward danger, for Augen needed his armor if he was to try to save his commander and the men under him.

The small detachment of guards and guarded slipped into the dark and cluttered arsenal, one of them hiding near its rear.

"You men stand near the entrance. I will...take a quick inventory and ensure nothing has been stolen."

The guards were lucky to be wearing visors, for the glares they were shooting their leader would have been unmistakable even in the darkness had their faces not been covered.

The same could be said for the snickers and chuckles that followed when Field Marshal Koder stumbled over a pair of spare boots and shin guards and into a large stack of organized long rifles, knocking them all over in a noisy and profane mess.

"Curses on this dark and disorganized room! General Lomat will hear of this when he returns. It is utterly shameful that he keeps such a cluttered..." A hand grabbed the whining officer's shoulder and jerked him away from the back end of the arsenal. Koder was indignant.

"How dare you lay hands on a commanding..."

The guard who had snapped out of his mocking spell covered the man's mouth and gestured toward the back of the dark storage facility. The other three men had already loaded their rifles and fixed their sights on the pitch-darkness of the back corner.

During the chaos of Koder's fall, something in the shadows had moved, something big enough to catch all four guards' eyes despite the spectacle in the forefront. For a moment of intense strain, all parties stared frantically into the shadows, willing their eyes to adjust, but they were too late.

A deep click preceded a mechanical whirring, and two glowing blue eyes illuminated the far end of the arsenal.

The soldiers understood that the eyes were not biological, but rather the visor of Augen's gothic armor beneath the helm, but such knowledge did nothing to soothe their nerves. They knew who wore the armor and what he was likely to do with it.

"Captain Di Gattchen, you are not authorized..." The guards, who shakily backed farther and farther back toward the exit, never had a chance to finish their sentence, for the cowardly marshal did not move, and a fully armored knight sprang from the shadows with inhuman speed and took advantage of his inaction with supreme efficiency.

Jerking the tail of Koder's decorative coat over his head, Augen pulled the disoriented official over his shoulders and flung him into the guards at the entrance.

Koder squealed as his body flew into the men he had assigned to guard him. All were far too surprised to respond effectively, save one who ducked aside and raised his rifle, but he too was not fast enough.

Augen drew no weapons against his former comrades and made a point to refrain from killing any of them, though many would likely spend a day or two in the infirmary with concussions.

The guard who kept his cool in the armory would certainly be among them, as the neo-steel fists of Augen's armor quite nearly split the man's visor into clean quarters with a focused blow.

Another guard tried to reach for his rifle but reconsidered after a long stare from the Templar standing over him.

Augen shook his head ominously, and the soldier lowered his hand, avoiding eye contact with the knight, who then commandeered his long rifle and flew toward the mechanical sector, where the Squires and explosives were kept.

Koder and the remaining two guards he bowled over would recover momentarily and sound the alarm, but Augen needed only to find a Squire and escape with some grenades in tow, and the men assigned to march in formation were too noisy and awkward to surprise him.

As they marched around one side of the keep, summoned by the screams and enraged howls of the humiliated field marshal, Augen simply went around the opposite side.

The guards posted to the lookout towers were already neutralized, so the escapee reached the explosive cache and mechanical bay completely uninterrupted, and by the time the troops had turned and marched back to where they started, he was stocked, loaded, and on wheels.

The Squire Transport Vehicles had all been stripped of their heavy armor to help build necessary extensions, quarters, and fortifications onto the dated stockades, but Augen had no interest in sustained combat for the Squire anyway. It would get him there, and nothing more, and he would do his work on foot.

The guards, who had given up their awkward, tight formation in favor of a staggered skirmish line, reached the bay just in time to see a stripped STV fly from the entrance and barrel toward them, blaring its horn all the way.

Augen slowed just enough to give the men time to dive aside but did not alter his course, and Marshal Koder, who was once again too slow to be a soldier, was struck by the corner of the fugitive vehicle's bumper and launched over the hood and roof of the STV.

He landed with a sickening crunch and did not get up, the only casualty of the knight's escape.

———————— ❖ ————————

Alexander strode through the halls of the Ivory Citadel and into one of its dozens of elevators, drawing salutes and silence wherever he marched.

It was amazing! After more than nineteen months of meticulous, unending work and fifteen-hour grinds, the War Council ended early, and the scheduled representative meetings were pushed back nearly an hour on the same day.

Alexander had free time and was so stunned by its manifestation that on a different day, he would have spent it pacing guiltily down the halls, wondering what he could be doing in the meantime.

But today was different. He had a burning desire in his heart to make things right with Catherine and still felt dreadfully guilty for hitting her nearly two weeks prior.

Though now, he was not certain how he would make amends or get to know their adopted children, he decided to take the old priest Nathan's advice and use his free time to acknowledge the original source of his power.

Once he was inside the elevator, instinct built by years of repetition guided the emperor's hand toward the "Ascend" button, but a moment of self-awareness and control corrected the gesture.

He was not returning to the palace or the military complex, where his self-inflicted schedule usually took him. He would go below the political superstructures and grace the eldest and subtlest of its manmade brethren.

Once the doors opened and the emperor of the Western World graced the room with his unexpected presence, priests, theologians, monks, and scholars of all shades froze in place and stared at the intimidating specter in the doorway.

"Rest easy, bearers of the scriptures of Deos. It has come to my attention that I have not given the source of your life's work nearly enough time. I am here to pay my respects and read from the words of Deos personally. It has been far too long."

Alexander's words echoed through the entryway and into the vast underground construct beyond, and the tension dropped.

The clergymen standing before him acknowledged his presence with a humble bow to the waist before going about their duties as though he had not visited at all.

Stained glass windows lining the ceilings and walls and lit by electronic bulbs created a magnificent hue of various colors that never darkened with the sun's passing.

The interior of the superstructure itself possessed an obvious relational kinship with Archaea's first cathedrals. However, it was not designed to be similar to such structures, but superior in every fashion. Decades of meticulous work during the Empire's rise to power ensured that it truly was the greatest of its kind.

Alexander needed no guide to get where he wished. For, despite the building's busy walkways and numerous branches stretching deeper into the foundations of the mountain, the legendary Underground Cathedral had an obvious core around which everything else orbited, as a galaxy dug from the bedrock would look should one possess the ability to see it all at once.

"Welcome to the Great Cathedral, my liege," Zavaden, head of the citadel's district, declared, shuffling into the hallway and straightening his highly decorative white robes. "You are perhaps the last person I expected to see here today! What may I do for you?"

The Exalted Bishop of the Underground Cathedral wore no facial covering or mask, for tradition dictated that those working in the name of Deos possess no anonymity.

Alexander tilted his head in slight confusion, for though Zavaden's words were friendly, his face seemed troubled as though he was caught at a distressing time.

"You bring news? About the visions?" Alexander posited gently. The bishop straightened his back and tilted his head up for a moment, but only maintained the form long enough to arrange his thoughts.

"No. No news. Just working with documents and monks all day... Do you wish for enlightenment on the prophecies of the empire?" When the emperor gave no immediate answer, Zavaden hastily changed the subject. "Well, we can deal with that later. I was planning on drawing up a resolution with some of the scholars and delivering our findings to you anyway. You don't have to give it another thought until then.

"I am still rather surprised at your sudden appearance, though. Do you not have work to attend to in the upper levels?" Alexander stepped at pace with Zavaden, who guided him as they walked one of the cathedral's exterior branches.

It took a moment for Alexander to realize that he was being directed away from the cathedral's core, but he was snapped out of silence by the revelation.

"I wish to read from the Words of Deos," he stated abruptly. The archbishop's back straightened, telegraphing surprise though he did well concealing it in his response.

"I see. If you have any questions about the Word, I assure you that I can answer them. There are hundreds of us working here to do just that."

"Thank you, Zavaden. But I would rather read it myself." With that, the two leaders altered course, and neither man said anything else for some time.

The relationship between the foundational floor of the Ivory Citadel and the remaining members of the Great Bastion was complicated, and the nature of the branches played out in their head officials.

Because the founders of the Empire desired to include the clergy in the structure of the dominion, numerous exemptions, privileges, and immunities were granted to the Holy Church and its acolytes.

However, enforcement of the law was accomplished almost entirely through the military and federal branches, creating an artificial link between the clergy and the military that could only be described as strained, but necessary regardless.

"Well. If you insist. The scriptures are currently unused, and presuming you keep your distance as is tradition, we can pull them from the Crypt."

Thousands of excerpts, commentaries, essays, and discourses on the scriptures could be found within the vast library of any imperial cathedral, most of all its colossal patriarch, where most works of this kind were conceived, but in the whole of the Golden Empire, there existed only one complete copy of the scriptures.

In the early days of the empire, fear of the Word being mistranslated or abused by the body politic kept direct access to the scriptures minimized or flatly prevented.

So, at the behest of Church leadership, long-dead and political rulers who were sympathetic to their fears, a suspended and heavily reinforced safe known as the Word-Crypt was forged and subsequently stored in the safest location Alampia could offer.

As mightier fortresses were built and technological advancements made, the sealed words were ceremoniously relocated from fortress to fortress until finally finding rest in the depths of the mountain below the Ivory Citadel, where, if Zavaden and his ilk had their way, the texts would never need to move again.

As the emperor approached the Crypt, which hung from a beautifully decorated yet physically imposing hydraulic system in the perfect center of the citadel's core, Zavaden motioned with his hands to a man sitting at a mechanical platform, and the hydraulics hissed to life.

One man lowered the safe, three more clergymen, each specially assigned for the job, were required to open the first hatch, and as the official head of the Church, Zavaden alone had the electronic key required to open the second.

The ceremonial ordeal was complex and time-consuming, and even then, nobody in the room—including Alexander and Zavaden—was allowed to touch the document. Instead, the exposed words of Deos remained suspended and visible only through a magnifying lens.

A simple remote control designed to dictate what pages became visible was granted to the emperor by the exalted archbishop, and the reading could finally commence, though only in the presence of the head of the Church and numerous guards who, like Alexander's bodyguard, would spend their lives guarding their place and never see life outside of it.

"At your leisure, my emperor," Zavaden said, stepping back so Alexander could use the viewing console.

Once the emperor was at the console, the handwritten words on the document jumped out at him, conveying stories of old, consultations for the present, and occasionally predictions of mankind's future. Though Alexander periodically recognized elements of the adages from documents put out by the clergy, there was something unique about reading the words of Deos without the input of others.

Alexander had no obvious plan for his reading and jumped about from story to story until something caught his eye, all the while under the scrutinous eyes of the exalted bishop standing behind him like a sentry.

"What is this?" Alexander inquired aloud, breaking a long and lonely silence. Zavaden shuffled forward and crouched so that he could read over the emperor's shoulder. His words were careful, and his tone focused. Every word out of his mouth was intentional.

"Ah. The Patriarch and the Judges. A compelling story about Deos meeting with a man He had conversed with in the past. The deity was on His way to a civilization He planned on annihilating for the pagan atrocities their culture promoted.

"Knowing that members of his family lived inside the capital, the patriarch bargains with Him in the hopes of the city being spared."

Alexander skimmed through the story. He could only vaguely remember the tale from his childhood studies, but as he read, it returned to him. "I remember it now. The negotiations failed, did they not?"

Zavaden shifted his weight uncomfortably, but did so in a manner that was unnoticeable to Alexander.

"I suppose they did. Why don't you move on to the stories of the ancient kings? They are far more applicable to you than this."

The emperor moved his hand to order the pages turned but thought better of it and continued to read. He wanted to finish the story. Zavaden sighed aloud and checked the time.

"He took them out..." Alexander finished with an invisible grin on his face.

"What?"

"I disagree with you. The patriarch asked for the city's salvation under certain terms, and despite the terms never being met, Deos saved the family." The emperor turned to face Zavaden, who stared blankly back at him. "Don't you see? Deos did consider the patriarch's request, his deeper one. He saved the family despite the superficial deal falling through."

Zavaden raised an eyebrow and stifled an indignant scoff. "I do not need to be lectured on the stories in the Word, and I do not see your point here. Deos struck the city with fire and ash despite requests from a man He considered righteous. Which brings me to..."

"Yes, but he saved the innocent," Alexander interrupted.

The bishop sighed to himself, succeeding in maintaining a calm demeanor despite an apparent frustration brewing within.

"I still do not understand how that applies to the Empire or the prophecies."

Alexander did not respond to the bishop, but stood up and shook the man's hand. "This has been incredibly helpful! I saw those prophecies as an imposition on a righteous Empire by a deity with no regard for the faithful, but perhaps it would be wiser if I let Deos choose whom He finds righteous rather than trying to save it all."

At this, Zavaden physically flinched, as though the emperor had tried to punch him. "There is no need to try to save it at all. The reason Deos struck the cities in the story was that they were pagans and guilty of horrific acts of perversity and violence, a people with blood on their hands."

"Doesn't every empire have blood on its hands?" Alexander calmly responded.

Zavaden sighed again, visibly frustrated by this point, but kept his peace. "In a sense, but our people live under the scrupulous and unwavering work of the Church. Times are different."

As the emperor and the bishop began once more to tread the vast halls of the cathedral, this time so that the visitor could leave in peace, Zavaden worked up the nerve to state what was truly on his mind.

"If I may be forward with you, Your Majesty? I am rather disappointed by your bleak view of the Empire. It is as if...you think all that we do in the Church is meaningless."

Alexander put his hand on the shoulder of the man standing beside him. "Friend. That is not what I meant to convey at all. Perhaps you are right. It could be that the visions among the clergy and the prophecies about the collapse of an empire do not apply to us or our time.

"But I think Nathan said it well. We should focus on being innocent in the eyes of Deos rather than simply trying to avoid the wrath that comes as a result."

"Nathan said that?" Zavaden said with a final, though less frustrated sigh. "Yes, he is among our more...grim-minded compatriots. I am personally not fond of him, but there is a place in the Church for his ilk just as there is for mine."

Alexander stepped into the smooth lift but turned once more to his clerical compatriot in an effort to alleviate the weight of their conversation. "Keep up your good work, Zavaden. We all still have something to learn, and now, thanks to your hospitality, a great burden of mine has been relieved. I will see you again, hopefully under similar circumstances."

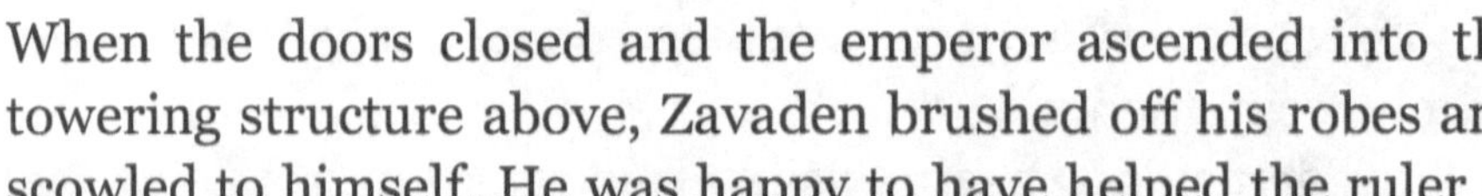

When the doors closed and the emperor ascended into the towering structure above, Zavaden brushed off his robes and scowled to himself. He was happy to have helped the ruler of the Western world and fulfill one of his primary roles within the Church, but there was much to the unexpected visit that disturbed him.

As the exalted bishop slid back into the heart of the magnificent cathedral, he pondered what Alexander's next move might be. He also wondered what to do about Nathan. The man clearly needed to be put straight, or silenced, one way or another.

Such a removal had to be done with tact, though, and potential methods for such action would be Zavaden's focus for the rest of the day.

CHAPTER 14

CONFRONTATION

Augen's heart raced furiously as he stood before the first of the Monster Ribauldequins and stared down its four dozen barrels.

The weapon itself was cleverly nestled into a wide alleyway where a mock building with paper-thin wooden walls was built around it. The edifice had more in common with a tent than the stone structures providing its two support walls, but from the exterior, with throngs of civilians lining the weak foundation, the false buildings were invisible to the outsider.

Augen would not have found them had he not witnessed the farthest one being built in the square Maveth Shedim's men used as a landing pad. Cross-referencing that location with the parade's trajectory on the balloon took only a moment during his escape, and he was grateful that he took the time to do it before grabbing his armor and making a scene.

Whether through impressive intel or incredible luck, the hidden rebel cannonry was placed to stretch the length of the parade, ending inside the same city square.

Augen stepped past the corpses of the unfortunate rebels ordered to guard the massive gun and work its loading mechanisms once the ambush commenced. He could hear the crowds gathering outside the building as the slow, rhythmic rumble of the military parade approached.

His time was short, and the knight realized that his original plan to foil the ambush by planting timed explosives would never work.

The parade's participants and their onlookers would be inside the kill zone in moments, and according to the parchment in his hands, five more guns were awaiting a radio signal to slay in catastrophic numbers. Even with minimal resistance, he knew that reaching them all before the parade was bombarded by a concealed Ribault would be impossible.

So, rather than trying to blow up the hidden guns, he decided to blow their cover instead.

He had never worked this kind of artillery before, for such deadly weapons were supposed to be extinct, a casualty of various de-escalation movements, yet here the rebels had at least five in their possession, and if they were anything like the one Augen stared at, they were not cheap replicas. They were authentic. After a minute of exploration and study, Augen found the hydraulic controls and tilted the massive barrels upward, as though they would be targeting aircraft rather than infantry. The tips of the barrels touched the roof of the weak structure and collapsed a portion of its thin ceiling.

"Deos, protect the people outside," he prayed silently. Then, after a moment of hesitation, he grabbed hold of the ignition lever and unleashed the Ribault's ammunition through the remaining ceiling and into the sky.

Pieces of the building flew everywhere as forty-eight rounds of hot grapeshot careened into the air with a hasty but consistent rhythm, blowing the thin, wooden roof into splinters and setting the rest of the structure ablaze.

The cheers of the crowd turned into screams of panic, and the drumming of boots clapping the ground in synch was muted at once. Augen knew that General Lomat would break up the parade as quickly as he could and disperse the platoons to minimize shrapnel and grapeshot damage before continuing the march.

The rebel surprise was likely spoiled, for the initial devastating volley was likely meant to strike the rear guard of the 7th and throw their support platoons into disarray, but its premature ignition did nothing of the sort.

Rebel soldiers, standing amongst the civilians, presumed that the ambush had commenced and drew their weapons, firing on the columns with small arms of every kind. Their uncoordinated volleys were met with the full force of the platoons' counterattack, and as the civilians fled, those who remained to fight were shattered in moments by the stoic 7th and their iron-jawed leader.

Despite this, Augen pressed on. The parade was over, and countless innocents were already saved from the crossfire, but he wanted more.

If Augen had his way, he would cripple Maveth and his forces to the point of unsustainability. The rebel leader would not get the best of him again, not if he had anything to say about it.

The next building was considerably less camouflaged, sticking out amongst its neighbors enough to keep the Templar from consulting his map before entering.

Having been ordered to stay inside the windowless structure until they received orders to fire their battery, the rebels within paced about, nervously arguing amongst themselves about what they should do next.

They knew something had gone wrong, but it was not until an Imperial knight dropped by, jumping through a hole he punched into the roof, that they discovered the weight of their predicament.

Augen carved his way through the panicked insurgents and began to rotate the illegal artillery upward once more. This time, the process was even smoother.

"Here's to your continued success, Maveth Shedim," Augen laughed to himself as the next barrage of shrapnel flew uselessly through the roof and into the sky. The second gun, which had been placed to shoot farther into the parade's core, had a cluster of spare shell drums sitting near the chassis' rear bracers. It was an expensive payload of explosives that Maveth would regret leaving so lightly guarded.

But the master tactician hiding nearby had already mustered his response, and as Augen tossed a live grenade into the munition crate, a colossal attacker stormed through the back wall and pinned the unsuspecting knight onto the machine he had just sabotaged.

"No snipers to save you this time, Templar," Goliath sneered as he pushed Augen's head toward one of the undetonated charges.

Had Augen remained where he was, the impending recoil of the barrel would likely have crushed his head, helmet, and all.

But the Templar's surprise did not remain, and rather than fight the powerful man's grip, he moved with his off-balance foe, causing him to stumble forward far more than initially intended.

Augen's quick response rendered his assailant's pinning maneuver useless, for Goliath was forced by the unexpected lack of opposition to recoil or risk losing his arms to the same mechanism with which he planned to kill Augen.

The rebel was quick to recover, grabbing the Templar by the breastplate and heaving him into the back wall—a grappling maneuver Augen would appreciate as the ammo case detonated, flinging both super soldiers into the alleyway in a ball of fire. Goliath, who was unaware that Augen had spiked a powder box, accidentally put himself between his enemy and the explosion, taking more of the impact as a result.

Augen was the first to slowly arise. His ears were ringing, even under his helmet and headpiece, and his head throbbed from the impact of the blast, but his foe was equally slow to stand, and by the time one knight recovered enough to do any damage, his opponent had done the same. So, after sixteen strange seconds of respite from both smoldering parties, the duel recommenced in earnest behind the flaming structure and its newly shattered cargo.

The narrow room of the building had kept Goliath from drawing his swords, for there would never have been enough space within for such weapons to be used effectively. Once the two men were outside, the giant's deadly weapons flew from their sheaths, and Augen understood that his options were dwindling.

He did not need to let his foe pin him down. He figured that the commander understood the risk of advancing too far, but there was still a chance that he would get overzealous and bring his troops into range of the three remaining death traps.

So, after a quick jab to the giant's chin and a kick to the chest for a moment of separation, he unhooked his mace and swung it with bone-shattering speed at his reeling foe. It narrowly missed, for Augen's pursuer was still dizzied by the exploding room, and the Templar seized on his enemy's daze to flee up the nearest staircase and back onto the rooftop.

As he looked for the next false structure, worry started to prick Augen's psyche, for it looked as though he might not accomplish what he set out to do. He may still die, and in fact, if he could not find a way to finish Goliath off, it looked like he certainly would, but such a fate would not be very meaningful if he failed to save those still at risk from Maveth's remaining ambush.

So, in a desperate effort to buy himself a few more seconds, Augen planted his feet and flung his mace toward the encroaching behemoth's head as Goliath crested the staircase behind him.

Goliath saw this coming and just barely deflected the incoming projectile, which grazed his shoulder brace and flew into the roadways below.

Upon impact, Goliath stumbled backward, dropping the sword he used to deflect Augen's projectile and nearly tumbling back down the staircase. Augen exploited his temporary advantage as well as he could, viciously swinging the edge of his shield at any weakness he could spot. He could not afford to give his enemy any time to recover.

Goliath nearly fell off the roof, but managed to catch the shield with his free hand and jabbed Augen's breastplate with the tip of his remaining blade.

The blow glanced off, too low to hit the armpit joint he hoped to fatally puncture. Augen recognized his efforts to target the gap in his cuirass and withdrew the shield to avoid a second, potentially successful attempt.

The tiny moment of respite was all the rogue knight needed to recover balance and throw the Templar back onto the defensive.

Augen no longer had his mace, the best weapon in his arsenal for striking Goliath down in his armor, and his foe adjusted form to compensate for the loss of his weapon with unnerving fluidity.

He did not need two blades to win a duel, and Augen recognized this as lightning-fast blows and stabs flew at him in flurries nearly impossible to block, even with both hands controlling his shield.

He feared his options were expended until he remembered the remaining grenades slung on his belt.

Of course! Even he cannot block an explosion with a blade! The thought did not need completion. Augen unstrapped an explosive, pulled its pin with his thumb, and let the fuse cook inside his hand just long enough to keep the giant from catching it and tossing it elsewhere. Finally, at the moment he believed advantageous, he tossed the grenade into the air between them and jumped back.

"Eat this, you freak!" Augen exclaimed, bracing for an unavoidable explosion of shrapnel.

Goliath panicked for a fraction of a second but regained composure and responded.

In his effort to maximize the damage of the shrapnel, Augen had tossed the grenade too low, so with expert precision, his foe slapped the metal projectile with the flat of his blade, sending it skyward with such speed that the explosion could not send particles through either knight's armor when it erupted.

Now was Augen's turn to panic, for in his confidence, he neglected to pull another grenade and had no time to repeat the maneuver, especially now that Goliath had seen it done already.

So, in a final futile effort to gain the upper hand, he struck his momentarily exposed foe with the end of his shield, knocking him a step backward before grabbing his shield with both hands in an effort to wedge its tip into Goliath's throat. But once again, Augen's experienced and massive foe got the better of him, sliding his blade smoothly along the root of the Templar's left arm as he flung himself forward.

With no plate armor in the armpit to hinder it, the long blade slid through the under armor, the triceps, the bone, and then the biceps of its target, cleaving Augen's arm almost completely off.

It is said that time slows down for those close to death, but for the Templar, it froze entirely.

He saw pieces of his life pass before his eyes in misty fragments. He saw portions of his lonely childhood, the angsty years of rebellion from his youth, and his days with Christine.

As he saw her image standing beside an unsure shell of a man whom she loved, regrets of his former life sprang into the forefront of his mind, and he realized that, beneath the burden and regret, he still did not want to die.

He knew it was right for him to do so; he understood that he chose his circumstances just as much as they were dictated by chance. Yet, seeing her again led his understanding of poetic justice to falter, and any death wish he possessed fell by the wayside.

Unbeknownst to him, he was falling now. First, the Templar, drunk with pain and shock, was knocked to the edge of the roof.

Goliath stood triumphantly over his latest kill until a well-aimed bullet struck him in the eye. The rebel stumbled backward, swearing and screaming as he went, but not without the presence of mind to kick his captive off the rooftop first.

A fabric roof that once crowned a market booth broke the worst of the Templar's fall before impact with the brick road below.

"To follow Him means to sacrifice your relationships, your lust for power, and even your will to survive." The words of the old man in Pallerheim rang through the knight's head as he lay in a heap on the roadway, largely unfazed by the fall, but nearly dead from shock and blood loss.

Chaos ensued around him as men of the 7th rounded up and executed the exposed rebels against the backdrop of a panicked, but largely untouched, civilian population retreating to their homes.

It is not fair, Augen thought. How can anything good come of this? Perhaps I will never know... Perhaps I don't deserve to know.

Though unnoticed by the dying Templar, a man crouched over him and bandaged his arm at the stump, cutting off circulation so that he would stop losing blood.

"Excellent shot, General," a sergeant of the Seventh exclaimed with excitement.

"Did I ask for validation? Push the men forward and watch for more false structures." Adjusting his headset to communicate with intel, General Lomat wiped his jaw on a bloodied sleeve and spoke with cold fluidity.

"Alert our new friends in the medical ward. Have them prepare for surgery and blood transfusions. Our Templar is going to need both."

❖

Augen slept, but what he experienced was nothing like the sleep he was used to. Initially, the nightmare memories he had grown to expect came to him in short, repetitive bursts, but as time went on, they faded away into a conscious nothingness.

No image came, no surreal sensation, no sound, yet somehow, Augen was acutely aware of it. He thought that the stasis would last forever, but slowly, he began to feel something else, a subtle yet nagging unease clawing at his soul.

He believed something was wrong, but he could not identify the source of his fear. He had forgotten about everything—his arm, his situation, his life, none of it was real in the abyss of that moment, just a weight on his consciousness and the recognition of its existence. The sleep his damaged and exhausted body summoned was technically restful, but incredibly unpleasant regardless.

When he awoke, several days had passed, and Pazkt Lomat stood over his bed, staring down at him and fidgeting with his decorative knife.

Initially, the commander said nothing, and Augen's eyes drifted to those who worked on his broken body. They were all women.

Their uniforms were black and red, adorned with large white crosses splitting their smocks in perfect fourths and speckled with coagulated bloodstains. They were Hospitaliers.

Noncombatant and legal in both empires from the day of its conception, the youngest of the holy orders brought hope for survival wherever military conflict, natural disaster, or pestilence of any kind emerged. They were the organizational and technological equal of their older sibling orders, but benevolent and loved by the populace rather than feared.

"He is stable," one of the doctors reported to her coworkers. "Neutralize his arm once more and strap it down. We don't want our work going to waste." A needle was quickly injected into Augen's already-numb right arm, causing the limb to disappear altogether from his mind.

A fit middle-aged woman leaned in to General Lomat's ear and spoke with less hush than she intended.

"You asked me to have him awakened. While the knight is conscious, he is your responsibility."

"I understand."

"You also understand the sacrilege of spilling blood on our grounds, and the punishment of such action before the law?"

"Yes." An uncomfortable silence filled the room as the woman stared at the knife in the commander's hands before slipping out with her entourage quietly following suit.

As the last of the nurses and surgeons stepped away, Pazkt Lomat ceased his fidgeting and moved to Augen's side.

"Augen Di Gattchen. That is your name, is it not?"

The Templar tried to respond but could only work out a nod.

"Clearly, I do not understand your kind..." the commander said, eyeing him over as though he were observing a monument or some kind of exhibit.

"How do the Templar implant such dedication and drive into you? Are all your brothers-in-arms so blood-crazy and focused that they would break out of prison to finish their mission, dooming themselves in the process?"

Augen gave no answer, but his superior officer did not wait for one. He stared down his nose with stone-cold eyes at the bedridden man.

"Are you aware that the man you struck with the STV during your escape was a field marshal, and that he is now crippled from the waist down?"

Augen did not answer and began to look about.

Vigor was slowly returning to his torso and head, and though he still could not feel his right arm, he moved his head enough to see that the severed appendage had been reattached to his body and was currently held together by a mechanical brace pumping blood, water, and several other fluids into the pale limb hanging from his shoulder.

The commander wiped his jaw and began to fidget with Augen's knife once more, but this time with a jolt of frustration.

"Since then, Field Marshal Koder has spent his every waking moment writing his colleagues and preparing official reports... He plans on pressuring your order into publicly executing you for treason."

Augen grunted aloud, but continued looking around the room, as he was unsurprised by this and had nothing to say. The wide stone structure he lay in was certainly not part of the stockades, and he wondered if it was commandeered by the Hospitaliers recently or built by them decades ago.

The commander did not take the casual response happily. "Do you not care? If he gets his way, you will be the face of treachery and cowardice for the empire, a political emblem of everything you aren't. And if I cannot help you..." In his frustration, the commander twisted the knife violently between his fingers and popped open the hollow hilt pocket in the process.

The hand-drawn image of Christine fell from the hidden stash and unraveled into the commander's hand. Augen ceased his obstinate scanning of the room and fixed his eyes on the picture as Pazkt Lomat did the same.

"Who is this?" he asked, this time with genuine confusion written in his eyes. Augen writhed in the first touch of pain he felt since awakening.

"She was once everything to me... I lost her."

The commander of the 7th stared at the drawing as Augen gave his response. "I see..." he said, spinning the blade dismissively in his hand and stopping only to stretch his shoulders and wipe his chin. "You do not really represent your kind, do you?"

The knight slowly shook his head once more, and his commander sighed.

"So, I have misjudged you again."

A cool breeze and an unnatural calm took hold of the room. The man standing at its base straightened his back and wiped his chin with professional dignity, then he removed his headpiece respectfully.

"I do not think I can help you out of this, but I will do what I can to make it easier." With this, the officer carefully replaced the picture in its holster, set the dagger down beside its owner, and turned away to the exit.

"I warned you about playing hero, but I am beginning to think that you were never playing at all. Deos be with you on your final journey." When Pazkt Lomat finally disappeared behind the door, Augen was left alone and wide-awake, capable of pondering his life but unable to change anything about it.

Realizing he would not fall asleep again, he gathered as much wit and professionalism as he could and shot a sincere prayer to his Maker. It had been a long time since he had done so, and he understood there would not be many chances left to do it privately.

"Well, I did as you predicted through your prophet. I climbed a great tower. I fell." He winced to himself as an instinctive urge to move his right arm was met with searing pain. "I saved many men, including ones with great power." He paused at this, trying to remember the last piece of the prophecy. "I do not recall setting any buildings on fire... Perhaps it has a deeper meaning that I missed?"

Augen rolled his eyes. He was rambling to himself at this point. Perhaps he just wanted someone to speak to in the lonely ward he was forced to occupy. The straps binding him prevented any pious postures, and deep inside, he still felt far from the eyes of his God.

"Perhaps you can make something of my life? I am well aware of what I have missed and wasted. Do you care enough to know, too?"

His eyes teared up as memories of his accomplishments and failures since Pallerheim flew through his head. Despite the heroics, it did not feel right that his story would end this way, not to him at least.

He grabbed the precious knife with Christine's image in it and clutched the blade to his chest with his free hand. He could not see the picture stored within, but it gave him some comfort to think of her while he lay alone in the cool stone room.

"I am so sorry. I wish I could have known the end of my choices. I wish Deos had come to me before I strayed from the path. Perhaps things could have been..."

A dose of drugs that had been temporarily nullified by the Hospitaliers returned with a vengeance, and without warning, Augen's mind faded into numbness once more.

A young lady wearing a face shield and adorned with the markings of the Hospitalier sat behind the door and wept silently for the unnamed soldier whose conversation and prayer she overheard. Her superior, the middle-aged woman, touched her shoulder gently.

"Your gentle spirit does you credit, sister."

"Such tragedy accompanies war. Do all men condemned to it face death with such regret?"

"He is not dead yet. Be wise not to underestimate the workings of Deos. My life is proof that He is never so far as it seems from those He loves."

"But what of the man inside? The Templar? I heard the soldiers say he will be condemned to death."

"Deos dictates all, including death, and nothing happens without His knowledge. If it is his time to die, then he will die. Let Deos judge. He will do a better job than you.

"Now go inside and make sure he is stable, check his wound, make sure that his arm can recover."

"But if he is going to die..."

"Then he will die, but our mission does not change. The circumstances will only affect you if you let them."

...

"Tell me more about Iba."

"Since the foiled parade attack, Barbasul has stabilized considerably. The rebel leader, some disillusioned former prince of the area, was spotted loading up and fleeing in the drones his men hijacked."

"Is that all?"

"That is the summary, but I am not aware of everything. There are so many different problems to keep track of every day, I often have to be reminded of when I heard them. The council is hiding details about the engagement from me as well."

"Why?"

"Honestly, I'm not sure. They are all very keen on avoiding topics that shame their roles, but I can read them better than they think.

"The casualty count was unusually high for the kind of conflict we expected. I think that it partially comes to that. It may also have something to do with the Cataclysm-Tech the insurgents possessed."

Catherine contemplated the words of her husband as he went on about the first dealings of his daily job. Deep inside, she shared little interest in the seemingly endless rebellions springing up across the planet or Alexander's work in organizing their inevitable ends. Such conversation felt barbaric for a woman who dictated the standards of high society in nearly half of the world, and if she was totally honest with herself, she saw the savage details of enforcement as below her station, but such feelings were tactfully concealed.

For the first time in recent memory, Alexander had declared a unique day of rest for all the denizens of the Golden Empire.

Though such a decision could be made by the top echelons of the Ivory Citadel, her husband openly mocked such an announcement as an amateur's justification for lazy living and an obvious hindrance to progress.

This mentality guaranteed constant work within the government, work that had not stopped since the beginning of his reign.

Despite this breach of normalcy, an undeniable fact pleasantly garnished the circumstances: The emperor could have done almost anything in his incredibly rare time off, but chose to spend it with her.

So, Catherine smiled and listened, more than willing to tolerate the topic if it meant interacting with her spouse like a normal wife.

"Are you going to find out what they are hiding?" she inquired politely.

Alexander stared thoughtfully into the distance and formulated his response before answering.

"No. I will not push it."

"Really?" she snickered. "That does not seem like you."

"Well, there are things in my work that I simply cannot cover thoroughly. I need to accept that. Unless you want me to go without sleeping again?"

Alexander's attempt at humor fell flat as Catherine's smile disappeared. "How could you even suggest that?" she retorted. Her eyes met his, and he could practically see a spark of irritation floating between them.

A twig snapped behind the couple, and Alexander spun.

"It is probably just the girls..." Catherine whispered with a sigh.

"I thought you said they were occupied?"

"They told me they were."

"You either eavesdrop correctly or step out from the shadows!" Upon the emperor's startlingly loud command, the youngest of his girls shuffled out from behind a nearby bush.

Catherine smiled weakly and motioned for her to approach.

"Lea? I thought you all had tutoring today with the guard. Are your sisters here?"

Lea shook her head vigorously, but her eyes, inexperienced in the art of lying, told another story through short glances at a different cluster of bushes.

Anger arose in Alexander's chest and began to boil into a much sharper command, one that would likely be accompanied by a threat, but a touch on the arm from his wife helped quench it before it could erupt.

Lea stepped onto the walkway nearest them and, unsure of what to do, curtseyed timidly to her intimidating audience.

"It...ended," was all she got out. It was a lie, and both adults knew it.

"Really?" Catherine interjected before her husband could. She knew why the young maidens were unwilling to show themselves and believed that, deep inside him, Alexander did too. The little girl nodded, staring at her own feet as she did so.

"What brings you out here then, child?" Alexander asked with a poise that surprised his mate.

She shifted her weight and shrugged, unsure of what to say in response, but Alexander did not push it further.

"Well, if you wish to spend your time crawling about in the garden, wear appropriate clothing. You will spoil your dress."

The little girl nodded in agreement, and the emperor took a knee so that they were eye to eye, then he pulled an exquisite diamond necklace from his back pocket and set it in her little hand.

"I know you were not the one who made the noise. Yet you were willing to take on the consequences for whichever of your sisters did. Loyalty and obedience are beautiful gifts to give a loved one, so I will grant you this to honor the strength you have."

Lea's eyes lit up, and she gasped slightly as the extremely expensive trinket slid into her hand. She started to speak, but Alexander put his finger to his mouth.

"Keep this safe. It can be our secret. And whatever you do, do not let your sisters take this from you." The girl nodded quickly, and the emperor sent her out.

"And keep off the flowerbeds," he yelled after her as she ran down the walkway toward her quarters. Catherine carefully embraced her husband and listened quietly for the others to join their sister. When the rustling behind the couple ceased, Catherine broke the silence.

"That was a beautiful necklace."

"I was going to give it to you." Alexander sat back down, and his wife seamlessly adjusted into a side hug, never letting her grip weaken or slide onto his flaws.

"I know. I love what you did with it, though." The couple shared smiles and sat in silence for quite some time. The day was young and the sun blasted the palace orchard with warmth, but Alexander had something eating at his mind.

"What am I going to do about the girls?" he sighed with a touch of pain.

Catherine sighed too, saddened by the death of their romantic silence but well aware of the conversation's inevitability. "I do not know," she finally said.

"Can I confess something? I was not ready to adopt those kids. I was going through so much change in my own life. So many responsibilities. I do not really see them as mine. Do you think that is normal?"

The couple did not move from their position, but much of the warmth left their embrace as Catherine coped with the words. In a way, she always understood this, but hearing them said aloud was insulting to her.

She had adopted the children in hopes of bringing him back into the family unit. It did not go as she had hoped. In a sense, it felt like he rejected them all.

"I am not sure. Nothing about our life seems very normal. But who am I to complain? We both wanted this."

"Normal or not, I will try to build a bridge to those children somehow. I owe it to them, and to you." The emperor relaxed as he finished his sentence, and his posture began to show it.

Catherine smiled in response, and though their unchanging pose prevented Alexander from seeing her face, he could feel her mood improve.

"So, are you going to get them all expensive jewelry then?" she inquired humorously.

Her spouse missed the joke and answered bluntly. "No, buying their love would be shallow and short-lived. It would also appeal to their worst nature as girls. I want to do this honestly, as Deos would have it done."

"I love hearing you say that. If I may give some advice? Let the girls get to know you for who you are. They understand your work ethic, but they never see the results of your work and motivation. Perhaps you could have them follow you during..." Catherine caught herself mid-sentence with a resigned sigh.

Between security issues, maintenance complications, and the potential distractions of having children in the middle floors, such a move could prove problematic or even disastrous. Her own brain debunked the idea before the words left her mouth.

She felt Alexander shift his shoulders so he could see her eyes, waiting for her to finish. She had a feeling that he understood what she was going to propose and recognized its logistical problems in the same manner she did. His interjection proved her suspicions correct.

"During my regular work schedule? I doubt that would go over well. The security complications of having children in the lower levels would be..."

"Yes, yes. I agree," Catherine interrupted, breaking her side hug and rubbing her forehead. "I just think that it would be wise to show them why you work so hard. Nothing can really replace direct contact, but if they saw how you affect the world for its betterment, I believe they would be far more forgiving of your distance."

When she stopped, the couple made eye contact again, and she could see his mind working to formulate a solution. She smiled and stood on her toes to give him a quick kiss.

"What if we went to the silo in Tyre?" Alexander said with a smirk. To this, Catherine visibly started.

"What? Leave the citadel?"

"It is a bit unorthodox, but far from impossible. The vessel in Tyre is already running engine tests! The girls would be enthralled." Catherine started to interject but was unsure of what to say. She admired her husband's obvious desire to turn a new leaf, but this seemed like too much, and in fact, it barely seemed like him at all.

"And with the wars in the ancient world dying down, this would be an excellent opportunity! I can temporarily restore the council's authority over the remaining military maneuvers and schedule a personal visit to our operational Void Race Silo in Tyre."

"Alexander..."

"We will have to be undercover, of course. But with some preparation, I can arrange this in a matter of days!"

"Alexander..."

"We will be gone no longer than a week, and the other meetings can be postponed for considerably longer than that. Naturally, some makeup work will have to be done afterward, but..."

"Alexander!" Catherine shouted, unsure of what to say but certain that something needed to be said. The emperor paused his monologue and waited for her to think of something.

"Do you not think you are taking this too far? You still have responsibilities here..."

She never finished her thought, for Alexander took her head in both hands and kissed her with a passion and joy alien to her. The moment seemed to go on forever, and when it came to its conclusion, she had forgotten what she was going to say.

"I have a responsibility here, too, and I am serious about it. I want to return to our days of youth, and though I cannot put an end to my role in government, I want to try to restore what we both once had. What you wanted when you married me..."

Catherine exhaled in a panic, her body realizing that she had been holding her breath for quite some time. "Can you really do that?" she finally got out.

Alexander was already striding to the door with the purpose and spirit of a man half his age, but he paused his purposeful march just long enough to conclude.

"I am the emperor of half the world! Believe it or not, my job comes with some benefits."

CHAPTER 15

A SHIFT IN THE WINDS

"Time is up, traitor! Are you ready to meet your demise?"

Augen's smile disappeared, and the young nurse, who had been tending to his wounds and providing him company for almost a full week, gasped and stepped away from his bedside as two men of the 12th stormed the room with vengeful pleasure smeared onto their countenances.

"The field marshal has finally assembled his request for your execution, and we have been given the privilege of escorting you to your ride."

"Yes, we hope that your flight to Diona isn't too uncomfortable." The guards laughed to themselves and motioned for the prisoner's brace to be unhooked from the walls. The nurse hung her head but did as she was told.

When Augen was pulled from his bed and hauled to his feet, the guards circled him like sharks, binding his arms and legs in shackles while the Hospitalier performed her last act of healing on him, praying silently for his soul and binding his arm to a strap on his back.

Her superior slid into the room while they worked, speaking softly with the prisoner.

"You are healing up nicely, but do your best to avoid flexing your triceps, for any excess strain will re-tear your wound...and we will not be able to help you again. Deos be with you on your final journey."

"Aww. You lovely ladies don't need to worry—he won't need time to heal, for he will not live long enough to recover entirely. Will you?"

The younger of the soldiers sneered at his prisoner and shoved his finger into Augen's exposed augmentation scar. The bound man screamed in agony, and the guard laughed aloud until he was struck from behind by the nurse, who packed an impressive punch for a woman her size.

The guard stumbled forward, swearing aloud and grabbing the back of his head. When he turned his body to counterattack, the canoness stepped between them, staring into the guard's soul with intimidating resolve.

"You need to leave. This is not a place for malevolence."

The other guard growled at his comrade and grabbed him by the arm, jerking him toward the door. "You couldn't control yourself, could you? Couldn't wait until we were outside?"

"What is your problem? They have no authority over us!"

"You do not know one of the oldest military codes in existence. Never, ever, cross the medical staff. For a day may come when you end up strapped to one of their beds, and no authority can protect you there."

The older soldier looked menacingly into Augen's eyes, but gently faced the women beside him.

"My apologies, ma'am. We will wait outside for the prisoner." As the guards stepped outside, the superior turned in silence to her underling.

"You need to learn restraint, sister. It is unwomanly and against the codes of our order to lash out in physical anger."

"I beg forgiveness, Mother Superior."

"Deos will forgive you, and I do too. Your desire to protect does you credit, but there are better ways to accomplish it. Now, where is the blade left by the commander?"

"I have taken it."

"Good. Now bandage his arms with some of our sealant-casts. Make those wounds untouchable for his trip."

"Of course."

"And do not keep the men waiting. Despite their spiritual weakness, they are still our guests."

"Yes, Mother."

Satisfied, the canoness nodded and left in haste, leaving the nurse to follow her orders in silence.

Even after the work was done, and the arms of her patient covered in a strong, sealed cast, Augen had not recovered from the pain inflicted on him through a second of physical contact.

"They will not be able to hurt you like that again," the nurse whispered as she finished the seal.

"We will see. It is going to be a long flight back to Diona."

The young lady nudged the knight forward, sliding something into his sling in the process. Augen tried his best to feel what the object was, and hoped that it was his blade, but he could not discern it with certainty.

"My brother was one of your kind. He always said that the worst kind of cruelty is to leave someone defenseless before his enemies. It is why he joined up after the..." As she spoke her mind, a palpable sadness began to hinder her words. Eventually, she gave up trying to talk, seemingly certain that the Templar understood what she meant to say anyway. The object in the sling was indeed his knife, the last piece of his old life.

"Please. For my sake. Use it only to defend yourself."

After a moment of melancholy silence, the knight nodded and left the kind nurse to her own devices.

At the door of the hospital, Augen was met by more than just the guards waiting at the doors. Numerous men from his old division waited to see him off, mocking his pathetic state and spewing insults at him.

Among the hecklers was Field Marshal Koder, screaming incoherently about his legs and fanning the anger of the men around him into a molten frenzy.

But in the back of the procession, behind the chaos and unnoticed by most besides Augen, a well-decorated, prestigious heavy-infantry division and their steel-jawed commander stood at completely motionless attention, and watched in silence as he left.

As Augen stepped onto the loading bay of the Moth meant to carry him back to Eros, where he would meet his demise, Commander Pazkt Lomat lifted his voice and the 7th Reds saluted in perfect unison.

They were performing funeral rites for the man who had saved them from death, but the cargo hold was sealed before he could watch its conclusion.

"One-way trip to Diona!" one of the prison guards inside jeered, mock-blowing a horn with his hands and mouth as the storage room pressurized and the old airship began clawing its way back into the air.

A second guard worked to strap Augen's free hand to the wall behind him. Augen would have to remain standing for the journey's duration or hang from his good hand at the wrist.

"You know. When I was pulled from my normal duties to escort a prisoner to his execution in Diona, I had a feeling I was going to see one of those new imperial super soldiers on the way. I could not have predicted that he would be the prisoner."

"It must be your lucky day."

Augen's response caught the arrogant man restraining him off-balance. The prisoner was not supposed to be the one making quips.

"Are you being smart with me?" The guard squared off with his prisoner and drew a baton from his belt.

His partner, the mock trumpeter, followed the man's lead, chuckling sadistically as he approached Augen.

"You do understand that we can punish you for nearly anything up here, and provided I give the proper excuses when we land, walk away untouched."

"You may be strong, but your one uninjured arm is not going to keep you safe chained to the wall."

"And you are not going to use force unless it is absolutely necessary. Right, Basan? Zadir?" The scornful laughs disappeared, and the mocking faces became disappointed ones as a third man stepped into the cargo bay.

"The prisoner was threatening us," Zadir mumbled to the newcomer, who took his place confidently between him and Basan without making eye contact with either of them.

"Chained to the wall with an arm tied behind his back? It seems rather pathetic that you took him so seriously. Perhaps you should look for another job?"

"He is a knight."

"I am aware. I was briefed on his status and his reasons for execution. I also had a short conversation with General Lomat."

"You spoke with Iron Jaw? Is he as ugly as they say?"

The newcomer, an older, dark-skinned man from the Southlands with a calm demeanor and superior rank compared to his colleagues, ignored his coworkers and continued his train of thought, never letting his studious gaze leave the prisoner's visage.

"He was court-martialed for refusing to follow orders, then broke out of prison to finish his mission..." The other two guards leaned in as he finished. "He severed the spine of a field marshal during his escape."

Zadir and Basan jumped back in tandem and fumbled with their batons, but the dark man just smirked.

"I have to give your kind credit—your dedication is admirable, though it is a pity that after all that work, you still failed your mission."

Augen glared into his accuser's eyes but did not respond, so the two scornful guards did instead.

"He broke someone's spine? Why didn't he just run for it?"

"Because his kind is not human anymore. The knight is a machine, without remorse or hesitation, cutting swaths into any living being foolish enough to draw the ire of his handler."

Augen was insulted by the insinuation that he was no longer human, but he wondered if there was any point in talking back, so he kept his peace.

"So, why are you standing so close to him?" Basan inquired nervously; his colleague was quick to interject before the NCO could.

"Basan, you are never going to be anything more than a guard. Did you not hear what Sakit said? He is like a robot; without his handlers here to give him commands, he is docile. Like a cow," the guard sneered, mockingly leaning onto Augen's shoulder as though they were old friends.

The man called Sakit took a calm step backward as the knight slammed his forehead into the skull of the man leaning on him.

Zadir yelped and stumbled away from the immobile knight, dizzily fumbling with his baton. Eventually, he stumbled into a corner and fell into a seated position.

Basan strode forward to strike the prisoner, but the dark man grabbed his shoulders to hold him back.

"I do not recall saying that you should touch him."

"He almost killed Zadir, Sergeant!"

"Do you really want to make him mad? Ok. Hit him with your stick. Let us see how far that will get you."

The sergeant released the rabid guard, who started forward, but contemplating the words of his technical and intellectual superior, stopped prematurely and dropped his club.

"What are we going to do then?"

"We will do what we are paid to do. Keep watch...and leave the prisoner be, unless he causes trouble." As Sergeant Sakit finished his thoughts, Zadir stumbled back toward Augen but was stopped by his extended arm. "You too," he commanded.

"If he is as inhuman as you say, why does it matter?" Zadir quipped as his NCO found a relatively comfortable place to sit amongst the various cargo crates.

"Because it is our duty to do so...and because everybody deserves some right to be left alone. Now, shut up and take a seat. This is going to be a long flight."

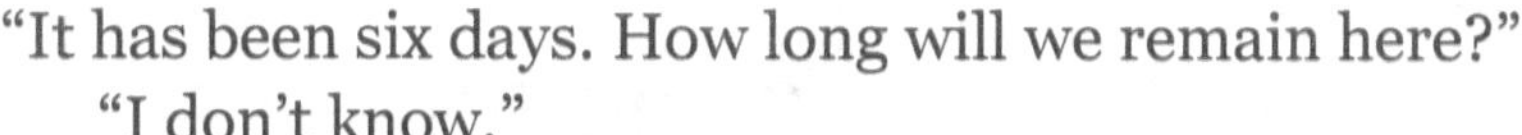

"It has been six days. How long will we remain here?"

"I don't know."

"Then what is our next move? If your income has been frozen, then all we have left is the hostage." Maveth Shedim sat in a dark room surrounded by compatriots of varied nationalities.

"I have more plans. We simply need to take the wisest path, and I have not yet discerned which one that is."

Behind him sat Goliath, who had squeezed into a comfortable position in the room and sat immobile, picking at his recently emptied eye socket and growling to himself.

The rebel foot soldier questioning Maveth was a middle-aged man of Byzican descent. Not old, but experienced, his facial features and posture boasted the angst and durability of a survivor's spirit despite years of hardship.

Though the man's cold demeanor and sharp wit had earned him a lieutenant's rank among his peers, he bowed his head to the exiled prince even as he questioned the man's strategy.

"The Empire's primary focus is efficiency and damage control. If we keep our heads low for too long, then it is quite possible that they simply replace the king and put us on a cold hit list. If that happens, everything we have done will be for naught."

Maveth nodded thoughtfully as the lieutenant spoke. Periodically, he glanced back at his colossal bodyguard, waiting to see if the wounded knight would interject. The giant never did, so no direct answer was given.

"I agree. We need to stay in the spotlight, but we need a method of mass communication that won't draw the wrath of the military onto our heads too quickly.

"According to our sources, the Media Guild Headquarters in Byzica has been recaptured by the empire. So, for the moment, we have no choice but to remain where we are until an alternative is found."

The soldier standing before him was clearly dissatisfied with the answer but remained respectful to his superior.

"Very well, my lord. You have my loyalty, but the men will not appreciate your answer."

A nod from Maveth sent him from the room with his compatriots, and only the top two figures in the ancient-world rebellion remained. The room sat in eerie silence for a short time as Maveth contemplated his next move and Goliath scratched his eye socket.

"I have contacts who are medically trained. If you request it, we can…"

"I am fine!" his captain interrupted with a growl. "The bullet is not in my head, and I did what little could be done by myself. Unless I get a blood clot, I will recover; the only thing that can really help me is time."

Maveth sighed in response, trying to build up the gall to push what was on his mind. "We are going to need more assistance," he finally let out.

At first, the giant slouching in the corner provided no response, but after an agitated sigh and a final frustrated scratch at his face, he let out another menacing growl.

"He will not be pleased."

"We just need intel. I will take responsibility for capturing it. There has to be an imperial facility housing such equipment."

"My lord will *really* not be pleased."

"Your superior understood the risks of his investment. It was only a matter of time before my own assets were frozen."

"If you run a mission from here, you risk exposing your location."

"I have friends who run safehouses in the Silver Empire, and by proxy, numerous backup plans should we be exposed."

When the fallen prince finished his answer, Goliath murmured to himself, seemingly out of deference. Maveth turned away and gave him a moment to collect his thoughts before saying anything else. Finally, the wounded giant slammed his fist into the stone wall beside him, cracking its outer seal.

"We may not need to contact my lord at all," he said with surprising composure. "I am fairly certain that the Empire has built a small base nearby. It will likely have what we need within its walls."

Hearing this, Maveth spun back to him.

"What kind of base is this?"

"No idea, but the local maps do not label it, so I would presume that it is some kind of observation base."

"And you know that it has what we need?"

"Intelligence facilities usually possess means of mass communication. Over the last three years, the Empire has scattered such bases all over the Western world. I happen to know that one of them was built on the island."

"And how do you..." Maveth stopped mid-sentence before probing too deeply.

Instead, he course-corrected his line of thought past his accomplice and back onto his mission. "Do you happen to know where this base is?"

Goliath shook his head and shuffled to the door. Once outside the building, he stretched his back and groaned to himself. Maveth followed him to the door.

On the horizon, his men caught a glimpse of a colossal storm hovering over the sea, sending angry growls to the dry world, warning of its approach.

"No, but Tyre is not a large island. I am sure your boys need something to do."

❖

"Is that the island?"

"Yes, it is, Lea."

"It looks dirty."

"That is because we are far away from home. The ecosystem is hotter and drier here."

"Is the water dirty, too?"

"Probably not, Lea."

"Are the people dirty?"

"Not especially."

"What about the food?" Catherine snickered to herself as her husband endured their youngest daughter's salvo of inquiries. Two of the other girls had their faces pressed to the windows.

Alexander's desire to take his family away from the Ivory Citadel had been swiftly and decisively executed. Various flight arrangements were made, as was a tour of the nearly completed Void Silo in Tyre.

He had even produced false identities for them to travel under. With such documents, the family could avoid attracting excessive attention or requiring a massive military escort.

Not that such measures were really necessary, since nobody outside the top floors of the citadel knew their real identities, but as in everything else Alexander did, he was thorough, and she respected him for it.

"May I do your hair?" The eldest of the girls, and the most adjusted to her opulent lifestyle inside the citadel, sat with her chin up and her knees together. Catherine silently bemoaned the girl's disregard for childlike pleasures but agreed to her request.

"If you wish to do so, Alli, you may," she responded, realizing that their postures were identical and that she was speaking as she normally would when being broadcast.

The artificial identities Alexander manufactured allowed the family to keep their first names, but Catherine feared that she had brought a third identity on board with her, one that even Alexander seemed to have abandoned better than her.

For years, Catherine dreamed of leaving the citadel, losing the burdens she and her husband had been chosen to bear. Yet, now that she was outside, her conscience felt ill, as though her very essence were tied to her home in Alampia and her spirit were now disembodied. Watching Alexander interact with Lea and fidget with some trinket in his left pocket, she wondered if he felt the same way.

"What are we going to do at the Silo?" Lea queried.

"I want to show you some of the Empire's plans. You see, without a goal to focus on, society can easily overemphasize the menial problems of everyday life. While it is no good for a leader to ignore small problems, it is also unwise to leave the masses to their own devices for too long. So..."

"So, you give them something to do while you fix the small problems?"

"Do not interrupt, Ven," Catherine snapped.

The second-eldest of the girls shrank slightly under Catherine's gaze, and her husband nodded in agreement.

"It is great that you are so quick to catch on. But your mother is right. You need to learn how to control your impulses should you wish to grow up respectable."

"And not be left scrubbing lavatories for the rest of your life," Alli muttered under her breath. Catherine, who was close enough to hear the quip, spun in her seat.

"Do you think such disrespectful comments will get you anywhere? You will shut your mouth unless you are spoken to."

"Catherine." Alexander smiled at his wife and touched her arm. The fire in her eyes was something he had not seen in a long time. He had always loved her passion, especially when it leaked from her usually professional composure.

"Your mother is..." He hesitated, trying to find the correct words before continuing. "Your mother is correct, Alli. Authority figures are owed respect, but...but the words I spoke to you, and to her, all those weeks ago are not." He paused again, hating the words as they left his mouth and toying with the contents of his left pocket to distract himself. The words were bitter and humbling, but they needed to be said, so he continued.

"I need to beg your forgiveness for my behavior as of late."

"Alexander, you don't owe..."

"Please, Catherine, don't interrupt. This is long overdue." Catherine let out a small growl but bit her lip, recognizing her own ironic breach of etiquette, and sat in silence until Alexander finished his thought.

"I have been a poor father to you and a poor husband to your mother, but I plan on changing that. Just as your primary focus should be on your family, mine needs to be on you, too."

An intercom buzzed to life and interrupted the emperor's apology. Via the device, an elderly man alerted the family of an imminent landing and disappeared just as quickly.

Alexander was tempted to stop and allow the interference to cut his talk short, but he stifled such desires and finished his thought.

"You wondered why I brought you all here. It is because I want to show you what keeps me so busy, so that perhaps we can understand each other when I am distant. When you see me in the projectors and on billboards, you can know what I am working toward, but please understand that I have no intention of taking you for granted anymore."

Lea hugged his arm, sliding her arms over his augmentation flaw and forcing him to bite his lip rather than cry out.

"Thank you, Daddy," she said. "I forgive you."

Carrol, the third child, did the same thing, and the older two girls nodded. The aerial cruiser touched down with a thud, and the excitement ratcheted back up immediately.

"I wanna go swimming!" Ven and Lea squealed in excitement.

"Quiet down. We can go after we reach our quarters. Stay together now," Catherine called after them as they piled down the chamber toward the doors. Alexander groaned and rubbed his arms.

"I see your numbing ointment is wearing off," she sighed quietly.

"It barely works."

"It is still better than your last medications," she said, waiting for him to recover. He was quick to do so. He stretched his back and shoulders and stuck out his right hand, beckoning her to take his arm, but all the while fidgeting with the three small vials inside his opposite pocket.

They were his backup plan, just in case he needed some extra energy. His wife did not know, and if things went according to plan, she would never need to know because they would never be used.

Deep inside, Alexander was ashamed of feeling the need to bring such medication, especially after his conversation with Nathan. However, he had understated his use of the drugs when they spoke, and after relying on chemical support as long as he did, he could not leave it completely, especially now that he was so far out of his normal routine.

"Shall we?" he said with a halfhearted smile.

She said nothing, but carefully took his arm and accompanied him to the stairwell, where they were met by a small bodyguard squad, a handful of attendants, and four hyper girls, jumping about and giggling with each other about swimming.

It was not exactly an emperor's welcome, but Catherine knew that was the point.

"I think things are starting to change for the better." Alexander smiled gently as they walked to the armored carriage awaiting them. Catherine was quite deep in thought, but allowed a smile once she was inside the vehicle.

"Yes, perhaps you are right."

CHAPTER 16

A STORM IN TYRE

The hours dragged on for Augen, who stood chained to a wall on what would likely be his last long-distance flight.

Initially, he kept himself occupied by observing a thunderstorm looming over the horizon; it was beautiful in its own right, and distracting enough to keep his mind off his current situation.

However, when a gust of wind shook the airship and caused it to list slightly, he tore his eyes from the porthole, granting his vision of the exterior. He could see that they were above the oceans again, and the thought of it made his skin crawl. So, with the window no longer providing any comfort, he had to find something else to keep his mind busy.

Though not well received by his audience, Augen chose to distract himself by speaking of the last three months of his life, of all that had happened in Barbasul, and of his strange interaction with the old man in Pallerheim. The dark-skinned man named Sakit seemed interested in Augen's story, and as the knight spoke, he found that the seas drifted away from his consciousness.

"You cannot possibly believe this idiocy!" Basan exclaimed after Augen's conclusion.

When his colleagues provided no response beyond a disinterested grunt from Zadir, Basan threw his head back and laughed dramatically. "Disappearing men, visions in the desert, divine intervention? Surely, this man has taken too many blows to the head!"

Augen posited no response, and Sergeant Sakit, who seemed entertained by the story, though not entirely convinced, kept his peace. The knight had no interest in provoking his captors and even while the sergeant was present, knew better than to provoke the hot-tempered guards.

Without commentary from anyone besides Basan, silence retook the room, and the looming storm began to beckon for Augen's attention once more. The thought of the water in the clouds nearby and the seas below caused his arms to itch painfully, but with his arms restrained, there was nothing he could do about it but squirm. His story had taken several hours to tell, though the knight had no way of telling exactly how long, and everyone's legs were getting tired.

"You weave a strange tale," the sergeant finally commented while finding a place to sit and tipping his head back.

"You mean *impossible*," Basan growled. When his second attempt at mockery fell flat, a spark of rage was kindled within him, and though he said nothing more, Augen could see the glow of an irrational spite emanating from the guard as he left the storage bay, pausing for only a moment to whisper something into Zadir's ear.

After a brief shuffle around the room and the reorganization of a chosen cargo stack, Sergeant Sakit pulled his cap down over his face and kicked his legs up.

"You certainly experienced much, for having such a short career," he quipped from under his cap. "I don't know if I believe your religious experiences, but I cannot deny the weight of your predicament. Especially near the end, with the hostages and the giant."

"I could not bear the blood of more innocent people on my conscience. Yet it seems that, in a way, I am doomed to carry such a weight regardless of my choices."

Augen's response fell on deaf ears as the NCO faded into unconsciousness.

Zadir sat silently on a crate, breathing evenly and keeping his eyes locked coldly on Augen. The guard seemed disinterested in what his prisoner had to say, so Augen made up his mind not to bother attempting conversation with him. "It is a shame," the knight finally muttered to himself after several minutes of silence.

Despite Augen's presumptions, the man reclining over the cargo crates was still listening. When the knight went silent, he decided to inject his own thoughts.

"I agree, it is a shame about those hostages. How ironic that King Jubanic was the only man to survive, the tyrant." He snickered to himself without moving his body, unaware of the prisoner's visually confused response.

A brooding drum in the distance announced the rapid approach of the storm, and the airship shook slightly as though it were afraid of its presence.

"Who is Jubanic?" Augen queried. He was genuinely curious but also desperate to remove the tempest from the forefront of his mind.

"You don't know his name? It is comical how little you Northerners know about the people of the ancient world. It is even funnier with you. After all, you did travel all the way down here to save him."

Augen sighed to himself as a second rumble tore his attention back outside. The thought of seawater had his arms itching again, but with one arm strapped to the wall and the other tied behind his back, he was unable to indulge in even the most basic efforts to relieve them. So, despite the embarrassingly obvious tension in his voice, the bound Templar forced himself to continue.

"And what makes your king a tyrant?"

"He is not my king, for my homeland is not in Babyl. Jubanic al Asad made a name for himself among all the imperial puppets in the ancient world when he declared himself head of the national clergy three years ago."

"Is that not blasphemy?" Augen's question was met with a slow shrug from the sergeant.

"Technically, yes. But imperial law allows for the temporary seizure of power to purge lands deemed culturally problematic. Shortly after his ascension to the throne, hundreds of local Imaums and scholars were rounded up and publicly executed."

"Imaums? You mean the ancient pagan religious leaders? Their false religion deserves to be quelled anyway." Augen's flippant response was met with a scoff from Zadir, catching him by surprise.

"He wasn't purging anything. The cathedrals in Babyl are still nearly empty every day, and your so-called 'pagan' cults abound. What he used was a political tool to remove the cultural leaders he saw as threats to his rule, nothing more." The sergeant lifted his cap and made eye contact with the prisoner.

"Your view of the ancient world's religion is not uncommon… It may even be correct," he continued calmly. "But their beliefs were never a factor in their deaths. They performed no treasonous actions and obeyed the laws of the land." Sakit paused before finishing his thought, seemingly hesitant to continue, but Augen's interest was discernible, so the NCO tentatively continued. "Before the law, they were just as innocent as the man you slew by mistake. Do their beliefs really make such a profound difference here?"

Augen shuffled awkwardly about with all the movement his restraints would allow. His itching arms and myriad injuries were largely to blame for the throbbing discomfort, but Sakit's words rendered his spirit stricken with a dire ache, and unlike his arms, there was no conceivable way for anyone to scratch it.

Satisfied with what was said and not expecting an answer, the sergeant leaned his head back once more and covered his eyes.

A deep rumble from the storm preceded a violent tremor and an apparent drop in altitude. The men in the room were briefly thrown into the air and slammed into the steel plating on the floor.

Zadir was the first to recover from the impact, leaping to his feet, flinging obscenities, and holding his lower back, which took the bulk of his fall.

The sergeant, who had fallen from the stack of crates and hit his head on the floor, was considerably slower to rise. Basan stumbled back into the room, gripping his wrist.

"The pilot says that the storm is on top of us," he yelled over the commotion.

"Really? I would never have guessed," Zadir retorted.

Sergeant Sakit's response was more useful. "What is our trajectory? Are we going to try to pass over the storm?"

"I don't know. It sounded like he was going to try."

"He has not made a decision yet? Did he not see the chaotic torrent coming?" Sakit exclaimed angrily.

"He said that the storm altered its course, that it was originally going to pass us..." Basan's response was unsatisfactory to the sergeant, who sped out of the room before the guard could finish. Basan gripped his hand and grunted to Zadir, who eyed Augen with dark intent.

"The sergeant is gone, and if it takes him as long to reach the helm as it did for me..."

"His footing is better than yours. The question is how long he will converse with the bridge crew."

"So, are we going to..."

Zadir, who already knew what his colleague was going to ask, ripped a piece of steel rebar from a nearby pallet. The ties holding the cargo down were loosened slightly as the thin metal rails were pulled out from beneath them.

"Yes," he interrupted calmly. "Now shut up and grab one."

Though Augen's attention was chained to the porthole and the deluge that had begun beating on its thick sills, the two malevolent guards were caught approaching in his periphery, and Augen's stance and eyes readjusted to the more imminent threat.

"I caught a glimpse of the fancy knife in your cast. How ungodly! Don't you know that prisoners aren't supposed to carry weapons? So, we will be taking it off your hands now. Unless you want us to consider you armed and dangerous?" Zadir sneered, approaching slowly with the steel beam clutched in his hands. Basan imitated his co-conspirator's movements on Augen's opposite side.

"My knife is an heirloom and the only remaining link to my old life. It is precious to me," Augen said.

He understood that such an attempt would not work before the words finished leaving his mouth. So, without hesitation, the knight appealed to something more basic. "The first man to touch my knife is getting his skull fractured!"

The men hesitated briefly, but they were not repelled.

"Threatening a guard? I perceive an imminent threat, Basan. Don't you?"

Basan nodded enthusiastically and tightened the grip on his weapon. A flash of lightning illuminated the room from behind the attackers, causing Augen to squint. His hesitation cost him when a rebar club struck his forehead.

"This is for threatening your betters!" Zadir shouted spitefully, winding back for another slug. The blow would have been worse had the lightning not caused his attacker to hesitate as well, but Augen's forehead began to bleed immediately.

Basan also swung his newly acquired club at the immobilized knight, but Augen was focused now, and his combat training would not permit an unanswered second blow.

Basan's swing was low, aimed at the lower torso, as was Zadir's second foray, and Augen blocked both blows with his legs, knocking his attackers off-balance.

Ironically, the impact of Augen's unexpected parry ripped Basan's weapon from his injured hands.

Zadir maintained his grip but was put off by the knight's rapid recovery. Winding back for a third strike, the guard overestimated his distance and was summarily corrected with a strike to the face from the toe of Augen's boot. As he stumbled backward, Basan tried to grab at Augen's cast from the other side. Augen twisted his hips and briefly caught the guard's head between the wall and his knee. It did not crush the man's skull as he had hoped, but it hurt, and Basan stumbled backward to hold his ringing ears.

"Is that all you got?" Augen cracked, hoping to make his opponents angry. He knew that emotional fighters were less calculating and more likely to miss his obvious weaknesses. It did not work.

"Get up, Basan! And keep your swings high. Strike downward onto his head and shoulders. He will not be able to deflect them with that bad arm."

The ship dropped again, throwing everyone except Augen back onto the floor. His shackled hand kept him standing, but he gained no advantage from this opening. He knew that, in truth, it was unlikely that he could beat them unless circumstances changed drastically.

"Why are you doing this? Are you really so insecure and desperate for affirmation of power that you kill those who do not fear you?"

Zadir stumbled to his feet and gripped the pole with both hands. "You are a dead man walking. Why would I kill you?"

Basan slowly found his footing again and prepared himself for another assault on the restrained knight. Zadir, who grew impatient at his colleague's incompetence, picked up the second length of rebar and shoved it into the clumsy guard's hands.

"I can teach you a lesson, though. After all, what is the point of having power at all if you are unwilling to wield it? Don't worry; you will still be conscious enough to comprehend your demise when we reach Diona. If you hand over that knife, I can lighten your punishment, but one way or another, you have had this coming for quite some time. Everyone wins, except for you, of course."

"You are a disgusting human being," Augen snarled.

"Sakit keeps telling me that. Yet, he has never been able to prove anything. I am unaffected by his opinions just as I am by yours. If the empire demands your death, why should it care about your short-term welfare?"

More blows followed, and this time, most of them found their mark. With his uninjured arm restrained, Augen could do little to keep the beating from being seen through, except to keep them off-balance and hope for help to come.

His attacker claimed that he would live to see the end of the voyage, but he did not trust Zadir to keep his word. So, as he did his best to minimize the damage of the incoming strikes, he slowly shifted his injured arm inside the cast until the knife concealed inside started to slide from its hidden pocket.

The iron cuff pinning Augen to the wall could not be broken, even by him, so he had no other choice but to try using his bad arm and coveted blade to drive off his attackers.

Just one moment would be all he needed, a moment of arrogance from Zadir or an advantageous tremor from the storm to bring him into arm's reach. Basan was a follower by nature, and if his sadistic coworker was struck down, he would back off.

Even the tiniest movements made his arm throb worse than the blows to his head. The beleaguered prisoner could not even tell if his arm was leaving the sling, but his agonizing efforts seemed to be his only option.

Another quake shook the Moth, and a burst of light illuminated the interior of the storage bay. Augen prayed silently, willing his bad arm to continue moving until he could take hold of his blade.

More tremors came, and the roar of the cyclone became constant, but no perfect moment came for Augen to end his attackers' relentless assault.

"You claim that you wished to save the innocent? You had all the power a man like me could have wished for, and yet, you could not even succeed at that. It seems I am not the only disgusting one here." As Zadir monologued, Basan briefly paused his attack.

"We should stop," he said.

"We will stop when I tell you to!" his counterpart snarled. Augen's head was bleeding, and his eye and neck were badly swollen. Had his body not been physically enhanced, he would likely have been unconscious or dead.

"I did what I thought Deos wanted of me..."

"That story again? Nobody here believes that Deos chose you for anything. You are just a big, brainwashed lunatic who was struck too many times in the face."

"You cannot tell me what I have seen," Augen responded coldly. "Your disbelief proves nothing, and no amount of physical abuse will make you right."

Zadir raised his rebar club once more, but Basan grabbed the bloody piece of metal by the tip.

"I said stop!" he yelled. Zadir scoffed and shoved Basan back into the loose rebar pile, which shifted considerably upon his collision with it.

"Have you lost your nerve?"

"We are going to get in trouble! This is not like the other times. The sergeant..."

"The sergeant will not do anything. Look at this storm! None of us is likely to make it out of here alive! Forget the consequences! Nobody cares about us, especially Deos! When I am done with the big believer, I will come after you next, you coward!"

There was no stopping what came next. Augen desperately tried to pull his arm from its sling, but it became clear that he was incapable of it.

His left triceps and the tendons tying that arm to his torso were so badly damaged that his meager effort to pull it from the sling nearly put him into shock, even without Zadir's help.

Augen's physical inhibitors were weakened when he became a knight, but it was clear that his traumatized body would simply not allow it.

A colossal blast of turbulence careened into the airship, which leaned heavily one way, its engines straining against the immensity of its elemental abuse, before rapidly overcorrecting in the opposite direction. The three men inside the cargo hold were thrown to one wall, then to its opposite. The belts and chains holding the cargo to the floor creaked and groaned under the unique pressure, but nothing fully gave way.

When the bipolar tossing finally ceased for a moment, the gravity in the room seemed to vanish, as though the ship had transcended the atmosphere and now floated in the Aether.

Augen wished that were the case, but he knew better. The hull of the Moth screamed maniacally with an ever-increasing pitch, and the water pounding the portholes ceased. The ship was not floating; its engines had failed, and the airship was now in free fall. The storm had apparently grown bored toying with the airship and had made up its mind to drown it. *I am dead,* Augen thought as his stomach flew into his mouth.

A shrill grinding sound replaced the squealing as the secondary engines kicked in and gravity returned to the room, but instead of pulling toward the floor, the force pulled Augen into the wall behind him.

Loose debris whistled through the air, and Augen did his best to stabilize himself, but his efforts were in vain. For a jarring about-face, yanked him away from the wall with such force that the shackle on his right arm bent over the support panels before snapping in half like a brittle tree branch.

The poor guards, who had the misfortune of not being tied to a wall like their prisoner, were flung around the room during the chaos, slamming into various stacks of cargo until neither one was conscious.

One final violent shake struck the cargo hold with such ferocity that its frame warped and rivets shot about the room like bullets. Then, suddenly, all was finally still.

CHAPTER 17

THE PASSION AND THE PAST

Sergeant Sakit opened his eyes and gripped a bloody gash on the back of his head. The room was spinning, and his eyes could not seem to focus on anything. His body demanded rest, but he ignored the desire and stumbled forward.

The breezeway he walked down was horribly warped and slowly filling with seawater from the nose of the wrecked airship.

The Eroan Moth had been flung into the sea, yet somehow, he had survived the calamity. A sharp pain in his hip bid him pause to check his battered body for broken bones. The moment of respite felt pleasing for the NCO, but he did not remain for long; he still had work to do.

A glance at the dark, twisted, gurgling mass of seawater that was once the airship's cockpit confirmed the doom of its bridge crew.

"The poor souls, may Deos receive them," the sergeant prayed before turning away and stumbling back to the cargo hold, where his two underlings were kept. He needed to know if they had suffered the same fate, and then he would find out how far he would have to swim to reach land with his prisoner, provided the Templar was still alive.

The cargo hold was mostly dry but horribly malformed. Various crates had broken their bonds and flown about in the turmoil, as had a large cluster of rebar.

The sergeant did not initially see living cargo, but the prisoner announced his presence by reaching out from a shadow and taking hold of the captain.

Sakit was already disoriented and would not have put up any fight had Augen wanted him dead, but rather than smash his body or fling him about the room, the Templar pulled him close.

"Is there any land nearby? There has to be land!" The knight was pale, bloody, and teary-eyed, and a bloody cloth was wrapped around his forehead. Panic was written all over his countenance.

A shift in the airship's weight churned the water and dragged the room slightly farther into the sea. The knight saw this and dropped his hostage, shuffling back into the corner farthest from the water. His left arm had been ripped from the medical strap that held it steady and was now dangling limply at his side. His other arm was bleeding at the wrist from where his shackle dug into his arm before its chain broke apart in the chaos and loosed him.

"What were those fools thinking, refusing to ascend? They have no idea what water will do to me!" the prisoner cried out, more to himself than anyone else.

Sergeant Sakit waded through the knee-deep basin at the low end of the room and scanned the horizon through a porthole. Nothing.

"Any idea where Basan and Zadir went?" Sakit queried. The prisoner provided no answer, but simply sat in the corner, hyperventilating, staring at the water, and scratching at his useless arm.

Sakit checked the opposite porthole and sighed in relief. The storm limited his vision, but even with a handicap, he could spot solid land through the porthole nearest the panicked knight.

"I will not die like this!" the detainee finally exclaimed.

"You will not have to. I think our pilot, foolish or not, managed to get us to Tyre before crashing. I believe we are on the beachfront. Or very close to it at least."

Sakit heaved one of the lighter crates and revealed the exposed arm of Zadir, who was crushed by the rebar stack he had loosened prior. Sakit swore to himself and continued his search for the other guard.

"Where is my knife?" the knight questioned aloud.

"You don't have one. Just stay up there, and I will try to find a way out of here," Sakit answered, assuming that the super soldier was delirious.

Another quick visual inspection, and he saw that the knight had clearly sustained some vicious impacts to the face. He sighed to himself, hoping that the bruises and cuts were the result of flying debris.

The airship had either landed on a sandbar or floated atop the waves, for the internal shifting had developed into a consistent pattern of relatively calm rocking motions even as the wind beat on the ship's exterior.

The sergeant began making his way to an exit, but movement on the far side of the room caught his eye. Altering his course, he waded through the water and found Basan pinned to the floor by a wayward cargo crate.

The guard's mouth popped barely out of the water, gasping for air as he tried and failed to free himself with a single unrestrained arm.

"Help me!" Sakit yelled back to the knight, who had crawled to the water's edge and retrieved a slender piece of metal from one of the shallow pools. When no response came, the sergeant gripped the fallen container and pulled it with all his might.

Nothing moved, but another small shift in the water pulled the guard's head completely below the waves, leaving only a cluster of bubbles to mark his fallen location.

Sakit pushed his way through the water back toward the prisoner, who sat in the corner farthest from the brim with a large dagger in his hands. His breathing was still quick and erratic, but the crazed panic in his eyes had vanished. He was responsive again, though only time would tell if that was a good thing for the NCO.

"Templar, listen to me! Basan will be dead in minutes if you tarry. I cannot help him out of the water."

"Good," Augen responded calmly.

Sakit began climbing toward the large man, but a cold glance in his direction stopped him dead in his tracks. His own adrenaline rush began to dissipate, and the blade in the prisoner's hand finally registered.

Where did he get a dagger? More importantly, what does he plan on doing with it? Sakit wondered, but that did not matter. He had to save his colleague, and that meant talking the knight down.

"You spent your life as a Templar trying to protect people, did you not?" His words reached their target and were rejected on the spot. Another cold glare from the armed prisoner preceded a slow shake of the head.

"I made a promise to protect the innocent. I owe the scum below the water nothing." The knight's change in demeanor announced the origin of the marks on his face.

Sakit sighed solemnly and kicked himself for leaving the prisoner alone with Zadir. He had worked many years with them both, so he knew of Zadir's violent tendencies and Basan's unwillingness to stand up to him, but regardless of whether Basan had followed in his colleague's abusive footsteps, Sakit did not want to see the troubled man die.

"Perhaps not. But you claim Deos saved you from death in Pallerheim. You said you had killed a priest? Were you truly innocent when He sent His man to help you?"

This time, his words struck a nerve, but Sakit feared it may have been the wrong one, for the knight arose and pulled the blade from his scabbard.

"Do not compare me with that deplorable excuse for a guard!"

Sakit stepped back, fearing that he may have gone too far, but if the Templar's story was true, and he believed it may have been, then he had no interest in letting the heroic soldier taint his name now.

"Why not! What makes you so special that Deos saved you exclusively?" A normal knight would likely have skewered the sergeant where he stood, and Sakit knew this. He was testing his own faith by testing Augen's commitment.

His prisoner was free, and somehow, he was also armed. The wise thing to do would have been to flee, but a hook in Sakit's conscience told him not to. Instead, he pulled his outer coat off and extended the article of clothing to the imposing giant.

"This is dry. It will help keep your bandages from getting wet. Please, extend the same mercy to this broken man that Deos did when he saved you."

The fire in his eyes slowly cooled, and he sheathed his blade, slowly sliding the hilt into a belt buckle before taking the NCO's coat.

"Tie my dead arm behind me, and put the coat on the other arm. Tighten the sleeve on my wrist as much as you can, and do not think for a moment that you can take Christine from me without losing your life."

"Who is Christine?" Sakit queried with no response.

The prisoner ignored his question, locking his eyes on the water he would have to cross and hyperventilating again.

Even with the seawater never rising above his knees, the knight was clearly fighting a complete mental breakdown as he timidly shuffled through the submerged space and approached the drowning guard.

With a great heave, the knight used his free shoulder and arm to shift the crate off the pinned guard.

Basan floated to the surface, unmoving. Sergeant Sakit pulled his comrade from the water and struck the man's chest with a closed fist until water spilled from his mouth.

After a moment, the near-dead guard gasped aloud and gripped his bad arm, choking on the remaining water in his mouth and rolling over on his own accord.

The sergeant did not wait for Basan to fully recover. He needed to find a way out of the airship. The ladder to the upper stores seemed the most reasonable way out, and miraculously, it was undamaged by the crash, as was the hatch leading out.

"Hurry, you two! Let us leave this deathtrap before the sea loses its patience and smothers us."

❖

Augen's head finally cleared up when his soaked shoes touched the dry beaches of what he had to assume was Tyre. His footwear gripped the sand, pulling as much of the coarse mineral compound with it as possible, and Augen was so relieved to see it that he had to fight the urge to touch the coarse minerals with his hands.

The Deathwatch Warmoth was designed to travel slightly beyond the bulk of Archaea's planetary atmosphere, hundreds of feet above even the mightiest storm. Augen could not understand why the pilot and his bridge crew chose to avoid doing so, even with the storm clearly visible on the horizon.

Enough anger toward the crew—their mistake was something they paid for with their lives. What a strange storm this turned out to be, Augen thought, dropping to his knees and thanking Deos for His apparent protection.

Not only did the Moth land on a sandbar that prevented the ravaged airship from sinking, but he soon found that, when traversed cautiously, the same submerged anomaly created a shallow walkway all the way to the beach.

He was thrown tens of thousands of feet into the ocean and never got wet above the waist.

The storm itself, which had so rapidly descended onto the airship earlier that day, was now caught by a mighty northeastern wind and flung toward the southern borders of the Silver Empire. He could still hear the terrible thunder bellowing in the distance, and the storm's black exterior was visibly less than a handful of miles away, yet where he sat, it was not even raining.

"Deos Almighty, your generosity toward me is unmatched. What have I done to deserve such careful preservation?"

As Augen prayed aloud, staring into a cloudy coastal sky and a sun he had believed he would never see again, Sakit, who had waited for the barely functional Basan to climb onto the sandbar before continuing, was now stumbling onto the beach with his remaining underling in tow.

The wind walling off the storm blew with such force that it quite nearly knocked over the two normal men as they stepped onto the beach, but to Augen, who had spent so many days penned up, it was the greatest thing he could imagine feeling, aside from perhaps a hug from Christine.

In the distance, he saw men running toward him, wearing uniforms similar to those of his guards, but even from several hundred yards away, Augen was confident that they were only lightly armed. Four poorly equipped guards were not a search party sent for a fugitive knight or a Templar hit squad. He was not their target; he was safe.

"I am a free man," he announced with a laugh. "I can go home."

"I cannot stop you," Sergeant Sakit responded, dragging his largely unresponsive underling up the beach.

"I can return to Eros."

"Indeed."

"And perhaps, I can finally work up the courage to..." Augen paused as he spoke, unsure even now if he would be able to face Christine and her father again.

He slowly rose to his feet, contemplating various outcomes of confession and whether it would be wise to come clean at all, at least regarding Steven. He had learned and suffered so much. Surely, he had atoned for his mistakes by now.

The condemned Templar slowly took a single step forward, willing his feet to create a pattern of similar movements, but the process was slow, as though his body shared the hesitancy of his spirit.

His mind was so overwhelmed by the possibilities and pitfalls of the future that when the men running toward the wreck reached Sakit and Basan, he did not compute their arrival. By the time his paralysis was finally softened, his feet had summoned only three small steps from where he had started the trek to his freedom.

"Where are you going?" he heard Sakit call out to the newcomers as they stopped for a moment to catch their breath.

"We have to fetch help in one of the seafront towns!" one of them gasped, eyeing the wrecked Moth on the waterfront.

"Our outpost fell under attack," another man, the fittest of the four, sighed, trying to keep his voice stable. "A group of armed men slew the entrance guards and took hostages. We were barely able to escape the onslaught. Is the man with you a knight?"

Augen heard the question and flinched. His back was still turned to the crew, and though he gave no personal response, his focus returned to the present with a panicked fury.

He could feel the sergeant's eyes on him and awaited his answer. The NCO hesitated in his response but tentatively continued.

"Yes. In a manner of speaking, he is a Templar." The response sent the men into hysterical excitement and brought the conversation and newcomers to circle Augen, who waited cautiously, unsure of how to respond.

"You must help us, Templar!" the guard exclaimed.

"It is not my mission," he responded, pretending that he still worked for the empire and was not previously traveling to his own execution. If Sakit kept the fact hidden from the newcomers, he certainly had no plans to reveal it.

"The outpost is a critical location for an imperial agenda," the guard responded. Augen stiffened his shoulders in frustration and spun to face the man talking.

"I do not care about your agenda! I am leaving! I have to get to Pallerheim! If your base is so important, then perhaps you should have fought for it rather than fleeing to find someone with the spine and competence to do your job for you."

Sakit eyed Augen intently but said nothing, and Basan, whose faculties had mostly returned to him by now, did the same. It seemed as though they were willing to let their former prisoner go, and Augen was more than willing to seize that opportunity.

The guards, on the other hand, were not catching on.

"Templar, you do not understand! We tried to fight, but there was another knight with the enemy, clad in black, bigger than any man we had ever seen, and wielding a greatsword with one hand. He spearheaded the assault and cut our garrison to ribbons. We circled to strike the enemy's flank, but a noble and his family were visiting the facility, and the enemy took them hostage. We could not get a clean shot."

Augen's heart skipped a beat, and his blood ran cold; his dead arm began throbbing violently, as though it wished to remind him of what happened to those who tried to fight Goliath. And who else could they be describing?

"Deos, why?" he mouthed. No one save Sakit seemed to notice Augen's change in demeanor, and the Templar tried to take advantage of it.

"I am sorry, soldiers, but I am badly wounded and could not help even if I wanted to, and if the men who attacked your base are who I think they are, then those who are taken hostage are as good as dead." Augen turned away from Sergeant Sakit, who seemed to expect something of him, and slowly began making his way down the beach.

At the behest of the sergeant, he had saved Basan from drowning, an act that put him at enough risk. Attacking Goliath without armor or the use of his left arm was suicide, and he would not dare throw his life away for some building.

The guards lowered their heads in defeat, but as Augen stepped away, gaining confidence with each slow stride, Sakit spoke up.

"Do you really believe that girl will take you back? That your life will just return to normal?" he yelled sharply at Augen's back. The Templar froze again, this time with a spark of rage in his eyes, but the sergeant ignored his response and strode to his side, speaking silently in hopes of providing at least a superficial modicum of privacy.

"This Christine you speak of is not your dagger, is she? She is the reason your heart is so set on returning to Pallerheim, is she not? You are not the man she knew, and you can never be that man again!"

"Leave it," Augen growled quietly.

His warning went unheeded. "Your past cannot be changed. There is no going back to the way things were! Whoever Christine was, the man she knew is now dead. You have a purpose here, so fulfill it. Or spend the rest of your life on the run."

"I said, leave it!" the knight barked, breaking his cold facade.

"I will not! Your insistence on living a fantasy will waste your life. Imagine someone like you attempting to be average. What a waste!" Augen growled again and began stomping away, but the sergeant reached out and grabbed his arm around the biceps.

The bandage covering his augmentation wounds held firm, and he was not in any pain, but in a flash of hatred and adrenaline, Augen's dagger was off his belt and hilt-deep in the sergeant's chest.

Basan stumbled backward in stunned surprise, and the newcomers did the same, drawing their weapons and yelling various conflicting orders at the rogue knight and each other, but it was Augen who was most confounded by his actions.

He ran forward and kneeled over Sergeant Sakit's body, inspecting the damage he had done. The blade had been buried to the hilt in his right lung, barely missing the heart, but fatal regardless. The NCO coughed up blood and gasped for air, trying to work up the strength to speak.

"What have I done?" Augen cried, staring at the dying man and seeing Steven's body lying in the sand, too.

The guards regained their senses and began loading their rifles and pistols, preparing to put the unarmored knight down for his crime, but Basan stopped them, beckoning the men to see the knight's next move.

"What have I done?" the knight said again, trying unsuccessfully to pull the knife from Sakit's chest without doing more damage.

The sergeant gasped hoarsely and raised his head to respond. "You have done what you are trained to do," he said flatly. Augen reached for the knife once more and tried to remove it, but a pained flinch from the sergeant made him recoil.

"I will avenge you, and use the blade on myself when you have passed. I will do what I should have done in the beginning," Augen said in an agonized tone.

Sakit's head fell backward, and he coughed up more blood. Augen knew there was no saving him, but the man responded nonetheless.

"I believe your story. I believe that Deos has chosen you for great things if you are willing to follow Him."

"And what a mess I have made of everything! If only I had died in that wreck!" Augen moaned.

"Everyone dies, Templar. I suppose you just get the unique chance to decide how. So, spare me your pity and your vengeance, and do what you promised Deos. Do your job. I think you owe me that...and yourself." His eyes rolled back in his head, and with one last pitiful effort to inhale, Sergeant Sakit lay still.

Augen straightened his back and stared into the storm, seeing his reflection inside the sinister turmoil beyond. The self-hatred he was familiar with returned to him, but the uncertainty he had also grown to know was strangely absent.

For nearly a minute, he quietly mourned the man he slew, but also the life he now recognized he would never have. He was not a family man, not anymore, and he recognized that he was unlikely to ever be.

So, after a long silence, he stood, pulled the knife from Sergeant Sakit's corpse, carefully cleaned the blade, and sheathed it.

The men around him backed away cautiously, but Augen had no interest in fighting them.

"How far is your base?" the Templar queried, breaking the solemn silence.

"A few miles? We were trying to reach one of the port cities down the sea bank," one of the guards responded as the men lowered their weapons and Basan strode to Augen's side.

"The sergeant told me what you did on the Moth. I owe you my life and will follow you to death. You will not have to worry about me turning you in after this," the guard whispered to him as they walked.

"I am done running from the consequences of my choices. Should I survive, I will turn myself in," he responded coldly.

Augen meant what he said, but in his heart, the Templar was nearly certain he would not have to worry about keeping his word.

He began making his way toward the base, with Basan and the guards following him closely.

Nobody in the group noticed this, but on the horizon, veiled by the violent rains over the sea and clothed in red, blue, and yellow sun rays, a Being shaped roughly like a man stood atop the chaotic waters, beckoning the mighty winds to fold the storm away from the shore.

CHAPTER 18

GROUND ZERO

"Clear!" a rebel yelled to the three men behind him. Though relatively undertrained, Maveth's men moved efficiently from room to room, shooting and stabbing the structure's mostly unarmed occupants until the central headquarters was littered with the corpses of unprepared engineers and steelworkers.

"It seems the giant did our job for us. I have yet to meet an armed man in this entire facility." One rebel smirked at his comrade as both men cleaned their blades on the soft fabric of a piece of furniture. The other two were digging through a group of cubicles, making themselves absolutely certain that no one else was in the room.

"What do you suppose the tower outside is?" one of the killers queried, nodding at the base's imposing central structure, which they could see through a window.

"I am not sure; it almost looks like a Skydagger."

"Skydagger?"

"You know, one of those factories where the old Warmoths were built."

"Do you think the Imps are making more of them?" The two men took a moment to gaze at the monumental structure while the other pair concluded their search of the room and approached to join them.

Below, other rebels rummaged between the various enclosures, looting the corpses that littered the grounds, and searching for the opportunity to make more.

"I doubt it. There's no entrance from the grounds. No doors, no windows, not so much as a porthole. Even the giant could not find a way to get in. Plus, I read that the Skydaggers were taller than this."

"Really? I didn't know you could read," one of the others chuckled.

"We should do the last floor and return to the plaza. Prince Maveth needs the space to be completely clear before he arrives with Jubanic in tow." A sigh from the man nearest him prompted a flurry of nods.

"Yeah, you're right. We shouldn't rush, though—it is quite likely that we will find some imps hiding upstairs." The men made their way toward the stairs, causing the youngest among them to sigh.

"Are the elevators still not working?" he asked.

"Last time I checked, I think the alarm system deactivated them."

As the intruders cautiously ascended the winding spiral staircase, the young one broke the silence again.

"What do you think they are going to do to that royal family?" A series of dirty looks from his comrades communicated their displeasure with his reckless mouth, and the boy understood that any more words would result in blows.

However, as they slowly cleared the top floor without incident, their tension died down, and the young footman's question wormed its way into all of their minds.

"I am not sure what Maveth is going to do when he gets here," the group leader finally let out, declaring an end to their forced silence.

The rest of the rebels lowered their rifles and tentatively resumed their search with less professionalism. They had crossed the bulk of the floor without a sound and were fairly certain that no one was hiding on it.

"There were children with them. You don't think that Maveth will…" the young one asked aloud.

"Tough luck for them if he does," the largest of the group quipped, turning a table and finding a horrified desk worker cowering beneath it.

"I got one," he said, casually drawing his curved blade and pulling a homely woman to her feet.

"It's a woman," the young one said.

"Yes, and?"

The captive squealed in horror and begged incoherently as he put the scimitar to her torso and began carving her open, but the young soldier gestured for him to stop.

"Why don't we keep some of them hostage like the royals? Perhaps she can tell us how to get into the tower?"

"Goliath ordered us to clear the building, not capture hostages for information. If Maveth wants to interrogate anyone, he'll have the giant do it," he said, and with a violent jerk, he finished his captive off.

The young man watched the gory episode unfold with obvious conflict written on his countenance.

The others did not appreciate his visual response. "What has gotten into you? You shot a man on the first floor. Have you lost your nerve already?" the big man said defensively.

"He could have been armed, and it seems different with…"

"With women? You cannot be so naïve! Women work for the Empire, too. Get used to the thought of killing them, boy, because you will probably have to…if you live long enough."

The big soldier squared off with his comrade as he spoke, but after a moment of distraction, the leader of the group threw a hand up, a motion that ended the arguing on the spot.

"Quiet down! Quiet! Do you hear that?" The leader gestured to the opposite wall, which shook slightly with a mechanical whirr before stopping suddenly with a thud. They heard a nearly identical, though slightly sharper sound coming from down the hallway.

"The elevator! Get back to the elevator!"

The four soldiers sped toward the top-floor elevator doors, where a single survivor, who had managed to elude their earlier search, used some kind of specialized key to awaken the slumbering platform while his hunters squabbled.

The doors slammed shut just in time to absorb a handful of light rounds from the attackers' rifles, and the whirring began once more, this time growing distant until it disappeared altogether.

"You two, finish the top floor! You, come with me!" Snatching the young man from the gaze of his associate, he nearly dragged the young soldier all the way to the bottom floor.

The duo could hear the rumble when they passed the bottom floor entrance, but rather than culminating in another thud and exposing its content, the mechanical platform continued descending until all traces of movements had vanished.

"We need to find the giant."

"Why now? Shouldn't we finish our orders first?"

"Not anymore. We have just discovered where most of the workers escaped. We may have also found the entrance to that tower. He will want to know."

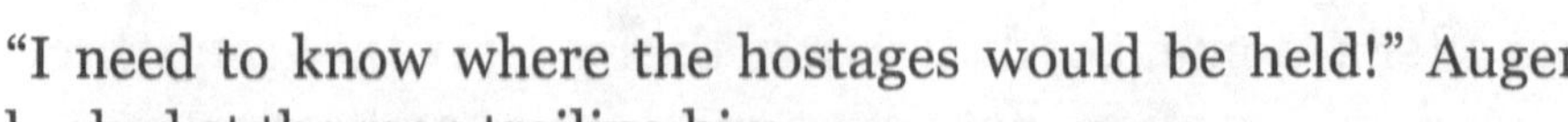

"I need to know where the hostages would be held!" Augen barked at the men trailing him.

The guards who tried to stay closest to the knight, including Basan, struggled to match his pace, striding across the dunes toward the fallen outpost and its likely doomed occupants.

A cynical focus emanated from the Templar's features. It appeared to his followers that the severity of his injuries did little to hinder his newfound drive to accomplish one more mission.

"If they are alive, they could be in any of the above-ground structures," one of the men answered, trying not to lose his breath in the process.

"I heard the invaders say something about keeping the Comm-Station in good shape," a different guard interjected. "It may be that they plan on holding the facility to ransom and broadcasting their demands to the public. If that is the case, and they have not yet accessed the lower floors, I would assume the hostages would be held there."

"What is on the lower floors?" Augen queried, tilting his head back just enough to read the physical reactions of the guards.

They squirmed slightly and exchanged brief, cautious glances with each other before answering his question. Augen noted this and assumed that a half-truth or lie would follow.

"Mostly storage containers, exhaust ports, and some mechanical hardware, nothing too special, but certainly expensive," the tallest of the guards finally responded after another tactful pause.

"If it is just a storage facility, why do you doubt their ability to reach it?" Augen questioned, convinced that they were hiding something. More squirming from most of the tired company confirmed his suspicions, but this time, the response was quick.

"Getting into the elevators would require a special key held by very few people on base. Almost every holder of such keys retreated into the basement the moment that the facility came under attack. It is unlikely that our assailants got hold of one."

The stormfront slowly began drifting away from the coastline as the wind picked up its tempo, growing so strong and consistent that the tiny troop along the beachfront struggled to keep their feet.

"Not now, Deos," Augen mumbled to himself as he watched his contingent stumble about behind him. For a moment, he considered leaving them behind, but he saw their struggle to assist and extended a hand to Basan instead.

"Grab each other's wrists! Form a train! Basan, take my hand!"

The guard hesitated but tentatively did as he was told. The others followed suit and in a matter of moments, the men following Augen had formed a small train of soldiery headed up by him, and like a locomotive, he tugged the troop off the beachfront and all the way back to their base with his good hand.

After some marching, a shout from a follower bid Augen to abandon the beachfront and begin up a nearby hill. When the marching caravan finally spotted their target, Augen eased his grip and paused, trying briefly to catch his breath and gather his wits. The establishment sat nestled among a cluster of dull hills, which provided little protection save limiting the station's visibility from a distance. Bunches of dry coarse brush had gathered around the area, rooted to the soil and unmoved by the wind. Augen recognized that, with a little luck, reaching their destination unnoticed by the raiders would be relatively easy.

"I see him! I see the giant!" one of the guards exclaimed to Augen, pointing at the plaza that sat amid a group of cubic buildings and some kind of strange tower.

Augen tried to match the man's vision and caught sight of the colossus strutting through the courtyard.

The "giant" they spoke of was the same man who had nearly killed him twice in Barbasul, the same man he could not defeat with a full suit of armor and two working hands. Augen could claim neither advantage now, and though it seemed that the monstrous rogue never recovered his second sword from their rooftop dual, he knew that if they came to blows, there would be no rescue this time.

Fighting the urge to look away, Augen pulled his followers into a tiny rocky crevice lined with the brown underbrush. The men crouched behind a particularly large water-stained boulder. Their leader kept his eyes on the colossal foe, knowing that he had to come up with a plan if he was to save anyone at all.

"Where is Maveth?" he muttered to himself as his rival ordered men about in the shallow canyon ahead. The drones were not present either. Was Goliath working on his own now? Either way, Augen knew he would have to bypass his horrible foe for as long as possible if they were to see any success.

"I think the hostages are in there," one of the guards whispered to Augen, pointing toward a building near the corner of the plaza. The entrance was closed, and the few exposed windows were dark and thin, but several rebels hovered near the entrance as though they were told not to leave its immediate vicinity.

"They are certainly guarding something in there."

❖

"What are we going to do?" Catherine whispered to her husband as the killers surrounding them briefly turned their backs.

The girls huddled behind her, the youngest ones crying silently, and despite her mental fortitude, Catherine fought the urge to join them.

Alexander motioned for her to wait a moment while he desperately tried to conjure a plan. The room's long-distance radios buzzed and whined to life as a number of the invaders attempted to harness the machine's power.

"I think we have it!" one of them announced excitedly to his partner.

"Good. Contact the prince." More whirring sounds followed, and the men standing over the hostages drifted away from their objective to watch. Alexander shifted himself subtly toward his wife and leaned in to her ear.

"I am afraid I may know who we are dealing with, and if my hunch is correct, we are lucky to be alive as it is. We need to wait for an opportunity to arise before we make any aggressive moves."

"Stop talking!" one of the rebels yelled over his shoulder. Alexander spun back around, dropped to his knees, and groveled like a coward to the man confronting him.

"Please, sir! I am extremely wealthy and can provide your master with a great ransom! If only you would spare us. Please! I am innocent! We were simply traveling through when..."

"I said, be quiet!" A blow to the face interrupted his pathetic cringing, and Alexander spun with the blow to face Catherine.

He met her confused stare, and the ridiculous facade of his cowardice disappeared into a stoic half-smile.

"What are you..."

"Shhhh..." he whispered, putting his finger to his mouth.

Another blow, this one striking a flaw on his torso, brought a more genuine reaction, but Alexander kept his eyes locked on his family. They all watched him questioningly, but he had already formulated a plan.

"Any more noise out of you and it will be far worse," the intruder growled before returning to the console to assist his associates. "Some nobleman," he muttered to an associate. "You would think a man of his size would have more fight in him."

Alexander took Catherine's hand and smiled, speaking as quickly and quietly as he could.

"I am feigning weakness. When I engage, move the girls to the back corner."

The door slammed open, and two more intruders, one with a surprisingly well-kept uniform and the other quite young for a soldier, burst into the room.

"I am sorry, sirs!" Alexander squealed to no response from the rebels, who were now distracted by the late arrivals.

"Where is Goliath?" the older newcomer inquired, briefly scanning the room and noting his absence.

"You should have passed him in the plaza," the rebel nearest the captives noted.

"We didn't see him," the young one responded.

The well-dressed soldier, who appeared to outrank his compatriots, nodded to the young man accompanying him and gestured to the door. The youth nodded back and took his leave to search for the missing knight.

The radio's ambient scratching was contorted into a consistent hum by its users.

"Prince Maveth! Do you read?" Initially, all eyes, including those of the hostages, were locked onto the radio. When a voice crackled into focus on the other side, Alexander's heart skipped a beat.

"It is him," he whispered to Catherine.

"Who?"

"The man behind the wars in the ancient world. Wait for my signal. We may have less time than I thought."

A sharp stare from the nearest guard silenced the couple, but this time, the silence alone did not appease him. "I told you, no more whispering! Do not make me separate you from your children! They may not fare very well on their own!"

Catherine gasped aloud and withdrew from her husband, but her face grew a fiery red.

"You would dare harm the children? You would need to kill me first!"

"That could be arranged!" the guard responded, drawing slightly closer to his captives.

Alexander tried to continue acting pathetic, but when the man drew to approach his family, his blood boiled, and he fought the urge to lash out. He knew that to maximize their chances of success, he needed to wait for the best possible moment to strike. Yet, with the slight encroachment of his captor and the nature of his threat, he understood that such a time might be running short.

Trying his best to maintain his docile facade, Alexander drew a quick breath, preparing to lunge into the man's body with all the force he could muster. His shaking hands tensed, and his fingers tingled with an intense adrenaline-fueled shock.

Though he was out of practice, the various martial arts he learned in his youth, paired with the element of surprise, would likely be enough to overwhelm the distracted terrorists, especially if he could get hold of one of their weapons immediately.

"Enough!" the well-dressed soldier barked to his compatriot. "Goliath ordered that we leave them alive, and unless the prince says otherwise, you would be wise to obey. Unless you wish to cross Goliath?"

The words must have struck a chord in the guard's mind, for he hastily withdrew, postponing Alexander's attack, but the man's furious visage and focused stare declared the end of further communication between the hostage family's members.

With everyone in the room silenced, the prince's frustrated voice ringing through the machine was all that could be heard.

"The drones and their pilots cannot handle this cursed wind, so for the moment, we remain grounded. When the weather dies down, we will be minutes away. What is the situation on your end?"

The rebels looked at each other nervously, each seemingly wondering who could summon the most appropriate response, until the sharp-looking newcomer finally stepped forward.

"The base is all but cleared out. We have a handful of stragglers who took refuge below the base in some kind of underground bunker, but your landing zone is clear. We have also acquired..."

"What is this bunker you speak of? And where is Goliath?"

Initially, another uncomfortable pause took hold of the rebel group, but the young soldier sent to find the giant jogged back into the room, sweaty and winded, almost immediately after Maveth's request. He shook his head when his eyes met theirs.

"Goliath is not in the plaza, and I could not find anyone who saw where he went."

"He is nine feet tall without his helmet! He could not have just slipped away!" the man working the radio snapped before spinning back and cautiously formulating his response for Maveth.

"Goliath seems to be occupied at the moment. We are not too sure where he is. The bunker is no threat to us, just some kind of reinforced cellar a few lucky workers have locked themselves into."

No response came, and the man in charge took advantage of the silence.

"Get back out there and find Goliath! You two, accompany him!"

"What about the hostages?"

"What about them? They are soft, spoiled nobles, hardly worth two guards. Just keep your distance and pay attention to them until you get further orders."

As the men poured from the building, no one caught Alexander cracking a subtle smile at his family. *Wait for me,* he mouthed to them.

This was the moment he had been waiting for. Only three captors, with two of them distracted by the machinery, was as good a chance as he could hope for. All he had to do now was wait for a moment to allow the men to clear the plaza and then...

"I am in the air and will be down shortly with the package. Have the machine prepared for broadcast." Maveth's voice echoed through the room, but before the uniformed lieutenant could respond, the plaza outside burst into chaos, gunfire, and yelling.

CHAPTER 19

DEALING WITH THE DEVIL

Augen's initial plan was to storm the plaza with all the speed and force his men could muster, in hopes of throwing the invaders into disarray. Such a strategy had merit, for the outpost was nestled within a pocket of the semi-mountainous landscape and received only a tiny bite of the otherwise crippling winds.

However, after further deliberation, he decided on a different approach, one that more closely resembled his efforts in Eris Port regarding the leather cannons. The guards would be split into pairs and maneuver behind various chokepoints of cover, creating a short chain of guarded checkpoints all the way to the shallow valley in which they currently resided. This mission was an extraction, not an invasion, and if the plan worked as Augen wished, he would be the only one to enter the plaza or any of the other buildings. He would bear the greatest risks and likely be the only casualty.

The guards understood the plan surprisingly well, requiring nearly no explanation and quickly moving into their spaces without being spotted by the marauders below. Augen's confidence was further bolstered when Goliath suddenly strode from his space in the center of the plaza to the hills opposite them, disappearing over the crest of one without ever looking back.

Such behavior was suspicious, but Augen chose not to ponder it. Instead, he took it as a sign that perhaps things may work out for him, at least regarding the success of his rescue mission.

There was certainly no better time to strike, so with his tiny crew in position, he slid down the hillside and crept toward the communication building. He had nearly reached the closest wall when he was finally spotted. A yell arose from within the plaza, and Augen's men responded accordingly, unleashing a hail of gunfire toward the man unfortunate enough to draw attention to himself.

Most of the lead missed their targets altogether, in part because of the firearms' designs and partially because of their inexperienced handlers. The few rounds that managed to land were ineffective, striking the center mass in well-armored areas or lightly grazing the wearers' limbs, leaving them physically unaffected.

However, the ear-bursting pops of the incoming gunfire shocked the soldiers in the plaza. The sound of each shot echoed across the shallow valley several times over, concealing the locations of the shooters and making the tiny ambush party sound considerably larger than it was.

Because of this, several of the rebels in the plaza dropped their weapons in panic, fleeing into the nearest building without a fight.

Many of the raiders found cover, but several of them faced the wrong way, convinced that the outpost was surrounded and firing at anything their startled brains thought could be an attacker, even when such phantoms were in the hills opposite their enemies.

The more level-headed of the rebels finally managed to return fire, but they too were unable to hit any of their concealed targets, and while their eyes were drawn to the hill, several of them did not even comprehend the knight barreling at them from their flank until he was far too close for them to do anything about it.

Fighting a group of men with only one arm quickly proved difficult and awkward, and Augen found himself unable to be as aggressive as he was accustomed to.

But even without the use of his left arm, the Templar overwhelmed his distracted targets without any dangerous injury, sheathing his dagger and switching it out for one of his fallen foes' scimitars and a sidearm that he tucked into his belt. He would be unable to reload the handgun once its ammo bar was emptied, but some kind of ranged capacity could certainly come in handy, especially if Goliath returned.

The building he wished to enter echoed with a brief flurry of gunfire from within, and a child's scream followed. *Confirmation enough for me,* he thought, kicking the door off its weak hinges and clearing the room as quickly as he could. It was surprisingly easy since no rebel in the room was alive by the time he entered.

A noblewoman stood in the corner of the room with four terrified girls huddled behind her. All five of them gasped at the newcomer.

"Stay back!" the mother exclaimed, drawing a large, curved sword from a rebel corpse.

Augen smirked and held up his working hand, initially because he found her resistance quaint, but also because he had two rifles trained on his flank.

"I am here to help," he said as calmly as he could. The large noble with the guns, presumably the lady's husband, scoffed.

"I know what prisoners' garb looks like. Your jacket fools nobody," he said, nodding for the girls to get behind him.

"I am not a mercenary, and I am not with the men who attacked you. I do not have the time to explain, but we have to go!"

"Girls, move behind me! Catherine, pull the small, red key from the slit in the comm station."

Augen's heart began to race as he watched the man's orders play out in front of him. The gunfire in the plaza was intensifying and growing coordinated. He knew that the element of surprise was all but spent for the men fighting for him outside. *This was supposed to be fast!*

"You do not understand," Augen began. "I am trying to help you!"

"Do you have the key?" the noble inquired flatly of his wife without taking his eyes off his target. It was apparent that he had no plans to come along peacefully. The man was quite large and seemed very capable of handling himself and his firearms. His chest was bleeding in three places, though none was bleeding heavily enough to be fatal. Augen wondered if the man had begun an augmentation.

"Yes, I have it," the lady answered hastily.

"It is a good thing those terrorists know so little about our machines. That access key would have gotten them downstairs. Put it on my belt," the nobleman chuckled, wincing slightly at his wounds and visibly contemplating what he would do to Augen.

The man's glare had a menace about it, but nothing brought more discomfort to the Templar than the familiar roar of incoming drones.

They could be reinforcements, Augen initially thought, but deep inside, he feared he knew who was coming, and it would not end well for any of them if they stuck around any longer.

Augen shifted his weight, considering the prospect of rushing the man and trying to take them all outside by force, but with only a single functioning arm to use in close combat, he was certain that even if successful, he would be shot several times in the process.

"We are out of time! I am here to help you!"

"Close your eyes again, girls," the noble said to his daughters before raising the firearms' barrels to shoot for the head rather than the torso.

Augen had less than a second to plead his case. "I am a condemned Templar, traveling to my execution in Eros for failure on the field, and by the grace of Deos, I was marooned here, where I may possibly atone for my mistakes. Even if it means death for me, know there are guards behind this building ready to take you away from the battlefield."

Augen's pride was hurt when he confessed his reality aloud, but that very pain may have finally gotten through to the people he was trying to rescue. The lady, who had been studiously observing his body language since she turned over the key to her husband, leaned in to his ear and whispered something that extinguished his resolve and lowered his rifle.

"You are sure?" he whispered back, considerably louder, seemingly unaware that he now had to compensate for the roaring drone engines outside. A nod from the lady and the man tentatively yielded.

"Where are we going, then?" he finally asked, eyeing the Templar with caution but keeping his weapons down.

"The men accompanying me have created a passage to the coast. If we can reach them in time, you should have a straight shot out of here!" Taking a hasty glance out the door, Augen spotted the three drones hovering overhead, seemingly unwilling to land in the weather conditions presented to them. His hopes that this convenience would grant them passage to safety were dashed to bits when a heavy round careened inches past his head and punched a hole in the wall beside him.

"Can that back window open?" Augen asked, ducking away from the door to prevent another such attempt on his life.

The noble answered by firing one of his rifles into the thick window pane and shattering it.

"Catherine, step out first and get ready to grab the girls. I will help them through." The lady hastily did what he asked, and Augen flinched when the lord stepped between the girls and him, raising his rifle once more to the knight's midsection.

"You will go last," he commanded bluntly.

"I was not expecting any different," he responded, putting up his sword-hand while he spoke. The noble began passing his children through the window and into the waiting arms of their mother, a handful of feet below.

"It will be faster if I can help," Augen said in frustration.

"I know your kind. Your efficiency is outdone only by your pragmatism. You were created to be killers and survivors, so I apologize for not caring about your survival as much as you seem to."

As he passed the last girl through the window, the lady below yelled up to her husband.

"We are clear!"

Augen smiled slightly upon hearing it and hastily responded.

"My men are on the hill! They are expecting you! Go up to them and follow the path!"

The noble glanced outside, and after watching his family run to a pair of guards waving for them to come, nodded his thanks to the Templar and stepped onto the windowsill, preparing to jump. But footsteps and yelling came from outside the door opposite, and Augen turned to see two rebels charge into the room.

"Run!" he yelled over his shoulder before turning and cutting down the pair as they tried too late to raise their weapons.

The next trio to enter was far better prepared, with the first having already drawn his hand weapons in hopes of buying time for his partners to get clean shots on Augen.

But they came in too close to each other, and rather than buying time for his comrades, he was thrown in their way and accidentally shot in the back. When his body dropped, the two remaining soldiers were quick to follow, for the second-long clearing granted by their friendly fire was exploited by a dual-wielding nobleman who put one down on the spot with his right hand and disabled the other with his left.

"I said run!" Augen yelled to the man behind him. The noble stepped back onto the window frame and gestured for him to join.

"My family just crested the hill. It is time for us to join them! Both of us!" he yelled.

Augen was taken aback by his change in tone, but the gratefulness expressed on the noble's face explained enough. He quickly strode toward the window, but a voice from the doorway stopped him dead in his tracks.

"Are you looking for this?" A cloaked figure in expensive armor strode through the door holding a whimpering King Jubanic in front of him. Maveth Shedim's face was covered by the same cowl he wore in Barbasul, but Augen could sense a sinister smile beneath the visor. The rebel leader shook his head in amazement.

"Where is your left arm? You could not possibly be the same knight I sent Goliath to dispatch in Barbasul. You don't happen to know where he is, perchance?" A long pause ensued, and the rebel chuckled to himself.

Augen slowly backed toward the window but paused again when the noble glanced outside and stumbled into the room, narrowly dodging a handful of light rounds flying at him from behind the building. They were surrounded, and Maveth clearly knew it.

"You know, the craziest thing happened to me on the way over here. I arrive by air with my quarry, despite the confounded wind, just to witness the mayhem below.

"My knight is nowhere to be found, and some hotshot has cut his way through my men and into the very room I need to use, freeing the hostages my men claimed to have taken, and in the process, possibly damaging the machine I need to use.

"By this point, I am contemplating a total abortion of the mission. A turn-and-burn if you will."

As the exiled prince spoke, Augen heard yelling from the hillside where his men once waited, and seconds later, the entire exit route he and the guards had established erupted into a flaming netherworld of heated phosphorus as Maveth's Hydra-Class Drone unleashed its fiery payload into the resistance below.

The unnatural light of the reaction illuminated the room with a hellish burnt-orange hue, and the heat was so intense that the rebels shooting at the nobleman from the back side of the building burst into flames without direct contact with the liquid fire.

Clearly not expecting the reaction to be so intense, Maveth flinched as the heat, light, and sound of the screaming metal flew into the structure through every crevice and hole. Augen did the same, remembering when his division of men faced the same hellish fate.

The short burst of agonized howling from the rebels outside drew a visible emotional reaction from Maveth, who mumbled something about the wind to himself before snapping back to business.

"Then, out of nowhere," he continued, mostly concealing the frustration in his tone, "I get a tip from a reliable source that the nobleman behind you is far more valuable than the one I currently hold. I am told that between the public deaths of him and his wife, I can change the face of Archaea's political landscape forever!"

Augen and the nobleman exchanged glances, and the man raised his guns toward Maveth.

"I don't know who you think I am, but my wife did not come with me to the base, and if you touch her or our children..."

"If it is any comfort at all, I have no interest in your children. Consider them already safe from my touch," Maveth shot back, pulling his hostage closer to his body so that a clean shot would be impossible. The king whimpered and provided no resistance.

"But, Templar," Maveth continued, "you have the opportunity to make a deal here that could get you your life back. This pig here has gravely wronged me, but if you help me take the man behind you, alive ideally, I can give this sniveling peon to you and let you both walk out of here untouched."

A sharp moment of silence pierced the room. Augen could hear the footsteps of enemy combatants arriving at the door, but Maveth commanded in his native tongue for them to stop, and the encroaching soldiers did as they were told.

This pause led the noble to panic, backing into the corner and adjusting his second rifle to aim at Augen again. Augen turned his head slightly so that his eyes could meet the noble's, but he made no other move.

"Who are you anyway?" he inquired gently.

The noble spat out his answer in a panic.

"I am no one of consequence!" he shouted at Augen before addressing Maveth. "And killing me will change nothing! The Golden Empire is greater than any one man...or king!" The noble aimed at King Jubanic, who squealed aloud and soiled himself, and pointed his second firearm toward his own head.

"Wait," Augen said, leading all in the room to pause. The Templar slowly turned his head all the way to face the noble.

"I do not know who you are within the government, and I do not care. I came here to protect a family man, and that is all you are to me."

The room filled with smoke from the hill, but the horrific heat was already dying out, with only the phosphorus itself still aflame and everything else absorbed by the soil. The Templar leaned in just enough to speak quietly to the noble, who stared back in stunned silence.

"If you survive, please honor that part of yourself, for my sake. Not everyone can have such a privilege. Now, get to the basement. You will have only a couple of seconds!"

The noble had no chance to respond, for Augen did not wait for a response. He leaped from the ground with all his might, clearing the distance between Maveth's hostage and himself and kicking the captive king into his captor with both legs.

With only one arm to use, Augen's physical stunt cost him, for he was unable to recover midair and had to land on his back and roll over to return to his feet. However, the impact flung Maveth and his captive into the back wall, and the sword the rebel held to Jubanic's back ran the cowardly politician nearly completely through.

As the prince and his prize tumbled from the door, the rebels awaiting them outside pulled their sights from the building's entrance, unwilling to risk shooting their leader or the package he held.

This moment of hesitation saved the life of Maveth's attacker, for once the one-armed Templar was on his feet, he showed no such hesitation but barreled from the doorway with a sword in hand and death on his mind.

By the time Maveth threw his bloody captive off and rose to his feet, the crazed Templar had stepped over them both and thrown himself into the ranks of the prince's men.

"Quickly!" Maveth yelled to several soldiers who stood near the landed drone he had arrived in. "Patch Jubanic up! We need him alive!"

Despite the chaos erupting in the background, several invaders lowered their rifles and did as they were told, running to the wounded puppet-king and dragging him back to the craft storing their extra equipment.

Those outside Augen's melee were unable to get a clean shot, for the Templar could not slay his foes efficiently enough to create an opening where he stood alone. Instead, the knight resorted to pushing, kicking, and throwing many of them around while his blade slowly did more permanent work on their numbers.

Unbeknownst to most inside the plaza, another man darted from behind the communication building toward the doors of the Central HQ with two rifles in hand and a key to the basement on his belt.

Augen's blind, suicidal fury dulled when the first clean shot punctured his lower torso.

Independently, the wound was unlikely to be fatal, but more stinging impacts quickly followed as the men he fought hand to hand became less numerous. Next, his working arm felt a sting, then a bullet lightly skimmed his neck, missing arteries and his spine but causing dramatic bleeding regardless.

His hand gripped his sword with such intensity that his muscles cramped and his limb grew rigid, making the prospect of drawing his sidearm or throwing his blade impossible.

When the fourth and fifth rounds put holes in his central torso and right shoulder, his mind began to panic, and he stumbled backward into the headquarters wall, irrationally hoping that the nearest structure would provide him cover and slow the coming of more wounds.

The surviving insurgents unlucky enough to face Augen's initial onslaught had finally cleared out and gained enough distance from him to avoid hindering those trying to shoot their attacker.

However, the rebels ceased their fire for a moment as their target tried to lean on his scimitar, clumsily snapping the blade in two, and collapsing onto the brick pavement instead.

Maveth also took a moment to observe, wondering aloud if Goliath would have taken such a beating before finally dropping. When the spectacle appeared to be over, he returned to the comms station, pulling several of his underlings with him.

The knight was visibly breathing but did not move, and most of the rebels exhaled slowly, turning to resume their previous business as the second drone finally landed and began unloading their now much-needed reinforcements.

A furious howl emerged from the comms center, and all eyes flew to Maveth as he emerged once more, cursing the interfering Templar, as well as himself for saying too much.

Before the second captive escaped through the window, he had taken the time to introduce the fragile radio equipment to the butt ends of his rifles, reducing the vital machines to a smoking heap of scrap metal and sparks.

"Stop staring and kill the..." Maveth paused mid-rant, unable for a moment to believe his eyes, before finishing his sentence with even more rage. "Kill him quickly! Before he gets away!"

The soldiers paused, too, gathering their wits with slack jaws as they beheld a knight, riddled with bullets, stumbling through the doors of Central Headquarters, before raising their firearms in tandem to finish the job.

Augen felt nothing and saw little, just blurs of black, grey, or red, with a vague sense of shape and distance remaining functional inside his mind, even if only in the abstract sense. His training and instinct for survival had miraculously carried him into cover, not that he was capable of doing anything useful with it.

The scimitar he used moments ago on his enemies was crudely broken but remained stuck to his hand regardless, for even if his mind could compute the pointlessness of a broken sword, he had quite forgotten how to drop it.

Instead, he meandered into the dark room with no specific purpose in mind, unaware of his enemies or friends, seeing instead the moments of regret his life had endured.

When a chaotic torrent of lead blew through the doors of the building, shattering them like glass, the knight would have been shattered too had it not been for an already broken nobleman who had taken his time getting into the elevator so he could dose up.

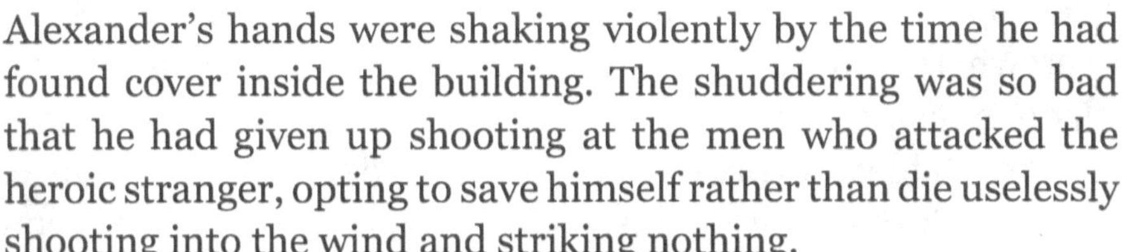

Alexander's hands were shaking violently by the time he had found cover inside the building. The shuddering was so bad that he had given up shooting at the men who attacked the heroic stranger, opting to save himself rather than die uselessly shooting into the wind and striking nothing.

The wounds his body had sustained, paired with the dose of natural adrenaline, struck him with a violent urge for more powerful chemicals.

The withdrawal struck him with such force that it took him four attempts to fit the key into the elevator lock. When the doors finally slid open, the gunfire had died down, and Alexander assumed the battle was finished.

Believing himself to be relatively safe, Alexander slid into the back wall of the elevator, dropped his guns, and pulled a vial from his pocket, biting its tip and revealing its needle so that he could inject its contents into his neck.

I am sure that Catherine and the girls are safe, he silently told himself, unwilling to contemplate the alternative.

He had watched them crest the hill nearly a full minute before the Hydra engulfed it in flame. *They have to be safe!* he thought. *They must be safe!* The words in his mind continued to repeat themselves like a broken recording, but a tiny whisper of doubt rendered the forced words of his internal dialogue irrelevant.

He had to escape from both the pain streaking across his body in waves and the thoughts denying him his hope, and by some master stroke of luck or fate, he had the means to do it hidden in his jacket pocket for the duration of the trip.

Rather than tapping the lever to close the elevator doors, Alexander sat in the back, slowly controlling his breathing and raising the needle to inject himself. *Deos can forgive me later, and so can Nathan and Catherine.*

Then, out of nowhere, the strange knight who saved him and his family stumbled into the building, bleeding everywhere, muttering to himself, and clutching a broken blade in his working hand.

The sudden surprise shocked Alexander out of his trance. Another dose of adrenaline pumped through his veins upon the sight of the violent spectacle, granting him another touch of clarity even without the drugs.

"Kill him quickly! Before he gets away!" a voice rang into the room from outside, and Alexander did not hesitate to deny the voice its satisfaction.

Dropping the vial and leaping to his feet, Alexander flew toward the staggering hero and tackled him just before the room erupted in a whirlwind of lead and fire.

The chaos was horrific, but the sensory overload Alexander's drug-diluted body would have felt under normal circumstances came across as a cold focus instead. His breathing stabilized on its own, and in a matter of minutes, both men were inside the waiting elevator, untouched by the deadly foray.

A pause in the barrage allowed Alexander's ears to take in other noises under the pitched whining of damaged eardrums.

He could hear the knight's silent rambling with slightly more detail, something about killing people and Impact Day, and he put together that the knight may have personally experienced the horrific occasion.

Something else interrupted the sadness he felt contemplating such things.

Within the building, he heard a second voice coming from beneath a pile of rubble. A rebel soldier, the young one who was sent by his dead superior to fetch the giant, was still inside the room when his leader ordered a barrage upon it. Ironically, it seemed as though he was the only one struck by the volleys and now lay under a fallen shelf with numerous bullet wounds in his lower body.

"Help," he muttered to no one in particular. Alexander picked up one of his rifles and took aim at the boy's head.

"This is for terrorizing my family," he responded. In a moment of strange clarity, the knight grabbed his hand and pulled the barrel down.

"No more," he said in a pained whisper. The emperor began to pull away, but with his next words, the dying knight convinced him to reconsider.

"No more dead children," the Templar repeated. Alexander glanced back toward his target, but after a moment of eye contact and a frustrated growl, he capitulated.

"You should find some new friends, kid," the nobleman said, kicking away a piece of rubble that had fallen into the elevator's threshold during the onslaught. With the metal shard removed from its inconvenient resting place, the automatic doors impatiently slammed shut, sheltering its inhabitants from the soldiers who stormed the building seconds later.

When the platform finally began to move, he set his focus on the grisly, murmuring guardian who sat with his back to the wall. He had finally dropped his sword and now clutched a knife he had carried on his belt, staring at its cracked hilt like it was the face of a loved one.

Alexander tore off strips of his shirt to bandage the obvious sources of hemorrhaging on the knight's body. When that was finished, he checked the man's neck and free wrist for a pulse. It was slow, dangerously slow.

The vials! he thought, picking up the one left on the floor but pausing before he raised his arm to inject it. A voice in his head bid him pause.

Those are *yours*, the voice said. You are the emperor of the West! Do not waste your resources on this peasant! He did his job to protect you. You owe him nothing!

The elevator hummed melodramatically as Alexander wrestled with himself over the vial until the Templar dropped his knife and arm.

The consecutive thuds of their impact with the floor snapped Alexander out of his indecisiveness. "What am I doing? Willing to give up someone else's chance for life?" he exclaimed to himself, staring at the glass object in his hand. "For these?"

The thought of such dishonorable behavior dragged with it a torrent of self-loathing and rage, and the emperor knelt over the near-dead man sharing the elevator with him, a new resolve burning in his eyes.

I am the emperor, and I owe men like him everything, he responded to the shadow in his mind before injecting the vial into the soldier's chest. This might not work, but I do not care. I will give him a chance.

The elevator slowed to a stop, but the slight tremble of the room was the only movement Alexander picked up. The knight was still...his eyes were out of focus and partially closed...he looked dead.

"No!" Alexander yelled, preparing the second vial and violently administering its contents into the man's neck. No response.

As Alexander ripped the cap off his last vial, the elevator doors slid open on their own. A tiny sliver of hesitation pierced his chest before he could administer the drug.

This is your last chance, it warned, but Alexander smiled mockingly to himself and snickered, "Not mine, his."

With an angry grunt, he raised his hand to strike his chest again, but the knight's eyes shot open, and with a flash of drug-induced focus, the one-armed knight knocked the vial aside and grabbed Alexander's wrist before he could use it.

"Who are you?" he inquired aggressively.

Alexander sighed in relief, partially because the knight could not use his other hand to hit him, and dropped the last vial, never to pick it up again.

"My name is Alexander Oladita. You saved my life; I was returning the favor."

The knight sighed for a moment, too, apparently recollecting his recent past and spitting out a large spot of blood in the process. "Augen Di Gattchen and I remember. Thanks," he said with a hint of sarcasm on his breath and his free hand now clutching his bloody chest.

Alexander picked up the wounded soldier's knife and handed it to him. Initially, the knight was slow to respond, but a glance outside the elevator threw him into a panic.

"Pick up your weapons! We are not alone down here!" he said.

CHAPTER 20

THE PIT

Augen's body was in poor shape. It seemed that Alexander had been able to keep him alive with some kind of medicinal booster, and his heart pounded violently as a result. The wounds on his torso had been crudely mended but were far from innocuous, and though his body had already begun recovering, he needed to rest if he wanted to survive. But at the moment, rest was not an option.

Alexander had reacquired his firearms and fixed his sights on the hallway ahead. A loud clanging echoed through the steel and concrete catacombs, and both men jumped.

Corpses lined the dimly lit hallway before them. Those in the narrower chokepoints had been run through, while those in the wider spaces had been cleaved nearly in twain. Lost limbs were scattered about on the floor, and streams of blood gripped the concrete like the sprawling roots and vines of a creeper.

The storage facility was never the haven they hoped to reach, for it seemed Goliath had found a way into the basement without the need of an elevator. Those who descended into its halls hoping to avoid bloodshed found themselves at the mercy of a far more deadly foe than the ones they fled from.

"Is there a practical way out of here?" Augen queried as quietly as he could.

"We just used the only one I know of," Alexander answered. Another loud crash in the distance ripped the duo back to attention. The ruckus seemed to be farther away than its predecessor, but it confirmed in Augen's mind that the noises were not ambiance, but artificial. Goliath was almost certainly still down there with them, though it seemed at the moment that he was unaware of their presence.

"We need to move," Alexander whispered. "Can you walk?"

"Yes."

"Then we can still take cover below the engines. Perhaps, with a little luck, we can locate an exit by using one of the exhaust ports." Alexander slowly took the lead, but another echoing crash pulled Augen into the front.

"I will go first," the knight said, trying not to cough too loudly between breaths.

"The main complex is up ahead. That hall will likely be quickest."

"How do you know?"

"Most major structures built by the empire are spirals. The hallways are designed to allow for coming-and-going foot traffic to traverse entire walkways without blocking each other."

"Major structures? I thought this was a storage facility." Augen's quiet conversation, between suppressed coughing fits, began to sound like an interrogation, and Alexander appeared to notice.

"It is a storehouse...of sorts. I should lead. I know this facility better than you." Alexander quietly shifted himself ahead, but Augen caught his shoulder as he passed.

"What are you hiding?" the Templar asked bluntly. Alexander shrugged Augen's hand off but tentatively responded anyway as they continued.

"My job requires that I hide nearly everything from everyone. Few people live the kind of life I have to, and few know what I do. Perhaps that is why the terrorists want my head."

Augen paused his own train of thought to contemplate Alexander's response. The words themselves were clearly meant to be vague, yet something in his tone suggested they were still personal to him, as though he was telling the truth, even if it was nebulous.

"I meant about the building," Augen clarified with a sigh.

Had the circumstances been different, he may have allowed such conversation to continue, but he had vowed to himself that Alexander's life would be spared, which meant that he was on a job.

A final dark chime pulsed through the hallways, deeper and more distant than its predecessors, before giving way to complete silence.

Hoping that Goliath had concluded his work and left the way he came, the pair hastened their pace considerably, clearing the curved hallways before they finally reached the core of the facility, and it was far more than a mere storage structure.

The colossal underground fortress descended nearly ten stories deeper than the floor they stood on, creating one open balcony after another, each slightly overlapping its previous level, creating a nautilus spiral of concrete and steel.

In the perfect center of the open chasm loomed a metallic monolith that seemed to hang from the unseen ceiling like a behemothic steel bat.

"Beautiful, isn't she? If only my family had had the chance to see it," Alexander whispered as they began to descend.

Initially, Augen gave no response, staring blankly at the artificial obelisk before him, trying to compute what he was looking at.

The center of the spiral was so dark, he could not discern any meaningful details pertaining to its bottom floors or the abyss below it.

As Augen's eyes slowly adjusted to the unexpected distance and darkness, he observed a cobweb of thin steel scaffolds stretching out from the shadows to touch the obelisk's lower layers. He also saw giant rubber and steel veins caressing the tower's outer surface before disappearing inside through various portholes.

As he took all of this in, it came to him that the so-called basement was not a small feature in the outpost's design; these floors were the entire purpose of its existence.

"What is it?" Augen finally asked.

"It is the future of our world. The result of more than a decade of meticulous planning and work. Sadly, I believe we are now going to have to destroy this one later."

The mechanical endeavor and precise engineering were undeniably stunning indeed, but as Augen studied the dark, lifeless rooms, noting the corpse-littered floors and the blood-stained concrete below, he hoped that Alexander was wrong about his prediction for the future.

A tap on Augen's shoulder snapped him out of his thoughtful trance and pointed him downhill.

"Exhaust ports will be on the bottom floor."

The pair began their march down the spiral, but Augen froze suddenly and grabbed Alexander's arm.

"Do you hear that?" he inquired.

"Hear what?"

The two stood perfectly still, taking in the faint yet foreign sound as it echoed up the structure's frame. A deep, rhythmic thudding ascended the stairs, passing the travelers by and heralding an imminent threat. They were footsteps, heavy, fast, and approaching with unnerving speed. Augen moved just enough to stare into the spiral's center, where he witnessed the source of the sound.

"Run! Up the stairs!" he yelled to Alexander, pulling them both upward as hastily as possible.

Four stories below, Goliath, who had apparently discovered their presence, careened up the staircase toward them, a dark shadow with a single eye fixed upon his new quarry.

"The path upward is a dead end!" Alexander yelled, following Augen but pulling his arm away and trying to reload his rifles.

"We will have to find a way, for there will be no success in fighting."

Augen knew he was speaking the truth, but after only one floor of sprinting, his wounds returned to the center of his focus, and he realized that running may not be an option either, even if they discovered an exit on the top floor.

"Is there a way to enter the central spire from the top?" Augen wheezed, coughing up blood, and unwittingly slowed his pace to speak.

His chest and legs were in excruciating pain, and though the drugs Alexander had administered kept him moving, he was noticeably losing steam.

The duo finally reached the top floor, with Goliath less than a floor below and Alexander beginning to show visible panic. He took a knee and hastily finished loading his last heavy round into one of his rifles.

"No. There is only one way out, and it is below us," he finally answered, fixing his sights on the attacking giant and unleashing his rifle's fiery breath into his torso. A lucky shot may have struck a joint in his armor and done serious damage to its wearer, but it was not so lucky.

Goliath felt the impact of the round, but aside from a moment of hesitation and an annoyed growl, Alexander's last heavy slug did nothing to prevent the giant's imminent arrival. Augen grabbed the nobleman's shoulder and tried to pull his attention to the large tubes hanging just over their heads.

"Quickly! Grab a hose, and use my knife to cut its restraints! You can get to the center and climb down from there."

Alexander, who had fixated on his approaching killer, paid no mind, checking his ammo bars to gauge how many small shots he had left. Augen grabbed his shoulder again.

"It is useless! The light rounds could never puncture his armor! Your only chance is escape!"

Alexander glanced at Augen's extended hand and the blade it clutched. Despite the imminent danger, he hesitated, seemingly realizing that Augen had no plans for his own survival. Hoping to ease his conscience, the knight flashed a weak smile. "Go find your family. I will be fine," he finished, hoping to dispatch the noble's resolve to fight to the death. While Augen found his own words unconvincing, they seemed to accomplish his mission. Alexander dropped a gun to free up his hand, but pushed the knife away.

"I will not need it," he said. Then he sprang over the nearest guardrail and off the ledge.

Using his gun as the crude handle of a makeshift zip line, Alexander rode the rubbery but taut fuel lines into the darkness and away from danger.

The restraints, which were not made to survive blunt impact, snapped apart when he struck them, hindering but never halting his trajectory until he finally found himself clinging to the outer layer of the chasm's central monolith.

Augen observed this with slight relief before turning to face Goliath, who now stood mere feet from him, watching Alexander make his escape.

"It seems that you made a real problem for my employer," he said coldly. Augen hesitated, unsure of how to respond and wondering why he was not already dead. As Alexander began his slow descent, the giant watched with amusement, visibly confident that he would meet the noble at the bottom of the obelisk without issue.

"He contacted me as I made my exit. He is convinced that you are the same knight I fought in Barbasul, but that cannot possibly be true," he continued. "There is no chance that he would be so stupid as to pursue us again, and even less chance that he could find us if he did."

"Why am I still alive?" Augen asked flatly, uninterested in the conversation. Goliath said nothing but turned to stare into his eyes with his working one. Even below his visor, Augen read surprise in his body language.

"A death wish? So, you are the Templar I fought?" he practically gasped. "Well, that does change things," he said, slowly drawing his blade and rubbing its hilt in both hands.

Augen sighed and tried his best to give a measured response. "You have me now; you can tell your boss that you finished the job. Just let him go."

"I am afraid there is no bargaining here, at least regarding your new... friend. I have been ordered to take him alive and kill you, but if you are the Templar I dueled in Barbasul, I need to get some information out of you first. Pretty standard questions, I am sure you understand."

The rubbing motion he made on his weapon became faster and more erratic, as though he was breaking in the weapon's handle before trying to use it for the first time.

This, of course, was not why he did it. The movement was a psychological trick used by both the Templar and Teutonic Orders, an intimidation tactic that Augen understood but found himself unable to disregard.

His body was broken, and he wished for it all to end, but even then, he could not help but feel unease at the sound of the leather and mail grinding against the steel of Goliath's blade.

"Despite your infuriating persistence, I cannot help but admire your dedication to following orders, so if you answer my questions satisfactorily, I will promise you a hasty and painless death. Do not stall—I still have to capture your friend."

Augen remained quiet but slowly pulled his knife from its sheath and gazed at its hilt, wondering if Goliath would allow him to see Christine's picture once more.

Goliath clearly noticed the blade but did nothing except shoot him a warning glance. A moment of contemplation brought Augen to give up on such hopes and sheathe his weapon. Seeing this, the giant continued nonchalantly.

"How did you track us? And why did the Templar send you here without armor or reinforcements?" he queried. "Is it the drones? Is there something in their electronic modules that makes us traceable?" A moment of silence, and Augen chuckled.

"I doubt you will believe me if I tell you, but since you have been generous..." he said with another short snicker that felt a touch more like a scoff. As he contemplated the past few days of his life, he found himself struggling to believe the words even as he spoke them.

"I was dropped onto the island by chance and stumbled across your little operation purely out of circumstance. I never tracked you at all. I never wished to see any of you again."

As the words left Augen's mouth, Goliath squared off with his one-armed target, assuming that the wounded Templar was playing games and preparing to punish him for it.

Yet, once Augen said it aloud, something else came into his mind, the supposed circumstances of his last few months of life, the miracles, the visions, the prophecies, and at that moment of bleak silence, a small sliver of Augen's doubt was purged from his soul.

"Apparently, Deos has always had a plan for me, even as blood remains on my hands." Augen did not realize it, but a large smile had crept onto his face, not out of mockery or arrogance, but because he was thankful, for so much had happened even in his short life since Pallerheim.

Deos had His eye on him. Though he could not understand why, there was no doubt in his mind that it was true, and more than that, it was undeniable. This realization hit him with an invigorating intensity far outpacing any medication or drug he knew of.

Goliath slammed the pommel of his sword onto the handrail beside Augen, bending its frame. Clearly, he was not amused.

"Do not stall! My patience wears very thin! I can make your life end slowly without needing to stick around!"

What the towering butcher said was also true, and Augen acknowledged it even as the grave knight grabbed his coat collar and nearly heaved him from the ground with a single arm.

"I asked Deos to make my death mean something—perhaps that is why He let me live this long," Augen continued calmly. "You see, I was put here to give the man below us a second chance at life."

Slowly pulling the handgun from his belt, Augen offered the weapon to his opponent handle-first. His foe recognized the symbolic gesture of surrender, and with little hesitation, released Augen's collar to take the weapon. Despite his submissive posturing, the Templar was now free to move again, and Goliath's second hand was now full, so he finished his thought.

"That is why I was allowed here, and it is why you are not going to take him."

The effect of Augen's deceitful maneuver was short, but with unnatural speed, he took complete advantage of it. In a blink, Augen redrew his knife and plunged it into the crux of Goliath's right hip flexor. The armor was thin and jointed there, and though such a wound would not be fatal, the blade easily sank into Goliath's joint muscles, rendering the giant's lunging leg all but useless.

The rebel howled in fury and pain before matching Augen's speed, striking his foe with his left knee to stand him back up and knocking him away with a vicious headbutt.

Augen stumbled back from the blows with a newly broken nose. He was able to keep hold of his only remaining weapon, but narrowly avoided tumbling over from the impacts to his face. Wiping the blood pouring from his face, Augen stared down the barrel of his own pistol.

"No good deed..." Goliath quipped as he pulled the trigger. *Click. Click. Click.* The pistol's ammo bar was gone, pulled from the weapon's barrel as Augen surrendered it.

With a second furious scream, Goliath flung the firearm to the wayside and into the darkness below, but by the time he adjusted his sword for a deadly gore, Augen had already closed the distance again, catching the greatsword at its secondary parry hooks with the tiny blade, preventing an accurate thrust.

Enraged, the monstrous butcher swung his cleaver toward Augen's torso a second time, then a third and fourth, willing the fierce weapon to run its target through and spill his guts as it had so many others, but the two combatants were far too close together for Goliath's zweihänder to work as it was made to.

In Augen's sudden bout of supernatural clarity, he saw himself parrying each assault even before the blows were initiated; he saw the angle of his enemy's blade, the exact target on his body for each dangerous foray to puncture, and precisely where he needed to counterstrike to render them irrelevant.

The greatsword was parried in one direction, then another, with its already off-balance wielder growing more enraged and awkward with every attack.

Such disorderly assaults played to Augen's advantage, allowing him numerous opportunities to strike back; however, with each of his cuts, it became increasingly obvious that a killing blow would be nearly impossible.

The brigandine armor Goliath wore was more than enough to deflect light-grazing blows and even posed the threat of catching Augen's blade and ripping it from his hand if he stabbed too haphazardly. Goliath's helmet, visor, and pauldrons were all but untouchable, and even with Augen's temporary positional advantage, his opponent proved more than capable of preventing any truly dangerous cuts.

In a moment of incensed aggression, the behemoth swung his cleaver horizontally with enough force to tear half a dozen men into perfect halves. The blade whistled uselessly into the concrete wall, splitting a small cooling pipe, which spewed strange gases into the air, but missing its intended target altogether. Augen took the moment of exposure to close in on his foe again, plunging the knife into Goliath's lower thigh just inches above his right knee.

Another scream from the giant heralded a crippling blow to Augen's back as Goliath also took advantage of his foe's overreach, driving the pommel of his sword into Augen's spine and breaking at least one rib in the process. The air in Augen's lungs disappeared, and for a moment, it felt as though it would never return. He was able to withdraw his blade again, but was lucky to accomplish even that.

Goliath was still too close to his opponent to effectively stab him, so instead of awkwardly trying to angle his weapon correctly for another clumsy maneuver, he took the moment of opportunity to create distance between himself and his foe, grabbing Augen with his left hand and flinging him down the walkway like a ragdoll.

The duel would have been over in that moment had circumstances been different, for with his newly acquired space, Goliath now had complete control of the fight's logistics and could have beheaded his opponent with a single well-timed swing before he could regain his footing.

Ironically, Augen was not the only one without footing. For though the Templar was dangerously slow to recover from the blow to his ribs, Goliath underestimated the damage his right leg had sustained and nearly fell flat on his face after his first advancing step. Both men were left using the handrails to slowly regain their balance.

Despite the temporary providence, Augen knew that the advantage was no longer his own, and it would not be long before the titan could adjust his fighting style and compensate for his new wounds. Augen was still left with only one functioning arm and a dagger; there was no true adjustment available to remedy either one.

"What are you hiding?" Goliath snarled, stumbling to his feet and slowly shuffling toward Augen, who retreated backward at the same pace. "You really are willing to give up your life for a stranger? What do you know about him that I do not?" Augen was taken aback by Goliath's sudden desire to talk again, but took it as an opportunity to catch some air.

"I do not know anything about him," he gasped, slowly trying to control his breathing and bring it back into equilibrium. "However, we both ended up here for a reason, and I would have done the same thing had it been somebody else."

"You lie!" Goliath growled, adjusting his blade and standing upright once more.

A glance at his rear flank and Augen noted that he had nearly reached the end of the spiral. A raised mechanical bridge to his left seemed to lead into the obelisk, but he had neither the time nor the knowledge of how to lower it. He was running out of space. *Alexander has an excellent head start now*, he thought. *I certainly hope that is enough.*

Goliath took a deep breath and tentatively limped forward, with each step growing slightly larger and more confident. Augen had a feeling the fight was over for him. He could try to get behind his enemy and continue stalling him from below, but recognized that was all it would be, stalling, delaying the inevitable. Augen's legs were wounded, too, and the medication Alexander had put him on was already fading.

A tube similar to the one Alexander had used to swing away now hung just a couple of feet above Augen's head. For a moment, he considered trying to follow Alexander's path, but recognized that even if Goliath did not catch him as he tried to clear the rails, he would likely be unable to scale the wall of the obelisk with only a single working arm and two wounded legs.

He looked longingly at the flexible cylinder as it passed, but another moment of clarity struck him, and he realized: If he could not escape or kill Goliath, he could at least buy Alexander and his family one more moment of respite.

The tube certainly had liquid running through it—he could hear it moving through the hoses when he passed under them—and perhaps, if he timed it correctly...

"I have decided that you are telling the truth," Goliath finally sighed, letting go of the handrail and raising his blade once more. "...at least, that is what I will tell Maveth...so I have no more reason to keep you alive."

Augen held up his dagger once more, but a moment of hesitation kept him from throwing it. The dagger meant so much to him; did he really wish to part with it? Even now? A final moment of hesitation, and he sighed, too.

"Goodbye, Christine. I wish I could have loved you as you deserved," he said aloud.

"What?" Goliath paused. The moment of stillness was Augen's perfect window of opportunity, and he seized it, flinging his dagger and its contents through the tube looming over Goliath's head and into the black abyss beyond.

Once free of the rubbery substance it penetrated, the blade curved slightly toward the monolith, as though the memento was attracted to it, before disappearing into the distance without striking the giant at all.

Goliath, who assumed he was Augen's target, braced himself to deflect the incoming projectile.

He quickly realized his mistake when the contents of the newly ruptured tube, some kind of black, mephitic, chemical compound, dropped onto his head with the force of a broken dike.

The noxious tide did not stop after emptying the tube's immediate contents but continued to spill forth, covering the floor and walls and dumping over the edge of the balcony onto the lower floors.

Suddenly, the once-black balconies were engulfed in flashing red lights, and a wailing alarm system announced the presence of some kind of deadly emergency.

"Air-quality, suboptimal. All staff, evacuate immediately!" a mechanical voice resembling that of a woman announced over a loudspeaker, and before Augen could compute her words and take in the new sensory changes, he began to feel light-headed.

Augen hastily limped away from the black waterfall that had buried his pursuer, but he stopped to reconsider his options when he passed a final hose, this one slightly higher up.

He knew he could not free-climb the obelisk, but perhaps he could still rappel most of the distance with the tube?

He doubted it would work, but recognized he could not descend the nautilus quickly enough to avoid suffocation. He needed a faster route, and at that moment, this was the only other option his mind could conjure.

The extra rifle Alexander left behind had been buried with Goliath in the spill, so he would have to use his good hand to grip the hose, but if he could break their restraints with blunt force as Alexander had, then he would be able to descend the tube relatively quickly by clinging to it with his legs.

Thinking of no better alternative, Augen carefully climbed the guardrail and prepared his body for a well-coordinated leap to relative safety.

"I can do this," he muttered, trying not to gaze into the abyss below.

A guttural roar from inside the cascading chemical dump reminded him that he had no more time for hesitation.

Goliath burst forth from the toxic shower and was somehow able to spot his fleeing opponent through the pitch-black liquid coating every inch of the rebel brute's body.

Unwilling to see his mission fail even under the dire circumstances, the giant limped menacingly toward Augen, sword still in hand, ready to finish what he started on the other side of the world.

Augen considered risking a foot race once more but chose instead to make his leap. His damaged legs throbbed, but he mustered enough strength to carry their wielder to his destination.

His hand clutched the rubbery tube, and for a moment, he feared it would give out under the strain, but his grip retained its fortitude, and the momentum of his jump allowed him to hook the duct with his legs without the need for abdominal work.

He was free of the floor, and Augen found that shuffling down his suspended line was easier and faster than he had presumed it would be.

By the time Goliath reached Augen's old launch pad, he could barely see the Templar shambling into the black abyss the way his accomplice had done minutes ago. The pressure for action was now Goliath's, and for the first time, time did not favor him.

Quickly surveying his surroundings and formulating his own exit strategy with what little he could see, he grinned eerily beneath his mask and waited for his target to break its joint as he watched Augen shuffle to the first suspender brace.

A well-placed heel kick snapped the weak bracer into two parts, and for a moment, Augen found himself harmlessly sliding toward the crater's center, but such ease was short-lived, for less than a second later, Goliath cut the line.

The tube jerked violently before going completely slack. Augen no longer needed to worry about breaking the remaining bracers, for when the pressure of his bodyweight pulled the hose taut, the girders gave way on their own, doing little to slow the free-falling soldier clinging to its end.

The plummet into blackness felt like it would never end. Augen retained the wherewithal to let his feet slide off the hose, a move that prevented him from falling upside-down. But the distance of the drop would certainly have been fatal had the hose not caught on a support beam reaching down from the ceiling to keep the heart of the nautilus sturdy.

Suddenly, the rubber vine Augen clung to went taut again, and his body was hurled horizontally into the side of the obelisk. After bouncing painfully across the steel face of the column, Augen found a small opening in the hulking mass of metal and anchored his foot into it as he had done in Eris Port.

When the rubber cylinder began to slip again, the knight abandoned his plan to use it, relieving his usable hand long enough to find a space on the tower he could comfortably grab that would not suddenly give way as his previous method of descent had.

A moment of respite came to the Templar as he dangled from the face of the strange object in the center of the chasm. The air was much cleaner now, and despite his fingers and ankle throbbing from the pressure of independently keeping him suspended, Augen was relieved that for a few seconds, he had a moment to think without Goliath present to interrupt.

Perhaps even now, it was not over. A glance about and Augen recognized the possibility of escaping with his life.

The nearest scaffold he could jump to was only a few stories below, but it was not directly beneath him, and to reach the safe route down, he would have to slowly shuffle across the metallic cliff nearly twenty yards before safely dropping onto the platform.

He eyed the face of the monolith and surmised that such a plan could be accomplished, albeit very slowly, since he had only one usable arm. With much cautious deliberation and a slow, calming breath, he made his first move across the mechanical precipice, shuffling his hand, then his feet from one viable gap in the machinery to another.

A deep, slamming sound rang from above, and Augen shifted sideways a second time and stole a glance back up the nautilus walls.

The darkness that had once veiled the bottom levels of the manmade crater now did the same to its upper tiers.

The upper levels were now illuminated by the flickering emergency lights, but nothing was clearly visible in the hazy red distance. Augen heard the black liquid pouring over the edges of each floor, making its own way to the bottom by any means available, but he could not place the source of the impact noise until it came again, closer this time and followed by a strained growl.

Goliath had chosen to test his legs and pain tolerance by leaping down onto each overlapping floor in hopes of outrunning the toxic tide. Augen could not see him but understood that his time was short.

"Wait there!" a voice arose from below, snapping Augen out of his strained reconnaissance.

"I told you to find the exit!" Augen responded, furious that the man he was trying to save had refused to leave.

"I already did! The same spot the giant entered through." As Alexander spoke, Augen heard the rattling of metal and caught the image of a large man pulling chains from a storage unit nearly six stories below.

A loud grunt from above preceded another booming crash. Goliath was still approaching, and Augen realized that if he was to maintain his pace, Alexander's help would be meaningless. The monster would beat them both to the bottom floor, and all would be lost.

"Leave the chains and get out of here!"

"I can toss them to you, and you can swing down!" Another thud erupted behind Augen, and this time, it was considerably closer. He stole one more panicked glance over his shoulder and beheld his pursuer standing on the balcony directly across from him.

Their eyes locked, and even under the newly formed layer of grotesque liquid covering the killer's body, Augen could sense a sinister smile forming under Goliath's mask and inside his posture, as he prepared to pass him with another jump.

Both of his targets were in sight, and unless something changed, Alexander would now be the first to meet his fate.

"I said, get out of here! Goliath can see you! And he is..." Another slam, and Augen's heart froze. Alexander was not listening, and death was now at the threshold.

Let there be no more death on my account! Augen thought. Then he kicked his feet out from below him and let go of the wall, plunging past Goliath, past Alexander, and all the way to the bottom of the pit.

Chapter 21

Spat from Hell's Mouth

Alexander watched the heroic soldier plummet past him, and for a millisecond, he and Augen made eye contact.

The soldier seemed relaxed, making no effort to grab the wall, slow his descent, or even protect his head from the impending impact.

When he struck the floor, a small set of plastic storage compartments shattered beneath his body but did little to break his fall. After the clatter died down, the entire structure went silent for a moment as both Goliath and Alexander stared at the broken form of a man lying on the floor beneath them.

"Well..." Goliath chuckled, breaking the silence. "...that makes my job a bit easier. To his credit, he put up a stunning fight for someone in his condition."

Another loud clang heralded the intruder's continued approach, and Alexander snapped out of his trance.

It was possible that Augen was still alive, but even if he was, both of them were still in grave danger—the sirens above continued their shrill warnings and the black fuel and lubricants were beginning to drip across the bottom floor, yet somehow, despite being covered in the oily liquid, the chaotic colossus sent after them was still functional. Though he walked with an obvious limp, he made his way around the final spirals with notable speed, for they were small enough to render shortcuts unnecessary.

"I suppose that matters little, though. A close failure is still a failure, regardless of effort or motivation," the rogue knight continued, slowly rounding the second-to-last floor as Alexander did the same on the scaffolding.

"I have never heard of such heroic motivation from your kind," Alexander responded, catching the giant's eye and gathering the chains he carried, careful not to let them catch on anything as he leaped from the final layer of scaffolding.

"I assure you that any such behavior is purely defective. Probably a result of the trauma I inflicted on him in Barbasul," Goliath answered, gripping his wounded leg but pressing onward.

Alexander reached the bottom floor first, gathering his chain into a roll and trying to decide whether he should try to escape or fight. Goliath seemed to read his mind and answered for him.

"You do not need to bother with him. I will make sure he is dead before I take you, though I will say that running will not get you anywhere either." Goliath's feet struck the concrete floor with enough force for Alexander to feel it, and moments later, he came into view. The behemoth was coated in the toxic fuel, but still breathed well enough to snicker to himself.

"It is a shame," he muttered, limping toward Augen and reaching for his torso to heave him up. "He could have been a great knight if only he had never acquired such idiotic sympathies."

That did it for Alexander, who dropped a portion of the chain roll and lashed at the giant with the tip he still held. The steel shackle struck Goliath with enough force to be felt beneath his armor.

"Idiotic sympathies?" Alexander yelled at his grease-soaked enemy. "He is everything a knight was created to become. Selfless, loyal, dedicated to protecting those who need protection..."

"...And a failure. I suppose that, too, is ideal in your eyes?" the massive killer interrupted, reaching again for Augen's body. Another scourge, this one timed well enough to hurt, struck Goliath's hand, making him drop Augen again.

"He is no failure. If he is dead, he gave his life protecting my family. That is enough in my eyes! I suppose a self-serving cur like you could never understand that."

The steel whip cracked toward Goliath a third time, but the beastly rebel caught the tip in his palm and, with a single swift movement, severed the chain with the parry-guards on his sword.

"I am not interested in what your eyes see! Our kind was bred to kill, survive, and strike fear into the hearts of the enemy. We are survivors and killers. A weak, privileged man like you could never understand the likes of us!"

Alexander tried to unravel more of his chain and strike again, but with a furious grunt, Goliath swapped targets, closed the distance between himself and his tormentor, and grabbed the chain again, this time just above the hand of its wielder.

With a quick twist, the rebel wrenched the chain from Alexander's hand and wrapped the steel shackle around his neck.

"Now, you have wasted enough of my time! One more interruption, and I will make sure you can never walk again! Maveth said to bring you alive; he gave no specifications on your functionality."

Alexander tried to respond, but Goliath interrupted him with a sequence of feral blows to the body and head. Then, with a violent twist, he flung Alexander into the bleak darkness beyond, so that any effort to make for the exhaust port would require moving past him.

Alexander gripped the flaws on his arms and chest, several of which had been struck during Goliath's lesson in respect, before slowly pulling the chain noose over his head.

Goliath saw Alexander do it, but did not care to waste any more energy on him. Instead, the killer limped toward Augen and pulled him up by the late Sergeant Sakit's tattered coat. A short pause, and Goliath chuckled to himself.

"How are you still alive?" He dramatically probed the unresponsive knight, prodding him with the tip of his blade and chuckling as the unconscious soldier drew weary breaths that continued despite his cold countenance.

Alexander grasped his bruised neck and coughed aloud. His tailbone throbbed too, but when he rolled over, he realized that Goliath had unknowingly thrown him onto the rifle he carried down there and dropped.

"Your strange resilience is becoming annoying," Goliath sighed, putting the tip of his cleaver to Augen's exposed throat.

"I could leave you in here to suffocate, but I really should be sure you die. May the emperor strike me dead if I am caught underestimating you a third time."

"Granted!" Alexander coughed, striding toward his captor once more and shooting a single round into Goliath's shoulder plate.

The bullet, designed for unarmored and unenhanced foes, did nothing... But the spark it summoned when shattering over his plate armor did.

The chasm, once shrouded in near-complete darkness save the dull flashing of the emergency lights, burst into a chaotic pyrotechnic display, with Goliath acting as the igniting ember.

The colossus dropped his weapon and captive as the fire stroking his armor tore the fabric of his attention away from everything other than its own chaotic existence.

Alexander dropped the gun once more and flung himself at the burning titan. Imitating the move he had watched Augen perform in the comms room, he catapulted himself from the ground and kicked Goliath in the chest with both feet, launching them both away from the near-dead soldier lying between them.

The conflagrant killer stumbled backward, tripped over a crate, and fell into the far wall, which was also covered in fuel and ignited in turn.

Alexander leaped to his feet and crouched over Augen, trying his best to hold the limp soldier's neck steady as he heaved the knight over his shoulders and made for the exit.

Goliath never recovered from his fall. Instead, he sat tearing at his armor as the electronic headset in his helmet exploded. The embers covering his body began to melt the leather in his brigandine armor, searing portions of the protective garb that were supposed to come loose together, thus trapping its wearer inside a molten cocoon.

Before leaping into the exhaust vent with Augen, the emperor stole a final glance back at the apocalyptic burn behind him.

The machine above would not be spared, and even now, it saddened him to think about it, but a slight burn in his lungs reminded him that he should save regrets and reorganization for later.

He hurled himself into the black concrete tube and, after taking a moment to readjust his grip on Augen, fled the blaze with all the strength he could muster. The vent was ashen black but scalding hot, pumping the heat behind them into the world above, just as it was supposed to do.

Over time, the exit port began to curve upward, making the ascent considerably more difficult, and just as Alexander spotted light in the distance, the ground let out a deep rumble and shook violently for a moment.

The fire reached the fuel cells... Here it comes! he thought, stumbling toward the light even faster but recognizing that a few feet of distance would likely do little good now. They were both likely dead men.

"Deos Almighty, please keep my family safe," he prayed silently before a screaming explosion and a burst of blinding light illuminated the tunnel behind him.

A hot and foul-smelling gust whistled through the exhaust vent, followed by an airborne fire that devoured what little oxygen was left in the tunnel and careened toward the outside world in hopes of finding more.

Alexander continued to press onward but found that his lungs no longer worked. His body was weak, and the toxic wind grew thicker and more violent by the second. Shoved from behind by the red-hot hurricane, Alexander lost his footing and began to collapse forward.

His arms, both spent keeping Augen on his shoulders, would not respond when he tried to catch himself. The vent steepened further, becoming nearly vertical, and even without injury or a three-hundred-pound man on his shoulders, it would have taken Alexander too long to ascend.

I believe this may be the end, he mused, falling onto his knees and staring into the light above.

"Let them know I tried," he finally said when the fiery tendrils reached the pair and lurched past them.

The heat was horrific, yet just as Alexander's vision faded away, he felt like he was moving again, floating toward a light that was neither artificial nor destructive.

...

Maveth was sitting inside a drone with a handful of his men, awaiting word from Goliath, when imperial reinforcements arrived from the town. The fire that his Hydra had started on the hill alerted the authorities, drawing the town garrison to the isolated base he and his men had hoped to attack without incident.

The captive king was stable, patched up by Maveth's lieutenant, and lying on the floor beside him. But he wanted the other man, the far greater prize who now kept him from abandoning his dangerous post, even as his enemies came knocking.

"Put down your weapons! Surrender or be fired upon!" the leader of the garrison commanded through a bullhorn from atop a heavily armed war Squire. The men with him set up several heavy guns and entrenched near the fort's entrance with small neo-steel redoubts to keep return fire from landing effectively.

Maveth disregarded the orders and reached for his short-range comms.

"Kaettel!" he shouted.

"Yes, my lord?" the radio responded immediately.

"Have you found the pipe Goliath spoke of?"

"Not yet..."

"Then disregard previous orders and return to our position. Do you have another Banshee Payload?"

"We do, my prince! One more volley."

Without glancing away from the radio, Maveth motioned for the pilot in his drone to start up their engines before the prince ordered his response.

"Good. The enemy is upon us. Unleash hell into their ranks. They will not see you coming. I do not want to take off with their guns fixed on us, so the pressure for action is on you! And Kaettel..."

"Yes, my lord?"

"Do not miss your target again! Ammunition is more valuable than a soldier who cannot use it."

Initially, no response came, but when it did, Maveth had already put away his speaker. His surviving underlings scurried about making preparations for a ground attack, but many of them had paused, staring at the buildings nearest them.

"What are you all staring at?" he shouted, stepping out from the belly of his drone and finding the answer to his question. Every building with an elevator was filling up with smoke. A glance at the central tower, and he ran back to his radio.

"Goliath! Respond! What is going on down there!" When no answer came, Maveth ordered the second drone to fire up its engines, too.

"Hold your position, but do not get too comfortable! The moment our Hydra strikes the Imps, load up. We are aborting the mission."

The airborne warmachine announced its presence through a melodramatic growl that echoed through the canyon moments before it burst into view from behind the mountain.

The assault drone cruised past the central spire of the base before slowing to a hover above the front wall, leveling its fire-spewing barrels at the encroaching guardsmen, and adjusting its view so that a single foray would shatter the entire force.

"Load up!" Maveth barked, believing escape to be a guarantee, but as the rebels grabbed their gear and loaded into the drones, the ground began to shake.

The tremors lasted for about three seconds before a deep rumble followed, and the entire plaza shattered like a dropped porcelain dish. The concrete transformed into a dusty semisolid and sank into itself, pulling the structures closest to the spire into the ground.

Maveth panicked and ordered his drone to ascend prematurely, but the pilot, who stared at the sinking fort and churning land in shock, was slow to respond.

This ironic mistake would save the pilot's life and those of his passengers, for seconds later, the central spire exploded, sending shards of fire and sheet metal the size of horses into the air and through the hull of Maveth's airborne beast.

The deadly shrapnel, paired with the sudden pressure spike from the explosion, flipped the Hydra onto its head. The craft's engines, which were not designed to compensate for flying upside-down, continued to run regardless of orientation and drove the overturned machine into the collapsing plaza all the harder.

The body of the craft was completely flattened, and the ignition caps on the main guns ignited upon impact, and the newly armed Banshee-Rounds flew chaotically from their barrels into Maveth's second drone.

Before any of the men inside could blink, the drone's interior fuel cell ignited, and the whole machine popped like a helium balloon.

With a slack jaw, Maveth witnessed the loss of both the aircraft and most of his soldiers, but his pilot had seen more than enough and pulled the only remaining drone away from the carnage as quickly as the craft would allow.

The soldiers outside the base were thrown onto their backs, and the commander was flung from atop his vehicle. They were badly shellshocked from the explosions but unharmed, left to watch the entire base sink into the soil in a bubbling chain of dust, fire, and smoke explosions.

When the smog cleared, the garrison watched a single rebel drone disappear over the horizon, but no one bothered to pursue it. The men were happy to be alive, but unfeeling in every other regard.

Catherine found Alexander lying outside a broken exhaust port. His ears were bleeding, and his whole body was covered in burns, but he was alive. It seemed as though the explosion in the distance threw him out of the tube along with its excess energy.

Of the heroic guards who returned to their posts to save them, all but one survived the airstrike, and just as they had managed to circle the fort to meet up with the newcomers from the town, one of the men saw what looked like two bodies fly over the brush line after the explosion. The subsequent search was short.

"Over here, but keep the girls back!" she commanded the men around her before crouching and embracing her husband. "Praise Deos! Please, don't ever leave us again," she whispered into his ear, unsure if he could hear her.

Another minute passed, and the knight who intercepted them turned up. His condition was far more critical, with most of the bones in his lower body broken and his left arm all but ripped from its socket.

"Get a hold of the city garrison and have them bring their Squires over here. These men need medical attention," Basan yelled to the others.

When the city garrison finally carried the two men on stretchers into the Squires, Alexander was awake, though barely functional and in horrible pain, his family walking by his side every step of the way.

Augen remained unresponsive to the field medic, but for a moment, while being carried to the transport, he opened his eyes. Above him, a beautiful blue sky streaked with gentle grey clouds not dissimilar to those on the beaches of Nethel, smiled down at him.

The wind was gone, and the storm that had followed him across Archaea was nowhere to be found.

EPILOGUE

Augen awoke to the jittery chatter of several young Hospitalier-nurses. Smiles and even a small cheer erupted from the small party when he began looking around and breathing consistently.

"It worked!" one of the sisters chirped.

"What will they come up with next?" another wondered aloud before they began restoring his bandages and checking his vitals with giddy enthusiasm.

Trying to scan his surroundings, he concluded that he was in yet another hospital. His body was almost completely covered in braces, casts, and bandages, and his left arm was gone.

Despite the intense pain he felt, and the abrupt realization that he still never got the meaningful death he wished for, he smiled to himself, physically straining to do so and disregarding the extra pain the action caused.

He had seen Christine again in his dreams, as he had so many times before, but for the first time he could remember, he coped with it. In his darkest moment, he acknowledged the tragedy and prayed instead of mourning, thanking Deos for the opportunity granted him in those days, regardless of what ultimately came of it. When she faded away, he wept as he always did, but with gratefulness, telling her goodbye and thanking Deos for her survival.

"Please keep her safe," he muttered, catching the ear of a nurse.

"We know what you did. You are a hero! And yes, they are all safe," she stated, tenderly adjusting a bandage.

"Enough talk!" An older woman entered the room and snapped the younger nurses back to silent attention, though their wide smiles remained even with their superior present.

The matron strode into the room and stared at his bed, trying and failing to suppress a smile of her own.

"Good. He seems to be recovering. Finish your work and sedate him. He is being transferred tonight."

Augen took a strained breath and chuckled painfully. "It seems I will never escape Diona...not that much is left of me to execute."

The young women smiled at each other, and chuckling began again until the matron snapped her finger, and they all went silent once more.

"Do as I said, and be quick about it," she ordered firmly before turning and leaving. "And excellent job, sisters. Expect commendations for keeping him alive."

The door slammed, and the girlish squealing began again, though never enough to hinder the efficient completion of their orders.

Augen glanced about, confused and hoping for an explanation. Initially, none came. Just as the sedative was injected into his arm, beside the blood transfusion and at least two other tubes also puncturing the joint of his remaining limb, the lead nurse leaned in to his ear.

"Based on who sent us these supplies to revive you, I have a feeling that you are no longer going to Diona."

More blackness followed, and Augen awoke once more, this time in a different hospital, this one far outclassing any facility he had ever heard of. The technology was advanced, the structure of the room was exquisite and epic, though poorly lit, and this time, he could see nobody in the room with him.

"Can you hear me?" a man questioned sternly from beyond Augen's field of view.

"Yes," Augen slowly responded, trying not to cough. He could hear shuffling from somewhere behind him, and the stretcher he lay on slowly readjusted itself so that he now partially sat up.

"I have a question for you, Augen Di Gattchen," another voice, this one modified yet strangely familiar, interjected.

"Why did you save the people in Tyre? Did you know their identities?"

Augen sputtered a bit and readjusted his weight as well as he could. His head was strapped to the bed, and even while sitting up, he still could not see anyone in the room.

"The family? It is complicated," was all Augen could initially muster for an explanation, but when no response came, he slowly forced himself to continue.

"I have done many things wrong in my life. I believed that I could do a little good before dying...and no, I did not know who they were. I still do not."

"You wanted to protect the family, rather than kill the terrorists? That is not what you were trained to do," the voice responded, seemingly frustrated with the response.

"I have been told many times that I make a poor attack dog."

"Would you do such a thing again?"

This time, Augen paused, unsure of where this interrogation was going, but opting to be honest regardless. "Yes. I believe it would be my duty before Deos to protect the innocent. I would not hesitate."

Nothing more was said for quite some time. Augen even considered calling out and asking if anyone was still there with him, but eventually, a final question came.

"Do you want to live?" The tone of such a question was impossible to read. Was it a threat? An offer? Was it hypothetical? Augen could not gauge it, but the words reminded him of what the prophet in Pallerheim had asked him, so he gave a similar answer.

"A month ago, I would have said no. However, it seems that Deos is far more invested in my life than He is in my death." Augen paused. "So, if I were to get the chance: Yes, I would prefer to live, at least until He decides it is time for me to die."

Another long moment of silence, but this time, Augen caught a portion of a whisper lingering in the air.

"Leave the room," the voice finally commanded.

Augen was confused by this statement until he heard a quiet stampede of footsteps echo away into the distance, the metallic clang of a large door silenced all other noises, and a shadow moved in Augen's peripheral vision just long enough for him to catch it.

"Are you going to kill me?" Augen finally asked.

The shadow emerged from Augen's opposite side, revealing itself and stealing his breath. The voice he recognized but could not place was that of the Golden emperor, who now, in all his splendor, loomed over him like a specter, staring into his eyes through a faceless visor.

In reality, the emperor was slightly smaller than Augen, but at that moment, he seemed larger than Goliath.

"Your...Eminence!" Augen stuttered, unable to say anything else.

"No, Augen. I have no interest in killing you." The emperor stepped behind the bedridden knight, flipping a switch that made the bed slowly turn toward him. "I want to offer you a job, one that no other knight could dream of ascending to."

As Augen slowly rotated to face the emperor again, he could not believe his ears.

"Your Majesty! I would certainly follow you to the end. Regardless of what is asked! But...why me?" His question echoed through the room, but no response came.

For when the emperor removed his helmet, Augen did not need one.

❖

Maveth sat beside the unique radio his former second-in-command once used to speak with The Contact. His forces, who were now whittled down to a mere handful of loyal guards, hastily packed up their belongings and prepared to move to another safehouse and await reinforcements.

Maveth wanted a word from The Contact first, knowing that such a man could grant him a new bodyguard. He did not know Goliath's employer, nor did he understand how the concerned third party could get hold of illegal weaponry, hand out knights on a whim, or possess access to sensitive information.

He had pondered potential answers before but had decided that while Goliath was alive, it would be best to remain ignorant.

Goliath was now dead, and it would be time for a new batch of recruits and weapons, and both outcomes would have to manifest through the man he knew only as The Contact.

"We are prepared to leave, my lord," the Byzican lieutenant who had confronted him a day prior said, bowing his head slightly when he entered the room. Maveth sighed and fidgeted with the radio. He had tried to reach out since then, but no answer had come yet.

"Very well. Start the engines." Once the man was gone, Maveth attempted once more to contact the man who gifted him his rebellion, and just moments before he gave up, a dark voice answered from the undisclosed location his radio was programmed to reach.

"Report," it commanded. Maveth sighed nervously and gave his answer.

"Goliath is dead. We were intercepted by the Templar from Barbasul during a ground assault. Casualties were...catastrophic, and our weapons are nearly expended. We still have Jubanic, but I am afraid we will need more resources if we are to make something of his capture."

"Did you grab the newcomer?" was all The Contact said in response. When Maveth said nothing, the voice repeated itself, this time with a dark emphasis, "Did you grab Blodian Altegard and his family?"

"No," Maveth murmured, realizing the lost potential in such a high-value hostage. "He escaped into the lower levels of the fort before it exploded. He is likely dead. We never got hold of the family."

His loyal lieutenant returned to the room but said nothing as both men stared into the speaker of the radio, praying for a response.

"I see," the voice concluded.

"We are moving to a new safehouse. I will send you the location," Maveth interjected, hoping to move the conversation toward the future.

"Do not bother relocating. I will keep your location hidden until I send you another bodyguard."

"But..."

"I will contact you again if I want you to move out. Until then, stay put! I will send you another, more competent second-in-command. One who would never be foiled by an acolyte of the Templar."

The radio went silent, and Maveth solemnly turned to his lieutenant. He knew from the moment he made his first arrangement with the unknown man on the radio that a day would come for him to pay the piper. He also knew it was unlikely for his so-called partner to allow such failure to go unpunished.

Insisting they stay put after a strike like this was no strategy. The Contact was not making renewed arrangements—he was severing ties, and it would be far easier to destroy a target that held still.

"You once vowed to give your life for me," Maveth whispered to the only man still in the room.

He slowly nodded and bowed his head once more. "I will keep such a vow. If you continue the fight for our people's independence."

Maveth grabbed the lieutenant's shoulder and smiled. "Then you are now Maveth Shedim. My armor is in the chest behind you, and the title is just a name, but both are yours as long as you can keep them."

"Best of luck, my prince. Let the sun shine favorably upon you."

As the man spoke, Maveth pulled a hood over his head and made his exit.

"And you, too."

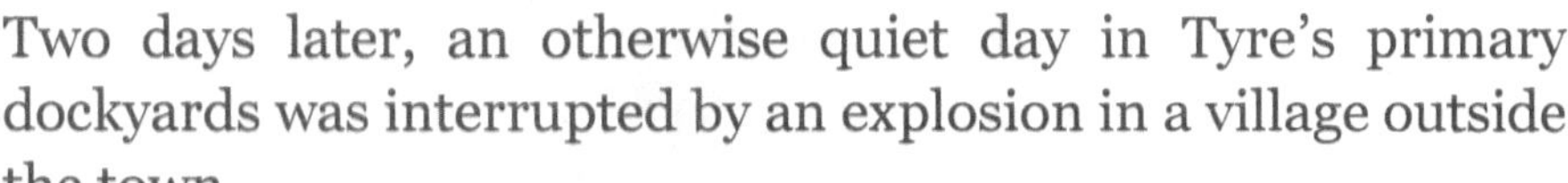

Two days later, an otherwise quiet day in Tyre's primary dockyards was interrupted by an explosion in a village outside the town.

The fire brigade and garrison, at least its uninjured remnant, would rush from their homes and quarters to extinguish the scorched remains of an imperial assault drone.

Those inside the village, including a rebel leader in an expensive purple cloak and his remaining entourage of armed insurgents, were all found dead, butchered by a single unarmored knight who disappeared into the shadows with their precious captive early in the morning.

In the knight's left arm, the former King Jubanic wheezed and moaned, complaining about his prior treatment at the hands of the rebels and whimpering to himself about the speed his rescuer made him run.

"We can just return to the town now. I am sure that the emperor will be relieved to know that I am alive and well. He may even grant me a new throne!"

"You misunderstand the purpose of my arrival," a white-haired Teuton with the exposed arm tattoos of the Inquisition finally answered, briefly slowing his pace.

"The emperor will not grant you anything because he will never find you. No one will. I have been sent to ensure it."

The busy garrison heard a single shot echo across the hillside, but Zhatka was right: The search party never found a body.

{Front} Object found in the ruins of the Tyre Void Silo, packaged for preservation as potential evidence. Local authorities were unable to agree on the origins of the damaged image or the means of its miraculous survival. The excavation team responsible for its discovery insisted that no container for the item was recovered. Further inquiries were planned but never executed as imperial forces confiscated all the preserved evidence.

ACKNOWLDGEMENTS

First, I would like to thank those who have directly influenced my world, starting with my father, who taught me self-discipline, how to organize my time, and how to persevere in times of frustration, never letting self-doubt or fear cripple my potential. Even in our roughest seasons, you have always been my hero.

On the other side of my parental coin, my mother accepted me for who I was, forgave my shortcomings, and encouraged me in times of frustration. You and Father made me who I am, and kept me on the straight and narrow through my formative years.

Now my brothers, Isaac, Aaron, and Eli, who kept me sharp, challenged me to better myself and provided one of the greatest Christmas gifts in history, a chance to push my hobby into the big leagues. You guys have always been on the precipice of success, and I thank you for believing in me.

Finally, to Jonny, the big brother I never knew I needed. You helped me build Archaea from the ground up, and it will forever bear your fingerprints. You have also been a role model and a genuine friend, and I will forever bless the day of our meeting.

Second, I must thank the people who helped make what was once a casual hobby into the competitive and sharp fictional work it is today. To my first professional editor, Michael Waitz, whose military expertise and exceptional feedback gave my work the professional flair it needed to really stand out. You also introduced me to my excellent publishers at Warrington Publishing, effectively becoming the spark to ignite my big break.

But even before my first step into the professional world, my life was full of people willing to help me better my work. Special thanks to Grandma Roberta, Hannah, Rain, and Hunter. You took time out of your own busy lives to invest in my work and see to its betterment. I will always appreciate it.

Finally, and most importantly, I wish to thank the one true God. The Master Storyteller and supplier of every talent in my possession, who brought the real world into existence and, for a time, walked with us mortals to show His empathy and care. May my work always honor You, and may my world be a faint reflection of Your boundless creativity and might. As you inspired Tolkien, Lewis, Chesterton, and Milton, I ask that You do the same for me.

About the Author

Caleb Franklin's story as an author is a strange one. An avid reader at an unusually young age, he plowed through elementary school with passing grades, an awkward personality, and little promise in the writing department.

Attending college to become a history teacher, he studied the great dramas of ages past, the grand inquiries, despicable treacheries, and myriad shades of complexities that drove our world's timeless heroes and infamous villains. Those characters embedded in his subconscious through years of casual development grew in depth. It was not long before they wanted to show themselves in his work.

Caleb lives in Oregon.

www.ingramcontent.com/pod-product-compliance
Lightning Source LLC
Chambersburg PA
CBHW021343310726
48971CB00001B/267